Also by C. M. Stultz:

Shadow of the Beast *

Coming soon by Eric J. Hull & C. M. Stultz:

Ash
(The Pendulum: Book Two)

* Available from Amazon

PYRE

The Pendulum: Book One

a novel by

Eric J. Hull and C. M. Stultz

ISBN: 978-1-517-00175-9

Cover design by The Scarlett Rugers Book Design Agency
www.booksat.scarlettrugers.com

For Robert B. Clark, Jr., who fired my imagination as a writer, and taught me all of the planets in the solar system. Thanks, Uncle Bert.

– Eric J. Hull

For Dana and Dawn, who always believed in *Pyre*; and for June, who's always believed in me.

– C. M. Stultz

PYRE

PROLOGUE

The old man's senses rang. Where there had been screaming and cursing and the crackle of exploding timber, there was the deadened hush of the pre-dawn forest; no frogs; no birds. His ears were scoured by the sharp sigh of his spade biting through the ashes as he finished covering her grave.

Nothing filled his nostrils but the faint odor of forest decay always present in turned earth. Where there had been acrid smoke and fear and the coppery tang of spilt blood, the gentle rains had come with the darkness.

He was terribly weary. Setting aside the spade he gathered his stained robes about him and settled himself on the low mound. Pressing grimy palms against his closed eyes sent showers of sparks dancing back into his mind, but they illuminated nothing. The images of the men on horseback, the battle, the awesome Blade of Rage in the hand of the young warrior King (and especially the imagined picture of Gwenlyn's face, frantic

1

with terror, cowering as the flaming house collapsed around her) had burned out with the wreckage. The few smoldering embers glowed dully in his eyes as he gazed at what had been his home. He viewed the emptiness in his soul with the same utter stillness with which he looked into the darkness before him.

His senses rang.

Time passed beyond his notice. The sun began to warm the surrounding hills and peaks; birds crept back and tentatively chorused. A hedgehog trundled past within two arms' lengths, paused snuffling at the charred corpse of a Fairen warrior, and waddled off into the brush. As the sun crept over the edge of the dark burial mound, tiny fragments of earth dried and whitened, frosting the grave with grey. As he stirred, the dirt shifted and rolled down into his sandals, tickling his feet. He started, grunting. It was then that he noticed the shaking form in the shadows of the trees to his left.

The youth's eyes were red and swollen. His clothes were disheveled, but spotless; no blood, no ash, a damning testimony to his absence during the night's terrors. His voice was hushed and quavering.

"Master ... are you injured? I - I've come back..."

The old man's eyes were the color of the ash. "Have you."

The boy staggered up and crossed the space between them; knelt, gaze cast down.

"When ... when they came I - we could hear them over the ridge and I left the house only for a moment to watch the battle. Your lady wife was sleeping and I never dreamed they would come this way and - and -"

Suddenly he was sobbing and speaking in a tortured rush, the words pouring from him like blood from an axe wound.

"Oh Gods I am so sorry I was watching from the hill and there were hundreds of soldiers and horsemen and blood and then that man with the screaming sword and they were burning everything and – oh Gifter! They ran into your house to hide! I don't even know if they were Fairens or from Edge, and then the others followed and they fired the house! There was nothing I could do. If I'd come down I would have been killed too, oh Master please forgive me there was nothing I could do and there was so much smoke and noise and blood, and I, I don't think they even knew she was –"

"Enough." The old man gripped the boy's shoulder so hard the bones ground together. This part of the story he already knew. He had returned from his night forage just in time to see the last of the burning. He dragged the boy to his feet. The youth whimpered and cringed away from him, but he grabbed the boy's chin and stared into his eyes, the last tatters of sanity dancing fitfully behind the old man's gaze.

"I shall. I shall forgive you if..." The darkest knowledge he possessed quietly joined hands with the grief and horror in his heart and began to chant. His words took on the singsong tone the boy had always associated with the casting of magics.

"I shall forgive you if you aid me this day, without question. I have a ... task. A gift to prepare, and I need you to help me complete it, Wil." His eyes smoldered, and he gripped the boy more fiercely. "It shall be the last I ever ask of you. Will you help me?"

Wil was afraid now, more than he had ever been while hiding. In the magician's gaze was the cast of madness. Swallowing, he nodded.

"Good. Gather some wood now, and kindling." The old man released him and turned away toward the ruins of the house.

"By fire, then," he said. "By fire."

He strode with deliberation toward the house, stepping past corpses darkening with restive carrion birds. Near the place where the doorway had been he upset his wicker forage basket with his foot. He noticed neither dead men nor discarded, now-useless herbs; he merely walked into the wreckage, unconsciously avoiding the places where walls had been, traveling the same paths he and Gwenlyn had trod for thirty years. Mists of ash rose about him as he shifted a fallen roof beam, tossed away a blackened drapery, searched through the rubble of his life for the things he needed now.

When he emerged he carried a small brazier and two pouches, smudged but unburned. He placed these beside the grave of his wife and plowed back into the wreckage. He emerged a second time with a six-foot iron rod, sharpened at one end. On the other was a bowl formed of three long tines. His third trip produced an iron weight on a length of fine chain. He walked over to the grave and stood, absolutely still, until the boy returned.

"So it begins," he muttered. "And so it ends."

He grasped the still-warm iron rod in both hands and with all his force plunged its sharpened end deeply into the grave.

The boy gasped and dropped his armload of twigs and sticks, then moaned in the back of his throat and began to back away, shaking his head in horror. Just before he took to his heels, his old master spoke in a quiet voice, almost like the one he remembered.

"Please don't leave me, Wil. I cannot do this alone." For just a moment there was a trace of humanity on the old man's face, though his eyes never left the grave.

Somehow, out of loyalty to a man who had been his teacher, out of fear of the old wizard's madness, or from an inkling of the terrible justice unfolding, Wil stayed his frightened legs, and bent to pick up the kindling with trembling fingers.

The old man let out a long breath, retrieved the brazier from the ground, and set it firmly in the bowl of tines atop the stake. He hung the weight from the far edge of the pot and took the wood from the boy, carefully arranging it in the pan before glancing up. "Have you flint and steel? Good. Strike the fire here, and step back."

The apprentice obeyed, and watched as his master blew the flames to full life and peered into them for a moment. When the old man spoke again his voice sounded odd, as though distorted by the heat.

"You have learned little enough, these years with me; I fear you have no vocation for the Art." He opened one pouch and spread its grey powder in a rough circle around him. "Still, you can manage what you must today." He scooped a palmful of grave-dirt into the basin. It sizzled. His lined face again took on its haunted cast. He wrote with his left forefinger in the air; a blue sigil glowed for a moment and then faded into nothing. "I had thought to find a haven from their foolish quarrels. Now they have come, and made me the greater fool." He emptied the second pouch into the fire, causing its flames to leap blue into the air. There was a scent of burnt citrus, and something else underneath it, something acrid, foul. The weight at the end of the chain began a slow pendulum swing.

He drew a long blade from his robes. The youth recognized it as an athalme, the keen knife used in rites to which he had not yet graduated. His master locked eyes with him. It was not a gaze he could have held for long. The old man's soot-smudged visage was alive with malice, and power.

"They shall pay. Both their twice-damned houses shall receive the gift we create this day, and both their houses shall burn in the hells they mete so lightly. Listen!" He spoke several words, harsh and foreign and resonant with power. "Say these words, Wil, and repeat them until the fire dies. After that you are free. But until then, repeat them, even after I cannot." He turned back to the hissing flames. "Such a malison as we now lay carries but one price. Say them!"

The words stuttered from the boy over a too-dry tongue, but in the saying, lent their power. The flames roared and pulsed, and the words began almost to speak themselves. Wil's mouth moved, the awful sounds came forth, but he no longer controlled any of it. The mage picked up the droning chant and stared into the heart of the flames where his pupil dared not look.

He bared his right forearm over the flames. Raising the athalme high in his left hand, in one swift, brutal stroke he laid open his wrist to the bone, blood spurting from the wound in crimson freshets. The flames roared eagerly and blossomed afresh, and began hungrily licking up the ropy spurts pouring down his wrist. The boy continued to chant, retching the abrasive syllables, unable to stop.

The blue fire blazed up to the mage's wrist and burrowed in. Wil watched as his master's veins blackened, fire creeping up his right arm *from the inside*. It spread like the roots of some hellish creeping vine, and when it disappeared into the sleeve of his robe and reached his heart, the old man was screaming the words, over and over, in time with the boy. The heat pulsed out from the mage's body in visible waves, distorting the trees and sky.

The knife tumbled from his grasp and half-buried itself in the dark earth, glossy vermilion and steel reflecting the raging fire.

Chapter 1
Aaren

The pennants of Greybeal Palace in Edge snapped smartly in the crisp morning air. Its three great wings branched east, west, and south away from its main gate; each branch ended in a tall tower, with the south tower the tallest. High stone walls closed off the two courtyards and rose into a great arch over the gate. Smaller walls extended from the east and west ends, spreading wide and stretching southward to encircle the township.

The windows in the upper chambers of the royal suite had all been flung open to catch the morning light and warmth on the eastern wing; but the anguished screams of its Queen drifted thinly down over the courtyard, eliciting sympathetic winces from the servants on their morning errands.

"*Push*, my Lady," urged the bloodied midwife. The old woman always wore a scowl, but this day it was graven deep with lines of fatigue and worry. This had been an abnormally difficult labor, over twenty hours, and showed no sign of ending soon. Although her replies to King Trever's messengers were non-committal, she feared the Queen and the child would not survive. The Telciens were a sturdy line, however, and she had delivered more than one infant from worse situations.

She gently probed Queen Alyda's swollen belly. Had the child finally shifted? For some hours it had not moved at all, and the midwife had feared it dead already. In the tiny but blessed pause between contractions she wrung out another cool cloth and wiped her Lady's face.

"The child is alive, and this next time you must help me. I know you are at your limit." *We both are.* She looked hard into the eyes of the Queen and found no strength, only despair. Alyda was young, barely nineteen, and exhausted almost beyond measure. Her own gaze hardened. "No. Perhaps not. It takes a certain courage to bear the firstborn of a King, and I have always wondered about your strength." She did not let her stare reflect the lie while she prayed. *Now, my Lady. You cannot survive another hour of this.*

The next contraction came. Biting down on the twisted rag, Queen Alyda squeezed shut her eyes, but not before the midwife saw a gleam of anger. *Thank the Gifter!*

"Now, my Lady. Now!"

At long last the child's head appeared. *It's crowning.* "Good! Another!" Several more inches. *My soul, it has no face! Ah, don't be stupid, woman, you've seen a caul before.* "My Lady, we are almost finished!" The next contraction brought the whole child forth, and it struggled in her hands. She tore the caul from its face, but it did not begin to breathe. Looking up for just a moment at her other charge, she blinked back a sudden bluish haze over her vision and answered the unvoiced plea.

"Your son is very much alive, Majesty." She turned him over to spank his struggling, bloody bottom. "And-"

The midwife burst into flames.

Her first thought was to get the crying child away from the fire. She quickly dropped him onto Alyda and staggered back from the bed, blazing arms outstretched in horror. Even as his mother reached clumsily down to hold him, he quieted, and the flames on the midwife died as swiftly as they had begun. The odd blue shimmering encasing her (*the color of his eyes?*) was the last thing to disappear. The pain of the burn finally penetrated her shocked nerves, and she collapsed onto the floor, smoking.

"Trever!" gasped the Queen, struggling with the umbilical cord. "Someone ... help..."

◆   ◆   ◆

In the adjoining antechamber, High Chamberlain Wildon's head swung sharply toward the doorway. "You! Check on them." The attending maid scurried into the room. Screaming, she stumbled back into the antechamber.

"What is it? The child? The Queen?" The girl stammered and pointed. Wildon grabbed her by the hair and forced her face to his. "What *is* it?" She was unable to respond. He thrust her roughly aside and strode into the bedroom, calling over his shoulder to his personal guard: "Summon the King."

Wildon's voice was low and gravelly, and his tongue was as sharp as his temper. He had a gaunt frame, and the grey streaks at his temples arced smoothly back to the dark leather cord with which he tied back his hair. His largish nose and keen politics had earned him the appellation "The Hawk" – though this name was never used in his presence. He spared the unconscious midwife the briefest glance and bent by the side of the Queen.

"Bring Trever!" she hissed, attempting to draw the child closer.

"Surely m'Lady is in need of more immediate assistance." His eyes never left the child. "One doesn't turn away a friendly hand in one's hour of need, good Queen." He reached for the boy.

"Snake! We will die first!" This was language she had never used with Wildon, but in her extremity her tongue was loosened. Grey motes danced fleetingly across Alyda's vision, and she fought furiously against the darkness. She was horribly pale, and at the literal end of her strength.

"As you will!" he snarled, just as the King rushed in.

There was a moment of uneasy silence broken only by the sudden squalling of the child. Trever gestured abruptly with his left hand and the teary maid bent to the stricken midwife. Trever knelt at the other side of the bed from Wildon. "Alyda?"

"I don't *know!* She was on *fire*, and then –"

"Perhaps, m'Lord, first things first." Wildon gestured at the bloody cord. He picked up the midwife's sharp blade and handed it to the King.

Alyda fainted.

✦   ✦   ✦

Two days later, it happened again.

The wet-nurse, a plump woman of indeterminate age and infinite patience, was tending the child in the nursery. Her screams brought the whole west wing running. By the time the three closest servants rushed in, the blue glow was gone but her long hair was still smoldering. These flames were hastily beaten out, and the hysterical woman somewhat calmed.

"I was just putting him down! He was being cranky, and I thought a short nap would do the trick, when ... ah, Gifter, again!"

The embroidered back of the scullery maid's blouse had begun to smoke, tiny flames licking gently at the yarn. She stood less than three yards from the crib. The wet-nurse screamed again, and the room dissolved into pandemonium.

Eventually, the King was summoned.

Upon leaving the nursery he climbed the circular stair to the south tower. He had only been up those stairs twice since the new mage had arrived the previous year. Trever didn't hold much affection for those who used magic arts. He was a man of direct action, and a pragmatist. Ironically, it was his pragmatism that had caused him to be persuaded to take a mage on after the last war with Faires. Lord Wildon had convinced the King that magical protection was in Edge's best interests. Trever had eventually agreed, and the mage had been appointed and moved into the tower ten months earlier.

Trever reached the top of the stairs and knocked on a great ironbound door. The hollow boom echoed back down the stairwell.

"Come in, come in," called a muffled voice. Trever pushed open the door. The room was cluttered and musty; the closed shutters over both windows had obviously not been opened for many months. Inlaid in the center of the stone floor was a great golden pentangle, surrounded by an unbroken circle of silver.

Pots and earthenware jars fought for shelf space with enormous leather-bound books, and all gave off strange and unpleasant odors. Behind a large table hunched a man with greying hair and mustache, gazing fixedly into a copper basin of water.

"Trever! Good of you to come. Come over here and have a look at this!"

"Actually, Vernor, I came on other –"

"Posh!" The sorcerer pushed up one sleeve and gestured imperiously to the King. "Where's the fire?" His dark eyes flashed sideways at his monarch. "That *is* the question, isn't it, m'Lord?" He beckoned again. "Look here, lad." He pointed to the bowl.

Trever ground his teeth but came around the table. "I see a plain bowl of water." He scowled.

The magician made a subtle gesture with his right hand, never taking his eyes from his King's. "Do you?"

Suddenly the water rippled, and no longer reflected the King's face. Instead came an indistinct view of the nursery. Trever watched with fascination, in spite of himself, as the scene with the wet-nurse played itself over again as it had been described to him. There was one significant difference, however. Just before each of his servants caught fire, a vivid blue glow emanated from the crib and lanced out at the unfortunate victims like lightning. As the child calmed, the flames died, and so did the unearthly light.

The water rippled, and again became clear. Trever raised his head. "So."

"Indeed. It is the young Prince Aaren."

The King exhaled abruptly and pushed himself away from the table, slopping the water. Turning, he stalked over to one of the shelves, picked up a strangely carved stone block and slapped it down again, raising tiny dust devils. "And what am I to do? Have my servants bursting into flames at the whims of a newborn infant? What are you telling me, Mage?"

The sorcerer had wandered over to his metallurgical workbench, and poked at a still-glowing mold. Drops of silver had splashed around the sprue and gleamed against the dark iron. The King could see distortion in the air around it, and was not at all sure it was caused entirely by heat. The Mage grunted and turned back to squint at his liege.

"When this cools, it should help considerably."

"But what *is* -"

"Ah, Trever, in good time. Come back to me in three hours. Visit the child. Be pleasant." He smiled. Reaching behind the bleached skull of what looked to be some sort of horned cat, he dug out a small vial of brilliant blue fluid and put it in the King's hand. "And here is something for Queen Alyda."

"What -"

"It will help her to find the strength to continue healing. Now leave me." He arranged his stained robe testily and turned his back on the King, busying himself with several crusted beakers. Visibly attempting to calm himself, King Trever turned and strode for the stairs.

"And close the door behind you!"

The door closed, not gently, and the Mage glanced at it.

"No respect for the sacred arts, well. Always in a hurry, a Sorcerer isn't called on until he's needed, no? Hmph. 'How fare you, Vernor? Join us for dinner, Vernor? Why thank you, Vernor, that was exemplary!'" He snorted, and focused the conjured yellow fire's light more carefully through a lens onto the mold. His eyes narrowed. For just an instant, his gaze turned inward, his face went slack, and the lens slipped from his hand. The clatter as it came to rest on the workbench brought his attention back to the task at hand. He shook himself, picked up the lens, and focused the yellow light again. "Not nearly as strong as it should be..." He stood for a moment, gazing thoughtfully at the pale fire.

Abruptly, he turned away. Rooting through a wicker basket, he dug out a tarnished metal pot of powder. Striking flint, he lit a mundane fire in a small brazier, set up a silver pendulum over it and tossed in a palmful of the powder. It flashed blue, and the pendulum swung wildly. The sorcerer scratched his beard and sat down in an overstuffed green wingback chair. The pendulum did not stop swinging. Vernor frowned.

"Now, by the Tempter, why would anyone else be conjuring Fire Magic?" He sat unmoving, staring at the swinging pendulum, for a very long time.

◆   ◆   ◆

Trever stormed into his council room, still fuming from Vernor's offhand dismissal. *He speaks so even to his King! Damn his arrogance! Damn all sorcerers, and all their works, too!*

He leaned against the great table in the room's center, drumming his fingers as he tried to calm himself. Magic was one of the realities of life, and its practitioners were, he gruffly conceded, necessary. They offered protection and counsel, healing and vision and power itself. Humility was seldom part of the package. Trever simply found it hard to trust in something he could neither fathom nor control.

His glance fell on the long, two-handed sword that hung from the high back of his own chair. *Even that.* The sword had been passed on to him by his father, and to King Crawford by his father; the kings of Edge had held it for as long as there had been men who bore that title. No one knew its origin, whether it had been made or found in Edge, or come over the mountains with the first settlers. The kings knew only its power.

The sword itself was ensorcelled. Each king taught his successor a word, as old and untraceable as the weapon, that invoked the power trapped within it. The blade howled with an unearthly song, and flames blazed along its edges. It made its bearer stronger, faster, and fiercer in battle, and imparted the same qualities to any who heard its cry. It seemed to feed off the anger of its wielder, and so it was called the Rageblade.

Trever laid his palm on its pommel, then slid his hand down to run his forefinger over the faint tracing of a pendulum engraved in the sword's hilt. *Now here is magic a man can count on. No vague prophecies or promises; just power that he can take in his hand and use when he needs it. But even this: can it be trusted?*

The King shook his head, clearing it of ire and suspicion. It was a fine spring day, much too fine to waste on such thoughts. "Stephen!" he bellowed.

His steward stood in the open doorway in an instant. "Yes, your Highness?"

"Send down to the stables and have our horses saddled." Trever buckled the Rageblade's belt around his waist. "And you bring our peregrines up from the mews. We're going hawking for the afternoon."

Stephen smiled. "At once, m'Lord." He hurried away, with Trever only a pace behind him.

◆   ◆   ◆

Vernor's gift came from its mold cool and gleaming in the evening lamplight, and also glowing faintly from the forces within. It was a wide silver bracelet, formed in two halves with their ends shaped to mate into a hinge. The mage sat at his bench and patiently inserted the pintle to join the halves, drilled holes in the open ends, and attached the clasps. The clasp mechanism was an intricate S-shaped, double-locking device. Vernor checked its operation several times.

He sent word to the King and Queen; they were waiting when he entered the nursery. Trever stepped forward. "Vernor, what is it you have devised? Will it work against this – this curse?"

Vernor regarded the King for a long moment. "I believe it will, Majesty." He produced the bracelet from his pouch and held it to the light for them to see. Smiling placatingly in the face of Trever's skeptical expression, he bent over the drowsing infant Prince.

The child stirred, but did not wake when Vernor closed the metal band around his tiny left biceps. The mage stepped back and drew forth the tinted lens he had brought from his workbench. He carefully aligned it to focus the lamplight on the armlet's clasp. When it settled, an amber circle against the silver, he murmured a quiet incantation in a strange tongue. The light seemed to pulse briefly; Vernor put away the lens.

He turned back to his monarchs. "I have done all I can do now. If anything in my power can prevent further manifestations of the ... problem, this will."

The King frowned. "What sort of magic is that, Vernor? I fail to see its significance."

"If I might explain, Majesty." He paused before continuing. "I still know nothing of this fire's source. Such things are spoken of in the Lore, but always in mystery. I know only that it comes from your son's body, and it comes when he is upset.

"This armlet I have created is a kind of barrier against such forces. While in place, it should interrupt the flow of energies through him and around him, and prevent his casting them out at others."

The King was only slightly mollified. "You say 'should' and 'if' and 'believe' rather a lot, Mage. Too much, for my liking. What will you do if this fails?"

"Try again, Highness. I shall study further, cast my net of questions wider. I will not abandon your heir, even if it means calling on the blackest of my arts."

When Trever spoke again, his voice was softer, his manner more thoughtful. "How long must he wear this artifice, Vernor?"

"I do not know, m'Lord. Mayhap for the rest of his life."

Chapter 2
Sare

The day the youngest Princess was born, she caught fire.

Queen Signe of Faires was brought to childbed attended by Obra, the wise-woman of King Gearld's court. Her labor was shorter and much easier than Queen Alyda's; this was, after all, her third birth, and Obra's skills were without equal in either kingdom. She coached and urged and comforted, and finally guided the small girl-babe into the daylight.

The child took a deep breath immediately her mouth was cleared, and let out a cry that was heard throughout the inner ward of the castle. She quieted when Obra lowered her into the tub of warm water that stood close to hand. Once she was bathed and swaddled, she was handed to her mother while the wise-woman attended to matters medical. Some thirty minutes passed before the King was allowed to enter his chambers.

He crossed the room in three long-legged strides, going at once to his wife. He took her hand and kissed her, his head dark against her blondness. "My dearest; all is well, then?"

Signe gave him a drowsy smile. "As well as ever, my Lord. We have a third daughter; not, I fear, the son you hoped for."

Gearld shrugged. "A light matter, and my hopes were not high after all this time. We shall make her a good match when the time comes, and the Proudlock line will continue whether it bears my name or no."

He bent closer to study the infant, who stared back at him with enormous newborn-blue eyes. "I see that as always, you have borne a child to take pride in, healthy and heedful. Though this one seems more delicate than her sisters; she *is* well..?" He turned and addressed the question to Obra, who nodded.

"Quite well, your Majesty. She merely echoes her mother's frame rather than yours. I doubt she will grow so tall as the Princesses Cillistra and Carola already begin to. But she is a fine, sound child withal. And with a fine appetite; she has already taken to the breast and fed."

"Well, good." Gearld turned back to the Queen. "Then, if I may take my leave, m'Lady, I shall announce her arrival to the council and have the white pennon raised to tell the city, and you may take your rest." He bowed his way out of the bedchamber to fond smiles from Obra and his Queen.

Signe shook her head. "Was there ever such a husband upon this throne? Resting does seem a good idea, though. Could you put her in the cradle please? Close beside the bed, so I can reach her if need be."

Obra lifted the little girl and moved the cradle closer with her foot. "Have you chosen a name, m'Lady?"

"Yes. She is to be called Sare, after my grandmother."

"A worthy name." Obra laid the child carefully down and began adjusting the coverlet. "And one that holds good omens for its bearer. How long did your gr – What, by all that is –?" An eerie blue halo had suddenly enveloped the little Princess. As they stared, it erupted into blue-green flames.

Both women screamed. Obra stood aghast for a heartbeat, then lunged down and scooped the baby from the cradle. She whirled and plunged Sare into the now-cold water of her natal bath.

For a horrifying moment, the flames lingered even underwater. Obra was forced to hold the infant's head beneath the surface as fire danced through her hair, across her forehead. The fire died, almost reluctantly, and Obra raised the gasping, squalling newborn and quickly examined her.

The Queen's face was transfigured with horror, her voice a muted quaver. "Will she – will she live?"

"Yes, I am certain. Her burns are not deep or widespread, thank the Gifter. Take her, Majesty, hold her gently and keep her lightly covered. I shall go and make poultices to draw the pain and begin healing."

Queen Signe gathered in her daughter, whispering and comforting as best she could. She looked up to see her own shock and disbelief reflected in the older woman's eyes. "Obra, you spoke of omens in a name. What curse or – or portent could *this* be?"

The reply was hushed and long in coming. "I truly do not know, my Queen ... my friend. I have never seen or heard of such a thing. I must study it, and consult all my sources of lore. But you have this promise: if an answer may be found, by whatever arts I may wield, I shall find it."

◆　　　　　◆　　　　　◆

Two days later, it happened again.

The infant Princess was sleeping, while her nurse used the time to work at embroidery in her own adjoining room. Suddenly, the child began to cry. Even as the nurse laid down her work, the cries rose higher to become screams of pain and fear. She rushed through the doorway, wondering at the strange light emanating from the tiny bed.

Sare's flesh glowed like a candle-tip with an unearthly radiance. Vapor curled from under her bandages, where Obra's poultices still lay. Her wispy hair smoldered. And playing over her contorted cheeks, her waving arms and plump, thrashing legs were lambent tongues of blue flame. They seemed to be growing in intensity.

The nurse stood paralyzed with terror, adding her screams to the sound echoing through the nursery. Long seconds passed before the noise of running feet galvanized her into motion. She snatched up a blanket from a nearby chest and flung it over the baby, rolling little Sare over and over, feeling heat that seemed to come from the very core of the girl's body. The fire died, Sare's skin grew cooler, just as other servants burst in.

Obra was summoned, and arrived just in time to see another manifestation of the horror flare up and fade after a few seconds. She set to work, calming the servants and dressing Sare's new burns, finishing as King Gearld and Queen Signe came in. While his wife comforted the child, the King drew Obra aside into nurse's room.

His face was drawn even thinner than was its wont, his voice pitched low and fearful. "Healer, what is happening to my daughter? What have you learned?"

"Little, I fear, m'Lord. I have searched through all that I could find of fire and dark magics, and found no mention of such events. It seems we face something new in the world."

"Can we do nothing, then? Must this curse continue until she dies? I refuse to believe that!"

"I did not say there was no hope, Majesty. I can tell you that it is some power outside Princess Sare causing these attacks. Of its source or meaning I know nothing. But I think that I may have found a means of protection against its advent. Even now, I am devising a talisman to shield your daughter. It should be finished before sunset today. While she wears it the power may not be able to reach her, as it does now."

Gearld pondered for a moment. "How long do you think she will be forced to wear this 'shield'?"

"No one can say, m'Lord. Perhaps for the rest of her life."

Chapter 3
Michael

The two brothers waited in the shed for their mother's screams to stop. Michael, four years the elder, held the trembling, five-year-old Jacob. He was so accustomed to Jacob's instinctive panic and misshapen limbs that he didn't even perceive them. His mind was on other things; this was not the first time they had waited out a birth in the tool shed. If it was like the other times, his father would soon storm from the house with a bloody bundle under one arm, returning later that night with the stink on his breath and still in a towering rage.

It was exactly like the other times. They heard their mother's cries turn from pain to grief, and the leaden silence of their father's disappointment and anger. The murmur of angry voices rose momentarily and the boys could hear their father.

"...woman! Even the soft-willed royalty in Faires can manage to produce a healthy daughter! Not this, this..." the voices sank again into the hum of their parents' despair. A moment later the house door slammed and Jacob hugged Michael tightly as their father's footsteps crashed off, past the two tiny white markers under the great elm and into the forest.   Those white stones marked the resting-places of the siblings that had lived long enough to be named. The others, like today, were stillborn or so monstrous that they lived only a few awful minutes and then perished.

Michael waited until he was sure that his father was well gone, then disentangled himself from his brother. "Come on, Jake," he whispered. "Let's go see to Mama." He led the younger child by the hand back into the house.

It was barely more than a shack. In the winter the chill wind swept down from the Nethals and found its way between the chinks in the logs. But it was springtime now, and the new green of the forest was warm. They stepped through the only door into the central room with its familiar fireplace, table, chairs, and the small bed the boys shared, then walked quietly to the other room where they peeked around the corner of the doorframe to look at their mother.

She lay on the tattered blanket, soiled rags clenched between her legs, weeping bitterly. She clutched a flask tightly in one hand. She did not look up at the boys. Michael glanced around the room, and began picking up. He righted a stool and sopped up the spilled water with one of his mother's shirts. He turned to Jacob. "Go fetch some water, Jake." Jacob looked out at the front door, eyes wide, then back at his older brother. "It's okay," Michael said. "He won't be back for a while." Jacob reluctantly picked up the water bucket from the corner and went out to the well.

Michael finished tidying as best he could, and went over and stood beside his mother. Using the sopping shirt, he began gently to wipe the blood from her legs. She stiffened for a moment, and then relaxed. Her sobs grew fainter, and her breathing less labored. Finally, she opened her eyes.

"Where's Jacob?" she slurred weakly.

"Fetching water." He didn't look up at her face.

"You're good boys." She curled up and drew the blanket around her. "That's fine, Michael. That's enough."

He stood with the shirt in one hand, then abruptly turned and stalked to the corner of the room, throwing the bloody garment to the floor. He whirled back at his mother, face red, eyes wet.

"Why don't you do it right! Papa is right, you're in league with the Tempter!" He glared at her, fists clenched at his sides. "Why can't I have a *normal* brother?" he shouted, just as Jacob staggered awkwardly back into the room, the heavy bucket sloshing on the floor as he tried to set it down with too-thin arms twisted out of true.

Jacob turned to him with pale eyes so full of pain that Michael couldn't stand it, couldn't stand to be near them, any of them, and he rushed from the room with an inarticulate cry, knocking his brother sprawling. His mother's imprecations were lost in Jacob's piteous wail, and Michael flung himself outside and into the woods, heading in the opposite direction from his father.

The branches tore at his arms as he ran, and he stumbled often as he tried to navigate through the rainbow of tears in his eyes. More or less by instinct he ran down toward the river, turned right and followed it upstream until he got to an unnamed little brackish creek that fed it. By that time he was quite out of breath and he slowed, wiping his face on his sleeve. He picked his way up the bank, following the creek deeper into the woods. Even though it was mid-morning, it grew darker here, and the songs of birds faded in the distance.

This was a part of the forest that most of the people shunned; but Michael had always found it peaceful, a safe haven from his family and the scorn of the other families in the area. The needles that blanketed the ground muffled his footsteps, and the undergrowth grew sparse. An hour later, he reached the great pile of mossy boulders that marked the spring. The trees high overhead grew so tightly together that it was almost as dark as dusk. When it rained, this place remained fairly dry, and Michael slumped to the loam beside a large black rock overlooking the pond that formed at the base of the boulders. It was very deep, deeper than the longest stick Michael had ever found to probe its depths.

He looked into the darkness of the chill water, wrapped his arms around his legs, and rocked, humming tunelessly. That was always comforting to him; he had in fact done little else for the first four years of his life. Eventually, his father had beaten some words into him, and then Jacob had been born. Protecting Jacob was what had really given him a sense of his own place. He couldn't stop his parents from their incomprehensible play of drinking, fighting, and reconciliation, but he could shield Jacob from the worst of it.

His father was a trapper, and spent more time away in the woods than at home, which suited his family well enough. There were other families nearby, but all had chosen a more solitary life away from towns and cities. One spring, when he was six, his father had taken him along to Faires to sell the winter pelts at the great market.

Michael had loved and hated the bustling town, so interesting but so terrifying, and he had unconsciously absorbed his father's frequently voiced loathing for the crowds and the "soft" people who lived there. They had spent the night, his father passed out behind a tavern down by the river, Michael hovering anxiously over him all night, jumping at the shadows of passing strangers and mongrel dogs.

The next day his father awoke in a foul mood and beat Michael with his belt for losing some of their funds, though Michael had no part in their keeping. They loaded their pack mule with supplies and headed out of town. As they were passing through the merchant district, they and the rest of the crowd were pushed rudely to the side of the street by royal escorts shouting, "Make way! Make way!"

Behind them rode two beautiful horses, splendid in their royal trappings. "Hail King Gearld! Hail the Queen!" shouted several excited pedestrians. Michael's father scowled furiously. The King and Queen smiled and greeted the people, but all Michael had eyes for was the little girl riding in the saddle with the King. She was dark-haired like he was, long tresses curled and shiny in the morning light. She looked untouched by the street dust, her emerald riding frock luminous against the charcoal flank of her father's stallion.

Michael had caught her eye, too. She stared at him as she passed, no particular expression on her face, just a frank stare at the little boy holding the bridle of the dusty mule in the gutter. Michael heard one of the guildsmen next to him speaking to another as the royal family passed by: "Just look at Cillistra! How big she's grown!"

"Yes," agreed the other, "A fine princess withal. And her baby sister Carola is an honorable addition to the family. No boys yet, but Signe's young, and the Proudlocks are a hardy line." The first man nodded his agreement.

Cillistra. The boy rolled the name in his mouth. It tasted exotic. *Cillistra.* They returned home without further incident, and without another word spoken. That was the first and only time Michael had left the forest.

He had thought of her often since, especially when he was at the pool. Today, though, his thoughts jumped and scattered, the anger and guilt of the day distracting him. He raged at his mother, and his father, and at himself. He tried not to think about Jacob.

Leaping to his feet he startled a small woodchuck not two armspans away that had been gingerly passing through the glade. It froze, staring at him with wide eyes. Michael was surprised to see it; animals also usually seemed to shun this place.

Stupid beast. It was probably soft in the head. Probably born of diseased parents, who abandoned it to the woods to die. Suddenly more angry than he could ever remember being, Michael lunged at the animal, scooped it up and savagely dashed its brains out against a mossy stone. He screamed at it. He screamed at his parents. Gripping the tiny warm carcass in his hand, he screamed at the world.

Things at the house returned to normal fairly quickly. Nothing further was said about the day of the stillbirth. But Michael felt compelled, over the next several weeks, to revisit the pool more and more often. It was strangely exhilarating, combining in the boy mixed feelings of pleasure and, often, rekindled rage. Twice he captured small creatures in the woods (his father's trapping lessons had taken well) and took them to the pool. Once there, he found it easy to work himself into a ritual frenzy and take the creature's life. After each killing he felt somewhat queasy, but mostly he felt a deep sense of pleasure unlike anything he had ever felt before. And after the second such incident, he discovered the cave.

He was washing the blood off of his hands in the dark waters of the pool when he first saw the pale green light. At first he thought it was a reflection, and glanced up, but it soon became apparent that the dim flickering was coming from deep under the water. Fascinated, the broken bird forgotten, he let the surface settle and tried to make out the light's source. It was no use. Realizing that the only way to find out what it was would be to swim down to it, he pulled his jerkin over his head and untied the cord that held up his breeches. Stacking his clothes on a boulder next to the pool, he carefully picked his way over the smooth stones and into the water up to his shins, where the drop-off was.

It was viciously cold. Taking a deep breath and screwing up his courage, he dove under the icy surface. The shock was sudden and enormous, but not quite enough to overpower his curiosity. He opened his eyes, and could see that the light was much brighter. He swam down, and to his astonishment saw that the bottom of the pool led to a sort of tunnel that angled up under the huge pile of boulders from which the spring came. The walls of the tunnel glowed an unearthly green, lighting the way with perfect clarity. Kicking back to the surface, he grabbed two lungfuls of air and dove back down.

The tunnel was a little narrow in places, but easily negotiated. As he followed it up he saw the surface of the water above him, and broke through into a large rock grotto, the walls of which were mostly black but mottled all over with glowing green lichen. The floor around the pool was comprised of variously sized white stones, which reflected the glow from the walls. There seemed to be something large at the far end of the room.

Michael climbed out of the water, shivering, and made his barefoot way gingerly over the white rocks toward the object at the far end. As he approached, it revealed itself as a large stone block, obviously carved by human hands, and inscribed with symbols he didn't understand. This wasn't surprising to him; he had seen writing before but had never learned to read. There were pictures too, stylized men and beasts including a great bear towering over the trees etched around it, and in the center a great pendulum, its suspended bob carved to look like it was ablaze.

Cautiously, he reached out and pressed the tips of his fingers against the damp stone. Without warning, his head was filled with a powerful voice, seemingly in conversation with itself. He caught it in mid-sentence.

...another. He is more powerful by far. We must act.

No! If we contact him ... take the chance of losing him ... He is too young, and our control ... weak.

Michael snatched his hand away from the altar, fully expecting the voice in his head to stop. But whatever contact had been made was far more permanent than that; the voice continued, obviously unaware of his eavesdropping.

... is responding to the Touch. He is the only entity in ... that has had the correct mental configuration to respond ... powerfully. If the Pendulum is to ever achieve its ... we must act now. He has come to us. Let us greet him.

Michael waited breathlessly in the silence that followed. Had the voice stopped? No, it had not.

Very well then. We greet the child. We ... indoctrinate him and with ... use of the Touch, we tame him. And make him ours.

Agreed.

"Don't be afraid." The actual voice was so sudden and unexpected that Michael fell backwards. Crying out, he glanced down to where he had cut his hand on the edge of one of the rocks. Only they weren't rocks at all, of course. They were bones.

All the way home, his mind raced. What had happened was so unexpected, and so much more immense than anything that had come before in his nine-and-a-half years, that he really couldn't get his mind around it all. There was a thing (things?) that called itself The Pendulum, and it lived in the altar under the pool. What it wanted from him was unclear from its spoken words, but frighteningly more apparent in its mind. What it said it wanted was to be his friend, to teach him things and make him powerful. And he believed that it would actually keep those promises. But what it really wanted was to make him its slave, for reasons Michael was still completely confused about. Many of the words it used were foreign to him, and he only understood about half of what it was saying to itself. But to do this thing, to own him, it was going to use what it called the Touch.

He shivered, remembering the feeling. It was exactly the feeling he had gotten when he'd killed the animals. The Pendulum had used it gently the entire time it had spoken with him, gradually increasing the pleasure, but never as much as he had felt it while at the edge of the pool. He knew from the overheard internal dialogue that it was doing this on purpose to make him like it, to make him want to come back.

And he did want to go back. It wasn't just the thought of something new, something wonderful and powerful that belonged only to him. It was the knowledge that he had a secret even from them (it?), and the fact that he could hear them think made him sure that he could take what they had to offer and escape whenever he wanted. He could actually hear them think! He marveled at the thought. Then another notion struck him, and he stopped dead in the path, suddenly cold all over. *What if they can hear my thoughts too?*

But no; if that were the case they never would have kept on thinking the things they did. They had absolutely no idea, he reassured himself. When he was outside the cave, back on the shore, he could still hear them, but much more softly; by the time he traveled down the steam five minutes the voice faded entirely. And so did the influence of the Touch.

That was the final piece he did not understand at all. Before he had left, they had encouraged him to bring more animals to sacrifice at the water's edge. They called it a tithe, another word he did not fully understand, but he understood their intent. They wanted him to kill more animals, and they'd reward him with the Touch each time he did.

Well, that sounded all right to Michael. That sounded, in fact, just fine.

When Michael was ten, and had known of the Pendulum for almost a year, they sent him on a journey. It would take five days, they said, to get there, and five days back. He waited until his father was out on a long hunt, and then simply told his mother that he was going to be away for a few days. She gestured vaguely and asked him why, but he just ignored her and she soon turned back to the much more interesting conversation she was having with the bottle.

Jacob was more difficult. "Where are you going?" he asked, pestering Michael as he packed provisions in a burlap sack. "What are you gonna do?"

"It's... I'm just going to be gone for a few days. I'll be back soon."

"Can't I come? Please? Why can't I come too?"

"I already told you, somebody needs to stay and look after Mama."

"She'll be all right. I wanna go!"

Michael stared at him. Jacob held his gaze for a moment, then dropped it, looking crestfallen. Without another word, Michael finished packing and slung the sack over his shoulder. Going to his brother, he hugged him fiercely with one arm. Jacob hugged him back awkwardly.

"It'll be all right, Jake. I'll be home before you know it." He threw a glance at their mother and walked out the door.

He traveled south along the river for the first two days, then struck east up into the mountains. He found signs of the ancient road the Pendulum had described, buried under years of forest decay and regrowth. Higher up, above the timberline, the road was easier to find, but he didn't think that people came this way often, if ever.

On the morning of the fifth day he came upon the ravine that had been described to him. He was dismayed to see that it had long ago been blocked by a rockslide from the steep cliffs above.

He spent the rest of the day trying to find a way around the blockage, but had to stop when it got dark. He checked his snares and found a rabbit, which he spitted and cooked over a small campfire just outside the ravine. As he ate, he looked up at the cliffs on either side, blocking out the stars that were just beginning to show. Perhaps there was a way to go around from the north, where the walls seemed slightly lower. He curled into his blanket and fell asleep.

His idea proved to be a good one. Exploring the rocks to the north, he managed to scramble up a narrow crevasse to the top of the wall. It was precarious, but he crab-walked eastward along the top, using the stunted bushes for handholds, until he passed the huge boulders and rubble that had blocked his way below. Descending was easier, the broken rock of the landslide reached almost to the top where he was, and it was less than an hour's work to navigate his way to the bottom of the ravine. He felt confident that he could make the return trip the same way.

The ruins barely hinted at the great stone structures that once stood there. Years of rain and the slow work of lichen had softened the broken columns and shattered cornices considerably. In awe, Michael picked his way over and around the great stone blocks, looking for the cave in the side of the mountain that the Pendulum had directed him to. He found it, mostly blocked by fallen stones, but clear enough in one corner, he figured, to squeeze through.

Knowing that a cave was likely to be inhabited, he hunted around until he found a dead juniper bush, brittle and dry. Scrambling up and crouching outside the opening, he struck flint and set it ablaze. Thrusting it before him into the hole, he worked his way past the rocks, and into the carved stone corridor that lay beyond. Seeing no obvious signs of habitation, he moved a little way down the hallway. On his right was an old torch set in an iron sconce. With the last of his juniper, he managed to light the gummy black end of the torch. It gave off a foul smoke, but threw enough light to see by.

Both sides of the corridor were broken with doorways; each door was old dark wood banded with iron. Michael tried each one, but all were locked. After five such doors on either side, the hallway turned to the right and stopped at a dead end. Nodding to himself, Michael held the torch higher and looked closely at the wall to his left. Just visible was a slight discoloration of the rock, about the height and size of his head.

He transferred the torch to his left hand and put his right on the odd patch of rock. Holding his breath, he pushed. Nothing happened. Bracing himself, he pushed harder. This time, the stone gave slightly, precipitating a grinding noise from his right. Spinning around, he saw the secret door pivot back into the darkness. He had to crouch to get through (an adult would have had to crawl on hands and knees), and the torch set cobwebs alight as he held it in front of him. A few steps farther on the ceiling rose and he could stand upright again.

The room was full of books. He stood in the center and turned in place, astonished that so many books existed. They were ranked on shelves, stacked on tables, and tumbled on the floor in disarray. Interesting, but only mildly so. What good were books, anyway?

One end of the room was different though, and he stepped over the books, holding his torch out before him, to see more clearly. It had obviously been the site of a fire; the furniture and some books were blackened and scorched. As was the skeleton, crumpled in the corner, seared in a cowering position, its arms covering its skull as if to ward off some grave danger. Michael shuddered. This was what he had come for.

Squatting beside the ancient remains, he gingerly reached in and poked with his torch at the dull silver medallion that hung on a chain from the neck bones. It was stuck, and he pushed at it harder. It came loose suddenly, snapping the brittle spine of the skeleton, the blackened skull toppling over and rolling right between Michael's feet. He jumped back with a cry. Muttering to himself, he reached down and grasped the medallion, holding it up in the torchlight to see. The moment he touched the cold metal, he could hear the Pendulum' voices talking to themselves as if he were right in the grotto.

He has found the augmenter!

So he has. Excellent. Now if he just follows the rest of his instructions and returns ... here, we will be well on our way.

... worry too much. Give him a slight Touch, to remind him to hurry back, and he'll never think to look at the books.

... child can't read anyway, they'll have no interest for him.

Perhaps. I hope ... don't underestimate him. Just to be safe though, a small Touch...

Suddenly, Michael was filled with that exquisite pleasure he felt whenever he tithed. He moaned, his eyes half-closing. It was wonderful. It lasted a short time, and then faded away. It made him want to kill something.

Lashing out with his boot, he shattered the skeleton, then stomped on the skull and the bones, grunting with the effort, until they were greasy dust. He finally stopped, panting.

Wiping the medallion on his tunic, he saw that it was embossed with the same picture of the flaming pendulum that was carved into the altar in the grotto. He slipped the chain over his head and let the cold metal rest against his heart. Turning to leave, he stopped, staring at all the books. *What good are they?* Well, that had become an interesting question.

He lifted one and flipped it open. Pages of symbols, written in a flowery, baroque hand. He opened another. The writing in this one was so crabbed and small that he could barely make out the symbols in the torchlight; but it had amazing diagrams of animals, many of which had been cut open, their organs and muscles displayed in intricate detail. Oddly, they weren't prepared in any way that matched anything his father had ever taught him about skinning an animal for eating or tanning.

He took that book, and two others with interesting pictures, and put them in his bag. That was all he could hold - this time. He stooped and moved toward the secret door. Looking over his shoulder, he made himself a promise. He would learn to decipher the symbols in these books. And he would come back.

Chapter 4
Learning

"Aaren, come here." Queen Alyda patted the red velvet cushion of her dressing room divan. The four-year-old prince stood in the doorway, eyes downcast, and shook his head.

Her tone became sharper. "I said, come here at once." He grudgingly let go of the doorframe and slouched over to lean against her leg. His lower lip protruded in an exaggerated pout. "Young man, your nurse tells me that there was another episode between you and young master Gregory."

"He, he, he was taking all the blocks. He was mean to me. I hate him." His lower lip trembled, threatening one of the renowned royal tantrums. Alyda picked him up and sat him facing her on the couch.

"You are a Prince, my son. Gregory is the son of one of your father's most important nobles. It would behoove you to act as one nobly born and not as a common bully when you don't get your way. There are not, after all, that many children here in the palace with whom to play, should you continue to anger those playmates you have. Do you take my meaning, Aaren?"

He looked her in the eye. "He was mean, and it was all his fault. They are my blocks." His eyes were fierce and blue and unrepentant. The Queen felt a sudden warmth flush her entire body. This happened quite frequently when he was angry. For just a moment, she felt as afraid as she knew the rest of the castle to be. He sat fuming, and she stared back at him, not trusting her own tongue for a moment. There was a pause.

Suddenly he burst into tears. "Why doesn't anybody like me?" he sobbed, holding himself stiffly erect at his end of the couch. The tears dripped down his face and darkened the red fabric of the cushion.

Her heart breaking for her son, earlier doubts forgotten, she swept him into her arms. His sobs were muffled against her breast, his tiny fingers curled tightly in the flowing fabric of her gown. "Oh, my boy, shh," she breathed into his hair, stroking his dark curls. "It will be all right. Shh, darling, I love you very much. It is very difficult being a Prince, but I will always be here to help you. Shh."

The artificial heat in her body died away, replaced by the pure warmth of her son in her arms. She rocked him, and held him, and kissed the top of his head. It was not fair, he was such a good boy, but the Gifter was fickle, and her son's road would not be an easy one.

✦   ✦   ✦

For once, the Keep at Faires was not hosting guests. The royal family was taking a quiet evening together in Gearld and Signe's chambers. Cillistra, the eldest daughter at age ten, was playing the harpsichord. Carola, two years her junior, was helping her mother with a tatting, and Sare, all four years of her, was laughing giddily, bouncing on her father's angular knee by the fireplace as he sang to her:

> "Three men sat on a blind man's hat,
> Two of them skinny and one of them fat.
> Three boys chased for the tail of the dog,
> Tripped over each other and fell in the bog.
> Three girls grew up to beautiful maids,
> Sweet in their dresses and sweet in their braids,
> And who does her Da love, as sweet as can be?
> The tiniest cherub, to bounce on his knee!"

The last line was the cue to toss her high and catch her again. She was laughing so hard that she started to hiccough. Signe looked up from her lace. "Gearld..." she warned.

"Ah, she's all right. Aren't you lass? Aren't you your Da's little cherub? Eh?" He grinned broadly and bounced her some more. Sare just laughed, but settled down and stopped hiccoughing.

Carola looked up at the Queen. "Mother, why does Sare get so hot sometimes? Like today. Is she bad? Because Helena said that she was bad and the Tempter made her cry to punish her."

Cillistra stopped playing, and Gearld and Sare turned to listen as well. Signe set aside the unfinished lace, and took Carola's small hands in hers.

"Darling, you little sister is not bad. She is as good as you and Cillistra are."

"I'm Da's little cherub!" Sare announced.

Signe smiled. "Yes you are. And sometimes when people don't understand things, it frightens them, and they say things that they don't mean. Your sister is a very special little girl, and those who love her most need to take extra care in protecting her from harm. Sometimes she does get too hot, but her necklace helps keep her safe. Would you like to help her stay cool when she gets too warm, as Cillistra and I do?"

"Yes," whispered Carola.

"Good. I'm sure she'd love you to help. Wouldn't you, Sare?"

Sare regarded her mother. "All right. Can we have ices now?"

"Ices! Yes, ices!" chorused the other two girls.

Signe looked at Gearld. "Well," he said, standing and throwing Sare onto his shoulders, "let's go see what Cook has in the still-room's cold box, shall we? Come on girls!" Cillistra and Carola bounded over to his side. He stopped in the doorway and looked back over his shoulder at his wife. "Is my favorite girl too big for ices?"

"*I'm* your favorite girl!" shouted Sare, as Signe laughed and joined them.

◆   ◆   ◆

In the four years Michael had worn the Pendulum's medallion, he had learned a great deal about its powers. First, it allowed him to listen to their constant bickering. He had learned to tune most of that out. Much of what they said to themselves was complete gibberish to him – he knew most of the words, but the context was just too foreign, and the sentences seldom complete. Occasionally, when they talked about him, he listened very closely, but most of the time he ignored them.

The second thing it could do was to allow them to Touch him, no matter where he was. He was pretty sure that they could tell when he was killing something, because that excited them like nothing else, and they rewarded him every time. He was also pretty sure that they could not hear his thoughts, as he had once feared. He had tested both theories at once, the first time they had ordered him to kill someone. That was also when he learned how the medallion could help him control other people.

He had been having trouble for some time with a group of boys from various families in the region. He would see them from time to time in the small hamlet where his family bartered for flour and salt and other necessities they couldn't provide for themselves. The four boys were all roughly his age, and never seemed to tire of teasing his brother.

"Hey! Lookit here! It's the monkey!" A caravan had passed through some years earlier with a trained monkey, something that had made quite an impression on all of the children around the hamlet. Jacob, with his unnaturally bent arms and loping stride, vaguely resembled the beast, and this had made him a perfect target ever since. Michael would step in, wordlessly throw a punch at the nearest boy, fists and elbows would fly, and Michael would end up going home with a bloody nose at the very least. But, he told himself through clenched teeth, so would at least three of them. And he was protecting his brother.

The largest boy, Taggart, was the worst, and the one that did the most damage. He had lately begun targeting Jacob during the fighting, which made Michael's job next to impossible. He couldn't take them all on and protect Jacob at the same time. After a particularly bad encounter where he had had a tooth knocked out and Jacob had returned home with an ugly black bruise swelling over his right eye, Michael had made a visit to the grotto. After the customary tithe and Touch, he swam in to deposit a raccoon's body with the others among the bones.

...than later. Animals hardly...

Duesedium romanicus? Instaglio orentis...

"You are bleeding," the Pendulum said.

"I got in a fight."

"Did you win?"

"No."

Aha! This is a good time—

... originally offered as part of the formal...

Yes, yes, I know.

"We can help you."

Michael cocked his head. "Help me? How?"

"We can make you stronger, and can make your enemies tremble before you."

And all you need do in return...

Before he realized what he was saying, Michael asked, "And what do I do for you in return?"

There was a terrible moment of silence.

How did he –?

...smart boy. Smart boy indeed.

"Watch your tongue carefully, boy. Do not anger us, or the consequences will be dire."

He bowed his head in genuine contrition. "I'm sorry! I just... I..."

"Enough. What you do is what comes most naturally to someone like you: Cut your enemies down like wheat before the scythe. Gather allies, and power, with our help. And kill everyone who stands in your path."

Yes, kill! Kill them all!

Michael shook his head. "I don't understand."

And so they told him.

The following week he and Jacob went into town on an errand for their mother. She did some embroidery, having a pretty hand with the needle when her hands were steady enough to thread it, and had finished a bridal veil for a young woman who lived nearby. They were to drop it off with her and bring back the two chickens that had been promised for the work.

Inevitably, as they passed the stables owned by Taggart's father, the cry rang out, "Hey lookit! It's the monkey and his monkey brother!" The four boys came ambling out of the shadows.

"Stay behind me Jake, like we talked about," hissed Michael. His brother tremblingly obeyed.

Michael waited, arms hanging at his sides. Sensing something amiss, three of the boys stopped short, but Taggart strode up and pushed Michael in the chest, hard. Michael stepped back slightly, keeping his balance; when he was sure he had the larger boy's eye, he *twisted* his mind, the way the Pendulum had taught him. He didn't actually grimace, indeed he didn't change expression at all, but suddenly all the color faded from his eyes, leaving them inky black. The medallion grew cold against his skin.

Taggart reared back, suddenly and inexplicably terrified and unable to properly focus on the monkey-boy's brother. Sound faded around him and all he could see were those eyes. He never saw Michael's punch coming, and even as it connected with his solar plexus like a hammerblow and doubled him up, all he could think of were those twin black pools of fear in front of him, and how he seemed to be drowning there.

The blow was far more powerful than Michael should have been capable of, and lifted the larger boy completely off of the ground. He landed heavily. Michael walked over and kicked the prone boy savagely in the head. He barely moaned. The other three rushed forward, then stopped aghast at the same sight that had felled their friend. Michael made sure each of them looked full into his eyes, and then quietly said, "Want some?"

The boys, almost drooling in fear, couldn't speak. They also couldn't seem to back away. They watched as Michael methodically kicked Taggart's head again and again, the blood pooling in the dusty street.

Finally, it was Jacob who cried out from behind him, "Michael, stop it! You're gonna kill him!"

Michael swung around and glared with full intensity at his brother, who shrieked and fell down backwards in fear. Instantly the blackness faded from Michael's eyes, and he stooped and picked Jacob up. "I'm sorry Jake, oh Gifter, I'm sorry. It'll be okay." He hugged his sobbing brother to his chest and murmured into his hair. "It'll be okay." He held his brother out at arm's length and made him look at him, at his restored brown eyes. "It's okay now, all right? All right?" Still sniffing back tears, Jacob nodded.

Michael turned back and spoke to the others, one hand still on his brother. "From now on, I'm the one in charge." They stared at him, eyes wide. "All right?" he prompted with just a hint of the cold anger they had seen a moment before.

"Yeah, sure. Right. Yes," they stammered.

"Good. Then clean this up. And meet me here to-morrow." He turned on his heel and led Jacob away, not bothering to listen to their hurried responses.

After delivering Jacob and the chickens back to the house, he went back to the pool. He undressed and swam inside the grotto.

"It worked!" he shouted, eyes catching the green glow of the cavern walls. "I killed him, like you said."

Liar! No deaths were delivered to us!

...the Original Act. Sycanthum seemed unable to provide...

"Did you, now."

"Y-yes. I did. That's his blood on my boots outside." He feverishly wondered how far he could bluff them. He really wanted the Touch; he *needed* it. But they seemed already to know that he hadn't killed the older boy. How could they know that?

...knows something. We should never have —

Silence! Your prattle distracts me. Focus on the boy.

"You lie. The power that the amulet gives you also delivers the truth to us. There was no killing this day."

Michael wasn't sure how much of the truth the amulet delivered, but he had a growing certainty that death flowed through it just fine. So be it. "I'm... sorry. I did not kill him. But the rest worked just as you taught me. They were so scared!" he exulted.

... will never work. He is too unreliable, too headstrong. We need more tractable allies.

... suppose. He is too strong-willed ...

...mandius alacayam...

... said that from the start. Use him now to bring others, and we will drink his death and be rid ...

Perhaps. A good idea anyway, to bring others now.

"Michael."

"Yes?"

"The time has come to widen the circle. Did you bend the others to your will, as we discussed?"

So they don't know everything. *Interesting.* "Yes. Yes, that part worked just as you said."

"Good. Then gather your troops and bring them to us."

Michael hesitated. "Why?"

"Do not question us! Deliver the others or suffer the consequences!"

Michael slowly nodded. "I will return tomorrow."

"With the others!"

Michael dove into the cold water.

That night he stayed up late, reading from his stolen books by candlelight. The spell he was reading about was a particularly nasty one, and required as an ingredient a human finger. Thoughtfully, he closed the book and stole outside.

He located Taggart's house easily enough, behind the stables. He crept in silently over the windowsill and found his way to the boy's bed, where he lay wrapped in blood-stained bandages, his breathing shallow and hoarse. He looked at the sleeping form for a moment, and then closed his fingers around the bandaged throat. Instantly Taggart's eyes flew open, and as Michael squeezed, he *twisted* his mind. The medallion grew cold. As his eyes darkened, everything he saw in the room looked to him as if it had taken on a silky glow. Immediately Taggart stopped struggling, his own eyes despairing and lost in the moonlight coming in through the window.

Michael squeezed until Taggart's chest stopped hitching, then a moment longer. Finally he let go. Dimly, over the victorious pulse of his own blood in his ears, he heard the Pendulum roar its approval. As he stood there, he was suddenly overcome with the Touch, vivid and powerful and perfect. He sank to his knees. The Touch eventually faded. Michael drew his small knife and looked at the dead boy for a long time, then slipped back out the way he had come - with Taggart's right index finger in his pocket.

He never did bring anyone else to the grotto. No matter how the Pendulum railed at him, he refused to share his secret. He killed for them, and secretly studied his books, and knew that as long as he was the only one, they needed him as much as he needed them.

Chapter 5
Companions

Darras, Lord Oswin of Edge, was celebrating his eldest daughter's seventh birthday when she surprised her parents more than they did her.

Jenora was tall for her age, with long russet hair and large hands for a young girl. She was sitting on the floor with her arms around her gift, a squirming mastiff pup. She looked up at her father with startlingly serious eyes. "Papa ... could I be trained as a warrior, like you?"

Darras was taken aback. True, for five generations the Oswins had been Palatines to the Kings of Edge. He had held the hereditary post himself for over fifteen years, serving as companion, confidant, and personal guardian to King Trever since they were boys. This tradition, and Darras' long friendship with Trever, had made Jenora, and later her sister Agnes, welcome at Greybeal Palace since Prince Aaren's birth. Raised as playmates to the royal heir, the girls had lacked for nothing, and were brought up to know and perform their roles in life as members of a noble house. But this was the first he had ever heard of such an ambition from little Jenora.

He looked to his wife, who could only shrug to signal her ignorance about the request. Considering carefully, he replied, "Well, I don't know, Jenora. Why would you want to?"

"Because I am the next Oswin. I should be the next Palatine like you are. And I want to be. I like Prince Aaren, even when he acts so spoiled. I want to protect him the way you protect King Trever."

It was a thought that had scarcely crossed Darras' mind before. He knew the regard Trever held him in. He knew that he and Kerwin, a fellow veteran who was the King's huntsman, were Trever's only close friends. There was no one closer to the King, perhaps not even his wife. Trever's marriage to Queen Alyda had been an arranged one, to seal an alliance with one of the southern kingdoms. She did her queenly duties well, and Darras knew that she held Trever's full affection – but perhaps not his full respect. Trever was a hard man in some ways, gruff as his father had been, and not one to spend much time worrying about others' feelings.

Yet, if there was to be another Oswin in the Telcien service, who else *could* it be? "But Jenora, do you really think you know what such a choice might mean? It takes years, years of very hard work..."

"I know, Papa." She smiled shyly before continuing, "I've watched you sometimes, when you didn't see me. You know I can ride already. And I made myself a wooden sword, and I practice with it every day. I'm really good!"

"So you are, eh? I just might ask you to prove it, you know." He smiled back at her. "I truly don't know, Jenora. A soldier's life is not all tilting and riding and practicing with swords. It's not all excitement and glory, either. It can be dirty and hard and dangerous. Would you really want to see those parts for yourself?"

Jenora's gaze was level and open. "But Papa, you've seen them, and you still serve the King."

Darras laughed and raised her to his lap, puppy and all. "I can also see that you won't be easily put off this course. All right: I'll make you no promises, but I will take this up with His Majesty when I'm next at court. The decision will be his." He caught Lady Oswin's eye again. She returned an exasperated smile and a shake of her head. He turned back to Jenora. "Will that do?"

She flung her arms around his neck. "Oh, yes, Papa! Thank you!" The pup, released, dug its claws into Darras' thigh and sprang to the floor. Jenora slipped out of his arms to leap down and chase after it, leaving her parents to their own discussion about her unusual aim in life.

Surprisingly, the idea of a woman warrior intrigued the King. He assented to Jenora's request, and immediately put her in the care of Leland, his Master of Arms. He also told her father that she might, indeed, one day assume her position as Palatine to the Prince, if her temperament suited the role.

It did. By the age of eight, she was the match of any ten-year-old boy in Leland's training yard, and an accomplished archer. She rode flawlessly, drilled with a half-sized sword for hours each day, and ran and climbed to build her strength and stamina. Her natural tenacity and cunning went hand-in-hand with her growing knowledge of tactics and techniques. She was indeed an Oswin.

Two years later, when Prince Aaren was six and she was nine, she was formally called before the King for her investiture.

◆   ◆   ◆

Aaren had been summoned to the Great Hall. His nurse dressed him in his finest, his puffed sleeves covering the silver bracelet on his left biceps. She smoothed down an errant cowlick of brown hair and looked him over. "That will have to do. Come along, your Highness, it's not good form to keep your father waiting." He nodded and reached up for her hand. "No, boy, from now on you walk alone, like a young man should." She silently repressed a shudder of fear at the thought of his touch, and her voice was sharp.

"Remember everything you have been taught." She walked over and opened the nursery door. "Come along."

He stood for a moment, staring expressionlessly at her with eyes that seemed very blue. She felt suddenly warm all over, but it was a feeling she had become so accustomed to over the last six years that she didn't even notice it. He stared at her for a moment longer (*willful child!*) and then went through the door and down the hallway, and she followed.

As he entered the Hall, his father's booming voice greeted him from the throne dais. "Aaren, my boy! Don't you look smart! Come up here and stand beside me. There are things I need to speak with you about." Without looking up he dismissed the nurse with a wave of his hand. She bowed deeply and retreated.

Aaren climbed the three steps and stood on the right, facing his father. Lord Wildon stood to the left of the throne, slightly behind the king. He looked severe, but then the chamberlain usually looked as though he had bitten into something that did not agree with him.

The tall narrow windows threw the morning light in stripes across the tapestries on floor and wall, leaving the dark wooden beams high in the ceiling in deep shadow. The three of them were alone in the great chamber. Aaren thought that his father's eyes looked uncharacteristically gentle.

"Aaren, you are growing up fast. How tall you are! Time seems to flow more swiftly with each passing day. And today is an important one. You shall leave here with someone to whom you may trust your very life.

"The Telciens have looked to the Oswins for loyalty, courage, and valor since before the time of your grandfather's grandfather. They are a steadfast line, deserving your highest trust and respect." The words were obviously deeply felt, and echoed a memory of King Crawford uttering them many years before. "Darras, Lord Oswin, has served me uncommonly well, in every capacity, since we were boys."

Trever raised his head and called out, "Enter, Jenora, daughter of Darras, and know your liege." The doors at the far end of the Great Hall opened, and Jenora strode forward, with Darras three steps behind. They both looked very fierce, Aaren thought, their burnished armor sparkling. They stopped at attention before the King, who stood to meet them. "Who presents this warrior?"

"I, Darras of the house of Oswin."

"Advance, friend Darras."

Darras and his daughter stepped forward. Jenora turned, stepped up to the first stair before the Prince and knelt. Aaren looked up at his father, who handed him the ceremonial broadsword. Concentrating on remembering all of the words, he turned back to the kneeling girl. He held the heavy sword in front of him, one hand on the hilt, the other under the flat of the blade.

"You are chosen, warrior, to be Palatine to the royal house of Telcien." Aaren's voice sounded very small after the throaty growl of his father, but it was steady and held the seed of command. He handed her the sword. She accepted it, then turned the blade down and touched her forehead to the hilt.

"This day I swear my loyalty, my honor, and my life." There was an uncomfortable silence. Trever cleared his throat and nudged Aaren with his elbow.

"Uh, rise, companion, and take your place at my side," Aaren finally blurted, but aside from a small blush he retained his composure. Jenora got to her feet, and lifted her eyes to meet his. They appraised each other frankly for a long moment, her fierce gaze met by Aaren's sober countenance. At the same time, they both nodded slightly.

"My liege." She joined him on the top step.

The king spoke again. "Darras, this warrior will become a superb addition to the royal house. You have served us well."

Darras bowed from the waist. "The Gifter provides." He straightened. "Now if it please the King, their training together can begin at once."

"An excellent idea. Aaren, go with Darras and join Master Leland now, and get to know your playmate as your Palatine. It is a long road you two begin today."

Aaren nodded and climbed down the steps, Jenora at his heels. "I am ready, Father." Darras spun on his heel and led them from the hall.

The King turned to his chamberlain. "So what do you think, Wildon?"

"A good match indeed, Majesty. She has attended to her training with a great deal of ferocity and determination, I'm told. These are good qualities in a Palatine. Lady Jenora has reason to love the royal house. And as the Prince is very ... strong-willed; perhaps it is good to match his temper with the compassion of the distaff sex. Time will tell, Majesty."

"Aye," Trever agreed. "Time will tell."

◆   ◆   ◆

Summers in Faires were glorious. Protected from the eastern ocean storms by the Nethal peaks, the days were long and warm, too warm perhaps but for the Wendlow River, curling down from the snowpack and cooling the farmlands to the north of the keep. From her window, Sare could see down the hill to the farmers at work in the fields by the river. But her gaze this day was directed across the river to the gentle swells of the hills to the north, the narrow road winding through them, and the promise of a picnic with her mother and sisters.

"Come away from the window, child, and get yourself ready," called Ilaine, her governess. Sare skipped over and squirmed into her traveling clothes, with Ilaine's exasperated help. "Stop wiggling, Princess, and you'll be sooner ready." Whenever Sare went outside in the sunshine, she needed to cover herself fully; the burns from her birth six years before had left her skin very sensitive to the sun's heat.

"We get to go swimming!" she said.

"So you've told me. That sounds lovely. Now, here's your sun bonnet - stop squirming! Let me tie the chin ribbons. All right. That will have to do." Ilaine eyed her charge critically. "Off with you then."

Sare squealed and ran from the room. *So sad,* thought Ilaine. *She will never be as beautiful as her sisters. The other children still tease her about her scars, though she has healed almost completely. Obra does wonders. But,* she reminded herself, *Sare is a princess, and with a joyful heart with twice the radiance of that spoiled brat Cillistra; she will make someone a fine wife.*

Sare stood on tiptoe and gingerly extended her palm to Killaern, her roan pony. The horse snuffled up the sugar with gentle lips and snorted comfortably. The stable master hoisted her up into the saddle and checked the panoply, tightened a strap, and nodded, smiling, to Signe. "All is well, my Queen." He nodded then at the three girls, splendid in their saddles. "Princesses, have a superb ride." The foursome turned and gently trotted off down the hill. He gestured to the two mounted men-at-arms, who spurred their mounts and set off, following at a respectful distance.

The morning delivered on its promise, the sky achingly blue, leant depth by small herds of wispy clouds. Sare thought that most of the clouds looked like either horses or rabbits, and said so several times. At yet another exclamation of the same observation, Cillistra turned in her saddle and glared at her youngest sister.

"What's that? A horse, you say! Well I never! Did you hear that Carola? That cloud looks like a horse! Do tell us again, Sare, and what about that cloud over there? Is that a horse too? No? A rabbit then. It must be." She faced forward again with an exasperated *harrumph.*

"Girls, let us be civil with one another," Queen Signe said from her place in the lead, not turning around. "It is too beautiful a day to be marred with bickering."

Cillistra turned again and glared silently at Sare. Sare stuck out her tongue and made a face, which made Carola, who was riding between them, giggle. Furious, Cillistra turned around and wouldn't look back for the rest of the journey.

"Just 'cause she's twelve she thinks she knows everything," muttered Sare, and Carola giggled again.

They stopped just before the sun was at its highest, under a grove of willows by a medium-sized stream. It was about a league off the road, and chosen for both its beauty and defensibility. The men-at-arms positioned themselves, one at the top of the hill and the other by the path leading to the stream from the road. Raiders and highwaymen had been less aggressive of late, but it was wise to take precautions.

They laid out blankets and unpacked their saddlebags. The kitchen had packed them roasted chicken, fresh loaves of bread, a wheel of soft cheese, and delicately flavored sweet wafers for dessert. Signe set out the feast and exclaimed, "Oh my. There is enough food here for ten. I think it would be nice if we offered something to Anton and... what is that other boy's name?" She smiled sideways at Cillistra.

"Matthew," sighed the girl.

"I'll go!" said Sare. "Let me take them some!"

"No!" piped Cillistra shrilly. "I'll go. You're too little, and besides, Mother needs your help fetching water."

"Oh, Carola can help me. Why don't you both go?" Signe quickly made up two bundles wrapped in napkins. Cillistra rolled her eyes, and Sare beamed. They each took one bundle and headed up the hill toward the men, still in their saddles.

Cillistra glared at her sister from under her long lashes. "You are such a pest. Why do you always have to follow me around?"

"*You're* a pest," said Sare.

"Honestly. Boys will never like you if you're always such a brat."

"*You're* a brat. Matthew likes me."

"Oh, please. Matthew is a handsome young warrior, and you are just a little girl with a big mouth."

"*You* have a big mouth."

They arrived at the top of the hill and Matthew swung down to greet them. "Well what have we here? Princesses? What brings two such beautiful ladies up to see me?"

Cillistra stared at him raptly, not saying a word. Sare looked at her sister, then at the young man. "Cillistra thinks you're handsome. I don't know about that. We brought you something to eat."

"Sare!" squeaked Cillistra, mortified.

Matthew laughed. "So you're not so sure then? Well, it is best to reserve judgment on matters of the heart until you're certain." He winked at Cillistra, who blushed even more furiously. "It is very kind of you both to think of me." He took the bundle from Cillistra's hands. "Many thanks to your mother as well. I'll just – Princess?" he stopped, suddenly alarmed as he gazed at Sare.

The other bundle had dropped from Sare's shaking hands, spilling its contents on the grass. Her complexion had gone unnaturally pale, with high spots of color dancing on her cheekbones. The amulet she always wore around her neck could be seen faintly glowing through her blouse. Her legs began to tremble and fold, and then she flushed deep crimson. She turned terrified eyes toward her sister. "*Cill!*"

The guard reached out to catch the falling child. "Don't touch her!" screamed Cillistra, knocking the young man aside and scooping Sare into her arms. She raced down the hill as fast as her long legs would carry her, past Carola and her startled mother, to the stream. Without pausing, she waded out into the chilly water and dropped to her knees, cradling the shaking six-year-old under the water, with only Sare's red, frightened face above the surface.

"It's going to be all right," Cillistra panted, out of breath. "You're going to be all right." Sare felt fiery, even through the fabric of their clothes and the cold water.

Sare nodded, panting. "It's - not - a bad one," she gasped.

Just as Signe splashed out to where they were, Sare suddenly relaxed in Cillistra's arms. The color of her face immediately began to fade toward normal. She began to cry, and buried her face in Cillistra's hair. "I've ruined everything," she sobbed.

"No, no, that's not true," Cillistra answered, hugging her close. "We just, we just decided to go swimming a little early, you and I, didn't we?" She reached over and turned Sare's face to hers. "Didn't we?"

Sare nodded, eyes puffy with tears. Signe reached in and took Sare in her arms, and carried her back to the blankets. Cillistra and Carola helped with her wet clothes, and made every attempt to keep their conversation light during the meal. But Sare was obviously exhausted, and even though she objected strenuously to packing up early, they all agreed that it was time to go home.

On the way Cillistra rode beside Sare. They didn't say much, just rode side-by-side back to the Keep.

◆   ◆   ◆

It had been raining for days. Michael and Jacob were cooped up in the house; their father was away trapping but due back soon, and tensions were high. The latest round of wrangling had ended with a brooding silence between the two brothers and their mother. She stayed in her bedroom, Michael hunched over a book in the corner, and eleven-year-old Jacob scuffed around the room sulking. The rain beat steadily on the roof, and hissed into the trees outside.

Michael hadn't been out with his followers in several days. He had acquired a small crew, mostly through intimidation, and had picked up roughly where Taggart had left off. The games they played with Michael at the lead were for keeps, though, and more than one solitary mountain traveler had added his meager belongings to the gang's pockets and their bones to the Pendulum's grotto. Not that Michael ever took anyone there still alive; that secret was still his alone.

Suddenly, the front door banged open. Michael spun around and Jacob cried out. Their father, returned days early, loomed in the doorway, rain running off of his sodden traveling cloak and onto the threshold. He was out of breath, and very angry.

"Get your Tempter-wrought carcasses out here and help me!" he growled. As Michael moved toward the door, his father shouted, "Well get your cloak then! We have a piss-load to do and not enough daylight to do it in." He glanced witheringly at his younger son. "You too, whelp. Gifter knows what use you'll be, but the river has swollen so high that I need all the hands I can muster to haul in the traps." He swung around and stalked off into the rain. The boys scrambled into their gear and hurried after.

It took over an hour to get to the place where the traps were snarled. Jacob could barely keep up, and Michael had to help him twice when he fell in the slippery mud. The entire way, their father cursed them, cursed the rain, cursed his wretched existence. When Michael asked him once to slow down, he was cuffed on the ear so hard his head rang. Blood dripped down his ear and mixed with the punishing rain.

Hauling the traps from the river was extremely hard work. Michael understood why his father had come back for him. It took the both of them to heave against the raging current and wrench the traps from the river's grasp. Once they were tossed on shore, Jacob pulled the drowned animals out and gutted them, stringing them together to carry back home.

As they worked their way down the river, Michael grew more and more enraged. His father's petulant ranting scoured his ears through the hiss of the rain and the roar of the water. They were up to their waists in the chill water, hauling on the rope of one trap that had become hopelessly tangled in a fallen tree, when Michael yelled, "Let it go! We'll never get this one!"

His father turned on him snarling (as he had known deep down that he would) and drew back to cuff him again. Without thinking, Michael *twisted*. His father, shocked and suddenly overcome by the instantaneous fear that came to all who looked into Michael's killing gaze, halted with his arm sticking up incongruously, looking for all the world like he was giving his son a friendly wave.

The roar of the water mixed with the roar of the Pendulum as Michael grasped his father's throat and pushed his head easily under the water. Everything stood out so clearly in his mind: the tiny splashes where the rain hit the river, the rough stubble of his father's jaw against his thumbs, the heat of his father's neck under his palms contrasted with the chill of the rushing water on the backs of his hands. And like heaven come to earth, as his father's thrashing ceased, the Touch coursed through him to his core.

And right in the midst of it Jacob flung himself onto Michael's back. The interruption was unthinkable; it cut Michael to the quick, and without hesitation he grabbed the feeble arms that tried to stop him and tore them loose, tossing his brother out into the river like a rag doll. Arms pinwheeling, Jacob managed a tiny scream before he hit the water. He bobbed up, coughing and choking, already swept away downriver.

He was still nearer the edge than the middle, and he slammed into the trunk of the fallen tree and was caught there, the breath knocked out of him. With his enhanced clarity, Michael heard one of his brother's ribs snap. Slowly, his bent fingers scrabbling weakly at the waterlogged bark, Jacob began slipping down under the half-submerged tree trunk.

"Jake!" Michael screamed, his eyes once again returning to their normal color. "Jake!" He threw himself down toward his brother, wading out as far as he dared, the current trying to snatch his feet from under him, trying to pull him under the tree as it had his brother. Only Jacob's head was still above water, his face beet-red, terrified eyes imploring Michael for help.

But there was nothing he could do. He watched his brother slide under the roiling water and vanish.

Desperately, Michael slogged back to shore and clambered over the log to the downstream side, looking vainly for sight of his brother. Agonizing minutes passed. He looked downstream, hoping against hope that Jacob might have slid completely under the tree and washed up again. But there was no sign.

He climbed up atop the tree and crawled out to where he had seen Jacob go down. On the upstream side, he saw nothing. Downstream, though, through the boiling currents, he thought he saw a pale flash. He plunged his arm down as deeply as he could, hanging onto a branch with his other hand. Nothing there but rushing water and the submerged slippery bark. Then, so briefly he almost didn't feel it, something brushed against his hand. It was Jacob's foot. Crying out, he groped another few inches, and felt it again. He clutched at it and pulled with all his strength.

In a sudden rush, he pulled his brother free. In doing so, he pulled himself off the log and into the icy river. Never letting go of Jacob's ankle, he swam desperately for the shore. He managed to find purchase, and dragged the cold little body onto the cold stones at the river's edge. Feverishly, he turned Jacob over, seeing muddy river water pour from between his brother's blue lips.

And suddenly, sickeningly, he felt the Touch again.

"No!" he screamed, flailing his arms as if he were having a fit. He screamed again, a long tortured keening as he writhed at the river's edge, his horror and the pleasure fusing into a horrific fire that bathed him in its awful heat. He kept on screaming long after the Touch had faded, hugging Jake's body to his chest, the rain washing over them both and vanishing into the whirl of the river.

Eventually, he stopped screaming. Some time later, he stopped crying. It was dark. His back and legs were terribly cramped, and he was chilled to the bone. The rain was still falling, but had lessened considerably. It was actually the muttering of the Pendulum that stirred him. With wet, cramped fingers he took the medallion from his neck and, standing, thrust it deeply into the pocket of his cloak.

It had come to him slowly, but with the surety of truth: he knew what he had to do next. Much of what he needed was in the ruins, but he knew enough to prepare Jake for the journey. He lifted his brother's body gently, and carried him up the bank of the river. He stooped and set him just as carefully in the black mud. It was very dark, and he could barely make out Jacob's body as he slowly, methodically, took handfuls of the wet clay and smoothed them over his brother. As he did, he sang the strange words he had learned in one of his stolen books. The song was of loss, and regret, and the savage insistence of grief. Forces moved through his fingers as he worked the mud.

By the time it was light enough to travel, it had stopped raining. The thick coating of drying mud covered the spindly boy and more, giving him the heft and symmetry in death that he had lacked in life. Fashioning a simple travois, Michael lashed Jacob down securely and set off for the ruins.

It took eight days. He almost thought he wasn't going to be able to get the mud-plastered corpse over the fallen rocks, but he managed. Standing at the crumbled entrance, he felt remarkably clear-headed. It had been years since he had been so focused, so empty of thought, and so empty of emotion. Not hearing the nagging voice of the Pendulum helped. The medallion weighed heavily in his pocket, but he did not touch it.

He took Jacob inside, lit the well-used torch, and dragged him back to the library. He had restored it over the years: righted the furniture, sorted the books back onto the shelves, and gathered the accouterments of magic to their places. Taking the medallion from his pocket, he tossed it into the corner, revolted by the sudden murmur of the Pendulum's voice in his head.

He thought of doing something more permanent, but found he couldn't bring himself to touch it again. When he was done here, he would go and tell them that he was through with them. No more killing for them, no more Touch. They would be very angry, he was sure, but he didn't think that they would kill him. He didn't know if they actually could. He did know their minds, however. They would threaten, but in the end they needed him more than they ever admitted out loud, and would hope that his reliance on the Touch would bring him back. He blinked, considering the idea. No, that needy part of him had drowned alongside Jacob and his father, he was sure. He had killed it too.

Turning back, he untied Jacob from the travois and laid him inside the circle of silver set in the stone floor. Going to a book-shelf, he took down an old broken-backed leather volume tied with twine. He gingerly undid the twine and turned to the page he wanted. He read the spell over several times. Nodding, the details memorized, he gathered what he needed and went to stand over the mud-encased body of his brother. His mind and heart still cold and empty, Michael began the casting.

It took longer than he thought, and was completely exhausting. By the time he reached the point in the spell where he was supposed to gather up much of who he was and invest that energy into the golem, he wasn't sure he could finish. But he was driven to do this, both to salvage what he could of his brother and to place a piece of himself where the Pendulum could never find it. He knew that his brother was dead, and that no matter what reanimation of the flesh he performed, he would still have killed him.

But he did it anyway. Because he could; because he didn't know what else to do. Closing his eyes, kneeling over the cold dried clay, he spoke the final words that gathered his life energy, and then he *pushed* it into his creation. A silent white flash behind his eyes drove him into unconsciousness.

When he awoke hours later, he sat up, rubbing his eyes. The torch had gone out. Feeling his way over to the table, Michael groped and found the flint and steel. He struck a spark onto a spare torch, held it aloft, and turned to look at what he had created.

The golem sat in the circle, staring calmly back at him with white eyes that lacked pupils. It seemed so large, its head on a level with his own though he was standing. *Did I make it grow like that? How?* Michael could feel the golem's presence in a way very like the way he was aware of his own body. He was not frightened at all. He knew with deep certainty that the grey creature before him was wholly enslaved; no, was a pure extension of his will. He held out the torch.

The golem rose gracefully to its feet and took the light. They stared at each other for a moment longer. Then they turned and left the ruins, the medallion glinting dully in the dust behind them, to go and face the Pendulum.

Chapter 6
Unfolding

"I don't think he's ready," said Queen Alyda.

"Why not?" bristled Trever. "The boy is old enough. I think he needs to be in the company of men a bit more."

"Does that have to mean unlocking the bracelet? Just have the ceremony without it."

"You know very well that the Age of Trust ceremony has always meant unlocking the bracelet to Aaren. It's been understood for years. The ceremony would be meaningless for him without that. And however well Jenora and Leland intend, the time for toy spears and wooden swords is past. Edge needs its Prince to let go the hem of his mother's skirt."

Sensing the inevitable outcome of the conversation, Alyda bowed her head. Perhaps he was right. The boy was almost thirteen years old, and had blossomed into a young man of whom she was very fond, if not wholly trustful. His heart held sway over his head all too often, and he had his father's temper. "Very well," she said. "I suppose you are right. I'll have the arrangements made at once. Perhaps at the Spring Banquet, in three weeks' time? It falls on his thirteenth birthday."

"Fine, fine. That's perfect then, isn't it? Just don't dawdle." He kissed her roughly but passionately, grinned through his beard, and strode from the room. Alyda smiled too, in the wake of his powerful affection, and called for her lady in waiting.

✦   ✦   ✦

The Spring Banquet was one of the biggest annual events in Edge. There was feasting and dancing, and special events like birth announcements, betrothals, and the Age of Trust ceremonies. The afternoon preceding it was frantic with scurrying help, and the smells from the kitchen tantalized everyone in the palace.

Jenora and Aaren left all the bustle to climb the tower to Vernor's study, and Jenora knocked on the great wooden door.

"Yes, what?" barked the mage's muffled voice.

They glanced at each other. "You sent for me," Aaren said. Silence. "It is Prince Aaren!" he added, then yelped as the door was flung open.

Vernor growled, "Yes of course it is. Who else would it be, eh?" He glared at Jenora. "Ah. You. You have some business here, girl?"

She drew herself up to her full height and looked down at the stooped figure. "Indeed I do, Mage. As the Palatine to the heir Prince on the day of his Age of Trust ceremony, I have urgent business being wherever he is." She stared at him. There was an uncomfortable moment of appraisal that Aaren seemed about to break when Vernor smiled and gestured into the room behind him.

"Very well then, very well indeed. Please come in, the both of you, we have important matters to attend to."

They followed him into the room, and stood by as he busied himself with something on the main workbench. Neither had ever been allowed in these chambers before, and the dizzying array of sights and smells was awe-inspiring. Aaren saw a shelf packed with glass jars, some of which seemed to hold a variety of preserved animals. He started to take a closer look when Vernor spun around.

"Pay attention, boy! No time for that! You know what tonight's ceremony means, don't you?

Aaren stammered, "Certainly. It symbolizes my journey from childhood to -"

"No, no, no, not all those bat droppings! I mean the phlogiston shield!" They stared at him blankly. "The bracelet you wear there on your arm, my boy. Do you know what it does, then?"

Aaren paused, considering. When he spoke he looked directly into Vernor's eyes. "Yes. I do. You created it when I was born to stop me from hurting people when I'm angry."

"What do you mean, 'hurting people'?" demanded the mage, staring intently at the Prince.

Again Aaren paused. "I can burn things."

"That is correct. And now your father thinks that you're man enough to control yourself without my help. He wants you to take it off. What do you think of that?"

Aaren's eyes locked with the magician's. "The King is always right."

"The King is as big a fool as any other man." Jenora stiffened, glowering. "Sit down, girl; I do not attack your liege or his father. Men are men, even those of royal blood, yes?" She did not answer. "Of course they are."

He turned his attention back to Aaren. "I didn't ask what *he* thought, I asked what you think."

Aaren considered. His deliberation startled Jenora, who was used to his quick, sometimes-thoughtless tongue. "I think that it is time to take my place at my father's side. I think that it is time to unlock the bracelet. I think that I am able to control the burning."

Vernor stared at him. "You think you can control it, do you?"

"Yes. Yes, I can. I've been practicing."

Again Jenora was surprised. *Practicing?* She had known for years of his ability to make a person uncomfortably warm when he was angry, but had never spoken of it with him. She knew it was a matter of great shame and personal distress to him. The thought of him exercising deliberate control over the power was disconcerting.

"Yes," Vernor rumbled, "I know you have. You've been playing with it all your life, and really concentrating on it for at least two years."

Aaren's eyes narrowed. "How do you know that?"

Vernor snorted. "It is my business to know such things. I also think you can control it. I know too that it is a much greater power than you imagine, and that you must exercise enormous restraint, lest it get control of *you*."

Aaren nodded. "I understand."

Vernor appraised the young man. "Mayhap you do, at that." He seemed to come to a decision. "And how do you remove the shield from your arm?"

"I cannot. It is locked, by your magic."

"Wrong! How do you remove it?"

Aaren stared at him, then down at the bracelet. There was a great deal of tension in the room. Jenora, without realizing it, held her breath. Aaren reached down and turned it on his wrist until the clasp faced up. He traced it with his fingertips. He looked up at Vernor, then back down at the bracelet. Gripping it firmly in his right hand, he closed his eyes. There was a pause. Behind Vernor, Jenora saw a pendulum swinging madly on the workbench. There was an almost inaudible *pop*, and Aaren opened his eyes.

What Jenora saw there frightened her badly. His eyes were a blue past blue, almost too bright to look at, and not the eyes of a human being at all. Then as swiftly as the transformation had taken place, the glow faded, and he was just her Prince again. In his right hand he held the open bracelet.

"I could have done that any time I wanted to," Aaren whispered, comprehension dawning.

"Yes, you could," said Vernor.

Aaren and Jenora spoke briefly as they descended the stairway outside Vernor's chambers. Both were bemused by the events upstairs, and both somewhat hesitant to speak.

"Is everything all right with you?" Aaren finally asked.

"Why?"

"It's just that you look, I don't know, troubled. And you won't meet my eye." They both stopped on a landing. The sky through the tall window was dotted with fleecy clouds, and the spring breeze was warm. It seemed to settle them back on more familiar ground.

"Some time - not today - we must talk about your ... power. It is a thing that you and I need to become accustomed to," she finally said.

"Yes. Things have changed. But I am still the same person as before." He looked at her, then down at the bracelet he had re-clasped onto his wrist. He wasn't ready yet to give it up completely. He had worn it all his life, and it was a part of him.

Jenora hesitated. "Yes, you are the same person, but today I realized that there are parts of you that I don't know. Our friendship, and my duties as your Palatine, demand that I know you better, that I may serve you better."

"Agreed. For tonight then, perhaps we may pretend that all is as it was before?"

"No, Prince, I think not. But I will be at your side, through this and all other changes that the Gifter has in store for us. Know that."

He grasped her arm tightly, and leaned in, his face very close to hers. "I do know that. Thank you." They stared into each other's eyes for a long moment, then he turned away, smiling. "I have less hours to prepare than tasks to prepare for."

"'Fewer' hours, Prince," she murmured to his retreating back, correcting his grammar automatically as she recovered from the proximity of his almost-embrace. For just a moment she had thought he was going to kiss her, and the thought had made her reel. *Get a hold of yourself, girl,* she chastised herself. If there was one thing she would never be his for, it was romance. She swallowed, and controlled her conflicting emotions as Master Leland had taught her. When the warrior girl had regained her composure, she followed her liege down the stairs to prepare for the banquet.

That night after the feasting, Vernor made a great show of formally unlocking the bracelet, with conjured fire and smoke and the same amber lens he had used thirteen years before. When he was done, Trever took great pride in presenting his son to the assembled nobles and ladies of the court.

Aaren, for his part, was gracious and regal, as befitted his new position as an adult. Jenora was asked to dance several times by the sons of nobles, and did so, enjoying herself; but always her eyes drifted back to her Prince. He sat on his father's right, smiling, speaking to the various people of Edge who had come. His eyes were very blue, and very human, and he was the most handsome young man she could ever remember seeing. Every so often his right hand crept down and toyed with the unlocked bracelet on his wrist.

◆   ◆   ◆

The Alatian dignitaries were in Faires again, from their smaller city in the mountains to the north. The Alatian people were primarily miners, and traders as well. Every few years they would make the trek to Faires to trade metals and ore for the prized Fairen horses and grain. It was the day of Sare's thirteenth birthday, and she was a little put out that her celebration had been postponed until after the traders departed, fully a week hence.

She was naturally expected at all of the events honoring their guests. Tonight it was a dinner given in the grand banquet chamber, also attended by several of the local merchants. It was a chance for the two groups of businessmen to meet and talk informally, and no one missed an opportunity to dine at the Keep.

Rodolpho, the Keep's majordomo, was in rare form. Cooks, scullery maids, and attendants of all sorts bustled through the halls under his critical eye. Sare caught up with him in the grand entry hall, supervising the placement of the banners and flags.

"Rodolpho?" she called.

He turned, saw who it was, and hurried over. "Yes, Princess? What can I do for you?"

"You wouldn't happen to have tonight's guest list, would you?"

"Not on my person, Highness, but of course I have it committed to memory. Had you a question about a guest?"

"Oh. Well, no. I mean, I'd heard that that awful boy from Alatia was going to be there, the one with the enormous ears, you know the one..." she trailed off, embarrassed.

"The Princess is undoubtedly referring to young Master Herris, who you can be assured has requested a seat at your side." She groaned and rolled her eyes, and Rodolpho added, "To which he was told that under no circumstances was my carefully designed seating arrangement to be reordered at the last moment, on the whim of some young pup. You are seated across the table and far enough down to be out of even his earshot, I believe."

Sare grinned and kissed him impulsively on the cheek. "You are a wonder, Rodolpho," she said, running off.

"As the Lady says," he agreed impassively, turning back to his work.

Dinner was actually quite entertaining. King Gearld had retained a conjurer/acrobat, who was able, it seemed, to produce colored balls from mid-air and then juggle them passably well. His jokes were somewhat off-color, to Sare's delight, and were principally responsible for his early removal from the room by Rodolpho.

She was seated between one of the Alatian nobles, an elderly man who was hard of hearing, and a young man named Jorge, who was Herris' age and, as it turned out, fiercely competitive with the other boy. He seemed to be perfectly comfortable looking at her; he neither ignored her scars nor stared at them, but gave her nearly all his attention, speaking naturally and with fine humor.

It soon became apparent that any devotion Jorge displayed toward Sare was met with a conflicting pair of looks from down the table; ingratiating ones to Sare, murderous ones to her companion. Sare was having a wonderful time. She made sure to put her hand on Jorge's arm when she spoke to him, and to laugh prettily at all of his jokes. In spite of her position in the shadow of her more desirable older sisters, Sare was a Princess of the royal house of Faires, and between her trained graciousness and beautiful green eyes, had her companion smitten before the dinner was through.

After dinner the party retired to the ballroom where six of Faires' finest musicians set the mood with a lively mountain tune dear to the Alatians' hearts. Jorge swept her out onto the floor, and she danced with him for the next three songs. She politely declined the fourth, and went over to chat with her sisters.

"Well, it seems someone has an admirer," smiled Carola.

"I don't know," said Cillistra, "I rather fancy the one with the ears."

"You are welcome to him, then," Sare replied.

"Not for me, sister, my plate is quite full."

"As always," noted Carola wryly.

"Meow, meow," Cillistra drawled. "Oh! Fireworks!" She pointed across the room to where Herris had stormed up to Jorge. There was a heated exchange, culminating in some minor shoving. Rodolpho materialized next to them and escorted them both to the door, despite their strenuous objections.

"How absolutely marvelous," offered Cillistra. The other two smiled and agreed.

Sare excused herself, kissed her father good night, and went off to her chambers. She was tired, and in spite of the evening, still out of sorts. Not one person had even mentioned her birthday, except her mother that morning at breakfast, and that didn't count. She opened the door and was surprised to see Obra waiting for her.

"Hello, child. Blessings to you and your house on your birthday."

"Obra! You are so kind." She ran and hugged her friend.

"I have something for you." Obra handed her a small package wrapped in gold paper.

"What is it?" Sare asked excitedly.

"Open it and find out."

Sare sat on her bed and gently unfolded the paper. Inside were several felt pouches, each drawn together with a string. Sare pulled the first one open and poured the contents into her hand. "Oh!" she gasped. The pouch held tiny silver beads, intricate and ornate. The next pouch held pearls, and the next beautiful tiny seashells. "What is all of this?" she asked.

"I know how much your embroidery and needlework bring you joy, and thought that with some special adornments you could make yourself something pretty."

"Oh, Obra, they're beautiful!" Sare carefully put the beads back into their pouches, then ran over and hugged her Healer friend again. Obra patted her on the back.

"The beauty I see is in the eyes of a young Princess," she said.

◆   ◆   ◆

Edmon the trader was pleased. He sat his horse, stopped for a moment at the roadside, and watched his three wagons trundle by on their great wooden wheels. They swayed a bit under their loads. He smiled at that thought: each wagon was filled to capacity by the finest fabrics he had seen in years. He had struck an excellent bargain with the weavers of Westfalls, far across the Steppes, for the best work of their looms.

His smile widened as he calculated his share of the expected profits. He was not yet thirty, was Edmon, and a venture as successful as this promised to be could easily move him into the upper ranks of all those who plied the trade routes and fairs each year.

A twinge of his natural caution gave him pause. *Sure you're not just counting pigeons before you've built the dovecote, lad?* But no, there had been nothing like this material at the spring fair in a long time; his goods were sure to be a sensation.

Well, we'll know soon enough, won't we? We'll be in Faires by tomorrow night. At that thought, his smile became an outright grin. There was a young woman in the city, a glover's daughter, who would be especially pleased to see him, and he, her. It had been over two months since their last evening together. He was setting spur to his horse when he heard the hoofbeats behind him.

He turned in the saddle and peered back through the mist, rising now as the sun began to set. In the distance, he could just make out two riders - no, three - coming up the road at full gallop. At that speed, they quickly became clearer, until he could see their dark clothing, and the weapons they all bore.

Edmon didn't hesitate. "Bandits! Run for it, around the curve and into the rocks!" He was already racing up the length of his small train as each of his wagoners whipped up his team into a quick trot. *Ah, but the beasts are tired, and oxen are not made for racing at their best. Better to be ready for the worst.* He signaled to the other mounted man in his troupe, a big, blonde Alatian named Hovarth, and the two of them fell back into a rearguard and followed the wagons with their swords drawn.

The wagons swept around the curve in the road, one of them skidding and bouncing off the rocky hillside on the left. As Edmon reached the curve, he heard cries of fear, the bellow of oxen, and a splintering crash.

He and Hovarth rounded the hill, and were forced to rein up their horses at once. A great tree had been thrown down from the hilltop, clear across the road. Edmon's first wagon had smashed into it; the two oxen lay moaning and lowing amid the wreckage, and the driver was dead, impaled on a branch. The second wagon's team was tangled in the debris, and the third had no way to pass.

Even as Edmon absorbed this, four black-garbed men leaped off the hill. Two landed on the wagons and attacked the drivers. One swept Hovarth from his saddle, and they both fell from the roadway and rolled down the opposite slope. The fourth clutched at Edmon but missed, and landed in a heap beneath him. Edmon killed him before he could rise, wheeling around again as he heard the horsemen coming on him from behind.

The two brigands nearest him were just that, big men with rough clothes and bright swords. The third, hanging back now, was all in black, with a mask of black mail over his face. Edmon had only a few seconds to see such details before his attackers were upon him.

He parried the first blow and returned it, backing away as they pressed him, both of them vying for an opening to strike at him. Their swordsmanship was less than his, but they were strong and quick.

His horse struck something and stumbled. *The wagon!* He rocked as the animal tried to find its feet. His guard slipped down for a moment, and the closest bandit laid open his throat in a bolt of fire and shock.

He was lying in the dust of the road, with horses' hooves shifting and pawing before his eyes. He felt the need to move, but could not. Between the horses' feet, he saw the brigand who attacked Hovarth climbing back uphill, wiping the blade of a long dagger with grass. He heard a voice above him, giving orders; he could not raise his head to see the speaker. One of the killers stepped up beside the horse, saying, "We can fit the goods from the broken wagon into the other two, Lord Michael. With the extra oxen, we can pull them even overloaded." The rider only grunted his assent.

The hooves moved away. A boot shoved against Edmon's back, sending him rolling helplessly off the roadside. He landed in a slide of dirt and rocks, looking up into the evening sky. *It's so beautiful; and why is there no pain?* He could feel the warmth as blood flowed down his neck, more slowly with each pulse. A last thought came to him with a taint of loss and regret: *Like this?*

♦   ♦   ♦

The bandit chieftain Olk grinned as he leaned forward in his chair. "You said that your master expected you to be made comfortable. Are you?" His followers, grouped near him and scattered about the longhouse, roared with laughter.

The small sallow man he addressed opened one eye as far as its bruising would permit. He did not strain against the ropes that held him spread-eagled on the dirt floor, nor try to move the small heaps of dry wood under each hand and foot. He rolled his head slowly, wincing a bit, until he looked up at Olk. "Jest all you please." His words came faint and slurred through his split, battered lips. "Only understand that no one contests my master's wishes for long. No one." He swallowed, and spoke more clearly. "You are making a mistake, Olk of Westwood. He comes. Beware him, and beware his wrath."

The cutthroats laughed again. Olk prodded his captive's ribs with the point of his sword. "You think I've never heard threats before? I've led these wolves twenty years, against all comers. And here I sit. My enemies are dead, and we grow rich. Who should I fear? Your faceless 'master'?" He sat back and smiled again. "We'll send you back to him with an answer. You'll deliver it, even with no tongue, and no eyes, and no hands for writing. He'll understand it all the same, and know that Olk rules here."

The small man closed his eye again, and shook his head carefully. "The only dead man I see here is the one with the large mouth. I have nothing more to say."

Olk stiffened and scowled. "Enough of this!" He gestured, and a crone shuffled over from the cooking fire and thrust the burning twig she bore among the sticks under the small man's left foot. Olk's smile was merciless as he watched the flame spreading. "I think you'll have more to say in a moment or two, my lad. So I say again: who should I fear, and why should I give up my seat to any man?"

"Because it is my will." The deep voice came from the longhouse's doorway. Peering through his henchmen, Olk could see only a tall man in black striding down the room as if it were his own.

The stranger stopped beside his bound servant, scattering the burning twigs with a contemptuous kick. A gleaming dagger appeared in his hand, and he knelt and began cutting the small man's bonds. Olk shook off his surprise and signaled to one of his lieutenants.

As Olk tried to see the dark man's features behind the black mask, his accomplice silently drew a knife and raised it above the intruder's back for a quick death-stroke. Suddenly the bandit was gasping and falling away, an arrow jutting from his throat. More than a dozen men burst into the longhouse, each one armed with a short, recurved horn bow. Their arrow-points roamed over the assembled company.

Olk was on his feet, roaring with anger, his sword rising to menace the masked figure that stood erect and unafraid before him. The stranger lifted his hands to still the disturbance all around and spoke again. "A final chance for you, Olk of Westwood. You rule here no more. I am Michael. Serve me, and share in wealth and power you cannot imagine. Refuse, and die."

"I serve no one!" Olk raised his blade and advanced. Powerful fingers suddenly clamped around his neck and wrist from behind; his sword fell to the dirt as his feet were lifted off it.

The inhumanly strong right hand let go of his wrist and spread itself over the top of his head. Its fingertips dug into his scalp and slowly turned his head around – while the other hand still held his neck immobile.

Through the mounting agony, Olk was barely able to register that his captor was a huge figure dressed in tight silver mail and a black mantle. Olk's head continued to turn, and his eyes squinted tight against the pain. As he began to scream, the last thing he saw was that his killer's own eyes were set deep, utterly white, and without pupils. Then everything flashed away in a hideous snap.

The killer dropped Olk's corpse beside his sword and moved to stand with Michael. Olk's followers watched it glide soundlessly over, and wondered at its size, its strength, and its grey, lusterless skin.

Michael tipped his head toward it, while his gaze pierced through his mask's eye-slits into every soul in the room. "My Shadow serves me well. I give you all the same choice that I gave Olk: serve me, or die. I offer you riches, or the grave. What say you?"

After a long moment, the largest of the ruffians stepped forward and laid his weapon at Michael's feet.

Chapter 7
Changing

The hunting party finally abandoned their search for a cave or other shelter from the downpour, and dismounted at a clear space among the trees. While some of Kerwin's huntsmen settled the hounds and horses, the others set to building a fire as he and Jenora erected a canopy for Aaren, the King, and Wildon. "Just step under here, your Majesties. We'll have everyone warm and dry in a trice."

Trever's beard streamed onto his surcoat as he doffed his light helm. "Warm, perhaps. I doubt we'll be dry again this night."

Kerwin laughed. "Perhaps, my liege. But do let me make the attempt, eh?"

Aaren had grown quickly. By age fifteen he was obviously destined to match the strength and size of his father. The years with Jenora had also taught him a measure of humility, and the maturity he had gained was at least partly credited to their friendship. He was still an impetuous boy, but occasionally showed the seeds of sterner stuff.

He stood and dripped and watched as the gamesmen tried to ignite the logs they had piled. Several times they managed to light the tinder, and a few flames would scorch the kindling Kerwin had carried all day in his pack. But the larger sticks and logs dampened the few tongues of red until they were no more.

Finally, Kerwin turned to the King. "It's no use, your Highness. The wood is just too wet, and we've nearly run out of dry tinder."

Trever grunted. "Cold food and wet beds tonight. Ah well, such are nothing new to old soldiers, eh, Kerwin? We'll just – Ah? What are you about, boy?"

Aaren had stepped out from under cover and moved toward the piled wood. His face wore a tentative smile as he spoke back over his shoulder. "May I please try something, Father?"

The King scowled. "And you know more than men who have spent their lives in the forests? Oh, very well, if you must."

The Prince knelt where Kerwin's man had been. Jenora noticed him working at his left wrist, and saw a gleam of silver through the gathering dark. Nothing happened for a moment, except that the boy's frame tensed as though straining at some invisible line.

Suddenly, a blue radiance sprang up to silhouette Aaren's form. It grew and spread as he rose, lifting his hands before him, palms down. The whole party moved forward to see better, then jumped back as blue flames burst shockingly from beneath the drenched wood.

The azure fire leaped into the air, several feet above the fire pit. It was brilliant, blinding, and eerily soundless. Jenora felt a shiver race over her that had nothing to do with the damp.

Just as swiftly, the blue flames died down and became quite ordinary, orange and red and yellow. The King and Jenora stepped forward again, to stand beside the Prince. They could see that the fire was in full blaze, and even the largest logs were completely dry and burning. Their clothes steamed in the heat.

Jenora glanced down and saw Aaren refasten the silver bracelet about his left wrist. He turned in the fire's glow, looking at his father, his eyes curiously empty. Trever looked back without a smile, his brows knitted and an equally unreadable expression in his own eyes. Then a grin emerged from his beard, and he clapped a hand to his son's wet shoulder. For just an instant, the boy stiffened at his father's touch. Then he too smiled, and without a word, they turned to face the comforting warmth.

Later that night, after the camp had settled for the evening and first-shift guards were sent out to shiver in the rain, Aaren turned in his bedroll and propped himself up on one elbow to face Jenora. His face was unreadable in the gloom, the only light coming from the embers of the fire kept fitfully alight by a soggy guard. They lay a little apart from Trever, his heavy snoring lending the night a certain rough comfort. Wildon slept soundlessly on the King's far side.

"Jen?" Aaren whispered, voice shaking slightly.

"Yes," she replied, just as quietly.

He didn't answer. She was suddenly sure that he was crying, and reached over and touched his shoulder. He lurched into her arms, and she held him, his tears hot on her neck. He didn't make a sound, but only held her tightly. Jenora didn't know what exactly was bothering the Prince, but she sensed that it had something to do with his display of power earlier. No one had made a single comment, but most of the party had given him a wide berth for the rest of the evening. Jenora thought of the emptiness in his eyes as he turned from the fire, and shuddered.

But this was a different man now. The past nine years had brought her ever closer to her Prince. She had come to love him, and was fiercely protective of him, and he was finally in her arms. She didn't want to move, to break the spell. She inhaled deeply the woodsy smell in his hair, and before she knew what she was doing, kissed him lightly on the top of his ear. He raised his head, and she stiffened, knowing that she had gone too far. She relaxed her hold on him and waited, embarrassed, for him to scold her or simply roll over without saying anything.

He bent forward and found her lips with his own. Jenora was stunned for a moment; there was a roaring in her ears, and then she pulled him tightly against her mouth, one hand on his broad shoulder blade, the other in his dark curls. They broke from the kiss and her breath was ragged. Aaren's hand stroked her cheek in the dark, and tentatively caressed her shoulder. He stopped. Jenora kissed him again, hard, and he kissed her back with equal fervor, his hand tracing a line down to cup her breast through her rough shirt.

Her senses were reeling. She felt as though she couldn't breathe, her body straining toward him through their bedrolls. They broke again, both breathing quickly now. He leaned close to her ear and whispered, "I love you, Jen."

"I love you too." He laid his head on her shoulder, his breath tickling her neck where his tears had so recently fallen.   She was still intensely aware of the weight of his hand on her breast. She didn't know what to do, but realized that whatever might happen between them it couldn't happen here, not ten feet from his sleeping father. She grasped his hand, lacing her fingers into his, and held it tightly to her, turning her back to him and pulling his arm over her like a blanket. Aaren moved closer and drew his knees up behind hers, pressing her close against his chest. He sighed deeply.

They stayed that way for a long time. Just before she fell asleep Jenora carefully disentangled herself from the Prince, so that everything would look as it should in the morning light.

The group broke camp the next morning, early. The rain still fell in a heavy drizzle. Jenora and Aaren didn't meet each other's gaze. After breakfast they saddled up with the rest and started back toward the palace. Aaren let his horse fall into step beside Jenora's. Both of them were already soaked. They were far enough from the other riders to hold a private conversation, and he smiled at her, sideways.

"So, Palatine."

"So, Prince." She smiled back.

"Thank you, for..." he struggled for the words. "For being my friend. I was feeling very alone last night."

"You are never alone," she replied. "I will always be beside you."

He grinned. "Yes, well we did get quite close to each other for a moment there last night didn't we?" His tone was light, and somewhat sheepish, which chilled her heart. Perhaps it hadn't meant to him what it had meant to her.

"Yes," she said carefully. "But of course we're still..."

"Right," he broke in. "Exactly. Things haven't changed at all." He seemed relieved. "Right, Palatine?"

"Of course, my liege." Jenora spurred her horse forward. The rain mixed with the tears on her cheeks, and her heart beat hollowly and hard in her chest. "Of course."

✦   ✦   ✦

Gearld was sick with worry, and furious at his inability to do anything about it. He paced the hall outside the room where his youngest daughter lay, and raged at the Gifter and the Tempter both, and waited for word from Obra. She had been tending to Sare since the latest, and worst, burning the night before. The door opened and Obra came out, closing it softly behind her.

Seeing the strain on her King, she immediately took him by the arm and led him down the hall to the room where Signe was waiting. She jumped to her feet and ran to her husband, clutching his arm. They both looked haggard, and desperate. Obra held Gearld's gaze. The rain outside the windows came down steadily.

"Sare will live, my liege. She is an incredibly strong young woman, more than even I knew. There seems to be a resilience and power of self-healing she possesses well beyond the norm." Obra shook her head. "She rests now, under as powerful a draught as I dared make for her. Tomorrow we will know more."

"But why now, fifteen years after you assured us the amulet would protect her?" Gearld demanded. Signe tried to quiet him, but Obra held up her hand.

"It is a fair question. I only wish I had an answer for you. I too thought that, aside from her odd episodes, she was protected from this curse of fire. For reasons we may never know, her thirteenth birthday seemed to mark a dramatic increase in the intensity of those attacks. Though never as intense as it was this time." Obra sighed, and suddenly felt every one of her years.

"The next may be worse. One day this may kill her. But not today. Aside from her own amazing recuperative powers, she has learned what little my healing arts have to offer, and this helps her too. I continue to research what I can, but I fear we deal with a powerful force completely outside my ken. I am so sorry; I have failed you in this."

"No," said Signe. "You have done as much or more for our daughter than any other in the kingdom could. Know that you have our love, and our gratitude."

"Yes, completely," the King echoed. "Thank you, Obra." He sank heavily to a bench and put his head in his hands. His Queen sat down beside him and laid her own head on his broad shoulder. Obra left them there to the sound of the rain, and went back to her chambers to study what more she could.

◆   ◆   ◆

Michael toed the medallion with his boot. The golem stood impassively across the chamber from him. Michael scowled, the torchlight throwing half his face into deep shadow. The books around him provided no comfort any longer, and he was finally ready to take the next step. Holding his breath, he bent and grasped the medallion for the first time in almost ten years.

...worry. We have the other artifacts; the Sword –

It is he!

What do we do? Should we Touch ...?

...I cannot believe...

...nictum domen...

... back, as you always...

I knew. In his heart he...

...Agenbath. Do not mistake my meaning, serpent, I...

Yes, a light Touch, just to remind ...

He gritted his teeth, fist clenched around the cold metal. Deep in his skull, he felt a warm tingle, but nothing like the pleasure from years before. He sighed, letting out his breath explosively. *It worked.* When he had placed that unnamed part of himself into his Shadow, who now stood at his elbow, he had hoped that it would somehow block their Touch. He had succeeded in overcoming his addiction to the sensation, and feared its resurgence. If it hadn't worked, he would still have gone through with this; but now they had one less power over him.

...something wrong.

Yes. Our connection is no longer...

...ozmen kour ti Michael enis hor...

He has done something to his mind.

Touch him again!

Again the tingle. *So.* He was protected, but they knew it. Or at least knew something. There was only one thing left to test. *Call it a peace offering.* He slipped the familiar cold metal chain over his head, feeling the medallion slither down and nestle below his collarbone, as though it had been there all along. Reaching into the burlap bag offered mutely by the golem, Michael lifted out the squirming hedgehog. He held it loosely in both hands, staring at its struggling form. Taking a deep breath, he tithed.

...or else the little one. If she...

DEATH!

Yes, death!

So that at least remains intact. This one may yet remain useful.

...still don't trust...

...Yellow. Yellow. Yellow. Yellow...

...lack of control. How will we guarantee his behavior now? He will not do what we want. We could offer him the Small Touch...

Too dangerous.

Perhaps. But it would give us more of an entry into...

Gathering his things, he led the golem from the ruin. What he needed to do next required more than his cruelty and magic could accomplish alone. Banditry was a small beginning, but he had his eyes set on the gleaming city of Faires. There was wealth there, and power, and something he had thought about for years, but never till this time admitted might be within his power to take: Cillistra.

He had gone this far, admitted to himself that he needed the Pendulum's help. It seemed that perhaps they had more to offer him. Now all he had to do was go and bargain with them again.

◆   ◆   ◆

Cillistra waited in the corridor until she heard Cook bang the last of the pots away and stomp off to her room. Slipping in the back, she glided silently over to the pantry and pulled open the heavy door, breathing deeply the familiar musty scents of the dried spices, the vegetable bins, and the tang of the cider barrels. Cook had doused the lamp, but enough light remained to pick her way over to the barrels.

Kneeling, she positioned the empty wineskin under a tap and carefully filled it with the potent cider. She took a healthy swig, and coughed. *Lovely.* She smiled, stoppered the bag, and was just turning to make good her escape when the light from a lamp and the sound of approaching voices startled her. Cursing silently, she pulled the pantry door almost shut. As the voices approached, she winced, recognizing one as her father's. Through the narrow crack around the door, Cillistra saw that her mother was with him.

"...and what are we to do? The Dark One's raids have become bolder with each passing season. Yet he remains so elusive! Those of his minions we do manage to capture know nothing." Her father sounded exasperated, and more weary than he ever let on in Cillistra's presence.

"You will find him, and you will capture him," her mother said, with conviction. "Give it time, Gearld."

"The longer we tarry, the stronger he grows." The King slumped onto a stool, his back to the pantry door. "He is a demon."

"He is a man like any other. You are acting like a child." Signe kissed him on the forehead. "I think you're hungry. How about some of Cook's nice ham?" She moved out of Cillistra's constricted line of sight to the sideboard. She returned with meat on a large platter, from which she began slicing.

"Don't want any ham," Gearld sulked. Cillistra almost giggled, imagining her father's scowl. A basically light-hearted man, his sullen moods were rare, and brief, and caused more merriment in his family than he would have preferred.

"What about that boy?" Signe asked.

"What boy?"

"The good-looking one that set the downstairs maids' tongues wagging this morning." Cillistra's ears perked up at that. She had heard of the young man visiting the Keep that morning, asking for an audience with her father.

"Oh, him. What of him?"

"He claimed to have important information about the Dark One."

"Every passing beggar looking for a meal has a secret map to the Dark One's lair," Gearld groused, tearing into a large hunk of the ham. "I don't have time to suffer such fools and still do what I must to track the fiend down." He chewed loudly on the meat he had turned down.

Signe looked at him. "Husband, may I speak outside my station?"

Gearld put down the ham. "You may speak to me at any time of aught that troubles you, my dear. You know that."

She sighed. "I do. These days though, I know that you are engrossed in your duties, and paramount to these is the capture of the Dark One. But I was there this morning, and saw the young man. John Winters was his name. He was..." she paused, groping for the correct words. "He had quite an air of intensity about him. Something in his eyes troubled me. And though well dressed, and moderately well spoken, he..." She frowned. "Whether you believe him or not, I think that you should speak with him. There is more to this young man than meets the eye."

Gearld regarded her. "All right. If he returns I will grant him audience." He stood, found a plate, and put the sliced ham on it. "Come, let us retire to our rooms, gentle wife and counsel."

She smiled, picked up the lamp, and joined him. As they passed into the hallway, Cillistra heard her father say, "And Signe? Thank you."

Cillistra waited until they were well away. *John Winters.* What a fascinating name. Tucking the wineskin into the folds of her skirt, she hurried up to the rooftop gardens. At night they were usually deserted, as they were now. She walked the paths, pausing at the fountain to sip some more cider, and found her way to the east parapet. Leaning against the cold stone, she watched the stars over the Nethals shimmer. Summer would be over soon.

She sighed, and drank again, the tipsy feeling spreading over her like a comforting blanket. Life in the Keep was so *dull:* the visitors, the dances, the lessons, her family. Sometimes she thought she would simply scream in frustration. Discovering the cider in the pantry the year before had helped somewhat, but always left her feeling wretched the next morning. It just wasn't fair. *Nineteen years old, practically a spinster, and each boy duller than the next.* They were all the same.

Lord Garret, Carola's beau, was a perfect example. Sincere, courteous, handsome enough (Cillistra was certain he spent more time in front of the mirror than Carola did), and utterly, utterly dull. Not that Carola was any great catch herself. Adolescence had not been kind to her, and no matter how she tried to stay away from Cook's pastries, her dress size seemed to be keeping pace with her age. Cillistra snickered, and took another swig.

This John Winters, now, he sounded interesting. It might be foolish to take her mother's word on anything, but still. Nodding to herself, she took the last long pull from the wineskin and headed unsteadily back down the stairs. If he did get an audience with her father, she would be sure to be there.

The next day, Cillistra felt her luck was changing, the world becoming a more interesting place after all. She was playing a new piece on the harpsichord in the main hall after lunch. Her father was going over some papers at one of the tables with an advisor, enjoying the music. The Keep's majordomo walked discreetly into the room and cleared his throat. The King looked up.

"Yes, Rodolpho?"

"The young man you asked about has indeed returned to request an audience. Shall I send him away?"

Cillistra concentrated on her playing.

"No, that's all right. Send him in," Gearld answered. Rodolpho bowed and left the room. He returned a moment later with a young man who, Cillistra had to admit, lived up to the hysterical giggling tales of the help. Dark curls framed a rugged face with a long, thin nose and full lips. Her mother was right too, though, he was dressed in an odd assortment of well-made clothes, as if he had inherited someone else's wardrobe and never been taught to sort it out properly. *No preening popinjay, he.* But at least he did not appear to be a stranger to soap, like so many of the horrid, awkward boys from town seemed to be. What a puzzle. She strained her ears to catch their words.

"Thank you, your Highness, for taking the time to see me. I assure you –"

"Yes, yes. You claim to have some information of great importance, I heard." The King regarded him stonily. "Who are you boy, and why should I listen to you?"

The young man's eyes flashed, but his tone remained civil and respectful. "I am called John Winters. I am but a humble merchant, from the western steppes. Recently arrived in your fair city, I learned of its troubles with the one they call Dark Michael." The introduction sounded like he had practiced it several times.

"We do not tend to call him by name, this Dark One," Gearld muttered, "but I know to whom you refer."

"As you say, your Highness." Winters inclined his head. "I was having a meal in a roadhouse just south of Faires two nights ago when I overheard a group of rough-looking men bragging drunkenly about their recent spoils of banditry. They –"

"Wait," interrupted Gearld. "What inn was this?"

"The, ah, the Crooked Raven, Sire."

"That's a low place, filled with the worst sort of rogues. What were you doing there?"

The young man stared at him for a moment, clearly at a loss for words. For just a second, he almost looked angry, and from where she was sitting, Cillistra thought that his eyes might have actually changed color, darkened just slightly. But she decided it must have been a trick of the light, because when she surreptitiously glanced up again they were still that lovely warm brown. "Well, ah, your Highness, being as I am a stranger in these parts, I was surely unaware of the nature of the establishment's reputation, ere I entered."

The King stared at him. "I see." There was a long pause. "And then?"

"Well, they also hinted at their affiliation with Dark Mich – with the Dark One. And they spoke of a raid they were planning on a holding north of Faires, this very night. They didn't say which one, but one of them mentioned a place called Sapling Fork." He stopped, looking like he was about to add something else, but then decided not to.

Gearld frowned. "Lord Callendar's estate is very near there." He continued to stare at the young man. Finally, he leaned forward. "There is something about you I can't put my finger on. I don't trust you." He sat back. "But I have no reason to distrust you either. And if the warning you bring us turns out to be true..." He stroked his short beard.

Coming to a decision, he called out, "Rodolpho! Find Captain Roman, and have him assemble a skirmishing party. We travel in one hour." He looked at John Winters. "And have him outfit an extra horse. We'll have a guest riding with us."

The young man's eyes widened. "What? You mean, you want me to –"

"Can you handle a sword?" barked the King.

Winters blinked, then slowly nodded. "Yes. As a matter of fact, I can."

"Then it's settled." Gearld stood and gestured toward the doorway. "Wait outside. I'll be along shortly. Rodolpho? Take care of our guest."

As John Winters was led from the hall, his gaze fell briefly on Cillistra, still playing in the far corner. He nodded to her almost imperceptibly as he walked out the great doors. Cillistra looked the other way, suddenly blushing.

Gearld gathered up his papers and dismissed his aide. Walking over to where Cillistra sat, he put his hand on her shoulder. "That was lovely, my dear. All four times. The next time you want to eavesdrop unnoticed, however, my advice would be to at least play more than one tune." He kissed the top of her head and strode from the room.

✦   ✦   ✦

The majordomo herded Winters out into the courtyard. "Wait here," he said frostily, and with a final withering glance at the younger man's clothes, popped back into the Keep. The door slammed, spurting little dust devils in the dirt at his feet.

Michael was furious. It had all been going so well. He had actually been granted an audience and the fool King was, more or less, buying his story. He had even stolen a look at Cillistra. The corners of his mouth twitched. *She is still so beautiful. All those years of thinking of her.*

But now the stupid King was dragging him along! This was not in the plan. The sacrificial sheep had been culled from his army, dullards and fools the lot of them, and sent on the raid as a "training exercise." The King was supposed to find them and thus validate Michael's story, and his new persona. Now it looked to be a good deal more difficult.

Well, he would have to just play along with it. When the time came, he could improvise. Perhaps this was a better angle than his original plan. Truth be told, though, he had not picked only the lowest of his troops, he had also picked those he deemed most dangerous and likely to die rather than be captured, including two that were addicted to the Little Touch, and could wield the killing gaze with some small aptitude.

So be it. He would ride into glorious battle with his new friend the King, and prove himself even more valuable. *The fewer survivors, the better.*

They mounted a party of twenty-six men, including Michael, and rode out to Lord Callendar's holdings. That minor noble was more than happy to help Gearld's troops arrange the ambush, even offering his two sons as lookouts on the north and south roads into the estate. The women and servants of the house bolted themselves into the cellar.

The ambush, Michael admitted to himself grudgingly, was as cunningly arranged as could be expected with little or no time to prepare. Callendar's knowledge of his land helped, but Michael also learned much from Gearld's tactics. This was already paying off in ways he had not imagined.

Just after the sun set over the Western Mountains, the hoot of an owl alerted the Keep's men that Callendar's son on the north road had sighted something. Within moments, a band of dark-garbed horsemen came thundering around the bend and onto the stretch of private road where Gearld's men lay in wait.

At the King's silent signal, oil-soaked hay bales were set ablaze, throwing a malevolent light onto the scene. As the lead horses reached the bottom of a small slope, four burly city guards heaved up the rope that had been lightly buried across the road, and tripped the two lead horses screaming into the dirt. The next two horses slammed into their fallen comrades, unseating those brigands as well. With a shout from Gearld, the party from Faires galloped into the fray.

The bandits were sorely outmatched. The men on the ground were cut down quickly, and the ring of steel and throaty howls of the dying echoed across the fields.

The numbers would have been almost equal, but the ruse of the rope gave Gearld's forces the advantage.

Michael did not hang back, but rather drove into the melee right beside the King. He dispatched one man on the ground and one on horseback in short order. As he swung his mount to meet the next attacker, the black-sashed brigand reared back in his saddle, his astonishment clear.

"Lord Michael!" he shouted, staring at his leader in disbelief.

Gearld's head snapped around. Blackness surging across his eyes, Michael caught the brigand's gaze and held it as he plunged his sword through the man's heart. "Here's a message for your Lord Michael," he snarled, wrenching the blade free and wheeling his horse again. He managed to clear the killing gaze from his eyes before meeting Gearld's. The King stared at him, consternation writ plainly across his features. Michael knew that this moment would decide if his plan would succeed or fail.

Gearld continued to stare at him. Around them, the battle continued. Not trusting his tongue, and mentally fighting against all of his arrogance as a leader, Michael dropped his eyes, bowing his head slightly. Then he turned and rejoined the fray, desperate to know the King's response, but sure that he had to play the charade out to the end.

The battle was quickly over. There were only two survivors among the outlaws, but both were badly injured and unconscious, and Michael did not expect them to awaken. The castle had lost but one man, and another half-dozen were bleeding from minor wounds. Lord Callendar's servants helped dress the wounded while the rest toasted the victory with Callendar's best vintage. The mood was jovial. Not many times had the men had the opportunity to strike so sound a blow against their enemy.

Michael had not spoken to the King. He accepted the handclasps and backslaps of the warriors, and drank to their health. He had even managed to sustain a small wound on his shoulder by deliberately deflecting the clumsy blow from one bandit enough to cut him, but not seriously injure him. He had correctly assumed that this would endear him to the men as much as his foreknowledge of the raid and swordsmanship in the battle.

Suddenly, a heavy hand fell on his good shoulder. Michael stiffened.

"So tell me, John," asked the King, "what you made of that bandit's words." The hubbub quieted, and Michael turned to face him.

"Bandit?" he asked, stalling for time.

"You know, the one that shouted 'Lord Michael!' when he came abreast of us." There were startled murmurs amongst the men.

Michael stared at him for a long moment. "Well, I assumed at the time that he was shouting his master's name as he prepared to assassinate the king of his enemies." Michael paused. "Which is why my blade tasted the black blood of his heart before he could work up whatever passes for courage among those demons, to utter that foul name again."

The assembled men roared their appreciation, raising their tankards and slopping wine over each other. Gearld's features finally broke into a smile. He nodded, releasing Michael's shoulder. "That's the conclusion I finally reached as well," he said. "I thought for a moment that the monster might have been among them, that we might have had the tremendous good fortune to finally meet him. But that battle will have to wait for another day." He took a goblet from a table and raised it to his men.

"To Faires, and the brave men who fight for her!" he roared.

"To Faires!" the men shouted back, drinking and laughing.

The King nodded at Michael, the small smile still playing across his features. He strode over to speak with Lord Callendar. As he passed Michael, he playfully ruffled the young man's hair.

Michael, too, smiled. He had won.

Several months later, Michael stood at the base of a high cliff, near the site of the forgotten ruins he had come to know so well. He gestured, and one of his lieutenants emerged from the gaping mouth of the new-cut cave Michael had been peering into. The man stopped and bowed to his master. Michael took the torch from the other's hand and strode into the cave's entrance, examining the walls and ceiling. "How does the work proceed?"

"Amazingly, m'Lord. We will have the connection to the upper level completed by tomorrow night." The man hesitated, then shook his head and spoke up again. "These – creatures – work faster than any three men could. They see far better in the dark, they can slither into places a rat couldn't, and they know every crevice of this entire mountain."

Michael turned. Even in the guttering torchlight, he could see the unease in his confederate's face. "Well they should know it; it was their home. And you don't like them, do you?"

The big man stammered, and could not meet Dark Michael's eyes. "I - I can respect them, and any use you make of them, Lord. But I cannot help the way I feel when I see them. They make my skin crawl." He hurried to add, "Most of us working here feel the same. I hope you understand, m'Lord."

Michael stepped closer. "I do. And you understand as well: I will make what use I choose of *any* creatures I must, to achieve my ends. You, and the others working here, and everyone who serves me must simply get used to the ... unusual. Is that clear?"

There was no way to miss the warning underlying Michael's words. The man nodded. "Yes, of course, Lord Michael. As you say, we will get used to them."

Michael clapped the other's shoulder. "Good. Now bring their leader to me. I'll await him outside." He handed his henchman the torch, and watched him disappear into the tunnel's depths before returning to his horse at the cliff's base.

In a moment, torchlight brightened the cave's outlet again, and stopped at the mouth as the man carrying it did. The other figure stepped out of the cave and went to stand before Dark Michael.

It blinked and shied a little at the daylight. Michael's horse also shied, pulling away from the creature, and Michael held harder to the reins. The being facing him was slightly shorter than an average man, and much slighter. The scales that covered its head and face were the shade of charcoal, while those on each of its bared arms bore a long yellow stripe bordered in black. It raised one hand; its three fingers were supple from base to tip, with no sign of joints. It spoke to Michael, its inhuman language rolling off a flickering, forked tongue.

Michael replied in kind, though more slowly. They conversed for several minutes. Then Michael nodded, closed his eyes, and *twisted* his mind in the new way the Pendulum had taught him - not the fear-inspiring way, but in the Touch-sharing way. The creature looked up at Michael, and its mouth spread in something like a smile, revealing bony plates instead of teeth. It shuddered. It knelt with bowed head before Michael, then rose and glided back into the cave.

Gazing off again to the North, Michael thought of Cillistra. He had gone to Faires several times since his first tentative visit, as he carefully built up the John Winters persona he used among them. Winters was a charming, if somewhat reclusive, general merchant and trader. He donated to the local Fairen charities, bought and sold in the marketplace, and had eventually received an invitation to one of the royal fêtes.

She was there: like a vision, like a dream; like a Princess. Michael smiled. In spite of his eventual designs on the Keep and all its occupants, he had fallen powerfully under her spell. She was beautiful, to be sure, but had a mischievous streak that became apparent to any who knew her long.

Michael, as John Winters, had grown to know her well. Of all her suitors, he was certain she found him the most intriguing. They danced together at the Keep, took long walks in the famed roof gardens, and (once!) he had impulsively kissed her. She had scolded him severely, but only after returning the kiss with a fervor that almost shocked him.

The time would soon come to ask for her hand. He was certain that he had made the proper impression on her simple-minded father. And once he had access to the secrets of the Proudlock clan, he could raise his army and take the city whenever he pleased. The latest gift from the Pendulum, the ability to imbue his top lieutenants with the power to *twist* their minds into the killing battle-glance and to receive the Little Touch, finally made it possible to raise and field a serious army, one that, even with lesser numbers, could take nearly any force it encountered.

Michael also realized, from listening to the Pendulum's conversations, that by giving this power to his men he also gave the killing force back to the Pendulum each time an underling slew someone, just as the death from each of his own killings fed them. And although they still spoke to no one but him, he was fairly certain that by extending the *twisting* power to more people, some essential part of the Pendulum's own identity extended out into the world. This was worrisome, but he didn't see any immediate danger. He also had the ultimate trump card of his eavesdropping; and when all was said and done, he didn't really have much choice. He needed them.

There was, to be sure, the other option, that of marrying Cillistra, waiting for the old codger to kick off, and assuming his role as King. *But no.* Michael made a moue of distaste. That would take far too long.

He raised his hand and his voice to his lieutenant, still standing in the cave's entrance. "I told them I was pleased with their work, and gave him what they most desire - though only a little of it. I think you will find their work progressing even better now." He paused, gazing up the face of the cliff. "I want their best efforts, and yours. Soon, this will be my home."

Chapter 8
Extending

It isn't enough. Michael shifted in the saddle as he descended into Edge down the Road from the Waist. The wagons carrying "John Winters'" trade goods trundled down behind him. *It just isn't enough yet.* He was twenty-three years old, and had more than a hundred men -- and unmen -- doing his bidding; his fortress was completed, a haven and center of power in the western mountains; but when you came right down to it, he was just a successful thief. He scowled.

In all the years since his father's death and his renunciation of - and eventual reconciliation with - the Pendulum, he had been trying to gain power and wealth. And he had; but it wasn't enough.

His Shadow was a constant reminder of his past, and wordlessly goaded him to ... to what? He didn't know. His name had gained a good measure of notoriety; he heard himself referred to as "The Dark One" or as "Dark Michael" more and more often. But power, real power, remained elusive to his grasp. He should have gathered twice the number of men by now, but it turned out that fear wasn't enough to keep them around. His leadership skills were rough and, he admitted to himself, inexplicably flawed.

And there was more, something else. During his last visit to the Pendulum, they had told him that he had something to fear.

Their tone had been more hesitant than he could ever remember it. "There are ... other powers at work in this world than you know. Parts even of ... us that have been used for other purposes, not ours."

Ah, bitter! Bitter...

... garadeos, yes. But he might yet...

"What sort of powers?" Michael asked.

"You have no need to know that."

...rivers of flame...

He must bring us back our fire...

"You need only know that these powers exist, and who wields them." An image formed behind his eyes: a youth with curling dark hair, dressed richly. "This is he. He has been given a power he does not understand. Its use does not strengthen us. And listen well, servant: If he grasps its true extent, he could thwart you – and even us. He must never do so."

Michael had rankled at the word "servant," but let it pass. "Very well. Who is he, and where?"

"He is Aaren, the Prince of Edge. You are our hands, our eyes, our voice. If you, and we, are to succeed, you must ... remove him."

Michael smiled grimly. "To remove a prince will be very dangerous. What will be my reward?"

Omarium rejacta! He dares...

Hush.

"If you do this, you shall be rewarded. We shall take back his power, and give it to you."

Of course we would never give Michael the fire. But he is quite clever. He may find a way to tap into it himself...

...of cornflower blue. I ached for her, even then...

That would never happen. He is only human.

Perhaps.

Michael thought a moment; thought about a power strong enough to cause the Pendulum to fear. This fire was something he meant to have. "Very well. I will do it."

He had prepared this caravan and told Winters' fellow merchants he wished to see what sort of pickings could be had to the East. So here he was, wagons loaded with the finest of his stores of cloth and spices and metalwork, approaching the city. It was still early in the year for traders to be coming across the mountains – the snows had barely melted enough to allow passage – and every home they passed, manor to hovel, seemed to offer up its share of gawkers staring at them in idle curiosity.

They asked directions to the field where traders usually encamped, and set themselves up for the night there, between the city wall and the river. Michael cleaned off the marks of his travel and changed into better garb, then went to present himself at the palace.

Within an hour, he was standing in the anteroom of Greybeal Palace, awaiting the King's convenience. The thin, dour-faced steward had told him that King Trever was very busy, but would come "at any time," and then left him alone. Michael passed the time by examining the various flags of Edge's allies hanging from the ceiling, and the antique tools nailed to the walls. He had tried to look through the room's high-set, narrow window, but could find nothing to stand upon – the only bench was firmly bolted to the floor.

As he paced, he heard a disturbance approaching from the inner chamber. The door burst open and a large, bearded, well-dressed man emerged, trailed by the steward and several others.

The group abruptly stopped as the big man eyed Michael up and down, then turned to the steward. "Who is this, Stephen? And what is he waiting here for?"

"Ah, I had forgotten him, your Highness. This is John Winters, a merchant from Faires, newly arrived here. Master Winters, I present his Majesty, King Trever of Edge."

Trever grunted. "A new merchant, you say?"

Michael stepped forward. "Indeed, your Majesty. I've come with my simple wares, to see if the people of Edge are as generous as I've heard." He amazed himself at the easy flattery; his months in Faires' court were standing him in good stead.

The King frowned, then shook his head and chuckled. "Well, if you've come so early over the mountains, you must have some ambition, lad. I've little time for niceties now. But welcome to Edge, and may you trade well here. This is my High Chamberlain, Lord Wildon." He indicated a dark, sharp-faced man on his left. "The Lords Oswin and Brighthope, and my cousin, Lord Branson." Three others, about the King's age, were on his right. "And my heir, Prince Aaren."

The boy stepped from behind his father and nodded briefly. He was slender and a bit shorter than the King, just beginning to grow into his hands and feet. Michael felt a thrill pass through him as he returned the youth's incurious blue gaze. *An unlikely vessel for great power! But we shall see.*

Trever gestured again. "You will already have met Stephen. He will see you settled and provisioned as you need. He will also present you to the head of our Merchant's Guild, who will explain our tariffs and customs to you. Now, if you will excuse us..."

They swept from the anteroom and down the hall without a backward glance, leaving Stephen to see the visitor out into the lowering dusk. As Michael returned to his pavilion and wagons, his thoughts were on the brief encounter. *So, now I know my target by sight. It remains to see how he is guarded, and how easily he might be taken alone. Ah, but that's for tomorrow. Tonight for my bed, and my dreams.* A vision of Cillistra flitted behind his eyes, and he smiled.

His smile had long vanished a week later, as he sat grumbling over his ale in the Riverside Tavern. He churned with impatience and frustration; he had been unable to find the Prince unguarded at any opportunity available to him. *I would swear they never let the brat step out alone! If he's not with the King, he has that damned red-haired Palatine tagging along. Even when he came to see my wares!* The Prince had, in fact, bought an excellent pair of gloves during his brief visit to Winters' pavilion – and the tall girl with the sword had stood beside him the whole time.

Truth be told, the trip had proved very successful for "John Winters"; nearly all the goods he had brought over the mountains had been sold. That only added to his problem: once his stock was gone, so was his reason for being in Edge.

He had had the palace watched, had Aaren followed every time he emerged. When that proved futile, he had even tried slipping into Greybeal himself, and bribing his way in. But neither bribery nor stealth had taken him past the too-loyal and too-diligent guards. He also discovered that a common merchant was simply not allowed much access to the royal family.

I need – a cat's-paw; someone who comes and goes there normally, and can be made to do my bidding. To that end, he had chosen the Riverside. It was a stylish place, frequented by the better tradesmen – and by people in service to the highborn.

It was his plan to eavesdrop on the loose talk among the servants and tradesmen, find one with a grudge against the palace, and bend him, or her, to his will, probably by using the Touch. He had listened to several such conversations already, but heard nothing useful.

He rose and went to refill his tankard. As he passed a table set back in an alcove, he caught the words, "... Lord Wildon..."

Michael leaned on the bar while the landlord drew his ale, his whole attention focused on the two men discussing the High Chamberlain. They were dressed in Trever's own livery; one wore the club and broad knife of a huntsman, dangling from his belt. It was he who spoke. "I tell you, when the boy lit that fire, the Hawk almost choked in his beard! I don't think he took his eyes off the lad for the rest of the night." He sat back and drained his mug. "And the next morning, he made sure to ride with King Trever between him and the Prince, all the way back to the city."

His companion nodded. "That explains it as well as anything, then. I only know that he avoids Prince Aaren as much as he's able. He doesn't seem to care much for Lady Jenora, either." The man chuckled. "Truly, he seems to have little use for youngsters at all."

"I wonder if that includes his own?" Seeing the
other's raised brows, the huntsman sat up and lowered
his voice slightly.   "You didn't know? Our fine
Chamberlain has himself a by-blow, got from a tryst with
some serving-girl years ago. She died when the boy was
born, or so I've heard. But Lord Wildon acknowledged
the lad, and took him in to raise. So perhaps he's not so
bad when all's said, for all his airs and ambitions."

Michael took his cup, and the other two he'd had
the barman fill as well, and stepped up to the alcove.
Holding out the three draughts, he smiled broadly and
said, "Your honor, sirs. I've been drinking alone till now,
and wonder if I might join you."

◆   ◆   ◆

Wildon turned the key and entered his home in the
city as quietly as he could. It was late, full dark outside,
and all the household was abed. Only three candles
burned to light his way down the hallway.

He passed down it to his study, shrugging out of his
cloak as he went. It was the first true day of spring, but
the night still bore some of the cold of the season past.

When he stepped into the study he saw that his
steward had left the coals alive in the grate, as instructed.
By their glow he was able to hang his cloak and find the
lamp on the mantle. He lit it with a twig of tinder, then
piled more wood on the fire and blew it into life with
the bellows. Taking up the lamp, he turned to his desk.

There was a man sitting behind it. He was young,
dark, and vaguely familiar. He seemed undismayed at
being found in another man's home at night. He put on
a disarming smile and raised a steady, empty hand.
"Pray, do not have me arrested or thrown in the street

just yet. I mean you and yours no harm. Quite the opposite."

Wildon moved closer, his right hand on the dagger at his belt. "If you mean me well, then why come skulking in the dark?" He set the lamp on the desktop and peered over it. "I know you, do I not? You're that trader who came from Faires last week - Winters, isn't it?"

The intruder nodded. "You have an excellent memory." He pushed back the chair and stood up. "I came at night because I wish to discuss things that might not bear the day. I wish them kept private, and I believe you will agree."

Wildon came around the desk, within arm's reach. "What 'things'? Whatever you have to say, get to it, and quickly, or I'll have no need to call the watch. I'll see you out with my own hands."

The other kept his innocuous smile, but suddenly his eyes turned ebon black. Wildon felt something wash over him, something between the cold of fear and the warmth of pleasure. The sounds of the crackling fire and the city night were gone, lost in the focus of those fathomless eyes. He almost lost himself there. But not quite.

With a gasp of effort he shook himself free of the paralyzing spell and lunged forward, taking the shorter man by the throat and pressing his dagger's point to the artery throbbing under his palm. "What in Tempter's name was that? Don't -" as Winters' hand began to move. "If you quiver, you die. Just answer me, and do it well."

The merchant spoke hoarsely past Wildon's gripping fingers. "It was nothing, only a gift I grant those who aid me. I only wished you to sample it. And I have other gifts to offer as well. Will you release me, so we might consider them?"

Wildon stood unwavering for a moment, then dropped his hand and stepped back, holding the knife ready. "I shall listen. But no more magic, on your life. Sit over there." He indicated a chair near the fireplace. As Winters went to it, he took his own seat behind the desk. "Now, you've thrice promised me some boon in as many minutes. Tell me what you mean."

"I can help you to acquire the things you want: power. A mighty name. A ... throne?" He smiled, mockingly now. "Unless I've heard falsely, and come to the wrong man."

Wildon stared at him, eyes icy. "Go on."

"Ah. I am more than a simple tradesman, Lord Wildon. I do far more than merely ply the roads and haggle for goods. I have power, very real, and the backing of forces still greater. I also have the strength of numbers who work my will." He steepled his fingers and looked at the Hawk over them. "I can be a most formidable ally, if an alliance would interest you."

Wildon cocked his head. "You speak the rankest treason. I should kill you at once." They gazed at each other for a long moment. The man's smile never wavered. Wildon snorted. "What sort of 'forces' and 'numbers' do you mean? The magic you tried to work on me? The mercenaries from the South I've heard about?"

"Before I can answer that, I will have to trust you more than a mere stranger might. And you will have to trust me as well. To that end, tell me: what think you, truly, of the Telciens that rule here in Edge?"

Wildon rested his chin on his fist, his eyes never leaving Winters, and pondered for several minutes. Finally, he laid down the dagger, folded his arms, and answered. "Trever is my King, my sworn lord. Never shall I speak ill of him."

"Yes. But what of his Queen, and his son?"

Again Wildon considered his reply. "Queen Alyda is not a strong woman. I would not rely on her overmuch if the need arose. As to the Prince -" His hand returned to the desk, and clenched into a fist. "- I know not what to make of him. He's touched by something unholy, and dangerous. All the kingdom knows it. I do not trust him." He glared at Michael. "And what interest is it of yours?"

Winters sat back in his chair, looking pleased. "Thank you for your candor. I will give some of my own in return. As to the Prince, I have my own reasons to wish him gone. You say, and I concur, that he is spawn of the Tempter. He needs to be removed.

"The forces I spoke of are both of this world and not of it. I can call upon powers older than the world we know, when needed. And in more common powers, I am raising an army in secret. Its size is not great; but believe me, you have never seen its like. When I am ready, it will sweep over these lands like nothing before.

"And when I do, I shall need men with me, men ready to take power and use it. I cannot be in both Faires and Edge at the same time. My heart, for many reasons, is in Faires. I'll need a man in Edge. A leader not afraid of power."

Wildon sat back, his mind whirling as ideas clicked into place. When he leaned forward again, his face was set in stone, and his voice carefully flat. "You are Dark Michael."

The man across the desk nodded slowly. "I am. Now, will you take your blade and try to kill me? Will you call for the watch?"

Neither of them moved for some minutes. The shadows in the room seemed to deepen as the small fire in the grate popped and ticked. Then Wildon picked up his dagger, and slipped it into its scabbard. He rose and went to his sideboard and poured two glasses of fortified wine. When he turned and offered one to Michael, he said only, "Let us speak more."

Chapter 9
Windfall

Michael was cheered by the morning sun, and by his own thoughts, as he rode at the head of his wagons on the Road back to the mountains. It was warm, the roadway was dry, and he had set things in motion that would take him ever closer to his goal.

He thought back to his meeting with Lord Wildon, two nights before. *What a rare man he is, my cat's-paw. Few, very few, have ever had the strength to resist the Touch. But even without it, we managed an understanding.*

Before he left that night, he had given Wildon a small box. "Keep this here, in your house. It will tell you when I have instructions for you. When it chimes, come to this room – and come alone."

His parting words had been equally to the point: "Bide your time, and do nothing harsh with your own hands. When I have made all ready I will tell you, and then, I promise you, you will come into your own."

Now, it was only a matter of time. He would return to Faires, continue his planning and gathering, and make his way with Cillistra. *Ah, and she is worth it, worth everything. In just a few days –*

His advance scout was coming back down the road, at the gallop. He reined up before Michael and raised his hand. "M'Lord. There's a small party approaching, just out of the Waist. They look well-to-do."

"How many?"

"Five men, two of them men-at-arms, I think. The others look like nobles or merchants. And two women, probably wives. D'you think they're worth a go, m'Lord?"

Michael thought for a moment. "Why not? Since Fate's put them in our path, we'll not ignore her." He turned to the train behind him. "Take the wagons off the road – there, into that lay-by. And get out your weapons."

When the wagoners and outriders all stood before him, he dug into a pouch at his waist and drew out a strip of heavy jawbone, set with large yellowed teeth. He moved his open hand over the bone, muttering too softly to be heard. In a moment, he put away the jaw and waved to the bend in the roadway ahead. "Their horses cannot sense you now. You know what to do. Up with you! To your places, and be ready."

Several minutes later, the first two men came around the bend, a woman just behind them. The emerald green of the woman's cloak against the black of her horse suddenly reminded Michael of something he couldn't quite grasp, but there was no time to think about it; as they rounded the turn, he gave the signal to attack.

The scout sprang from the brush at the trail's side, seized the older man's bridle, and wrenched his horse's head around. The animal bleated in pain and staggered. The rider reeled in his saddle, trying to kick his attacker and draw his sword. Another brigand leaped from an overhanging tree branch onto the horse's withers, and clamped his arm across the man's throat. They both tumbled from the beast's back into the dirt.

The woman cried out, "Darras! Oh, help him!" She spurred her mount forward, but was stopped by yet another man bounding into the path. He quickly struck the second nobleman out of his saddle with a heavy staff.

The two men-at-arms galloped around the bend, their swords drawn. A fourth and fifth of Michael's wagoners plunged from the trees to meet them.

The ambush was over in minutes. The two remaining travelers were also waylaid and dealt with. The bodies were moved out of the Road, the horses stripped of their gear and added to Michael's train. While his wagons were brought up and loaded with the spoils, he examined some of the smaller takings.

He glanced with a practiced eye at the bracelets and pendants, and then handed them to one of the wagoners. The last item he held up into the sunlight. The gold of the signet ring flashed back to his eyes, worked into an ornate letter "O".

Michael nodded to himself. *Oswin.* Family of the royal house's palatines. He slipped it into his own purse. With a wave of his hand, he set his caravan moving again. He had been right: it was indeed a fine day.

Chapter 10
Contriving

For weeks that spring, all of Edge had been humming with talk and interest. When finally three heralds made their way down from the mountains and reached Greybeal, the rumors were confirmed: King Gearld was indeed coming, himself, to see King Trever.

By the time Gearld and his entourage came into sight, the Road was lined with the curious and the idle, staring and pointing. No one cheered, but neither did anyone fling curses or other offenses. Gearld found that encouraging; perhaps some of the old grudges were truly forgotten, or at least laid aside.

Greybeal's pennons were flying, and a fanfare was sounded as the King approached. The palace gates stood open, and Trever himself stood just inside them, with Prince Aaren beside him, and a tall auburn-haired girl at the Prince's side, a sword on her belt and a black cord around one shoulder. *That must be the girl Palatine, Lady Jenora. I've heard that she's recently orphaned.* They came forward when Gearld stopped his horse, and paused respectfully while he and his escort dismounted. Then Trever raised his voice, though he came no nearer. "We welcome you, King Gearld of Faires, and your companions. Our hospitality is yours, by the customs of our people. Come and be received."

Gearld drew himself up and answered, "I accept your welcome, King Trever, by our customs. My companions and I thank you." Trever's steward came forward and called to the stable boys and attendants gathered around, seeing to the visitors' mounts and baggage with brisk efficiency. The two Kings fell into step toward the palace, with Aaren and Jenora a pace behind.

"So, what brings you here, Gearld? Something grave, I wager, to lure you across the mountains in your person." Trever turned his head to his son. "Aaren, run ahead and tell your mother that the King is here. Give her time to make ready," he added with a laugh.

"If you don't mind, Trever ..." Gearld touched Aaren's elbow to keep him a moment. "I'd like the Prince to come with us. What I have to discuss concerns him as much as it does us. I wish also to send for my legate here in Edge, and have him join us. If you'll give me an hour to clean off the worst of my travels, I would like to meet with both of you, and any other advisors you choose to have attend. Will that be suitable?"

Trever studied him for a moment, plainly intrigued. Then he nodded. "Well and good. We will meet in the council room, then. Stephen will show you all to your chambers, and fetch whatever you need. When you're ready, he can show you the way to the meeting. It promises to be - interesting."

As promised, King Gearld entered the council room at the appointed time, bathed and clothed more regally than he had been in the courtyard. He took his place at the side of the table opposite Trever, with the Fairen legate on his right and the Lord Mayor of Faires, also cleaned of the effects of travel, on his left.

For his part, Trever had seated Wildon at his right hand, and Aaren at his left. The Prince looked from face to face, but was able to read nothing in any of them beyond a sense of gravity.

At Trever's nod, Gearld rose. "Thank you for receiving us so promptly. King Trever, I bring serious news, and a suggestion that I hope will be equally serious.

"As the Lord Mayor can attest -" Gearld indicated that worthy, who rose and bowed. "- we have been troubled of late in Faires. I will let him explain the matter to you."

Trever sniffed. "Briefly, I hope?"

The Mayor raised an eyebrow, but otherwise ignored the slight. He was a short, lath-thin man who nonetheless bore an air of great dignity. "Your Majesties, my Lord, my information is quickly told. Only last week, we concluded the Spring Fair in our city. It is normally our second greatest of the year; only the Harvest Fair in autumn is better attended. Each year, merchants and guilds from every kingdom within reach by ship or caravan come to the Spring Fair. They know that all who attend will be eager to see their wares and buy them, as well as just to visit and enjoy themselves, after the leanness and enclosure of winter.

"This year, fewer than half of the usual attendees arrived. Only one trader from Seahale came; none at all from Alatia, or Qualls. Few, even, from Edge traveled over the mountains. Had you noticed this, your Majesty?"

Trever stirred in his seat. "Yes, we have heard talk among our tradesmen here, saying they would not hazard the journey. And you know why as well as I, I'm sure."

"We do, your Highness. It is because of the Dark One. His attacks have increased so much this year past that people fear to travel beyond their own homes. Indeed, we received news that he had waylaid one caravan from distant Westfalls, on its way to our fair. The two men who reached Faires to tell the tale were the only survivors." The Mayor looked to King Gearld, who nodded. Bowing again to his hosts, the Mayor took his seat.

Gearld cleared his throat. "It was this development that precipitated my decision to come here, and prodded an idea that I had been only mildly entertaining till now." He paused, as though uncertain of his ground – or careful of his next words. "The last time you and I met face-to-face, Trever, we came together to find an end to the strife between our lands. We both saw how wasteful of resources and lives the wars had been over those evil years, and tried to stop them. And we succeeded."

"As I remember," Trever mused, "it was you who suggested those meetings, too. What suggestion do you have this time, to solve your problem?"

Aaren felt his own embarrassment rise. Was his father deliberately trying to insult the Fairens? He watched as King Gearld took a deep breath and gathered himself before continuing.

"Is it only 'my' problem, Trever? Is the Dark One not also raiding on this side of the mountains? Does the terror he inspires not also hover, even if more lightly, over your own people?" He did not mention Lord and Lady Oswin by name. He didn't have to.

Trever's eyebrows came together - a sign, Aaren knew, that the dart had found its mark. "Agreed, he preys upon both our kingdoms alike. We do what we can to counter him, as I know you do, but I swear he is a will-o'-the-wisp. He will not be trapped or pinned down. By the Tempter, he's seldom even seen! But what do you propose we do differently?"

A smile flickered briefly on Gearld's face. "'Propose' is a good choice of words, Trever. The Dark One's power - truly, even the size of his forces - grows by the day. Unless we can present a greater power against him, he may become a genuine threat even to our thrones. So my idea is a simple and profound one: unite our kingdoms."

Wildon burst out, "Unite them! How?" Remembering himself, he looked first to one King then the other. "Forgive me, your Majesties, but how could such a thing be done? Which of you would rule the other?"

Trever's voice also carried an unpleasant edge to it. "My Chamberlain asks good questions. What do you have in mind to work this, Gearld?"

Gearld raised a placating hand. "I assure you, I never mean for either of us to dominate the other. My thought is more for the future, though its effect will be felt at once. I suggest that we announce that one day, our lands will be one kingdom, ruled by our children. I suggest that they, our heirs, marry and join the two lands. I have come to see if the idea is one you would consider."

Aaren was literally rocked back into his chair, his mind awhirl. *Marry!? One of the princesses? Which one? I've never even met them!* He struggled to compose himself, hearing Gearld continue behind the thumping of his own heart.

"Think of it, Trever. The effect it would have on our citizens could only be heartening, to suddenly see twice the power to stand against the Dark One and all other threats. And as for him: would it not give him great pause, to see us allied, presenting him with a united front against which he must batter? Can you see the advantage?"

For once, Trever was slow to speak. He sat with eyes unfocused, thoughts obviously milling in his head. Aaren watched him, his own thoughts gradually calming, but uncertain what he hoped his father would answer. Finally, Trever laid his hands on the tabletop. "I would consider it, if the terms were good and carefully outlined. What details have you prepared?"

"Only that we will continue to rule separately for our lifetimes. I wish to proclaim, as soon as we can strike an agreement, that Prince Aaren will marry my daughter Cillistra when he reaches the age of consent. When you and I are both gone, they will be King and Queen of a joint kingdom, Edge and Faires together. And we will be preparing the way to that for the rest of our reigns. The terms can be devised by people versed in such things, such as my representative here."

Again, Aaren's thoughts were a jumble of vague images and stories he had heard third-hand. *Cillistra? She's the eldest, a few years older than me. Isn't she supposed to be very beautiful? Or is that Carola? And isn't there a third princess? But married! How would that be ...* Dimly, he heard Wildon whispering something into Trever's ear. He shook his head and forced himself to pay attention. They were deciding his life here!

King Gearld was leaning forward, catching Trever's eye and waiting. Finally he spoke up. "What do you think? Is it something you can agree to, at least in principle, and set the diplomats to arranging the terms? I hope we can find this easier than ... our last attempt at accord." He added this last with a reminiscent smile.

Trever returned the smile, obviously remembering the same things from that time. Then he turned to Aaren. "Well, boy, what say you?"

Aaren was taken aback; his father so seldom asked his opinion of anything. He plumbed his feelings for some moments before answering, carefully, "The idea rings true, Father. Our kingdoms together would make a most formidable union. I, uh, believe I would be happy to... to marry... if you think it best."

Trever turned back to Gearld. Both men were smiling at Aaren's discomfort. It seemed, in a way, to make the moment more human. "Agreed, then. Prepare the details, and we shall speak again."

✦   ✦   ✦

At Aaren's summons, Jenora came into his chambers already very curious. She had seen little of him for several days; he had seemed to spend nearly all his time in the Kings' company, where her protection was hardly necessary. She had heard rumors of some very secret and important bargaining - all the palace hummed with rumors, often contradicting each other - but frankly discounted them as unreliable. She was eager to know if the Prince would tell her the whole story, unvarnished.

When she entered, he was seated at his writing table, with his chair turned to face the door. He didn't rise, but merely waved his hand to beckon her in. "Please close the door, will you? And draw up that chair, where we can talk quietly."

She did as he asked, watching him closely. His businesslike, almost brusque manner was plainly only on the surface; beneath, she sensed something else, perhaps nerves, perhaps uncertainty about what he would say, or how she would react. She was more curious still, and a little disquieted.

"I have two things to tell you. Big things. After I tell you, I have a favor to ask, too. I hope you can help me with it. I hope ... you'll still want to by then." He suddenly sat back and grinned self-consciously. "Listen to me! You'd think I was going to drop the moon on you, when actually I expect you'll be glad enough of both of them."

She smiled back, more at ease herself. "Not if you don't get around to telling me them, your Highness."

Aaren shook his head and leaned forward again. "Well enough, then. The first is about your future; our future, really. I've discussed this with my father and all his advisors, and they agree with the idea. When I am King, someday, I want you to be my High Chamberlain – that is, if you would want the job." He chuckled. "It will mean you'll have to put up with me even more than you do now. But what say you?"

She felt herself flush, felt the surprise of it race through her with a start of excitement. It took her a moment to find words. "Why ... it would be an honor, my Prince. Of course I will, if you wish it. But do people really agree? There's never been a woman Chamberlain before."

"No, but neither has there ever been a female Palatine, and everyone in the kingdom knows you've held that place well. No one objects, not even the King. The post is yours." He held her gaze for a moment, his smile reflecting hers. "Now, about the second thing..."

He hesitated, averted his eyes a moment, then looked up into hers again. "We're going to Faires next month, you and I and my father. We're going there to meet the Princess Cillistra, King Gearld's oldest daughter, and to hold our - our betrothal ceremony, Cillistra's and mine. In two years, when I'm of age, I'm going to marry her."

Jenora sat, stunned. It was as if he had drawn forth a weapon and struck her: shock, disbelief, shortened breath ... she felt them all, and felt the earlier flush drain from her cheeks; but no pain; not yet. She heard Aaren's voice going on, almost rushing on, "It's what King Gearld came here for, to arrange this, and my father agreed. I really think it is the best thing for both the kingdoms. It's certainly the best thing I can do for them. Think what it will mean: no more wars, no more rivalry, and twice the power against enemies like Dark Michael."

He paused. "Jen, say something. I'll need your help now, more than ever. What do you think about all this?"

What do I think about it? How can I say what I think? What I feel? Can I tell him what I feel – about him? If I do, what can he say? She shook herself, mentally, dredging up all the discipline that her training had ever taught her, all the coolness of mind she had ever achieved, and let it take control. *Fool! You always knew something like this would come. It's his duty; and it's yours, too. There was never any other way it could be.*

She met his gaze levelly, and swallowed once before trusting herself to speak. "I understand, now, what all the talk has been about. Quite a surprise, I must say. And you agree too, I presume?"

At least he had the grace to blush. "Yes. I've never met her, and never really thought of getting married, of course. But yes, I agreed." He laughed, embarrassed. "I hear she's very beautiful, you know. And as I said, it will make both lands stronger, and that must be a good thing. For the rest," he shrugged. "For the rest, I only hope she and I can tolerate each other, or better. I suppose it's the price of being a Prince."

She forced herself to return his smile. "Yes, I suppose it is." There was a long, awkward pause. Finally Jenora spoke again, saying the first thing that came into her head. "You also mentioned a favor you would need?"

"Oh, that. Well, as you know it's customary for a couple, at their betrothal, to exchange gifts. I was hoping you would help me choose something ... something appropriate. I've never bought anything for a girl before. I mean, except my mother. And you. But that's not... I mean, this is different." He wouldn't look at her. "Will you help me?"

She stood, surprised to find that her feet kept their balance. "Certainly, your Highness. It would be my honor." The room around her was suddenly a strange place, and she had to consciously look around to find the door. "I'll give it some thought. And I'm sure there are a hundred preparations to make for such an important trip. I'll see to them, starting now, if I may go."

He followed her out, and stopped to lean in the doorway. "Jen ... thank you. I'm going to need you a lot in the next two years, I think. I'm really glad you'll be there for me."

She felt her control slipping, and held her face firmly in check before replying. "You know I always will, my Prince." She turned away. She heard the door close behind her before the pain came, an engulfing wave that made her stumble as she hurried down the corridor.

Chapter 11
Bad Tidings

Vernor drummed his fingers on the tabletop, chin in his left hand. The circle of silver set into his floor glowed with an almost imperceptible white light, while the red tapers set at each point of the pentacle within flared and flickered in the darkened room. The flames danced again as the fire imp inside the enchanted circle threw itself against the white wall of force. It cursed and flew at the other side, bounced ineffectually off the light and knelt, panting, in the circle's center. Vernor drummed his fingers, barely stifling a yawn. The tiny imp smiled bitterly and made an obscene gesture at the mage.

Placing both hands flat, Vernor rose and walked around the table. He circled the caged elemental, fingers laced over his belly, and nodded.

"Now. If you are quite through battering your worthless carcass about, let us discuss the terms of your release." He stopped and faced the fire imp squarely, although he did not meet its eyes. The relative size of the creature didn't negate its fundamental nature. As a member of the demon family, its hypnotic gaze was as potentially dangerous as that of any of its kin.

It hissed. "I owe you nothing!"

"True enough," Vernor replied, "but as I have you bound here indefinitely, you - listen to me, Imp!" It had begun another careful circumnavigation of its confine, casually swinging its forked tail at one candle. "I *do* have you bound, Demon, and require the answers to five questions before I release you."

The imp stopped what it was doing and spun to face him, little tufts of fire at its temples. "*Five!* The accepted penalty is three! My Master will hear of this!" The red-fleshed creature literally fumed. "Never! You'll get three because you caught me off guard, and not a question more. And be thankful for even that!"

The mage smiled. "While you are hardly in a position to argue, three it is. But none may be couched in riddle."

"Oh!" shrieked the imp. "You dare!" It swelled to almost four palms high, thrice its former size, and then subsided. "You are a horrible little man, and I spit in your eye!" The demon spat, and a tiny drop of fire splattered against the white barrier. "You will get two answers straight, and the third as true prophecy. *And*, I hear all the questions first!" Its tiny breast heaved with indignation.

Vernor knew that he had pushed as far as he reasonably could. He nodded. "Done." Going to a cluttered worktable, he drew forth a linen scroll and peered at it.

"One. What manner of fire magic mirrored mine during the creation of Prince Aaren's bracelet sixteen years ago, and who was responsible? Two -"

"That's two questions!" barked the smoldering imp.

"Hmph. Very well, I'll settle for 'Who?', then ask the person myself." The imp shrugged. "Two. Other portents have indicated that Aaren will need to use his powers to save a life, very possibly his own, yet will be bound against doing so. What is the nature of this impediment?"

"Hate to make you look like the jackass you are, *human*, but doesn't he wear a locked bracelet of your own construction?"

"That bracelet has been unlocked for some while, Demon. He wears it now by ... hmm ... by force of habit, I suppose. At any rate, that is not an effective block to his powers. You'll have to do better than that. The third question." He looked back down at the scroll. "Is the Prince's forthcoming trip to Faires with King Trever a safe one? Specifically, what dangers await him?"

The fire imp stared at him incredulously. "Oh that's *all*, gnarled one? You wouldn't like the given name of a Major Demon, or perhaps immortality as well? By all that's unholy, these questions are *much* too broad. You may choose *one*." Giving a magnanimous wave of its hand, it crossed its minute arms over its chest and kicked at a red candle, which of course didn't budge.

"The deal is *made*, Demon." Vernor picked up a silver holy symbol and dangled it nonchalantly so that spears of light reflected into the circle on the floor. The imp cursed loudly as one nicked its tiny buttocks with a hiss and a curl of smoke. Rubbing its scorched regions, it did an elaborate dance trying to avoid the moving reflections, and screamed.

"You will burn for this, I promise you! I - *yow!* - I will answer your infernal questions, son of dogs! But put that damned thing away!"

Vernor pocketed the charm. "You are more accurately a damned thing,' Imp." Now it would not meet his eyes. Walking to the center of the pentacle, it squatted and looked the other way, grimacing furiously. Vernor turned his green chair toward the imp and settled into its gentle contours. He waited.

The demon closed its eyes and made a sigil in the air that glowed softly orange for a moment and then faded away. It opened its eyes. It looked pleased for the first time.

"To answer your first question: the wise-woman Obra of Faires. To your second: nothing shall stop him using his power, save his own conscience," the demon chuckled. "And as to your third:

> "From sudden rock, from hammer-blow,
> Beware the death by Stone.
> From icy Water wending low
> The sea would claim his bones.
> By Blade, by Bolt, by Steel, by Fire,
> The Prince his fate will seal.
> In roiling flame, his own dark Pyre,
> He'll scream and never heal."

The terms of the bond being fulfilled, the fire demon spat again and vanished, a tiny fireball imploding with a *snap!* leaving only an acrid memory in its wake.

Vernor sat very still. Bad poetry aside, the sheer diversity of threat was daunting. While a prophecy by demon would obscure or cast false light on the foretold events, it did not lie. The Prince *was* in danger from a plethora of sources. Vernor considered that.

Counseling the King would be little help. Not only would he have difficulty believing the threat real, he would, by his nature, be helpless to prepare for it. Tell him that a scout had detected an ambush party lying in wait, and they would be summarily dispatched. Warn him of treacherous townsmen and he could go prepared. But vague portents of undefined threat delivered by a sorcerer would merely frustrate Trever, and he was likely to ignore them.

The Prince? *Perhaps.* Just a boy, though his sixteen years had been packed with experience. Headstrong, arrogant, but he had turned the spoiled nature of his childhood into a challenge to himself; approaching the tolerance and patience of his friend and teacher Jenora was important to the lad. *And good for him.* He had, Vernor mused, the potential to be a greater king than his father.

If he lives to fulfill his destiny. Vernor's face went slack for a moment, as it had many times before, his eyes inward and empty. Somewhere deep in his mind there was the thin sound of distant screams.

After only a few seconds, it was gone, leaving him the sense of having just awakened. He shook himself and groped for the chain of his interrupted thought.

Kerwin, then. The King's tracker, personal aide, and oldest friend, now that Darras was gone. Some mistakenly thought that Wildon was the closest man to the King, but Vernor was well aware of the dual nature of *that* relationship. Kerwin, now, was a man who respected magic, would listen closely to the mage and, the old man knew, put the life of the King or Prince before his own.

Finally, having Jenora along would enhance the Prince's safety immeasurably. She loved the boy, that was obvious, and would protect him as surely as Kerwin. It did not occur to the mage that this trip, whose sole purpose was to introduce Aaren to his bride-to-be in Faires, might be painful to Jenora. Even if it had, it would have made no difference to him.

Joints complaining, Vernor hauled himself out of the comfortable chair and began cleaning up the accouterments of the Ring of Force. He gathered up the red candles and packed them carefully between his grey candles and a stained box of rough, grey, leathery strips. Thoughtfully, he pulled one of the oily strips out of the box and tapped it lightly on the edge of the wooden shelf. Lost in thought, he walked back toward his writing table, abstractly gnawing on one end of the dried meat, its unremembered saltiness causing him to drool just a bit.

"Well, Imp," he munched, "we'll just see about all that."

Chapter 12
Visit to Faires

Jenora smiled, drew a deep breath, and promised herself that she would retain her detachment. This wouldn't be as easy as she had thought it would be. If only he would stop going *on* about it so!

"She's supposed to be the most beautiful girl in their kingdom! Did you know that her hair reaches below her waist? Kerwin told me that a messenger told *him* that her skill on the harpsichord is a marvel to hear. Do you know how much farther? Gods! I should calm down a bit," he stuttered, heedless of the look in his friend's eyes.

"Yes, Prince. Perhaps giving your tongue a brief respite would allow your entire overwrought person some rest." She tossed her chestnut hair, warrior-short, and tried to keep the edge from her voice. "It's still another six hours, at least, to camp."

The party was just reaching the Waist, and the horses were forced into single file. Kerwin and the King followed their six guards, Jenora and Aaren brought up the rear. The roaring of the Wendlow drowned out the Prince's vexed reply, and Jenora was left, more or less thankfully, to her own troubled musings.

It seemed stupid to dwell on it, but ever since childhood she had entertained fantasies of marrying Aaren. After all, it wasn't that vain a notion. She was the eldest daughter of one of the noblest houses in Edge, descended from the same founding chieftains who had settled the valley with Aaren's ancestors. The death of her parents had necessitated the transference of her title and lands to a steward, and made her a ward of the royal court; but she would take over the management of her holdings upon her majority, early next year.

Just a year, she thought, wincing, *before my Prince's wedding to the foreigner.* Aaren was her best friend, her first kiss, and her sworn liege. It rankled her to sit blithely by and watch him moon over some silly coifed harpsichord player who, in all likelihood, didn't know a parry from a paring knife. She well understood, and approved, the necessity of binding the kingdoms of Edge and Faires together against the threat of the monster who had murdered her parents. It was the part about losing her Prince that rankled.

"Huh. Just five minutes of hand-to-hand with me, just *three* minutes, and see how fine her long raven hair looks." She knew it was childish, and she knew Aaren would be horrified, and she knew the water drowned out every word she muttered. "And what a stupid name. *Cillistra.* I think I'll name one of the new mastiff bitches Cillistra. A fine name for an animal." She smiled bitterly, but it really didn't make her feel any better.

About an hour later, Aaren slowed his mount and dropped back to ride close beside Jenora.

"Jen?" he said, softly enough that only she could hear.

Sensing his desire for a private conversation, Jenora fell back slightly from the group. "Yes?"

"I've been thinking."

Heart in her throat, she kept her voice level. "What have you been thinking, Prince?"

"About my power," he said. "To burn things."

Her mind raced to catch up with his direction, and her heart sank back down to its normal home in her breast. "Yes?"

"Well, you know that occasionally I experiment with it. Not often, and not, well, not very *much* of it."

"I'm not sure I take your meaning."

"Remember that time when I started the fire on the hunt last year?" He smiled. "That was the night you and I –"

"Yes, I remember," she interjected.

"Yes, well, other times I'd just tried lighting smaller things, like tapers or a bit of moss or things like that. To see how it worked. It always frightened me a little bit, Jen. Especially after that campfire."

She cocked an eyebrow. "Why?"

"It's just that I don't know how big it could get. When I think about it, it's like when we used to build little earthen dams on the stream behind the archery range. Remember?"

"Yes..."

"Well, if you notch just a little out of the top, the water comes out gradually. But you have to watch it, and plug it up before it widens too much. If you don't, then the whole dam collapses, and all of the water comes rushing out at once, and the dam is destroyed."

They rode in silence for a bit. Jenora was chilled. "Do you mean, Prince, that the fire might hurt you if you let it grow too great?"

Aaren frowned. "Hadn't thought of that. No, I don't think so. But it might get too big for me to control." He squirmed in his saddle. "And there is another thing." Sensing his discomfort, she waited while he struggled with the words.

"When I do it, when I burn something, it feels... good. And the fire wants to be bigger. When I started the logs at the campfire it was the biggest one I'd ever tried. I'd been practicing, and I thought I could manage it, but when I let it go, it was as if the thinking part of me was stilled. I don't mean that I was swooning or anything. It was just that the fire spoke very loudly to me, and the voice of my reason, the controlling part that you and Master Leland have taught me, was suddenly weak and very far away.

"I almost let it go. And I don't know what would have happened if I had. Most everyone sees my ... ability ... as a curse from the Tempter, I know, because it frightens them. But I keep thinking that maybe I have it for a reason. That it could be a useful power if I could only learn how to manage it.

"Since then I have only started small fires. I think that each time I use it, it gets easier to bend it to my will, but it's hard to tell." He sighed. "I could use your counsel, Palatine."

Jenora rode in silence for a moment, the Wendlow roaring distantly below them. "I do not know how to answer you. I think that you are wise to fear it, if what you say is true. And I agree that slow experiments are the more prudent course. I would have to say that our most valuable ally in this would be the mage Vernor. He knows much about such things. Have you spoken to him?"

Aaren frowned. "Actually, no. After that meeting in the tower on my thirteenth birthday, he left me uneasy. I'm sure he means well, but his manner disturbs me. I get the feeling that I am being tested." He smiled ruefully. "Your advice is wise though, as always. We'll seek him out when we return from Faires." They fell into a brooding silence then, and eventually caught up to the rest of the group.

✦　　　✦　　　✦

Three days later, they descended into the valley of Faires. In honor of the visiting royalty, the town had turned out with splendor. Colored flags rippled softly from a hundred rooftops, and babes were held aloft to witness the young Prince's passing. The main road was lined with wildflowers and firepots. Red and green and yellow smoke drifted lazily into the mountain air. Everyone was dressed in their finest, and on most faces were curious smiles. To Aaren's young eyes it looked spectacular. "They really know how to put on a show," he whispered to Jenora.

"They've had a lot of practice, Prince. This is the city of fairs, eh?"

He nodded, eyes wide.

Pulling up in front of the massive main gate to the Keep, Kerwin bellowed up at the guards on the wall. "His Royal Majesty King Trever of Edge greets King Gearld of Faires and requests traveler's sanctuary for the night!"

"Be it known," replied the chief of militia, splendid in his polished armor, "that King Trever, his kin and men, are always welcome in the house of Proudlock, for as long as they choose to remain." He saluted smartly and the two rows of honor guard lining the archway below snapped their long polearms upright, green and white standards fluttering. The way clear, Trever and his party rode between them into the courtyard.

Kerwin was uneasy. There was no sign of any hostility; all the faces surrounding them were, in fact, beaming or respectful, as befitted the station of the bearer. But there were just too damn many of them for his liking. Vernor had been quite agitated when they spoke, and the old mage was seldom mistaken. The King's tracker slowly scanned the entire crowd. *Nothing.* He turned to his liege and nodded curtly, once.

Trever agreed with his friend's silent assessment, though Kerwin's obvious jumpiness was contagious. Edge and Faires were truly at peace, now, but Trever remembered with clarity a time when that had not been so. Unconsciously, he rubbed the spot on his upper thigh where a Fairen arrow had pierced him, some eighteen years ago. He glanced at the flagpole, the flag of Edge flying just under the flag of Faires in honor of their visit. He smiled through his beard and thought with satisfaction that some years hence, this order would be righted.

They reined in before the stately columns of the main house and dismounted. Stable boys, freshly scrubbed and attired, darted forward to care for the horses. Led by Trever, the party climbed the five steps to the doorway and passed one by one beneath the ornately carved stone lintel. They were met by the Keep's majordomo, Rodolpho, as tall as the King but more slender. His voice was measured and possessed a strong Fairen accent.

"Most welcome men, and," he slipped in with the barest hesitation, "Lady of Edge. King Gearld and his Queen Signe extend you every courtesy and privilege of their House. We are honored."

His attention turned to Aaren. "Most especially do we hope your stay a pleasant one, Prince Aaren." The barest flicker of a smile graced his gaunt visage. "Princess Cillistra respectfully asks you to accept this small token of friendship." He proffered Aaren a box no bigger than the palm of his hand, wrapped in paper of the deepest blue. It was tied with a single silver cord.

Aaren looked around anxiously for a moment. Jenora tapped the nervous Prince on the shoulder and handed him his saddlebag, barely suppressing the urge to roll her eyes. Gratefully, he undid the flap and withdrew a present of his own, wrapped in yellow and gold, slightly the worse for travel.

"Um ... thank you ... that is, thank *her*, I mean, this is for her. Too." Awkwardly he shoved the package at the steward, stepping back and blushing furiously at the ground. The solemn steward cleared his throat politely, still holding out the blue and silver box in his other hand. Almost dizzy from mingled embarrassment and excitement, Aaren lurched forward, grabbed the box, and stepped back again mumbling his thanks.

Rodolpho cut in smoothly, "You all must be weary from your journey. Please be so kind as to follow me, and you will be led to your chambers." He gestured with his right hand and a chambermaid skipped forward and curtsied. "Mary, show these gentlefolk to the green suites." He turned back to the party. "King Gearld has asked for the pleasure of your company at his table this evening. Would two hours from now be convenient?"

"Fine, fine," rumbled Trever. "Which way to the baths, girl?"

She curtsied again, hands clasped behind her back, golden ponytail bobbing. "If you would follow me, my Lord."

Handsome boy, though very young, thought Rodolpho, as the party from Edge trailed after the chambermaid. *Not yet as arrogant as his father.* Rodolpho, too, remembered the old conflicts. *It is a good thing, this marriage. The Dark One makes gains by the week, and we need the strength of Edge.* He straightened his vest with a precise tug, and noticed two of the help idly gossiping as they stared after the retreating party.

"There are, I am quite certain, tasks of a particularly odious nature worth assigning to anyone in need of the work," he said to the foyer in general. The room was suddenly empty. Rodolpho's expression never changed, but inwardly he allowed himself a tiny smile, and started up the stairs to the Princess's rooms, tapping the yellow package with one bony finger.

The dining hall was immense – *bigger, even,* Aaren thought, *than the one back home.* At one end of the great stone chamber was a hearth tall enough to walk into. Two pigs and a calf were spitted and turning slowly inside it, by the efforts of two junior cooks whose perspiration glistened in the glow of the fire and the many torches lining the walls. Between each torch was the flag of a different kingdom or province that had, at some time, been hosted in this room. Over the tremendous fireplace hung the banners of Faires and Edge. A horseshoe of great oaken tables ran round the perimeter, draped with embroidered linen. Elaborate candelabra cast golden light over each few feet of tablecloth, and burnished goblets and flagons caught the light and sent if off in myriad gleams. Servants bustled from the doorway in the far end of the hall, heaping platters of food onto the crowded tables. The benches were three-quarters full as Aaren, his father, and Jenora were met at the great arched doorway. Rodolpho bowed deeply and turned to the room.

"His Royal Highness King Trever of Edge; Prince Aaren of Edge; and the Lady Jenora."

Gearld rose from the head of the master table at the curve of the horseshoe and called out, "Trever! Welcome! Bring that boy of yours over and pull up a glass! Antony!" He turned to the servant hovering behind him. "Pound the bung off the special reserve for our honored guests from Edge." The man scurried off to the kitchen. By the time the three had seated themselves at the table, two burly young men had manhandled a wooden cask into a cradle against the wall and driven in a tap.

The King of Faires stood again. "Honored guests. May I present my wife Signe, Queen of the Realm, and my lovely daughter Carola. Cillistra will be along in a moment, I think." He rolled his eyes and the men at the table laughed.

Glasses were filled. Trever stood and raised his aloft. "To Faires and her royal family, and their special reserve!"

Murmurs of "Hear, hear!" and "To Faires!" accompanied the draining of the first glass. Numerous other toasts followed, and within the half-hour Aaren was feeling positively giddy. It had been quite a while since he'd had so much wine at one sitting. Delicate pastries and marinated tidbits of beef allayed the onslaught of insobriety somewhat, but the main courses awaited the arrival of the Princess.

And arrive she finally did. A general hush descended on the revelers. Heads began turning toward the main doorway, and Aaren turned in his seat to see as well. What he saw stopped his heart in his throat.

She was stunning. Ebony tresses flowed languidly over ivory shoulders; her off-the-shoulder white gown, inset with pearls and glittering stones, looked drab against her luminescent skin. Three handmaidens accompanied her, each bearing a single lit taper; the golden light seemed twined and braided in her hair, sparkled from her gown, and dazzled the Prince.

She caught his eye, and the corners of her mouth lifted, transforming her from an artist's dream into a very human, beautiful woman. All conversation had ceased. The crackle of the great fire and the muted sounds from the kitchen filled Aaren's ears, while Cillistra, as she intended, filled his eyes.

Jenora, too, was absorbed in watching the Princess as she turned toward the head of the table. There was one odd thing though. All of the people in the room were staring at the Princess save one. Down the table, a handsome young man with long, dark curly hair was staring instead into the fire, his expression unreadable. From the particular spot in which Jenora sat, his eyes caught the fire behind the slaughtered pigs and threw it back balefully, as if a freshet of blood had caught the young gentleman full in the face. It lasted just for an instant; only Jenora saw it, and her revulsion was sudden and inexplicable. She was chilled. Later in her room she would remember a snatch of poetry from her lessons:

"...eyes like red-stained breakers on a twilight beach.
I think the sunset image now so terribly apt.
I cannot tear my eyes away,
and the light fades with gathering speed."

And then it was gone. His eyes were brown and lustrous. His gaze too finally turned to the eldest Princess, who looked out from regal, even haughty, green eyes, and her curtsy to the royalty from Edge was subtle and flawless.

"By the *Gods*, Gearld, that can't be one of yours!" boomed Trever. "Methinks this lovely Queen of yours conjured the lass whole from herself with nary a by-your-leave from *your* unfortunate face! Well, come here, lass, and introduce yourself!"

"Cillistra, Princess of Faires," announced Rodolpho, testily. That barbarian King had simply ruined the moment. There was a timing, a pace to these sorts of proceedings. And he knew upon whose head the Princess's wrath would fall for the abrupt end to this carefully crafted spectacle. He crossed his arms over his chest and frowned fixedly over the heads of those at the table.

Gearld rose and the rest of the men followed suit. "Daughter. I would present our guests. King Trever, the Loud." There was polite laughter. Trever bowed deeply, and winked. "Lady Jenora, Palatine to the Prince." They each appraised the other coolly, then Jenora acknowledged her with a slow and deliberate nod.

"And, of course, Prince Aaren, heir to the throne of Edge. My daughter Cillistra."

Aaren opened his mouth to speak, but no sound came forth. She allowed no more than a polite – and pointed – moment of his gawking before breaking in smoothly, "We are delighted to have you with us, noble Prince. I have long looked forward to this meeting." She approached him, her movement fluid and graceful even to herself, and extended her hand. Sheer habit guided the Prince to take her cool pale fingers in his, bow and kiss the air above them. She could feel the heat of his blushing face, and deep within her, an aversion was born. It was a very small thing, and it never showed in her face, but this rugged-looking youth was hardly the Prince of her fantasies. He seemed to gather the worst traits of both court dandies and town ruffians. And he certainly could not hold a candle to the passion she had known with her previous suitor, the merchant John Winters.

It had come as more than a shock to Cillistra when her father had ended that courtship some two months earlier, when her marriage to the Prince from Edge had been arranged. Indeed, she had not yet decided, within herself, whether it *was* actually ended. At any rate, this bedazzled boy would have to come far to make of himself a suitable replacement. She freed her hand, and gestured with it toward the table. "Come; sit and dine with me, so we might talk and know each other better."

Aaren nodded mutely and followed her to the seats reserved for them between the two Kings. Inwardly, she shook her head as he held out her chair. *It appears that the burden of the talk will be mine, unless I can free his tongue!* She smiled. *Barbarian.*

◆   ◆   ◆

Michael sat across the room, watching the emotions he could read like no other play across Cillistra's face.

His brown eyes were guileless and his face, framed by black curls, only smiled gently at the royal couple. His lean, well-muscled frame shifted as he watched them. His left hand rested lightly on the table linen, his fingers tracing the raised designs on a silver table knife of the house of Faires.

But behind the sparkling innocence of his gaze was a seething maelstrom of frustration and hatred. Just as the Pendulum had predicted, the boy had managed to thwart his plans. And here he was, a mere stone's throw away, again under the watchful eye of that cursed girl warrior – and half the Fairen elite guard. But that, he assured himself, would be remedied soon enough.

He repeated to himself, as he had a thousand times before, *this marriage will not take place!* He had worked too long and invested too much to be thwarted by these obscene pretenders to royalty. He would kill them all, slowly, and he would laugh as he crushed the life from their children.

He, too, remembered the shocking meeting he had had earlier that spring, when he was summoned to Gearld's antechamber.

"Good to see you, John," the King had rumbled, clapping him on the shoulder. "I fear I have difficult news. You know that I have approved of your courtship of Cillistra these past months, and were times different, I would be giving you my blessing even now." Gearld stepped away and faced the merchant fully. "I am sorry, John, but circumstances have changed. I am leaving for Edge tomorrow. I hope to arrange a marriage between the eldest son of Edge and the eldest daughter of Faires, to take place two years hence." He paused, as if studying the man before him for a reaction. "I'm sure you can already understand the importance of such a union, especially considering the growing threat to both kingdoms from the Dark One."

Michael had looked at the King in astonishment, for once caught completely by surprise. Being unprepared happened to him very seldom. One of his spies would die that night for his incompetence. The rest of the conversation was a blur of anger and frustration, which he had not bothered to hide, as it was just the reaction the King would have expected of him.

Even tonight, the pathetic Fairen King had shaken his hand warmly and thanked him for coming. Inwardly, the jilted suitor's thoughts ricocheted savagely between fantasies drenched in blood and those involving Cillistra. *No son of dogs shall have that woman. I would kill her first.*

To those around him, he joked, chatted, complimented the royal couple, and ate heartily. He cut into the thick rare roast with gusto, droplets of crimson dotting his knife. He was, as all Fairens who knew his merchant persona agreed, charming and full of life. *And full of Death!* Inside, Michael raged, tearing into the meat again.

Chapter 13
Meetings

The morning was Jenora's favorite time of day. She had always been an early riser, enjoying dawn's freshness and solitude. Today, she made her morning toilet in the dark. By the time the sun began greying the walls of her chamber she was well into her second set of exercises.

Most of the other members of last night's banquet would still be sleeping off the alcohol consumed during the meal, but Jenora drank seldom, and never much. Pulling on a heavy singlet and woolen hose to ward off the early chill, she set out for her daily run. New to the Keep, she did not yet know her way to the training yard, and so decided to circle the perimeter of the structure.

Halfway around the west wing she saw a narrow stone staircase leading up the wall, presumably to the roof. On a whim she veered onto the stairs. By the time she gained the roof she was winded, and stopped for a moment to admire the view.

The stairs had led her to an enormous roof garden. A fountain in the center was surrounded by sumptuous, painted wooden benches; white stone paths radiated in five directions, one leading to where she stood panting with hands on her knees.

The garden was over half a furlong on each side. There were shrubs, flowering hedges, even fruit trees. In wonderment she walked past lilies, roses, honeysuckle, and a hundred flowers she couldn't name. Some were just beginning to turn tightly wrapped night buds toward the east.

Emerging quietly from behind a plum tree, past delicate pink blossoms opening in the still air, she saw someone halfway around the fountain from her, facing the Nethals in the east. The sun was rising behind Maltern's Hounds, the multiple peaks sharply etched against the vermilion sky. Not wanting to disturb the other – a woman, she could now see – she stayed where she was, the gentle splashing of the water concealing her slowing breath.

As the light grew stronger, she noticed the woman's dress. Its bodice was of deep green velvet; it had puffed sleeves of green satin, a narrow waist, and lavish embroidery. A scarlet sash descended from left shoulder to right hip, emblazoned with intricate green-and-white abstractions of the Fairen coat of arms. From where she stood, the skirt looked full and pleated, and of the same velvet. The woman's hair was covered by a tight-fitting cap made of silk and feathers.

Fascinated, Jenora stepped closer. The brilliantly colored feathers were tiny, and woven into the beads and pearls and precious stones with golden thread. The predominant color was green. It sparkled; when the woman moved her head Jenora realized that her beads and feathers fell in long chains like tresses, just past her shoulders.

She came around the bench, saying, "Excuse me for intruding, but that is the most beautiful - oh!" She gasped, for the girl's face was a ruin. White ridges of old scar crazed across her brow and cheeks; fissures of fresh burn, angry red, mapped her throat and chin, reminding Jenora of the flood plains of Edge in the dry season. It was shocking, and she started back.

For a heartbeat the girl's brilliant green eyes levelly held her own. Then she rose and turned away. "Forgive me," she whispered," for upsetting you." She began to walk away, somewhat stiffly, as if in pain.

Jenora had never been more embarrassed in her life. Her reaction had been thoughtless and insensitive; but while she didn't have the social graces of Queen Alyda, she was determined not to be thought a complete boor. Blushing furiously, she called after the girl. "Please wait!" The girl stopped, but did not turn around. "I am so sorry..."

"Your pity is unnecessary."

"No! I didn't mean sorry for you! I mean ... that is, I am, well, what I meant to say was -"

"Please do not trouble yourself, m'Lady. It was a mistake on my part to come here this morning. Do not ... try to make things different than they are." She began walking away again.

"Please. Please stay. I just wanted to know about your beautiful dress. It is -spectacular." Again the girl stopped. "My name is Jenora. I am profoundly ashamed of my behavior a moment ago. Please. Come back and talk with me. Will you?"

The girl stood unmoving for a long moment. Then she sighed, and turned back. Smiling, although it obviously hurt to do so, she extended her hand. "I am Sare. It's an honor to meet you, warrior of Edge."

Startled, Jenora took her smooth, dry hand. It was cool to the touch; the sun had provided little more than light yet. "You know of me?"

"Oh yes." They sat on the bench, facing the garden this time, backs to the golden light. "I have heard of you for years. I always thought that a girl warrior was a strange thing." Jenora almost retorted, but let Sare finish the thought. "And an enviable one," Sare added. "Don't you find it difficult to compete with the men, who are stronger?"

"Not really. Strength is a many-faceted resource. While I cannot pull back the great bow as far as King Trever, my aim is better at any distance I can reach. Strength is not just brute force; it is the application of the proper force at the proper time. While a strong man may lift a great boulder with only his mighty arms and back, the stronger man uses a lever and saves himself the trouble. As Master Leland has often said -" She broke off suddenly. "I'm sorry. You asked a simple question and I give you an entire lesson. I suppose I am asked that question a lot. Forgive me."

"Not at all! These things have always fascinated me! Sometimes I dream ... well, sometimes I dream that I am a great fighter too, killing monsters, defending the Keep. Making my father proud." She stopped and looked away. There was a moment of silence.

"Well, why not? Men are recalcitrant, but manageable. Just smile sweetly and compliment their prowess and they'll teach you something in spite of themselves." Jenora chuckled.

Sare was still looking the other way. "These days my smile seldom has that effect."

"Oh. Of course. I didn't mean ... Oh, damn. Sare, I apologize for being so direct, but it seems this is going to get in the way of our conversation again and again. Please forgive me, but who are you? How do you come to be the way you are?"

"Ah," Sare said. "Why I am the way I am." There was a long silence. The sun crept across the garden and warmed the flowers, their scents mingling in the warming air. She looked closely into Jenora's eyes. After a moment, she stood and stepped back a pace. "Will you walk with me?"

"Certainly." They turned down one of the white paths.

"I am the youngest of my sisters. You have of course already met Cillistra and Carola."

"Oh!" interrupted Jenora. "You, you're the third princess! My apologies, your Highness, I did not recognize you. I thought that you were abroad, or, or something. It is a part of my duty to Prince Aaren to know the territory we visit, but information about you is scarce"

"No apology is necessary, Palatine. The last several years have been difficult for me and for the royal family. It became easier to just draw back from the public eye. My burns... have worsened." She stopped, knelt, and ran the back of her fingers along the unblemished white petals of a hyacinth. Her back was to Jenora.

"From time to time, since I was born, my body heats up for no apparent reason. At times it is so bad that I catch fire." She said the words very matter-of-factly, but Jenora sensed a tension underlying the girl's horrible revelation.

Very carefully, she replied with what she hoped was the same control, "How awful for you. What do you do when it happens?" She knelt beside Sare and put her hand lightly on her shoulder. Sare stiffened, and Jenora made to draw her hand back, but Sare reached up and clasped it back to her shoulder. There was a pause as the women gathered their thoughts.

"Thank you," Sare finally said. She turned and looked again into the young warrior's eyes. "I have not told that story often, and no one has ever responded with a touch. You are not repulsed." Jenora shook her head, not trusting herself to speak just yet. "I do not know how to tell you ... You asked what I do. I do nothing. It comes, it burns, and it goes. I wear this," she said, releasing Jenora's hand to pull the amulet from inside her bodice, "and it protects me from some of the fire's effects. But in the last few years things have grown worse. More frequent, and more powerful. And so, I keep to myself." They walked a bit further, and stopped to rest on one of the benches, watching the sun play in the droplets of the fountain.

"I am not hiding. It is not shame." Sare frowned and looked to see that Jenora understood. "But my family entertains people, in the great Proudlock style. That's part of who we are. And I make strangers uncomfortable. I stay away of my own accord. I think that it is better this way."

Jenora considered all this for several moments. "You are the most remarkable person I have ever met. I have never heard a story of greater bravery."

"No, it's not like that, I'm not brave at all. I'm terrified every time it happens. I walk in fear of the time it will happen again."

"You *are* brave, braver that the most valiant soldier because you live with your fear. It is one thing to cast fear aside in the heat of battle, and another altogether to live with it every day of your life." She shook her head. "Sare, I - what is it?"

Sare was wincing slightly. "The sun is high now, and perspiration stings my burns. I'm sorry, but I must go indoors." She rose to leave. "And you will surely be wanting your breakfast."

"But you haven't eaten either. Come down to the kitchens with me, we'll talk more as we eat."

Sare shook her head. "I do not feel comfortable around strangers these days, and there are many about right now. I usually eat in my rooms. Perhaps ... perhaps you would join me?"

Jenora smiled hugely. "I would be delighted to! Let me bathe quickly and dress, and I'll come to you ... where is your chamber?"

"In this wing, second floor. Just ask if you lose your way." Both girls were smiling. "I will see you shortly?" She frowned. "You don't have to come."

"Please say that I can, Princess!"

"Most certainly you are welcome."

"Good. I shall hurry. Order something big, and we'll talk till dinner!" She laughed, and sprinted away down the white path.

Sare turned and walked carefully down another path to a doorway, stepped into the blessed coolness and leaned against a wall with one hand. She was very happy. This strange warrior-girl from Edge was both nothing and everything like she had imagined. With a deep breath and a growing lightness in her heart, she started down the stairs toward her room.

As the days passed Jenora marveled at what she had learned since she had met the youngest Princess. Sare's story was astonishing, and to her surprise the girl who had lived it was becoming one of her closest friends. There was a depth of passion, and a clarity of purpose, that informed every word Sare spoke, and Jenora spent as much of her time with Sare as her other duties would allow.

She found herself torn between her desire to explore her new friendship and her need to be with Aaren. Suddenly she realized that she could combine these things; why, Aaren would find Sare just as enchanting as she had, Jenora had no doubt. She wondered why the thought hadn't occurred to her before.

It took two more days to persuade the Princess to allow the introduction. At last Sare relented with a bemused smile; it was obviously so important to her new friend that they meet. Jenora went alone and found Aaren in his room, penning a letter to Queen Alyda.

"Hi, Jen. *Fairing* well?" He chuckled and she made a face.

"You've been waiting to use that, haven't you, Prince? Gods. At any rate, put down your quill, there is someone marvelous you just have to meet."

He set down his pen, blotted the paper carefully, and put on his surcoat. "All right. But I have to be downstairs for another of Rodolpho's luncheons with the Princess in an hour." He rolled his eyes.

"Cillistra's luster is wearing off so soon?" asked Jenora.

Aaren laughed. "Not yet, my friend. She is truly the most beautiful woman I have ever met. But I must admit that her company is enchanting in smaller doses." He frowned. "Sometimes I get the feeling that she doesn't much care for me." He shrugged. "So who is this mystery man I am to meet?" They headed out of the room and down the corridor.

"Not a man, sire. A woman." She smiled and started down the stairs to the west wing.

"Well, well. Another Fairen beauty?" He waggled his eyebrows.

Jenora stopped so suddenly that Aaren bumped into her on the narrow stairway. She turned and looked up at him.

"My Prince, please listen to me as your closest friend." She looked so solemn, so earnest, that the smile disappeared from his lips and he nodded gravely.

"Of course."

"She is not ... a beauty. Her name is Sare, and ... and she has the kindest disposition I have ever encountered, and she is the gentlest, most honest... Aaren. She is Princess Sare, third daughter of the House of Proudlock." She paused, groping for words.

"I wasn't sure they really *had* another daughter."

"She is ... scarred."

Aaren cocked his head. "What do you mean?"

"From fire. All her life, Prince, she has lived in fear of a grave curse. At times, unpredictable in their occurrence or duration, she suddenly begins to burn. She carries with her terrible scars from these episodes. It is a wonder she has lived.

"But the woman who has emerged! You know I don't make friends easily, or lightly. But next to you, I now count her as my closest friend. For the two weeks we have been here I have been discovering the depths of her spirit. Aaren, do you know the term 'soulmate'?"

"Well, yes, I suppose..."

"That is what I feel she and I have become. I would have introduced you sooner, only ... only she ... would not agree."

"Why not?"

Jenora paused, hands trying to shape the words in the air. "She has learned to be invisible. Her features, and more truly the frightening manner in which they have been molded, necessarily set her apart from not only the royal household, but from everyone. Gearld and Signe are fair rulers, and good parents, but it became obvious to everyone that the less Sare called attention to herself, the easier it would be for throne and family alike. She is very alone." Jenora thought of every dance she had attended back in Edge, the banquets, the tourneys; all the kinds of events these last few years that Sare had only watched, if at all, from a narrow window or high tower, or heard muffled through the halls of the Keep.

Aaren wore a faraway frown, and she knew what he must be thinking. He knew well the embarrassment of a family associated with an unusual curse. All his life he had been the one whispered of, the one just-noticeably shunned, the one feared. Even before unlocking his bracelet at the Age of Trust he had learned not to speak of his power. Jenora felt a quickening in her heart at the thought of her two friends, so similar and so alone, being suddenly able to share those feelings of isolation with someone who would truly empathize. And for the first time she felt the quickening of a small, hidden fear.

"Let us go, Jenora. I am suddenly eager to meet this Princess."

Her eyes narrowed and Jenora hesitated a moment longer. "Aaren, please, do not mistake my meaning. But your ways are sometimes ... most times, mayhap, somewhat abrupt." He frowned, although he knew she spoke the truth, and she plunged on, "This is a woman of quiet. She is not timid, though she may seem so; her strength is greater than I have words to describe. But she fears you. You are handsome, and ... aggressive, and quick to put your thoughts to tongue." She grasped his chin and looked deeply into his eyes until she was sure of his complete attention.

"For me, Prince, think long. Be gentle." She brushed aside the glimmerings of doubt like a mental spider web. Some seemed to stick to her hand. "It is very important to me that you two become friends. Then, I think, I would be the most fortunate woman in either kingdom. Just... think before you say, or do."

She could almost hear him cut her off with an embarrassed, "Well enough, your point is made;" but instead she saw him swallow his irritation. "Lead on, then. My tongue is on its shortest tether." They both smiled, and Jenora turned and led the way down the stairs.

◆   ◆   ◆

They stopped outside the door to Sare's chambers. Jenora put her hand on his chest, impulsively kissed his cheek, knocked and disappeared behind the closed door. He waited with a half-smile; cherishing his friendship with Jenora, unreasonably beside himself in anticipation of meeting this secret Princess. He ran hasty fingers through his hair. There were muffled voices from behind the door; he strained to hear but could not. At last it opened.

Jenora stood to one side and motioned with her left hand. "Aaren, my liege and friend, this is Sare, Princess of Faires." Aaren stepped into the room.

Her face was, as Jenora had warned him, momentarily shocking. *But her eyes...* They were green, vivid, emerald green, the color of mossy rocks under a crystal stream in the hottest hour of day. He didn't know how it could be, but looking into her eyes Aaren *knew* her. It felt like the lost last piece of a puzzle had suddenly appeared and snapped into place. He bowed, unable to look away, his consternation writ plainly on his face.

"Princess."

Sare, too, was astonished. Like Jenora, he was so different from what she had imagined. His blue eyes held hers gently, and she felt her right hand taken up in his. Never lowering his gaze, he kissed the back of her hand. It was a brief, chaste kiss, but the answering flush that raced through her body was most certainly not. Aside from her attraction to him as a handsome man, something she was even then attempting to suppress, there was a maddening feeling of familiarity. It was as if she wanted to remember something but couldn't quite put her mind to it.

"Prince."

Jenora turned from one to the other. They were both acting so oddly. It was almost as if... "Have you already met?" she asked.

Neither answered her for a moment, though both looked as though they were about to. Aaren had opened his mouth as if to speak, and Sare had half-raised one hand. They stared at each other. Finally, head cocked to one side Aaren said, "No, I don't believe I have ever had the pleasure." Sare shook her head in agreement. They both laughed softly, not out of embarrassment, but at the peculiar situation.

Jenora could not imagine two hearts more dear to her than these, and felt the sudden mysterious blending of their tempos. She rejoiced at their meeting, but in a distant indefinable way she feared for their future. She shook her head, puzzled by her own strange thoughts. It wasn't as if anything had changed, not really. Aaren would marry Cillistra. Her own friendship with Sare would grow, and now that they'd been introduced, Jenora was certain Sare and Aaren's friendship would blossom as well.

Aaren and Sare seemed to suddenly become aware that they were staring. Both flushed, and cast their gazes away, but could find nothing in the room on which to fix their eyes save one another. He grinned. "Jenora was right."

"Oh? About what?"

"About there being someone marvelous that I had to meet."

"Yes, I guess she *was* right." Sare smiled.

"What?"

"She said you had a silver tongue, when it wasn't stunned to silence."

"Oh, that's not fair! She told you all about me, but I know nothing of you."

They gazed at each other for another long moment. Sare shook herself and, remembering her manners, invited the Prince and Palatine to sit. Sare and Aaren took opposite ends of a small divan in her antechamber, folding themselves unconsciously into familiar, even intimate positions unbecoming two royals at their first meeting. Jenora pulled over a low-backed embroidered chair and sat across from them.

"So what do you want to know?" Sare asked.

◆   ◆   ◆

Three hours later Sare closed the door softly behind her new friends as they took their leave, and then leaned against it, mind whirling. *This is so silly.* She'd only just met him, but she felt more comfortable, more *at home*, than with any boy she had ever met. No wonder Jenora loved him. He obviously held Jenora in the highest regard too, even loved her in his own way; but the love he held for his warrior companion was of a different sort entirely than the one Jenora held for him, Sare thought. Jenora, Cillistra, and now, amazingly, herself. *Popular fellow.* Twirling a string of beads and feathers around one finger, she walked over to the window and looked out at the clear night sky.

✦   ✦   ✦

Wishing Jenora good night, Aaren closed the door to his room and sat on the foot of the bed, pulling off his boots. *What an amazing conversation. What a fascinating girl.* He never had been able to place the tantalizing sense of familiarity he'd felt, though. It was strange. She was absolutely unique, he had never met her or anyone remotely like her, but it was as if he knew her from... *Well, from a dream.* That was close to the feeling.

And she was *funny.* He smiled, remembering her playfulness and jokes. She was never cruel about it, but her deadpan observations about the household of the Keep and its current guests were hilarious, and hit the mark with deadly accuracy. Her uncanny impersonation of his own father nearly doubled him over with laughter, and he thought Jenora was going to wet herself, she was laughing so hard.

What a delight. Folding his clothes over the back of a chair, Aaren marveled at his luck. He climbed into bed and blew out the candle. *A beautiful bride, and a sister-in-law who brightens the room in every way her older sister does not.*

✦   ✦   ✦

Calm but troubled, Jenora wished the still bemused-looking Prince a pleasant sleep. She leaned back upon his closed door for a moment, trying to find purchase in her turbulent thoughts. She made for the stairs and left the Keep, down the curving path to the river. She walked along the water for hours.

All but the servants were asleep when she returned that night; no one saw her climb wearily to her rooms.

◆   ◆   ◆

Three days later Aaren turned around, then turned again, while Jenora stood to one side and scrutinized him from hair to shoe. Finally she nodded. "You'll do, I think. At least we've done our best."

He frowned and flushed at the same time. "'Your best'. I'll remind you that I picked out these clothes myself, and packed them, too. I chose them because they could travel without damage, and still be – suitable."

"With no help from Queen Alyda, my Prince?" She laughed when he blushed more deeply still. "Actually, you look very handsome, and more than suitable. Is it time to go?"

Aaren saw Rodolpho entering the room and bowing. "It would seem so. Stay close to me, I pray you." They followed the steward out, down the stairs, and across the courtyard to the Keep's high-vaulted chapel.

The royalty of both kingdoms was waiting there, the Kings standing near the altar, and Queen Signe seated with her ladies, Carola and Sare in pews to one side. Sare was wearing another one of her amazing creations, an intricately stitched blue-green gown with embroidered bodice, and a matching cap with her signature tresses made from sparkling beads and tiny feathers. She smiled at Aaren and Jenora as they entered.

But Aaren scarcely had time to notice the witnesses, as Cillistra entered through a side door, draped in white silk and walking on the arm of Gearld's own High Chaplain. She stopped before the altar and faced the cleric as he mounted his step, and Aaren hastened to stand beside her.

The Chaplain lifted his hand over the royal couple, and addressed the Kings in the formal Scholars' speech. "Do thee consent to this betrothal of thy heirs, as a lawful contract, before man and the Almighty?"

Both Gearld and Trever answered solemnly, "We do," and the Chaplain bent his gaze upon Aaren and Cillistra. "The vows thee take this day are of the future, an exchange of promises as binding as a marriage, but they do not constitute a true marriage. Do thee understand?" At their assent, he turned slightly toward Aaren. "Thou, Prince Aaren of Edge, dost thou consent and promise to wed this woman when the day comes, by our laws and the providence of the Gifter?"

Aaren glanced at Cillistra, whose eyes remained lowered, then cleared his throat. "I shall."

The Chaplain addressed a like question to Cillistra. She raised her face to look at Aaren, but her expression and tone were unreadable as she replied, "I shall."

"Then I declare this betrothal lawful and consecrated. Be ever mindful of the vows thee have made." He lifted his arms in benediction over them.

Aaren turned and moved closer to Cillistra, but her hand on his chest stopped him. Her words were as formal as the churchman's. "I thank thee for thy promise, my husband-to-be. Now I must retire. I shall see thee this evening."

Aaren frowned for an instant. It was the custom in Edge for the betrothed couple to kiss at the end of the ceremony – often the first kiss they would ever exchange. He didn't know if that custom held in Faires as well, so he quickly nodded and kissed her hand instead. "Until tonight, then." She swept off without a smile or a backward glance.

Gearld and Rodolpho also seemed somewhat surprised, but shrugged it off and came forward with Trever and the Queen. Gearld clapped Aaren on the back, his other hand on Trever's shoulder. "That was well done! My thanks to you both. Now, if you like, we can repair to my hall and discuss the setting of a date for the greater ceremony."

Trever agreed for them both, and Gearld and Signe led them out. Aaren looked back from the doorway, to see Jenora seat herself among the other women, still in the pew. She began conversing with plump Carola, and with Sare, as the chapel door swung closed.

◆   ◆   ◆

A week's passage found Aaren and Sare strolling beside the river, enjoying the summer afternoon and each other's company. For once, Jenora was not with them; she and Kerwin had been detailed to begin preparations for the royal party's departure from Faires, five days hence.

The Prince and Princess stepped into a small glade that bordered the Wendlow, and stopped to watch the sunlight play upon the water splashing over a rocky falls only a few feet below them. Vireos sang and darted after insects between the trees. Sare sat down at the very edge, where the mist rose up to envelop her like a cool coverlet. She turned to Aaren with a laugh, and he felt something within him turn inside-out.

From the instant he had first seen Sare, her scars had seemed to fade and become less a part of her with every moment. Most of the time he scarcely noticed them; they were lost in his inner vision of the girl who was quickly capturing his heart in spite of the vows spoken only days ago. Now, though, he saw them clearly, and found himself moving to sit beside her, searching for words to ask the question that had sprung into his mind. He needed to take care; he did not want to hurt her feelings.

"Princess ... Forgive me if I am clumsy. Jenora has told me how you ... how you came to be burned. But do you know any more than you told her, anything of how it happens?"

Sare did not answer for long seconds, only gazed down at the falls. Then she met his eyes levelly and spoke with no pain in her voice or her regard. "I wondered if we would ever speak of this. No. No one knows. There have been stories and whispers, of course. I've heard some of them. Some say that I am being made to pay for some sin of my ancestors. Others say that some wizard or demon laid a curse upon me at birth, for reasons none can know. I've even heard it said that I am a creature of the Tempter myself, and this is the way he's marked his own. I only know how it has changed me, and set me apart." She considered for a moment. "When it happens, I'm terrified, and wonder each time if I'll die. Yet underneath ... sometimes, underneath the fear and the pain, I almost feel as if something were there, something I could touch and hold and use, almost like ... like a gift." She looked at him. "I know that doesn't make sense, but in the healing time that follows, there is something more going on than I have ever learned from all my years spent learning such things from Obra." She looked back at the water. "I don't know, Aaren. I truly don't know."

He took her hand and held it quietly in his own, staring into the swirling eddies with her. "You could never be any Tempter's servant. Only the Gifter could have created someone as good and wise and – and loving as you are." They sat, the warmth of the morning on their shoulders. "I've heard the same things said about me, all my life. I understand what it is to be apart, and to live under a cloud as you do."

Sare turned to him dubiously. "You? How?"

He let go her hand and turned to face her fully, legs crossed in front of him. "I also live with a curse – or a gift, if you could say that. I've done so ever since I was born." He held out his left arm. "This bracelet was made for me, like your amulet, to help control the power that comes through me at times."

She fingered the bracelet, tracing its shape and its clasp, then looked back into his eyes. "You burn?" she whispered.

"Not ... like that. I'll show you." He rose and went to a nearby cottonwood, rummaging around its base. He returned with a handful of small twigs and dry leaves, and carefully arranged them on the ground before her, several feet away.

His right hand was already upon his bracelet, as it often strayed when he felt tense. He turned it up and touched its clasp. His fingers hesitated of their own accord, as if reluctant to move. *Why would that be?* He dismissed the thought with a shake of his head, unlocked the circlet and slipped it off.

Holding his hand over the tinder-pile, he crouched closer to it. "Watch." He could feel the power in himself, waiting, desperate in its own insistent way to course down his arm. There was a new note in it, though, a burning tingle in his flesh, a throbbing in his head unrelated to his own pulse.

He looked up at Sare. There was something amiss with his vision, too; she seemed surrounded by a faint, shimmering blue glow. *Is it the mist, catching the sunlight?* He blinked twice, but the blue aura remained. *And why can't I hear the birds, or the water?* All around him, he realized, was an unnatural stillness; the whole of this small world was waiting, suspended – and it was wrong.

Something's wrong, all wrong. His heart was beating faster; the unreleased burning in his arm was becoming painful. Through the haze, he saw that Sare had grown pale, her eyes enormous. Faintly, her amulet glowed on her breast. *There's something about her eyes ... her face...*

Abruptly, he kicked the leaves and twigs over the drop. Fumbling in his haste, he closed the bracelet around his wrist and locked it. His hands shook. He bowed his head; the throbbing died away, the burning in his arm faded. After a moment, he was able to raise his eyes and meet hers.

She was no longer pale, and her amulet was dark. She looked up at him with nothing in her gaze but curiosity. "What..?"

He sat beside her, took her hand again. He forced himself to smile, and took a deep breath to steady his voice. "I can make fire," he said.

Chapter 14
Passage

Jenora was tightening the straps on Canticle's bardings when she heard King Trever growl, "Now where has that son of mine wandered off?" She and the big mare both looked up at the King's voice.

Trever was standing some twenty feet away, near Aaren's horse, Chance. The piebald gelding was fully packed, saddled and armored for the return journey, but his rider was nowhere in sight. Master Kerwin, to whom the question had been addressed, only shook his head. "I've no idea, your Majesty. He was here and busy as the rest not half an hour ago. Perhaps he's taking a last farewell from his betrothed?"

Rodolpho, overseeing the departure, overheard and joined them. "Would you like me to send someone to search him out, your Highness?"

Jenora piped up, "I can go and find him, my liege, if you wish."

Trever scowled. "If you would, please tell the Prince that I intend to leave within the quarter, whether he is ready or not. Plenty of time for mooning about when we're riding." Jenora left the courtyard, hurrying toward the west wing. She had a good idea where Aaren might be.

When she reached Sare's door, she knocked softly. A young chambermaid answered, telling her that Sare was not in. "I believe she was going up to the roof garden, m'Lady."

Jenora mounted the white stairs in the growing dawn light. As she came out into the garden, the sun broke free of the Nethals. Birds were beginning to sing, the morning buds were opening; it was so like that first morning in Faires that she stopped and breathed it in, remembering.

They had been in Faires little more than a month, yet so much had changed, it seemed a year. She had watched Aaren and Sare together often; neither would think of leaving her alone too much, no matter what was happening between them. *And something certainly has happened, hasn't it, girl?* The depth and power of the relationship they had come to in a few short weeks amazed her, even as Sare's impression on herself had. There was simply no denying it.

Her own feelings of betrayal lingered, somewhere unacknowledged down inside her. It would have been a difficult thing to see her Prince married to a cold foreigner; but to see his heart swept up so effortlessly, and by a woman she loved as well, was on a completely different scale. Yet for Jenora, pain had always been a source of strength. Where another might have let her disappointment grow to swamp their friendships, her love for Aaren and her faith in Sare led her to the acceptance she needed. They would always be hers; only the circumstances changed. Drawing a deep breath, she turned and surveyed the rooftop, looking for the two figures she knew would be here.

✦   ✦   ✦

"I'll miss you," Aaren said, as they leaned side-by-side on the stone parapet, gazing at the mountains that loomed up before them in the crisp morning air. "There is something so..."

"What?" Sare turned her head to look at his profile, her beads clicking softly against her cheek.

"Nothing," Aaren sighed. "The Gifter is mysterious, and we cannot know His reasons." He turned to face her. "Your sister does not care for me. So be it. We will build a proud kingdom nevertheless. Oh, but if things were different –"

"No," Sare interrupted, putting a finger to his lips. "No. Things are as they are. And I have two precious new friends to rejoice in."

Aaren smiled and took her hand in his. Gently he traced the ridges of scar with his fingertips. "What strange friends we are." He looked into her eyes. "We both live in fear; yours the greater, of course. But I feel as though I've found, for the first time in my life, someone who understands."

Sare returned his gaze, the warmth of his touch filling her with the courage to speak her mind. "Aaren? I want you to promise me something."

"Anything."

"I want you to promise not to use your power again." Aaren cocked his head to one side. She continued, "If it is as dangerous as you fear, as potentially uncontrollable as you have hinted at, then I believe you should not put yourself in the Tempter's way. I fear for you." And suddenly she was in his arms.

174

I fear for both of us. They thought in unison, unaware that the other was harboring the same fears, unwilling to broach the same unthinkable conversation. They held each other tightly, the slight morning breeze bringing the scent of snow from the Nethals.

✦   ✦   ✦

Jenora was surprised to glimpse only one figure, over near the farthest northern corner of the garden. She moved closer, peering around the intervening trees, and stopped when she realized that there were indeed two there.

They were so closely entwined that it was easy to mistake them for one person, standing silhouetted against the sunrise. Aaren's arms engulfed Sare's small form, his hands moved softly down her back, and their faces merged in the kiss. They were alone, all the world extinguished in each other.

Jenora found herself retreating several steps, stepping behind a nearby juniper. *I saw this happening, but even I didn't know what they had come to.* A small stirring of envy and anguish roiled inside her, but was crushed by a greater recognition. *He is to marry her sister. Oh, Aaren, Sare, what could come of this?*

After a moment, she came out from behind the juniper, calling Aaren's name. By the time the lovers came in view again, they were standing apart and Sare was straightening her cap and feathers.

Aaren raised his hand. "Over here, Jen. I guess it must be time, eh?"

"Yes, and your father is less than serene about it. We should get back to him with no delay. I'm sorry,

Princess, but as you know, kings seldom have to show patience."

Sare rushed to her, sweeping her into a warm hug. "Then quick farewells it must be! Go safely, my dearest friend." She drew back to look into Jenora's eyes. "May the Gifter guide you safely home, and send you back to me soon."

"That I promise you. Keep yourself well, until I see you again." They embraced again, then Sare turned to Aaren.

They exchanged no words, only gazed at each other for a moment before Aaren smiled and turned away, taking Sare's answering smile with him. Jenora followed him back down the stairs, to rejoin all those waiting for them. Sare remained behind; Jenora's last sight of her showed her sitting on the same bench where they'd first met, her small hand extended in a wave.

✦   ✦   ✦

Aaren's mind whirled. The clanking of Chance's barding provided rhythmic counterpoint to his thoughts as they jumped and scattered, reformed and leapt away again. The Nethals were glorious, black and purple etched white against the morning azure. Aaren didn't notice. Chuckling and rushing against the ebony rocks, the Wendlow foamed half a furlong below the King's party. Oblivious, the Prince saw only the face of Sare, heard only the soft rustling of her beads. Everyone except Kerwin was smiling at the morning; even the King seemed well satisfied.

Kerwin noticed again the fresh spoor of six or more horses, only hours old. He peered up the sheer cliffs, and down to the water, seeing only slick rock. He almost said something to Trever; but the royal smile was a rare thing, and he didn't want to break the quiet and solitude. He decided to say nothing. Lost in their own thoughts, the party of ten, with the six guards in the lead, rounded the huge outcrop of granite known as the Blinder and continued single file into a narrowing part of the pass.

✦   ✦   ✦

Michael and his Shadow dismounted and tied their reins around the gnarled limb of a stunted alder. Retrieving a crossbow and an ebony box from his saddlebags, Michael gave them to the golem and turned its eyes to the escarpment before them. Its head slid from right to left just once in a series of tiny, precise motions as it recorded every detail of rock and crag. Then it began to climb. Michael followed, careful to match its every move and toehold.

Half an hour later they reached the top of the ridge and turned south toward the Wendlow Gorge. Minutes before reaching the edge of the great cleft they could hear the roar of the water; glancing at the sun, they slowed and began to pace the top of the cliff, scouting a suitable place of concealment. Michael cast his gaze at the opposite cliff above the trail. He could just make out the still forms of the men lying in wait. He raised his left arm and held it aloft for exactly three beats of his heart, then let it fall again. A bandit stood and repeated the signal. Everything was in place.

The golem stooped and effortlessly scaled the damp rock, settling itself onto a narrow shelf between two small outcroppings of granite. Michael slid down behind it and wedged himself in.

Unslinging the crossbow, the golem sighted along its empty groove at the trail. Then it cocked the bow, rested it on its knees, and slipped the catch on the ebony box.

Nestled inside the box were three glittering icicles. Their chill radiated from the opened box and frosted the golem's fingers as it slipped one into the crossbow. Michael smiled. *One for the King. One for the Prince. And a third in case we need to improvise.*

✦   ✦   ✦

Sare clutched her amulet in her right hand and skipped down the side stairs from the roof garden. The clear gem was cold against her palm, chilled by the morning air. Her heart, as she looked out of a tall window facing the road to Edge, was an inferno by comparison. Aaren and Jenora were scarcely an hour gone, and already she ached at the thought of the time before their next meeting. Never in her sixteen years had she been so filled with joy, and joy's tense companion, longing. She couldn't possibly make them out at this distance, but just looking up the road connecting her to her new-found friend and her Prince made her feel closer to them.

The morning breeze off the river stirred her feathers lightly and she smiled, her scarred mouth still tingling at the ecstasy of the forbidden kiss. Closing her eyes, she hugged herself and drank in the cool smells of the morning: tilled earth from the east, baking bread from the royal kitchens, the dogwood blossoms and juniper mixing deliciously in the summer wind.

It was almost too much. She really thought her heart would burst at the memories of his eyes, his smile, his touch. She let out her breath explosively, not even aware that she had been holding it. Taking a long last look at the pass, she turned and continued on to the south wing and Obra's quarters.

The wise-woman was sewing a torn cloak in the light of the morning sun as it angled through her open windows. The room was small, its colorful tapestries and rugs catching the sun and glowing with a brilliance matched only by the smile on Sare's face. Obra smiled in return and nodded as her favorite royal daughter knocked politely at the doorway, curtsied, and came into the room.

"Do I disturb you, gentlewoman?"

"Not at all, child, come in. What is it," marveled the healer, "brings such a rosy flush to a young princess's cheeks this cold morning? Surely not just the mountain air?" Her eyes narrowed as Sare blushed but held her gaze. "Methinks, child, that impish Cupid has some small role in this! Can it be true? Are we in love, then?"

"Oh!" whispered the girl, putting a hand to her mouth. "Does it show so very much?"

"You would think to hide something of the heart from Obra!" She shook her head and put down her sewing. "Foolish girl. Come over and sit beside me." Sare did. "Well? Is he handsome?"

"Handsome! Oh, more beautiful than the oak in fall, he is *magnificent*! Obra! His eyes are so blue..." she trailed off, her expression describing him far better than her words ever could.

Obra put her right arm around the girl and hugged her. "My tempestuous, darling child. Old Obra had almost forgotten the passion of youth. It has been a very long time since a blue-eyed boy has stolen *my* heart." Her smile softened, her eyes turned somewhere within. Hugging Sare closer, she said, "I am very happy for you."

They sat for a moment, sharing the silence and the morning and Sare's joy. She absolutely *tingled*. She drew breath for another deep sigh, squeezing her hands together, and remembered the reason for her visit.

"Obra." Pulling away slightly, she turned toward the wise-woman. "A very wonderful knowledge has come to me, and with it, freedom and joy I cannot begin to describe. This, I mean, besides Aaren." The Princess did not notice her friend's eyes widen at the mention of her lover's name. *Oh, my dear. There is heartache coming on here. Oh my dearest child, leave it to you to find love with one pledged to another. What are we going to do?* She listened as Sare described her suspicions of a strange link between her and the young Prince.

"We spoke of fire many times. He also has been shadowed all his life with a curse, only he *sets* fires, simply willing them to burn. This power frightens him; I think he is afraid that he cannot control it. Also," Sare began, but stopped, twisting the amulet in her fingers.

"Also?" Obra raised a questioning eyebrow.

"Well, I think that whenever he sets one of his fires, by the power of his mind..." again the girl trailed off. She would not look up.

"Gifter preserve us!" whispered the wise-woman, eyes widening. She made the connection herself, and it had the ring of truth. Her mind spun. *Why this horrible link between two innocent children? Was the Prince as guileless as he seemed? And how could this startling new revelation help her protect the child she loved so well?* She chose her words carefully. "And what does he think of this, your blue-eyed love? He must be filled with remorse."

Sare frowned. "Actually, I have not told him what I suspect of our bond. I almost mentioned it to Jenora several times, but I - he - that is, I didn't want to ruin..." the girl wound down, clearly tangled in her thoughts. "But he did promise me to never use his power again. I told him it frightened me and I was afraid that he would be terribly hurt if it got out of control." She looked up at her friend, smiling fiercely. Tears brimmed and ran over her ravaged cheeks.

"Obra, I need you to promise me, on your life, not to tell a soul of this ... this connection. It would only cause our kingdoms grief, at a time when we so much need to heal and grow together. As he promised me, so must you." She slipped her pendant from her bodice and over her head, and held it out. "Enchanted and given to me in love, so I return this to you, Obra. My pain is over."

"I ... promise," said the healer, sure that her princess's pain, the kind that left scars on the heart instead of the skin, was far from finished. But love was not all joy, and that was for later. "I am happy for you all over again." She took the girl's hands in her own, the proffered stone glowing softly warm in the embrace.

✦   ✦   ✦

Michael saw the royal party round the corner of the trail from the west. The golem moved nothing but its eyes. Most of the party, still single-file, had drawn their cloaks about them, as the sun had not yet angled into the steep chasm. The Wendlow roared through the channel deep below, louder than a raised voice – or a signal.

The attack was swift and brutal. Boulders larger than a man's head crashed through the vanguard of the party, sending three soldiers and their mounts plunging over the cliff. They did not have time to scream.

Dark shadows hurtled close after the rocks, and a fourth guard went down, a sword through his neck. He fell from his mount and was kicked over the side, clawing at his spurting throat. The other two kept their mounts, but the killers seated behind them were busily plunging bloodied daggers

The surviving members of the royal party met their silent attackers with hastily drawn blades. The Palatine had stayed in her saddle, but Aaren had been pulled down, thrown off his assailant, and struggled to his feet. Ahead of them, also afoot and back-to-back, Trever and Kerwin fought desperately against the black-garbed bandits. The only sound louder than the river was the clash of steel. The golem's eerie gaze tracked the battle, right to left.

Aaren, at the end, was sorely outmatched. Two burly warriors attempted to engage him simultaneously, and alone either could have carved through his defenses. The width of the ledge put them in each other's way, however, and Aaren was barely able to hold them as they pressed him back toward Jenora. His piebald was whinnying nervously behind the two bandits; most of the other horses had either pitched into the river or bolted.

Suddenly, Aaren whistled a shrill three-tone note. His gelding nickered and jogged toward him, shoving between his master's attackers. The ruse worked perfectly. The bandit nearest the edge grabbed frantically at Chance's mane and took a handful of it with him as he plunged shrieking over the side. The other man was pinned against the stone wall, and Aaren ran him through. The thug snarled through blood-foamed lips as he died, saying something even Michael's sensitive ears couldn't make out over the rushing of the river – and the faint, tingling surges of the Touch that were coming to him now every few moments.

He felt these ghost Touches whenever the Pendulum rewarded one of his minions to whom he had extended the power of the killing gaze. He vaguely understood from overheard Pendulum conversation that it was through the amulet he wore, but even more through the power of his own unique mind, that the Pendulum could reach the others.

The red-haired Palatine looked enraged. Her every protective instinct must have been stoked to a fury, and her blade flickered like bloody fire. There were two men before her, and behind them the king's steed reared and snorted. The first bandit's assessment of the girl was an underestimate. He died. The other, hooded attacker between her and the king's mount advanced smoothly over the body of his fallen companion. The uncovered right half of his face was discolored and shiny, and for a moment the woman was plainly disconcerted by the fact that he was *scaled*.

He moved with deceptive speed, feinting and writhing out of her reach, his thin blade flickering out to touch her forearm, her thigh, her knee. She couldn't turn her horse on the narrow ledge; her furious blows always reached the air where he had just been.

Michael could see that the reptilian creature was playing with her, tiring her and waiting for the blood to slide down and interfere with her grip. The creature laughed, exposing bony grey plates where there should have been teeth. In a desperate move to finish off the snake-faced man and aid her Prince, she leaned far out of the saddle to her right. He slid easily around to her left, raising a vicious strike at her exposed side. A scream of pure agony escaped her as she realized the cut would score, leaving Aaren vulnerable.

King Trever dispatched a lanky and somewhat slower bandit with a lateral chop to the abdomen, his tremendous strength and enchanted blade nearly cutting the man in two.

Michael's eyes widened at the sight of the Blade of Rage. *An object of power: I must have it when this is over.*

The King took a grazing cut above his left eye from the next attacker, who leaped forward immediately over his fallen comrade. Blinking the stinging blood away, the warrior King delivered a rain of terrible blows. The man died, his body kicked aside as the next assassin pressed the attack. The mammoth Rageblade was drenched in crimson. The Touch was a steady throb in Michael's heart now.

Behind the King, a wiry man Michael assumed to be the huntsman, Kerwin, faced five men. He had taken several small cuts and was weakening; swordplay was obviously not his chosen vocation, but two more bodies were already sweeping downriver from his end of the fracas. A third joined them as Kerwin drove his broadsword into the bandit's throat. It stuck fast in the man's collarbone, however, and was wrenched from his grasp. He barely avoided following it over the edge.

Drawing his dagger, he tried to parry his next opponent's opening blow. It was obvious that the dagger was going to be useless against the bandit's axe. As the blade arced for his neck, he dove straight into the edge, screaming to his liege, "At your back!" and burying his own small blade neatly in the killer's right eye.

Kerwin's head bounced twice on the wet rocks, and was lost in the foam and whirl of the cold river. Michael turned the golem's eyes to the King, as he waited for the proper moment.

Trever glanced back as Kerwin went down behind him. He set his back to the wall, the great sword held stiffly out before him, the tiny flaming pendulum engraved on its hilt catching the morning light. Glancing once each direction, Trever muttered a word into his beard.

Light sprang from the long blade, as blindingly bright as the sun overhead, as the fire of the King's wrath blazed from it. He swept it in an arc before him, and it made an inhuman shriek as the air parted along its edge. The bandit on his right was flung back violently into the man behind him. The smoking body of the bandit to his left crashed into Trever's own rearing mount. Terrified, the grey lost its footing and toppled, crushing the bandit behind and rolling helplessly off the ledge and into the Wendlow.

Michael noticed peripherally that the outlaw crushed by the king's mount was his serpent-man, but did not pause to look any further. The power of this Rageblade was not to be underestimated. Reaching out to his Shadow, he told it to rise and take aim. It lifted the crossbow to its shoulder, locking its terrible gaze on the King's heart.

Now.

✦   ✦   ✦

(*glowing – warm*)

It struck Sare and Obra both in the same awful instant, the realization that the enchantment of the stone was being summoned. The Princess staggered up from her chair, holding the glowing amulet at arm's reach, as if it were a poisonous insect she dared not drop.

It began to pulse.

A high keening began in the back of Sare's throat, terror and bafflement fighting for control of her taut features. When the stone pulsed, it meant that energy was being absorbed at the highest rate, and that any more would begin to leak through its protection. It had only happened a few times in all her years. She could feel the stubbled hackles rising on her neck as the room began to shimmer. Drenched in perspiration, she sank to her knees, the keening escaping her mouth and sliding up the scale of hysteria; her eyes fixed in horror on the brilliant gem. The pulses were becoming so fast that the amulet seemed to flicker, incandescently white.

The feathers around her face began to smoke.

Suddenly, finally, Sare threw back her head and screamed. It was a ghastly, tortured wail of fear and of burning agony, and most especially of betrayal. Blisters sprang from her skin, and flames from her body. She drew a ragged lungful of searing air and screamed again. And again. And again.

Obra was helpless. Her own horrified shrieks reflected from the chamber's rough stone walls with the girl's, and she watched in agony as her Princess charred and crackled, the heat blasting from her in powerful, stifling waves. This was the worst it had ever been, and she knew the gem was scant protection from the fire's awesome intensity. Knowing that the amulet was the only thing keeping the writhing girl erect, Obra watched as Sare began to die.

The Princess's beautifully embroidered clothing was in flames. Pieces charred and wafted aloft in the wind of the fire, and what was exposed beneath tore Obra's heart from her breast. She screamed at the fire. "Stop it, stop it, stop it, you *monster, you're killing her!"* The girl continued to burn. *"You're killing her!"*

Their screams echoed down the walls of the palace, chilling the souls of all who heard them.

◆　　　　　◆　　　　　◆

Aaren spun around in time to see a dark tableau silhouetted against a blinding light. He heard his father's sword shriek, and it awoke a red, primal lust for killing in his heart. *He's invoked the Rageblade!*

In the same instant of terrible clarity, he saw the killer about to claim Jenora's life, and in the next heartbeat the King's grey crushed her attacker into the rock. The whickering blade was partially deflected, and its flat struck her cheekbone and slammed her head into the wall. Blood jetted from the bandit's mouth and narrow nostrils, splashing Jenora's leggings. Aaren noted with revulsion, as he leaped over the corpse and his friend toppled from her saddle, that the dead bandit's protruding tongue was forked.　He quickly knelt at Jenora's side.

King Trever swept the howling sword around again, and two more bandits tasted its flame, their blazing bodies quenched seconds later in the black water. The tip of the Rageblade tapped the cliff to his left. Fragments of blasted rock rained down on Aaren and Jenora. The Prince brushed them off as best he could; the superheated bits of stone could burn flesh or set cloth ablaze.

Shielding his eyes with his forearm, Aaren squinted up at the bolt of lightning wielded by his father.

In that instant a pale flower of ice blossomed from the King's chest. White spread from the wound with sickening speed, and just before the ice reached Trever's mouth he roared, and tried to lift his frozen arms. He could not. The flames on the sword died with the King, and he fell forward onto his face, his hair and beard rimed with frost.

To Aaren it seemed as though time had slowed to a crawl. He was supernaturally aware of the dead men and blood on the littered path; his father's icy hand clutching his frozen blade; three bandits still standing a few feet beyond the fallen King; and the weird grey archer across the river reloading his weapon, eyes on the Prince, his dead father, and his helpless friend.

His left wrist felt very heavy. Aaren heaved himself onto his knees and saw the strange archer cock its crossbow. He touched his bracelet. With awful, slowed perception, he saw one of the killers smile, and saw a second milky bolt nocked into the groove of the bow. Aaren realized with numb horror that he didn't know whether Jenora was unconscious or dead. He was alone. The bowman raised his weapon and took aim along its stock. Tears spilled down Aaren's upturned face.

His lips began to stretch over his teeth in a rictus of horror and grief and sick hatred. With a strangled sob he released the catch at his wrist.

And they burned.

With a heat more intense than from any magicked blade, the brigands were claimed by fire. The ledge across the river exploded in a flash of blue and orange.

As the bolt of blue flame lashed across the river at him, Michael flung himself back. As it struck the ledge, he barely had time to hurl the body of the golem between himself and the blaze.

On the narrow trail below, dead and living became as torches, flesh pooling and running together with the molten metal of their armor and weapons. Aaren's eyes were squeezed shut, his hands stretched forward, palms out, and blue fire played from his fingers over the blasted corpses. He couldn't stop. Like a powerful muscle clenched in involuntary spasm, the horrific heat poured from his body. It just went on and on.

The rock itself caught fire.

The roaring in the river was indistinguishable from the roaring in his brain, but what obliterated Aaren's reason and drove his mind whimpering into tighter and tighter circles was the gentle sound of whispering beads and rustling feathers.

He could hear them burn.

Chapter 15
Sare's Dream

Sare was in a hurry. Her green skirt flared around her ankles as she strode down the Avenue of Flags. Instantly recognized, she returned the nods and waves of the Fairens going about their midday duties. Arnaud, the florid-faced armorer, panted, "A greeting to y'er house m'Lady," as he pumped the massive bellows of his forge, rippled arms soot-covered and oily with his effort. She thanked him but did not slow down.

Turning onto a passing road, she greeted Lord Jankor, a noble from the foothills; Syntha, wife of the palace baker; and Old Tilly, a tutor of her youth. She turned right again onto the Central Way. Here she saw still more people that she knew by name. It did not seem odd that she met so many friends and acquaintances; as royalty, even semi-secluded royalty, she had had occasion to meet much of Faires' populace.

Sare continued to hurry down the roads she had known from birth, bearing signs ornate or simple; the people who saw her dramatic features either turned away or called her by name, as was their wont. She was used to this dichotomy, and felt beneath her hurry a pleasant sense of belonging. That some of those who called or turned were, in fact, dead, did not register with her at all. They were not unwholesome in appearance, and were so familiar that in her hurry she merely responded as if to a friend not seen for some time.

Sare knew she was late, and yet it seemed necessary that she travel every street in the city, and see again everyone she had ever met. In the back of her mind a tiny disquiet was born; and as she moved on she became more and more convinced that she was really saying good-bye.

The scene shifted in that effortless way that dreams twist the shape of things; the sky lowered and blackened, the air sharpened itself against the jagged Nethals, and suddenly her summer clothes were no match for the grey chill filtering down from a smudged and sullen sky.

The muted light made the buildings around her seem unfamiliar. Perplexed and a little frightened, she cast about for a landmark or, of course! a street sign. She approached the corner signpost with a smile that withered on her lips. Its surface was charred black.

She loped to the next intersection. This sign too was burned beyond recognition. Perhaps some catastrophe had occurred in this part of town of which she had been unaware. Frightened more deeply, she began to run, trying to escape this burned and brooding section of a place she no longer believed was Faires.

Seeing someone in a doorway, she stopped hard, the charcoal dust spurting up in tiny clouds at her feet. Turning toward the stranger, she stifled a gasp. She's burned too! But it was only her reflection in the glass, and as she drew closer to the smoky mirror, she saw that this last burning had eradicated her features completely. Her hair and ears and nose were gone; only her green eyes broke the smoothness, like gems set in rippled ivory.

191

Turning her head from side to side in amazement, she wondered at the being staring back. It was clearly no longer human. It would make no difference if the creature even had a name, and her sudden inability to remember her own was somehow appropriate.

The burned girl turned away from the glass.

Behind her the scene had changed. Burned shops and gritty paving stones had transformed effortlessly into fragile greenery surrounding a tiny stone well. Pink and white tiles radiated from it in concentric circles. Its bronze cupola sported a weathervane, burnished beak pointing resolutely eastward in the still air. But it wasn't the blank stare of the metal bird that drew the girl's gaze, but the brilliant blue eyes of the man sitting on the edge of the well. He too was featureless, and he wore a silver crown. As she appraised him he rose to his feet, and they stared at each other for a long moment in the silence.

He extended his hand.

The faceless girl looked over her shoulder once, not in hesitation, but more to verify that which she was leaving. Her reflection regarded her calmly from smoky glass and char. She turned forward again. Green skirt dusting the tiles with grey, she walked to him and took his hand in hers.

From their palms, tiny blue flames fluttered and spread, licking up their arms with the barest flicker of warmth; again, she was burning. She looked up into his calm blue eyes and let go a lifetime of fear. The flames caught at her clothes, and feathered from her head: golden-blue hair. It was beautiful, and inevitable, and very, very sad. Blue fire tears dropped from her ivory face, scattering like quicksilver on the tiles.

He drew her close and she closed her eyes; breathing the fire, holding the flame.

◆   ◆   ◆

Obra dipped a cloth in the cool water of the basin and pressed it gently against the ruin of Sare's forehead. The girl shuddered in the depths of her sleep, muttering and weeping. Obra looked at her frail, wasted form and wept too, cursing the Telcien name even as she waited to see if her young charge would survive the night. If she did, Obra would have to ponder long the wisdom of her promised silence. If not, all would know the beast's treachery.

Chapter 16
Retreat

Michael stopped at the base of the cliff to catch his breath. His Shadow stumbled away from him and leaned against a large stone. Its grey flesh was ridged and blistered in many places, burned black in others; its mail shirt had melted away over two patches of char, and the long doublet underneath still smoldered.

All this Michael could see only dimly in the fading daylight. It had taken hours to climb back over the ridge and trek north along its length; the long descent to their waiting horses had been a slipping, heaving nightmare, made worse by his fear that darkness would come before they reached the ground.

The golem's act of deflecting Aaren's lethal fire had exhausted almost all of Michael's energy, magical or otherwise. The golem could barely stand or walk on its own. He had supported it all the way. During the climbing, he had often been forced to bear its weight as well as his own, or to brace its hand or foot in some tenuous hold while it moved. He had led the climb down, trying to recall the way they had come up, and struggling along slowly and with total concentration when he could not remember.

Now they were down. As he stood gasping, the throb of his exhaustion and the pain of his own burns crept gradually back into his consciousness. The sense of defeat was almost as paralyzing as his fatigue. He limped to his horse and rummaged through his saddlebags for the few medicaments he always carried. When he had used them, his wounds were less painful, but his weariness only ached the more. *We'll have to make camp soon and sleep. But I wish to be away from here, as far as we can be, before then.*

Offering his shoulder, he helped the golem to its horse and into its saddle. Then he also slowly mounted, and led the way back into the waste that lay before them. He could do nothing about the damage to his Shadow until they were back in his retreat, with the tools and lore he kept there. *I will have to see to it,* he thought grimly, *that he is made much more resistant to fire.* It rode in patient silence behind him, tightly gripping the reins in one hand and the saddle in the other to stay mounted.

As the last of the daylight faded, Michael turned and looked back at the jagged crags they were leaving behind. His mouth tasted of ashes. His roiling thoughts relived each chaotic moment of the ambush, and the inconceivable thing the bastard Prince had done. *Son of dogs! So that is the power the Pendulum spoke of. How did that mere boy come to possess it? And how might it be stolen and made my own?* He had to know. *The single most important target...* Michael swore under his breath. If his spies or his reading or the Pendulum itself would tell him, he must know.

Chapter 17
Homecoming

The sun was about to disappear behind the Nethals when Jenora and Aaren rode down from them. They came through the western gate of the palace grounds, leading a third horse. Over its back it carried saddlebags containing the scorched bones of King Trever and his faithful Kerwin; from its saddlebow hung the sheathed Rageblade of the kings of Edge.

Jenora sat stiffly upright, though she looked worn and tired. Her head and cheek were bandaged. Aaren gazed straight ahead, his face a mask of control. Neither seemed to notice the people gathering around them or the mutter of questions and concern rising in their wake.

They reached the forecourt of Greybeal to find Queen Alyda and Lord Wildon coming down the steps to meet them. The Hawk stopped and watched as they dismounted, while the Queen ran forward, her bewildered eyes darting from the riderless horse to Jenora to her son. She laid her hand on his arm, her voice quavering with the unasked. "Aaren?"

He turned, blue eyes eloquent and filled with pain. "Lady-mine...Mother..." He reached for her, holding on as hopelessness and grief poured forth, inconsolable.

The news raced outward from the palace, by word-of-mouth and royal messenger. When King Trever's funeral service was convened a week later, every noble house in Edge was represented, as well as many from Faires.

There could be no lying-in-state. The King's bones were sealed in a coffin of gilded wood, its lid carved with his likeness. The procession of allies and friends filed through Greybeal's Hall of Hearing. Some paused to touch the coffin; some spoke briefly to Aaren or Queen Alyda.

Jenora held her place through all the long afternoon, greeting and announcing nobles and freeholders, merchants and guildsmen. Her gaze, too, frequently strayed to Aaren and Alyda. *I should be with them. They are my family, as much as my sister. I share their pain.*

The Queen sat rigidly in the High seat, her own usual place vacant beside her. She was cordial to all who addressed her. Her composure slipped only for a moment, upon meeting the obvious empathy welling from King Gearld and Queen Signe. She stepped down and spoke with them longest, clasping hands and blinking away tears.

Aaren stood stiffly between the thrones, staring over the line of mourners to Trever's casket. Jenora wondered at the rigidity of his face and body; he looked taller and more mature than she had ever seen him. His only slip also came when Gearld and Signe spoke with his mother. He closed his eyes, and turned away his face as if in shame.

Wildon the Hawk hovered beside the great doors, conversing with each visitor as he or she exited. He smiled sadly, pressed flesh, spoke consolingly, thanked them for coming. His eyes seldom left Aaren and the Queen.

Jenora remained where duty posted her until the last person had passed, the last condolence had been offered, and the doors were formally closed. At last she stretched and joined the other courtiers gathering around the Prince and Queen descending from their dais.

Wildon reached them first. "Your Majesties; their Highnesses King Gearld and his Queen asked that they be provided chambers, as they wish to remain in Edge overnight. I took the license of having the suite usually given royal visitors prepared for them. If m'Lady Queen would care to spend more time with them..?"

"Thank you, Wildon." Alyda looked weary and drawn as she turned to her son. "Would you like to see them, Aaren? You may accompany me."

"I think not, Mother. I should prefer to go to my own rooms now, alone. Perhaps I'll rest for a while. But do you go and visit them; it will do you good. And please ask them, for me, how fare their daughters?"

"I understand; rest well, my son. Jenora, will you escort me?"

"Certainly, your Majesty." Jenora took the older woman's arm and received a grateful clasp in return. She looked to Aaren as he held the door, but he would not meet her eyes.

Wildon called after them. "I believe I shall remain here, your Highness. I wish to confer for a time with some of the Council members. Things will be different now, and we need to be ... prepared."

Alyda stopped, and turned to stare at him. He held her gaze, his face carefully solicitous. "Very well," Alyda finally said. Wildon bowed. She and Jenora stepped out, Aaren behind them. The Prince turned away, down the corridor to the west stairs. The closing door framed a scene that troubled Jenora vaguely. The councilors who had remained were clustered around Wildon. He was speaking to them, his face measured and grave. But for a moment, his glance fell, and lingered, on the throne.

The King and Queen of Faires returned home after two days' visit. The news they had given Jenora of Sare was guarded: she was still unconscious, but she lived; for how long, no one could say. Queen Alyda seemed fleetingly heartened by their aid and counsel, and promised even closer relations between the royal houses in the future. But after their departure, the royal mantle seemed to weigh upon her greatly. She accepted the burden of rule by becoming still more quiet and inward than before.

Aaren, too, turned solitary. He spent a great deal of time in his chambers, writing letters that he refused to discuss with anyone. He rode Chance daily, pushing the beast hard over the entire kingdom, through the fields and farms and the wild lands around them. Jenora sometimes saw him standing for hours at the escarpment's rim, gazing across the flat plain and marshlands to the sea beyond. Every evening would find him looking from a high window of the palace, past the gardens and stables to the Nethals, to the West where the darkness settled last.

Chapter 18
Year's End

Three months passed with affairs in this same order. The news from Faires was unchanged. Jenora concentrated on improving her fighting skills; her horsemanship and lance-work became nearly unmatchable. She began wearing mail every day, throughout her practice with horse and halberd and sword.

Near the end of one such afternoon, she and Master Leland were fencing, advancing and retreating, both dripping sweat and breathing hard. Jenora was growing wary; Leland seemed to be engaging her more and more in the low line, as though to keep her attention centered there. Knowing him well, she suspected a trap in the making. *Perhaps, Master, and perhaps not!* She allowed herself to be drawn further, watching his intent brown eyes.

She saw the commitment to move in those eyes an instant before his body followed suit. He abruptly feinted low, then came up into an overhand cut aimed at her sword arm. She caught it upon her blunted blade, and for a second they stood straining against the crossed steel.

Leland clapped his gloved left hand upon his sword above their juncture and heaved with all his weight, easily pushing Jenora backward.

But she had already begun falling away the moment his hand came up, taking two quick steps back. Leland couldn't maintain his balance against the lack of resistance, and stumbled forward before quickly catching himself. As his blade dropped, Jenora swung her own up and across his forehead just at his hairline. The impact staggered the Arms Master and sent him to one knee.

Master Leland shook his head, his face clearly showing his astonishment. "That tactic defeated the finest Fairen swordsman I ever met, twenty years ago at the battle of Lake Fount. How did it not fool you?"

Jenora lent her hand to help him rise. "I have had too many years of learning how your mind works. You know you are famous for secret thrusts and subtle tricks."

Leland shook the hand he still held. "Well done, m'Lady. Will that be enough exercise for you today?"

"More than enough. Shall we meet at the same time tomorrow?"

As they hung up the practice gear, Master Leland seemed distracted, as if debating within himself. Finally, he turned to his pupil. "Lady Jenora, tell me ... have you heard of anything troubling Queen Alyda?"

Jenora considered the question for some seconds. "I do not know what you mean by 'troubling' her, Master. She seldom takes part in the lighter court affairs, as was her wont – she did not attend the Harvest Masque, for one. But it *has* been only a quarter-year since –"

"I know full well that she still mourns good King Trever, and carries that sadness about with her. I know that she leaves much of the day-to-day rule to Lord Wildon, who is most capable. But I have heard other things, things that disturb me. It is rumored that our Lady Queen is not truly in good health, that perhaps her grief has served to unsettle her mind. These are worrisome thoughts, with more than a year before Prince Aaren could assume the mantle. Do you know aught of them?"

"Nothing, Master Leland. Where does one hear this talk?"

Leland looked embarrassed as he shrugged, "Oh, it is only the things a man overhears when he works with the guards, or moves among troops each day. I would not say that these ideas are widely spread; but they are being spoken, though no one can say by whom."

"Then be reassured, Master. No one is closer to the Queen than I, except her son. She has nearly been a mother to me these past years. I tell you that she is fully fit to rule, especially with the able support of her High Chamberlain."

Leland smiled. "Yes, the Hawk is very – confident, shall we say? Very well, we shall speak no more of it. Will you come at the same time tomorrow?"

"Certainly; and have your tricks well-prepared. I shall be on my guard, I warn you." She left him laughing softly behind her, his concerns apparently relieved.

Winter came harshly to Edge that year. It brought early snows heavy to the fields, with ice jamming the river. It laid a cloak of overcast and gloom on the kingdom, locking everyone indoors to brood beside fires that gave scant warmth.

Despite her assurances to Leland, Jenora found herself watching the Queen more closely than before. It seemed there could be some substance to the rumors Leland had reported. Alyda did seem distracted at times, less certain of herself than she had once been. The unusual cold afflicted her more than it did others; she often did not leave the royal chambers for days at a time.

Aaren remained as distant as before, keeping to himself and suffering within. She came upon him one afternoon in the palace's library, paging through a volume of colored plates in a desultory way, paying little attention to the exotic beasts depicted there. He glanced up when she entered. "Hello, Jen. Been in the stables, unless my nose is wrong ..?"

She drew a chair close to the wide hearth and settled into it. "You're not wrong. Canticle has been favoring her left foreleg ever since we were attacked last summer, and this cold only made it worse. I was wrapping it with a warm plaster. And I nearly froze myself in spite of the braziers out there!"

Aaren smiled stiffly. "Yes, I'm here mostly because this is one of the warmest rooms in the palace. I think all the books must help keep out the chill and damp." After a moment, he spoke again, his voice lower, without looking up from his book. "Jen... about this summer..."

It was the first time he had said those words. She answered as casually as she could, "Yes?"

"While we were in Faires ... I learned something – that is, I might have learned something. But I wasn't sure, there was no way to *be* sure..." He closed the book and turned on his bench to face her. "I know you must know what happened between me and Sare. You must have seen."

She nodded. "Yes, I did." She said no more, not wanting to interrupt if he was finally willing to speak of all this.

"Well, there was ... more than that. More than just the way we - we fell in love. Sometimes, when we were together, I could feel ... something. I could feel this power, whatever it is, that I carry. It was ... reaching out, reaching from me to her. I could almost see a glow around her, the way - the way things glow just before I set them afire. It was there, Jen. It was real. There is something that connects us, and I think I understand it now. I think ... I think that when I burn things..." He stopped, and then whispered, "I burn her, too."

His speech had faded almost to a murmur at the end, but Jenora had heard it all the same, loud as a thunderbolt. "Oh, Aaren." She sat motionless as the horror of what he meant swept over her. "Dear Gifter, how could such a thing be? And so, when you ... in the pass –"

"Yes! Oh, gods, Jen, what I did! How, how could I do that, when... when..." He squeezed his eyes shut in his gaunt face, as if he could hide from the knowledge he did not want. She rose and went to him, sat on the bench beside him and put her hand on his steel-taut arm.

He raised his head, his face torn with pain. She could only look at him in mute horror. He collapsed against her, clinging tightly as all the grief and guilt burst from him in wordless waves of sobbing. For a moment she sat stiffly, the repercussions of his story still crashing through her mind. Finally, she put her arms around him, held his shaking form close to her, and softly stroked his hair.

Chapter 19
Spring

The winter was brutal, but surprisingly brief. The snows began to melt fully a month earlier than usual. The Wendlow became strident with the cracking and grinding of ice, and the falls glistened with it. People ventured out slowly onto ground turned marshy and soft, loose around its stones.

Within weeks, the peasants were planting the fields to take advantage of the extra growing time. There was some concern when the river rose steadily up its banks for several days. No serious flooding resulted, though, and Edge settled into the normalcy of tilling and crofting, trading and statecraft.

In Greybeal Palace, the early spring was also most welcome. Aaren emerged from his solitude; though he remained more solemn and indwelling than the year before, he once again took an interest in life, and an increased interest in the affairs of the kingdom. There was also news from Faires: Sare had awakened a few months earlier.

Jenora took the first opportunity she could to plan a trip to Faires. Aaren absolutely refused to accompany her

"My duties to my mother, especially during your absence, are paramount. You go." He smiled wanly. Although she knew that it was not his real reason, Jenora acknowledged the truth in what he said. It was better to have someone watch over Alyda, and the palace.

"Have you any messages for the Proudlock Keep then?"

"No. Well, of course convey my regards to King Gearld, Queen Signe, and my future bride. And..."

"And?" she said, gently.

"Nothing." He kissed her forehead. "Gifter speed you, my Palatine."

Jenora regarded him as he walked away from her. "No one blames you for what happened, Prince. No one."

He paused for a moment but didn't turn around. "I do," he said.

As soon as she arrived in Faires, Jenora paid her respects to the King and Queen, and asked after Sare. "She's in her chambers," Signe replied, smiling. "She's been asking about you constantly ever since she heard of your arrival. Hurry now, before she drives poor Obra to distraction."

Jenora hurried down the familiar corridors to the west wing. She knocked, and the door fairly flew open at her touch. Sare launched herself into the young warrior's arms with a shriek. Jenora gasped, and gingerly hugged her friend. Sare held her more tightly. "It's all right. I won't break!" Jenora clasped the other girl closely to her then, and they both fell back into the room, laughing.

Jenora held her at arm's length and looked at her. The burning had taken all of her hair; her face was somehow simplified, stripped to its minimal components. Her nose was now a tiny pugged nub, her mouth drawn thinner and tighter, her lips barely defined around it. Her ears also were reduced to small circlets. Sare's skin seemed now to barely cover her skull. Her cheeks and neck and hands were shiny and seamed with thin white scars. But her eyes were emerald and radiant, and she seemed strong and otherwise healthy. Jenora shook her head. "I thought I'd never see you again."

"I'm all right now. Obra and the Gifter have made me well." She looked with deep love at the old woman sitting by the window, working an embroidery frame.

"Welcome, Lady Jenora. It is good to see you again," Obra said.

"And good to see you too, Obra. You are a miracle worker."

"It is not my skills that brought this child to where she is today, but the strength and determination in her own heart." Obra nodded. "That is not simple modesty on my part. Sare possesses great courage, not to mention a pig-headed stubbornness the likes of which I have never in all my years seen."

"*Obra!*" cried Sare.

"So I have often told her myself," agreed Jenora. They all laughed.

Sare took Jenora's hand. "Come and sit down and tell me *everything*; that is, if you're both through calling me names."

"I think that is my hint." Obra rose and put her needlework away in her sewing bag. "I'll see you later tonight, Lady Oswin." She kissed Sare on the top of her head, patted Jenora on the shoulder, and closed the door behind her as she left the room.

The young women flopped down upon Sare's bed. Jenora marveled again at Sare's obvious health. "You look so good."

Sare's eyes clouded briefly. "I guess if you don't mind bald women covered in scars, I look just fine," she said, with some bitterness.

"That's not what I meant! I am just so happy to see you alive, after all of the horrible stories that we heard, and here you are, looking so strong."

Sare relented. "I know. Actually, my feelings are more mixed. Of course, I feel so incredibly fortunate to be alive, and in a way I can't explain, I awoke feeling stronger than ever. It's as if having gone through these last months, I know that I can weather anything. And this –" she paused, looking at the back of her hand, "– this is different too. Maybe I'm used to it. Maybe it's because there is no pretense any longer of growing up as beautiful as my sisters." She looked up at her friend, her green eyes flashing. "I am no one else but me. I am the third daughter of the King, and I think it's time I started acting like that person."

Remarkable, thought Jenora. "All by yourself, you have learned lessons Master Leland is still despairing of teaching me. I have missed you very much, Sare. As have others."

There was a moment when both girls seemed to hold their breaths. Neither looked the other in the eye. Finally, Sare broke the tension.

"And how does he fare?" she asked quietly.

"He is ... distraught. The death of King Trever, of course, and worry for his mother, the Queen."

"Oh, they told me. I am so sorry. It must have been ... terrible..."

Jenora looked away, kept her gaze out the window to the fields beyond the castle. "I failed my King. I didn't even manage to save my Prince. The only thing that stood that day against Dark Michael's killers was Aaren and his..." She stopped, still not looking back at Sare. "He did what he had to do up there, alone in that pass. I know that he suspected your link to him, even before it happened. But he had no choice. He knows this. But he won't forgive himself for it." She finally looked back at Sare, whose face was unreadable. "I think that he is far less healed than you."

Sare's eyes were far away. Finally, she got up and went to a small wooden chest against the far wall of the room. She carried it back over to the bed and spilled its contents onto the embroidered coverlet. Out of the box spilled dozens and dozens of letters, all addressed to her, all unopened. The royal seal of Edge secured each one. Sare dropped the box to the carpet and sat back on the bed, spreading the letters out between them. She gazed at the letters and Jenora thought she saw anger, pain, longing, and finally resolution, pass over her scoured features. She looked up, and Jenora reached over, took her hand, and gripped it tightly. Without a word Sare took the first of the letters from the bed, gently opened the seal, and began to read.

Back in Edge a fortnight later, Jenora found the Prince again in the library. He was bent over a history, reading by the light from the tall unshuttered windows in the far wall. He looked up as she came in, with a saddlebag over one shoulder, and freshly scrubbed after her long ride back from Faires.

"So, Palatine," he said.

"So, Prince." She walked over and moved a chair next to him, turning it to face him. She laid the saddlebag on the table next to his book and sat.

He glanced at the leather bag. "What do you bring me?"

"Letters of state. The Seahale agreement, signed by King Gearld. Some items for your mother." She stared at him.

He didn't move to open the bag. "Anything else?" he asked, the strain in his voice belying the passivity of his features.

"Open it and see."

Aaren reached out and undid the clasp, withdrew a packet of papers tied with a red ribbon. He untied it, and sorted quickly through the letters in the packet. He stopped suddenly, dropping all of the papers to the table save one, a green envelope sealed with crimson. It was addressed to him, and had a single dove's feather set in the wax seal. With hands now openly shaking, he slid his finger under the seal and opened the letter.

Aaren -

I have no idea how to begin. I am terribly sorry for your loss, and your mother's. Jenora tells me that the Queen's health is not what it could be. Please know that my thoughts are with you both. Now more than ever, I suppose, our two kingdoms are in need of a link to strengthen them.

Jenora told me what happened last summer. I do not pretend to understand the nature of the curse that binds us to one another, but I do know that you would never hurt anyone, including me, if there was any other choice. I hope that one day we can again be friends. Please look for me when you come for your wedding to Cillistra next spring.

Always,
Sare

He read it twice, then folded it carefully and smoothed it out on the table before him with both hands. Tears dropped quietly onto the paper. He stared straight ahead, at nothing. "She does not love me."

Jenora did not know what to say. In her heart, she believed that each loved the other a great deal, but she also knew that Aaren's highest duty was to Edge, and that his marriage to Cillistra was of paramount importance. She was really beginning to despise that woman.

Chapter 20
Intrigues

Cillistra lay back languorously on the turquoise cushions and stretched. It was a calculated move, and the renewed appreciation in John Winters' eyes as he gazed on her naked ivory skin was proof to her of its success. He started across the bed toward her with a hungry smile. She smiled back, but at the last minute slipped out of his grasp and into her chemise.

"No time for heroics, John, I have to get back before I'm missed." She held her dress in front of her coyly, tilted her head down and looked up at him through her lashes. Her ebony curls slipped over her shoulder and framed her face exquisitely.

His smile turned wry, and he sighed. "You are a slippery fish, my love."

"Time to put away the pole and fish another time," she responded silkily, stepping into her dress. "It wouldn't do to be caught with the King's daughter less than a year before her wedding."

His face darkened. "That will not happen. We will find a way, my minnow, for our love to overcome even an obstacle of that magnitude. The pretender Prince will drown in his backwater kingdom, and you and I will rule Faires together."

Cillistra looked up in alarm. She and John had been lovers for some four months now, since shortly after her betrothal ceremony. It still amazed her how smoothly and easily he had accomplished her seduction – though truly, she had not been at all reluctant. But still, she both loved and feared him when he spoke that way. She had no doubt that he believed exactly what he was saying, that he intended to have both her and the throne. The thought of marrying the inelegant Prince revolted her more now than ever. John was everything that Aaren was not: older, cultured, brilliant, and ambitious. Ever since the first time they had danced, she had been smitten by him.

Everyone she knew agreed, too. It was a shame, the courtiers said, to have to give up your true love for an arranged marriage to a foreigner, no more than a rude boy, really. Oh, Aaren had received some sympathy after the tragedy of his father's death, but it didn't change the facts. Cillistra suddenly felt a wave of despair.

"But it can't really be that way, can it? I mean, I must marry him, if our kingdom is to survive. Faires was weakened in the war with Edge, and now the Dark One threatens us anew. I love you, John," she said, her passion plain, "but I just don't see any way out of this." She sat abruptly on the edge of the bed, her dress not yet buttoned, hot tears of frustration rolling down her perfect cheekbones.

He stared at her silently for a moment. Sliding over, he took her in his arms. He was warm, and his strong embrace comforted her, but not enough to dispel her melancholy.

"Minnow?" he whispered softly in her ear.

"Yes?"

"What if there was a way? What if I told you of a way not only for us to be together, but to rule Faires, make her strong again, and eventually even rule Edge?"

She drew back and looked into his eyes. For a moment they were the laughing brown eyes she had loved to gaze into for as long as she had known him. Then, like a mirror pond smoothing out after a pebble has marred its surface, they changed. They became deeper, darker, almost black. She felt herself falling, the vertigo palpable and thrilling. She fell into that gaze and believed him, utterly and without reservation. Along with a brittle stab of crystalline fear, she felt a sudden deep pleasure suffuse her. It was like nothing she had ever felt before, and at the same time like coming home.

"But, how..?" she breathed.

"I am going to tell you some wonderful secrets," he said. "And this is the first: my name is Michael."

◆   ◆   ◆

Jenora found more causes for her earlier concern after she returned to Edge. Though she saw no outward signs of peril, she grew increasingly worried over the changes in Queen Alyda. The Queen became more withdrawn with each passing day, taking a less and less active role in the rule of Edge. She complained of discomforts and sleepless nights, of spells of weakness, and others of paralyzing indecision.

Quietly, Jenora took up a closer watch on Alyda. She arranged that the Queen's food be prepared and handled only by a few, trusted members of the palace staff; it was always carefully tasted before being served. She consulted with Vernor on the kinds of spells and magics that could be directed to a person's harm. He cast charms to detect and counter such influences, with inconclusive results.

Though the Queen seemed to slowly worsen, the government of Edge continued to run smoothly. Wildon the Hawk took on increasing responsibility without cavil. He appeared to be everywhere, helping prepare for the threatened floods, entertaining the annual delegation from Seahale, even presiding over a shire-court dispute between two noble houses. He gained a measure of respect, perhaps even affection, previously denied him. The people began to speak his name more and more, to praise his dedication and even-handedness.

His duties, it seemed, included visits to the drilling yards where the troops mustered and trained. Jenora often saw him there, moving among the tents, jostling with men and horses, pausing to speak with some of the commanders and men. He appeared to take special interest in the houseguards, watching them parade and practice.

By midsummer, Wildon had become the *de facto* ruler of Edge. In Alyda's name he had assumed nearly every power of the crown, and administered them all fairly and efficiently. This situation was not unknown in Edge's history; several times in the past, High Chamberlains had acted for monarchs incapacitated by wounds or illness. Indeed, it was the very reason the office existed. The populace, impressed by Wildon's assurance and capability, accepted his actions and gave little thought to such lofty matters.

Summer proved to be as kindly as the winter had been harsh. The days were long and fair, and only rarely hot. The afternoons and evenings were warm and lovely. Even Wildon thought so.

One particular midsummer evening gave him more than usual occasion to appreciate the season. He was walking through the streets of Edge near dusk, passing from light to shadow to light again.

It was an evening to make a poet even of the Hawk. The air was warm and fragrant, filled with inviting scents from the nearby market district and punctuated with stronger odors from the tanneries or the odd refuse-heap. Dust motes shimmered up and down the shafts of sunlight lancing between the close-set buildings; the streets had been newly swept to prepare for the summer-fair travelers.

The city's shops were just beginning to close. All about, people were lowering awnings and raising counterboards to shutter their storefronts. Several nodded and even smiled at Wildon as he passed, and he returned each salutation in kind. Dogs and cats lounged on doorsteps and windowsills, too indolent to chase the poults that sporadically darted across the lane.

Wildon had chosen to walk to his destination, rather than to take a carriage, because he delighted in his city in summertime, and because he wished to take thought unencumbered by any court interruptions. His thoughts matched the season and what he observed on his way; they were gratifying, and promised of coming fulfillment.

His destination tonight was also unaccustomed: he was going home.

Wildon's family home stood in the city's east end where his great-grandfather, a successful furrier, had built it. That man's son had become the first Lord Wildon when he was granted a small manor and its holdings for his service to King Trever's grandfather.

The present Wildon had spent little time on those lands, except in his youth, and scarcely more at the house he now approached.

Now over a century old, the house was as solid as the stones that formed it. Its pitched roof rose above the smaller homes and shops crowding round it, four stories high, echoed by the peaked arches of its windows and doorframes. As Wildon drew near, the sunset turned its white facade roseate and touched silver to the black wrought-iron of the door straps and latticework.

He opened the great oaken door, and was swiftly greeted by his steward. The elderly retainer helped Wildon remove his boots and left to polish them, while the master donned his slippers, rose from the bench and entered his salon.

A ten-year-old boy was playing with wooden soldiers on the broad carpet. He looked up as Wildon came in, his brown eyes alert; he neither smiled nor frowned.

Wildon settled into his chair at the dining table's head and lifted his hand. "My boy; how have you been since my last visit?"

"Well, Father." The boy laid his soldiers back into their box and carefully shut its lid. "The new foal is almost big enough for me to ride. And Walter says you said I could have a sword for my birthday next month."

"I did indeed." Wildon smiled. "That warrants a hug for the benefactor, don't you think?"

The youngster came to him and accepted a brief embrace. Wildon ruffled his hair as he stepped back, holding his gaze. "You must practice often with that sword, and later with larger ones. Learn to use it well. I plan great things for you, you know. You will be a power in this kingdom one day, and must be able to hold it." He eased back in the chair and motioned his son to the seat beside him. "Now, what does Cook have for dinner?"

The boy's first smile crossed his face. "Pheasant and fish, I think. He was hurrying all around this afternoon after the page told us you were coming."

"Well, go and fetch him, and we'll see what he was able to find."

As his son hurried out, Wildon rested his glance on the cold and empty hearth. *Great things, indeed. If you knew the half of it, my son, you would be amazed.* This and other thoughts were turning in his mind when a small bell sitting on his mantelpiece suddenly chimed once, softly. He sprang up from his chair, regarding the bell, then turned and left the room.

His son was returning up the hallway. "Cook and Bess are coming with our dinner, Father."

Wildon strode past without pausing, speaking over his shoulder. "Have them set our places. I will be with you in just a moment." He continued down the hall and stopped at the door to his study. He waited there until the boy had gone before unlocking the door and slipping inside.

As always after the bell rang, Michael's Shadow stood in the corner nearest the garden window, like a piece of statuary come indoors. The last of the sunset shone on its mail and faded into its grey skin. When Wildon approached, its right hand rose slowly and extended a single parchment. Wildon took it, and the golem fell back into immobility.

The Hawk unfolded the sheet. As he read the black, untutored handwriting, he seemed to hear the writer's voice speaking the words in his ears. He had heard that voice only a few times, but always it came to him with these rare messages, as it did now.

> *Our plan nears completion. It requires your*
> *hand to strike the blow that sets it finally in*
> *motion. I am in readiness. Strike soon.*

Wildon laid the note into the study's fireplace and ignited it with a quick stroke of flint. The tiny flame cast strange shadows across the golem's impassive face; the room had grown darker in the last few moments. The Hawk rose and went to the writing table where he pulled forth a piece of parchment and wrote:

> *I also am nearly ready, and shall strike in a*
> *matter of weeks at most. I will then await*
> *your bidding.*

He blotted the ink, folded and sealed the letter with plain wax – no signet – and handed it to the golem.

With scarcely a sound, the Shadow turned, opened the window, and slipped out. Wildon watched it vanish into the dusk as he closed the window. He never even saw where it scaled his garden wall and departed. His thoughts were elsewhere. *Aye, within weeks the power will be in my hands – and then we shall see what this unholy alliance of mine shall bring.*

✦   ✦   ✦

In their chambers carved within his mountain, Michael and Cillistra sat on opposite sides of his great bed, the distance between their rigid backs dark with tension. The single lamp cast its yellow glare across the rough rock walls, the irregular shadows suggesting fantastic shapes and forms. Cillistra looked into the shadows and saw faces, mouths agape. She saw a broken crown, and a horned beast. She closed her eyes. "No horses and rabbits here," she whispered.

"What?" he asked.

Without answering, she tore open another packet of the dreaming powder and emptied it into a glass of water on the night table. As it foamed, she drank it down, grimacing at its bitterness.

"Again?" Michael's tone was stern with disapproval. "That's your third."

She turned to him, the familiar torpor of the drug already feathering out in her mind, blunting the sharp edges of her morbid thoughts. "Yes," she said simply. But it wasn't her third. She wasn't sure exactly how many she had drunk, but she knew there had been more than three. Her eyes were dark and glittering with the effects of the powder. "I look at you, and I love you, and I feel this terrible knot in my stomach." He did not turn around. "What you want, what we both want ... it's not so terrible, is it?" He didn't answer. "Simply to be together. Every time I come here, I betray my father and my house. And yet I cannot stop."

She upended the glass and let the last of the bitter dregs slide down onto her tongue, which already felt numb. *I wish all of me were that numb.* "I love you, Michael. But I'm terrified of the violence." There was a long pause. She put the glass back down on her nightstand and ran her fingers through her long curls over and over, fascinated at the dark tresses flowing over her white fingers like river eddies. "So much killing," she whispered.

Finally, he turned. His face was drawn, though still somewhat slack from the draught he had taken with her earlier. "Yes?" he said. "The killing? Is that what frightens you?" His eyes were cold; he gripped the coverlet with white knuckles. Her growing distance over the last several weeks had obviously not gone unnoticed. "It is who I am. It is the only way to achieve my goals."

He watched her play with her hair. "Our goals," he amended, more softly. "Am I to lose you then, so close to our triumph?"

She lay back on the pillows, looking up at the ceiling, deeply in shadow. Her hands still twisted her hair. The drug gave her the courage to speak the truth she would not have otherwise dared. "I feel as though we are already lost," she said. "So many will die to make this thing happen, I can't bear to think of it. Every time you order your men to slay another caravan, or eventually to take larger prizes ..." she shuddered, swallowed, and continued, "you drive yourself further from me. This is not what I thought it would be. You are not who I thought you would be." A single tear slid haltingly down her cheek.

"You would prefer John Winters?" he sneered, voice shaking, though not entirely with anger. "Or would you prefer the wretched son of a wretched trapper, and a hovel in the woods?"

"No." Her voice was beginning to slur just slightly. "None of that matters. I only want you, and to be together, and for the rest of this nightmare, and, and intrigue, and ... death. To go ... away." Her mind was slipping deeply into the dream state. *Too deeply.* She had, she thought in a far-removed way, taken far too much. *Far ... too ... much...*

His eyes lost their iciness, and he slid over and embraced her. "I know I'm losing you." He buried his face in her hair. "I can't bear that, but I must ... I must finish what I have started, surely you understand that?" His hands held her tightly but tenderly; the pain and the passion in his voice were plain.

She marveled at his words. He had never seemed so, so vulnerable. From a long way away, she sensed him moving, his weight and heat pressed against her, holding her close, trying to bring her back. *But I don't think I can come back this time.* It was all so sad. "Goodbye," she tried to say, but wasn't sure she had uttered the word aloud.

Michael leaned over and saw all of the empty packets of the dreaming powder littering the table and floor. "Minnow?" he said, a growing alarm in his voice. "Cillistra?" He sat up and gripped her by the shoulders. Her head flopped limply to one side. Her breathing was very slow.

From what seemed like leagues underwater, she watched him shake her. She couldn't feel it at all. His mounting distress might have been touching, if she could have still managed the energy to feel touched. But all she felt was sadness and distance, and a slow sinking into the dark. She could see his lips move, but she couldn't hear his voice. Even breathing seemed much too hard, and so, with a sigh, she stopped.

The last thing she dimly saw before the brilliant flash of light engulfed her with its roar was her lover making strange gestures over her body, then flinging himself down to cover her. Then the light came, no gentle glow but a searing extension of Michael's power, blasting the shadows from her mind with the enormity of his love, manifested physically in a wave of energy that reached down to where she was lost and saved her, taking her in his burning arms and bringing her back to the surface where he waited, his tears mingling with hers as they clutched each other in the darkened cave.

◆   ◆   ◆

Michael's Shadow was crossing the fields of western Edge after leaving Wildon, skirting the fringes of the settled lands. The blackness of the night hindered it not at all; it was being drawn home to its master as firmly and surely as a length of chain being reeled back onto its capstan. If any thoughts passed through its mind, they were of a nature no person could name or recognize.

It was fully repaired – or healed – from the damage done by Aaren's fire a year ago. It was, in fact, even stronger than before. Michael had cloistered himself with the golem for two days after their return, neither eating nor drinking, casting spells and molding its clay until, when they emerged, it appeared exactly the same as the day he had breathed life into it. He had it clothed again in new mail and fine clothing, and set it again to tasks like the one it was performing now.

As it approached the foothills of the Nethals, preparing to avoid the guards posted at the mouth of the Waist, it abruptly stopped and stood, motionless, in the pale light of the quarter moon. The will that had been pulling it home had slipped away. The connection between it and Michael, the energy that flowed into and animated it, was utterly gone.

Moist patches grew on its grey skin, softening as the chain mail sank into it. Deep under the clay, in the thing's skull, a tiny spark of thought flickered, too subdued to be panic, too unformed to be more than a dull plodding wonder. It turned its white eyes to the East and opened its mouth. Jaw agape, its entire form began to shift slightly, to slide and shrink. Droplets of mud pattered at its feet.

And as swiftly as the energy had gone, it returned. Michael's will rushed back into the vacuum it had left behind, as powerfully and irresistibly as the tide. His Shadow straightened, its skin hardening again. It closed its mouth with a snap. Shaking the dried clots of mud from its mail, the golem began to move again, westward into the hills, home to its other, true self.

Chapter 21
Equinox

Early autumn came, bringing near-record harvests from the fields. Produce flowed up and down the Wendlow valleys; the ship owners of Seahale filled their holds and grew rich, and the trade market in Faires was the busiest and liveliest of many years.

When the Harvest Masque was held again at Greybeal, it seemed to bring an extra warmth, a special glow to the palace and grounds. After the death and cold of the previous year, the celebrants who came from every manor and guild in both kingdoms felt that they were truly celebrating something.

Jenora, too, was caught up in the occasion. The costumes and decorations were more exotic, the conversations more intriguing, the wines and foodstuffs more lavish than she could ever remember. She met a young man, the son of a minor noble from Faires, who was talkative and cordial; more important, he was *tall*. He was tall enough for her to be comfortable dancing with him, and they spent much of the evening doing just that. Even the music felt magical.

Yet something wasn't quite right. Jenora pondered that impression while she and young Falder sat for a moment. The answer came to her at once: *Where is Lord Wildon?* He had been much in evidence earlier, playing the proper but convivial host, dancing with all the ladies and shaking every hand. Now, he was nowhere in sight.

The musicians began another tune. Young Lord Falder came up and took her hand. "Come on. You promised me at least a few more rounds." He led her back onto the floor. As they whirled to a lively measure, Jenora glimpsed Wildon. He was standing at the far end of the Hall, still in the lavishly feathered costume and plumed hat he had worn, perhaps in deference to his nickname. He looked to be speaking to someone, but a column hid the other person from view.

Jenora's angle of sight changed abruptly when she and Lord Falder twirled into a different spot. Wildon was talking with a man, not costumed, but wearing the tunic of a palace guard. He turned, and Jenora recognized him as Malcomb, one of the house guards. Wildon smiled and nodded after him as the guardsman left the room.

Jenora wondered briefly about this converse, but soon forgot it in the enjoyment of the night. Young Falder left her with promises to write, and perhaps to visit in the spring.

She retired to her chambers with an unusual lightness of spirit, still hearing the music of the dance.

A month passed, the leaves fell, and with them a young woman's spirits. Though she worked diligently at her arts and studies, Jenora found the turning season more and more oppressive. Perhaps it was only the memory of the last winter, but she was dreading the dark months to come.

She rode Canticle often, both in the lists and in the fields. In the lists, her work with both sword and lance drew admiration from every warrior in Edge. Even Master Leland admitted that he could teach her little more.

In the fields, she enjoyed riding the boundaries of the kingdom. The big mare was graceful and tireless, with an easy carriage that allowed her rider to relax in the saddle. They made a fine team. Jenora often went out to spend time with her sister Agnes and see what was being done on their manor's lands.

She was returning from one such trip, listening to the wind rustle through the stooks in her fields and smelling wood smoke from a crofter's chimney. It was a fine evening, so she had taken the long way around the edges of her land to where a wagon path met the great Road. Just as Canticle stepped onto the firmer surface, Jenora noticed two mounted figures at some distance to the east.

They were not riding, but holding their horses close together and obviously talking, though she could not see their faces well enough to identify them. She held rein and watched for a moment, noting that one glanced her way with no apparent sign of recognition. They did not move either to approach or leave, so she turned west and rode off toward the city bridge.

What subject could be so private as to need a place like this for its discussion? She wondered why it aroused her interest at all. They might have been two friends who had met on the way. But her pleasure in the evening was gone, her feeling of portent returned in full strength.

✦   ✦   ✦

Two days after taking part in the conference on the eastern road, Malcomb walked the corridors of Greybeal palace on his normal patrol. His thoughts were of many things as he approached the north wing. They were of ambition thwarted and encouraged, of parleys and promises, kept and broken.

In a little-used area of the tower wing, near Vernor's stairway, he stopped. A moment's listening assured him that he was entirely alone. He removed a loose wall brick. In its niche was a tiny bit of vellum, easily disposed of in the flame of a lamp or torch. He drew it forth, and read the only word upon it: *Tonight.*

Chapter 22

Coup

Three hours later, near the end of his watch, Malcomb paused outside Aaren's chamber, listening for steps in the hall or sounds from the room. No one was approaching; only a chair creaked beyond the door. He opened it and quickly entered.

Prince Aaren was seated at his writing table against the side wall, quill in hand and a long sheet of linen paper before him. He turned as the guardsman closed the door. "Oh, it's you, Malcomb. Do you need something?"

"Nothing of import, my lord. Your mother only wished me to look in on you before she sleeps." He strode forward. "Have you been writing?"

Aaren moved as if to cover the page. "It's a letter. A private one. So if there is nothing-"

Malcomb drew his sword, hoping the youth's own voice would cover its rasp. It partly worked; Aaren had only stiffened and half-turned before the brass pommel crashed into his head, just above his left ear. The impact pitched him and his chair to the floor.

Bending over the still Prince, Malcomb thrust a hand beneath the boy's nostrils. He was still breathing, though slowly and shallowly, and blood was creeping from under his hair and down the nape of his neck. The blow had not been intended to kill.

The guardsman stooped and lifted the unconscious youth, carried him through the arch to the sleeping-room, and dropped him onto the bed. Moving quickly, he drew forth flint and steel and carefully lit the lamp on the stand. Then he arranged the body on the bed so that Aaren's right arm was extended to the table.

Malcomb raised that arm, moved it a fraction, and dropped it. Aaren's hand sent the lamp clattering to the floor, its oil splashing over the burning wick and spreading across the rug, instantly aflame.

Aaren never stirred. Malcomb watched for a moment as pungent smoke began rising from the blazing fibers, as the flames began licking at the thick coverlet of Aaren's bed; the Prince did not move.

Malcomb examined the scene one last time. It was to appear that Aaren upset the lamp while tossing in his sleep. With luck, the boy's strange power might even be invoked by the pain and fear of burning, making the fire all the greater. He nodded, turned on his heel, and strode to the door, pausing to listen before stepping out into the empty passage.

He returned to his post at the juncture with the main corridor. It would be necessary to raise an alarm eventually, of course; but give the fire time to grow and engulf a royal bed, the smoke time to choke a prince's life away. Malcomb smiled. The job had been smoothly done. Wildon's reward would be generous – indeed, it had better be. *Captain of the guard, perhaps even Chamberlain? After that, who knows? There is much within reach of a capable man with –*

Footsteps had been approaching for several seconds as he mused, he abruptly realized: a brisk, martial pace around the nearest corner. She was upon him before he could gather himself, nodding as she swept past, on her way to Aaren's door. Malcomb stopped and spun around. "Lady Oswin!"

◆ ◆ ◆

Jenora paused and turned, puzzled by the insistence in the man's voice. "Yes, Malcomb?"

He moved closer. "I only meant to say, m'Lady, that Prince Aaren asked that he not be disturbed tonight. He is writing a letter, I believe."

"I understand, but I am afraid that I must speak to him. We have had news from Faires that King Gearld and Princess Cillistra plan to visit at month's end to discuss the wedding's formalities. We must all begin to prepare their welcome." She smiled. "Don't worry, I will tell him that you tried to dissuade me."

She turned and went on, with Malcomb only a step behind and desperate for some idea to hold her. Suddenly, she stopped, staring at the smoke that oozed around the doorframe.

The sound of a drawn sword electrified her; she whirled, striking upwards with a full sweep of her left arm. Her mailed forearm struck his bare one cruelly, making her stumble back two steps but deflecting the stroke that might have disemboweled her.

Malcomb cursed and shook his wrist, but came on. Jenora snatched out her own blade and met him with a lateral parry. He moved in, pressing hard, forcing her to give ground. He was obviously stronger, a veteran man-at-arms. If the growing bruise she could see weakened his sword wrist at all, his skill compensated for it. His blade moved from low cuts to high to midline with equal facility, keeping her on the defensive. An almost mad fury burned in his eyes.

He made a sudden spring and swung his fist at her face. Jenora ducked, felt his knuckles graze her forehead, saw him follow up with a straight thrust. She beat his point away bare inches from her breast, and drew her dagger left-handed.

I haven't time for a long fight, Aaren is in danger. Perhaps one of Master Leland's tricks..?

Malcomb was pressing more cautiously, watching both her blades. She engaged his sword with her dagger's quillions and aimed a cut at his left flank, inviting a high blow. It came; Malcomb jerked his blade free as he evaded hers, and swung an overhand stroke to her head. Jenora swept both weapons up to entrap his sword between their crossed blades. In the instant that he was so immobilized, she drove her knee solidly into his lower belly.

Malcomb gasped and fell back, trying to bring his point into line. She lunged to his right, striking his sword high and catching it against her blade's forte. Her right foot came down behind his to prevent any retreat. With all her strength, she stabbed her long dagger beneath his upraised arm.

It plunged in to the hilt. Malcomb gave a gargling cry as he collapsed, wrenching the haft from her grip. Jenora spared no thought for her weapon, nor for the twitching body. She threw open Aaren's door, wincing at the rush of smoke into her eyes. Crouched below the worst of it, she scanned the room as she moved to the arch, searching for the Prince.

The smoke and heat were worse in Aaren's bedchamber. Its tapestried walls were ablaze; only her boots protected her from the burning carpet. She rushed to the bed and found Aaren lying in a ring of low flames. His bedding was charred from the floor up; flames flickered on the coverlet and burned sullenly all around him, yet he remained completely untouched.

She bent over him. His breathing was labored, smoke had blackened his face, and congealing blood covered one side of his head. Still, he lived. A glance told her why; the bracelet on his wrist reflected the flickering lights of the fire, but it also glowed softly with power from within. She whispered, "You wrought better than you know, Vernor," even as she grasped Aaren's arms and raised him up to lean on her.

She stooped and caught him across her shoulders as he fell. Taking as deep a breath as could be managed, she heaved and half-rose. The flames on the bed leapt and reached for each other as Aaren left them, but Jenora had little time to notice. Coughing, staggering beneath his weight, she somehow turned and made her way out through the door.

Carefully she laid him down on the floor tiles, her mind racing as she inhaled lungfuls of clean air. An attempt had been made on Aaren's life, by a trusted guardsman. If a man like Malcomb could be suborned, then the stakes and the prizes in this game, whatever it was, must be great; perhaps even the throne of Edge itself. Anyone could be a conspirator.

If that is the case, if someone wishes the Prince dead, then perhaps he should remain "dead." With sudden resolution, Jenora pulled her dagger from Malcomb's body, stripped off his belt and tunic, and dragged him into Aaren's rooms.

It was harder to see or breathe than before, but she worked quickly. She wrestled the corpse upright and draped its torso across the blazing bed, bent and swung its legs up as well. The ceiling beams were igniting now, the flames all around were more intense. There would be no identifying the body after a short time. *Let Malcomb take the place of the man he betrayed, and perchance help to keep him alive.*

She turned to go, and noticed another object untouched by the fire. Hanging in its sheath from a hook near Aaren's doorway, the Rageblade was surrounded by flames, but unharmed. The pendulum inscribed in its hilt glowed scarlet, as if to catch her eye. It was too fine a thing to leave behind, and Aaren's heritage as well. She snatched it down and ran, bent over, back into the hall.

After a moment taken to recover her breath and eyesight, she looked Aaren over carefully. He was still insensible, but breathing more easily now. He seemed uninjured except for the clotting, bruised wound on his head.

Jenora strapped Malcomb's belt around one of Aaren's shoulders and slipped her arm through it. She manhandled him up against a wall, and locked her other arm behind his loose biceps so that he leaned back against her shoulder blades. With the dead man's sword and tunic tucked in her belt on one side and the Rageblade on the other, and the unconscious Prince dragging behind, she shuffled as fast as possible down the passage.

It took several minutes to reach a stairwell, and a bumping, stumbling eternity to go down and reach a door. Once outside, she laid her precious burden among the hedges and ran to within earshot of the night watch; she took a deep breath.

"Fire! Fire in the west wing!" Her shout echoed off the palace walls, and was taken up by the watch. She waited only long enough to be certain that the alarm was given before slipping back into the building's shadow.

Aaren lay as she had left him. There was nothing for it but to hoist him again and half-carry, half-drag him away, down into the royal gardens. By the time she could no longer hear the tumult at the Palace, she was shambling and nearly exhausted.

She lowered the Prince into the cover of a dividing wall and slumped beside him. They were safe for the moment, but where to go next? Whom could she trust to give them shelter while Aaren healed, and she found out the meaning of this night's events? Slowly, an image formed in her mind and coalesced into an idea. Rising wearily, Jenora settled Aaren more comfortably and headed for the stables.

She led two horses from their stalls: Malcomb's nervous black and her own trustworthy Canticle. It was only a few minutes' work to saddle them, hang the Rageblade from her own saddlebow, and gather extra horse blankets and a good coil of rope. No one challenged her; it seemed all the equerries and grooms were off fighting, or watching, the fire.

In moments she was back to Aaren, heaving him across Malcomb's horse and covering him with a blanket. She paused to kiss his cheek. "Just a little farther, my Prince, I promise." She regarded his soot-smeared face with concern. "Just don't die, after all this." She mounted again, took up the other horse's reins, and struck out to the river.

They reached it in a short time. As usual, its banks were lined with boats drawn up or moored for the night. These sturdy little craft plied the Wendlow's length every day, carrying the commerce of city and kingdom alike. Jenora had always respected the watermen. Now, she left a stack of coins on the dock after carrying the blankets and rope aboard one light boat.

Getting Aaren aboard was more difficult, but she managed. As she stretched him on the blankets laid in the bottom, he moaned and tried to turn over. Jenora started, then smiled broadly, and with renewed energy covered him warmly and set a saddle pad beneath his head.

She uncoiled the rope and made it fast to the bowsprit. The other end she carried up the bank and tied to the bow of Canticle's saddle. She secured the black's bridle to her own saddle's cantle.

When all was ready, she pushed the boat out into the stream and swung astride her horse. A tug set Malcomb's black in motion; Jenora turned Canticle west and let her set her own pace. The boat moved well upstream. Darkness would keep both horses picking their way carefully; the river would narrow as they neared the mountains; they would reach the foothills by dawn.

As she bound the guardsman's tunic and sword with his belt, she thought ahead to getting Aaren across the mountains. But that was a problem for tomorrow. She pitched the makeshift bundle into the river and leaned upon Canticle's neck. It would not be the first time she slept in the saddle...

Chapter 23
Exile

The royal family of Faires was at supper when one of the city sentries was admitted to the Keep, asking to speak with King Gearld privately.

The King rose from his table and went out to meet him. The man, Fenton, was known to him as a reliable sort, not given to unwarranted alarms. After formally greeting the King, he drew Gearld aside and reached into his blouse as he spoke, with the accent of Seahale, his birthplace.

"Y'r Majesty, I was standing m'watch at the eastern gate when a woman just came up to the gate out of the dark. She was unarmed, and she spoke me fair, asking only that y' come there and talk with 'er, from inside the walls. 'Er only condition was that y' come alone, except for me, and tell no'ne. F'r token of 'er good faith, she threw me this." He held forth a signet, bearing the device of an elaborate "O".

Gearld took it and looked it over; it was vaguely familiar, but he couldn't place it in his memory. He pondered the puzzle: If this was some sort of trap, it was an odd one for the likes of the Dark One; and who else would be setting traps for kings? "Very well. I shall ready myself and meet you at the gate in a quarter of an hour. Until then, stop nowhere and say nothing to anyone, no one at all, agreed?" The sentry assented, and left bowing.

Gearld made his excuses to his family, armed himself with sword and dagger, and threw on his hooded cloak to conceal them as well as his face. He strode quickly through the streets of his city, growing more curious with each step.

Finally he reached the eastern gate and climbed the gatehouse, finding Fenton alone as ordered. "She signaled a minute ago, y'r Majesty. She's in those trees just past the frontier." He pointed to indicate where. Gearld peered into the gathering darkness, but could see nothing. "Light your lantern, and give it to me." The sentry quickly did so, and the King waved it out the portal several times.

After a moment, two people on horseback emerged from the trees. They rode up beneath the walls and stopped. One called up, in a woman's voice, "Is it you, your Highness?"

Gearld called back, "It is. What do you want here, coming in stealth and secrecy? Tell me quickly, or be on your way."

"We wish only to come in, so you may know us better. We are alone." She chuckled wearily. "No army hides behind us."

Her voice seemed even more familiar than the ring she had sent. Gearld considered for a moment, then turned to Fenton. "Open the gate. If this is a trick, it's far too subtle for any villainy I can imagine. But stand ready to give the alarm."

Minutes later, the two rode into the city street, and the gate was closed behind them. Gearld and the guardsman descended and stood before them. The woman was dressed in sooty, mud-splattered doublet and hose and boots. The other rider was a cloaked man, equally soiled, who seemed barely able to sit his horse.

The woman dismounted. The King went forward to meet her. She knelt in the torchlight, and he was astonished to recognize her. "Lady Oswin, what..?"

She looked up into his eyes. "By the laws of our peoples, I beg sanctuary of you for myself and my companion." Her voice dropped to a whisper. "Highness, it is Prince Aaren."

Gearld's mind spun. What calamity could possibly have befallen Greybeal, to bring its Prince and Palatine to his doorstep? What could it mean to Faires?

He gathered himself; whatever the causes, tradition now dictated his actions. He met Jenora's eyes and formally replied, "I do grant your plea, by the laws of our peoples. My ward is yours, and your companion's." He extended his hand and raised her up, still confused. "What do you here, m'Lady?"

She smiled wearily. "We thank you, Lord King. There is much to tell. But the most important thing is that no one else can know that the Prince is here. In Edge, they think him dead, and he must remain so until we know whom we can trust. And he is injured. Have you some place we might live, in secrecy, while his wound heals and we decide what we must do?"

Gearld thought for a moment. "Yes. One of our grain merchants was waylaid and killed by the Dark One last month. He had no family, so his house became property of the Crown. It lies near the northern wall, apart from nearly all its neighbors. You may hide there, and I will send you aid you can trust. Will that do?"

"Wonderfully, your Highness. Thank you. Can your man here guide us? I want the fewest people possible to know that anyone even arrived here tonight."

"I am sure he can. I'll speak to him, and find him a horse." Jenora remounted while Gearld sent Fenton to request a mount and a replacement sentry from the city patrol. She spoke quietly to Aaren, placing her hand on his arm as if to bolster him and keep him upright for a short time longer.

The guardsmen returned quickly, and in minutes, Gearld was alone in the street. He walked more slowly than before back to the Keep, where he rejoined his family at their meal, and sent a messenger to the healer Obra.

◆   ◆   ◆

The next morning, Jenora was awakened in her borrowed bed by a careful rapping on the house's rear door. When she opened it, she was greeted by Obra and, to her surprise, Sare, standing a few paces back and holding a large wicker basket. Obra greeted Jenora briefly and entered, but Sare hung back on the doorstep. "I begged Obra to let me come. Please let me stay, and see him. I really can help, you know."

Jenora stepped out and embraced her. "Stay and be welcome, Princess. It's so *good* to see you! If we trust anyone in Faires, you must know it is you. Come in, we'll wake him if Obra hasn't already."

They entered the solar room where Aaren was sitting, head bowed, on the bed Jenora and Fenton had moved there the night before. Obra was gently removing the bandage Jenora had roughly fashioned. She bent close to see the wound on the side of his head. "Hmm. It seems to be closing nicely. Lady Jenora must have cleaned it well."

"Yes, when she stopped the first night beside the river. I was still unconscious. When I came to myself, she said it had been more than a day since Malcomb struck me."

"There is much bruising, but I do not feel any softness to the bone beneath. How has your sense fared since you awoke?"

"My head aches, inside. Sometimes I grow very dizzy, and my ears ring. I fell from the horse once."

"I think I may be able to help with that." She turned and motioned Sare to come forward.

As she rummaged inside the basket, Aaren raised his head and saw who held it open. His face went white and completely still, as though he had received another blow to his skull. No word came from his open mouth, only a soft, indrawn gasp.

Jenora studied Sare. She could see the flash of hurt in the Princess' eyes, but none of the anger or bitterness of the spring. For a moment, she thought that Sare would turn and leave. But then the Prince slowly raised his hand and held it out to her, almost fearfully. And Sare took it, and sat beside him.

Aaren slowly drew back her sleeve, seeing the deep scarring all along her arm. He tentatively lifted his fingers to her face and brushed aside her strings of feathers, tracing the new damage, the lack of hair against his touch. His voice came hoarsely and barely audible. "I did this ... to you ... my fault..."

Sare nodded gravely, once. "I know. We understand now what you and I are to one another, what it means to use your power." She took his hand again and held it, waiting for his eyes to meet hers. After a long moment, they did. "And I *do* understand, Aaren. Everything."

Aaren bent his head again, and his words were muffled. "But how *can* you ... can you ... forgive ... ever forgive..."

Sare flung her arms about him, drawing him close. "Hush, love, I do. I do understand, and I do forgive you. I am well and healed, and now you must be too." For a moment he didn't respond, but finally she felt his tense shoulders loosen, and he embraced her in return, weeping.

Jenora stepped close and took Obra's arm. The old woman looked up, then at her two patients, and nodded. Without speaking, she and Jenora left them to begin a different kind of healing.

An hour later, Aaren lay down to rest again. Obra had him watch a pendant intently as she swung it for several minutes, murmuring in another tongue. When she finished, she reached out and closed the lids over his staring, sightless eyes, and laid a small blue stone upon his forehead. His breathing was abnormally deep and regular, and he made no movement.

She rose and turned to Sare and Jenora. "He will sleep very deeply now, for all the day. When he wakes, his pain and giddy spells will have left him, and he will grow steadily stronger again." She smiled. "He will also be very hungry. We shall have to bring more food from the castle, Princess. And I am sure you will want to eat, and hear the story Lady Jenora told me over breakfast while you were - otherwise occupied, about how they come to be here and why. I shall leave you the key your father gave us to the back gate. Meet me tomorrow morn at the Keep's secret postern, and we will check on our invalid together. If he is as well as I expect him to be, he will need no more of *my* arts." She arched her eyebrow at Sare, who blushed and smiled.

Sare chided the old woman for her teasing as the three said their fond good-byes. She sat at the scullery table, while Jenora prepared some of the food they had brought, and told her about that astounding last night in Edge. When Sare had eaten and the story was done, they sat on, considering what should be done next.

"Queen Alyda should be told that he lives, and quickly," Sare said. "If what you tell me about her health is true, the blow of losing Aaren could mean her end."

"I agree, Princess. I would have sent word sooner, but I was alone, and had to see Aaren safe. Now that he is, I can see no reason why I shouldn't be able to return to Edge and speak to her secretly. I could always say I had been visiting my sister these past few days; Agnes and her husband would confirm that without asking why. No one knows that I killed Malcomb and saved Aaren, though some may wonder where Malcomb has gone. If I can resume my normal place at court, perhaps I can discover who it was tried to arrange Aaren's death."

"But who would want to kill Aaren? And why? Most of the people here in Faires are only too glad there will be a King on my father's throne when he leaves it, and glad as well for the alliance. Is it not the same in Edge?"

"A week ago, I would have said 'yes'. Now, I must wonder about the whos and the whys. It must be someone with something great to gain, to take so great a step. Perhaps even Dark Michael is behind it. All things may be more apparent when I am home, and can see how the land lies. But I will remain here a few days more, to be sure the Prince is safe and recovered."

A sudden thought came into Sare's mind: *But what about Cillistra? Should I not tell her, too, that Aaren lives?* She said nothing to Jenora; that decision was one she would have to make as a sister, and a Princess. It was not one her friend could help her make.

They talked on, of matters less consequential. Jenora asked Sare to try to acquire a fresh set of riding clothes that might fit the taller girl, for her return journey, and a change or two of clothing for Aaren as well. Sare told Jenora of Carola's approaching marriage to Lord Garret, a noble some years older who had courted her for several years. They washed the dishes together, and repacked the basket for Sare to take back to the Keep.

They checked on the sleeping Prince, finding him deep in the healing trance Obra had placed upon him. They talked some more, and finally lapsed into a friendly silence that went on for some minutes. Then Jenora rose and took Sare by the hand. "Now come out to the garden. You've asked me often enough to show you some warrior-craft, and there's no one around to see us practice. Let me show you a few things."

Sare readily agreed, and the two went out into the autumn sunshine. Jenora showed her three defensive counters she could learn quickly, against an overhand blow with knife or sword, against a choking attack from the front, and against a choke hold from behind. Sare practiced all three for over an hour, learning to block and throw Jenora to the grass from each angle, until she could react with the correct motion against any one of the three attacks without stopping to think first.

As Jenora picked herself up for the last time, she laughed. "How quickly you took to that! Are you sure you've never practiced these arts in secret? Should I be jealous of some man-at-arms for stealing my best friend?"

Sare blushed. "No, no, I assure you, this is my first attempt. Who but you would teach me, and not be afraid of hurting me? No, it's just as if … you've shown me how to tap into some strength inside of me that I never knew was there. It's a wonderful feeling; is that how it is for you? I want … I want to thank you."

Jenora hugged her. "You've always been the strong one, Princess, the strongest woman I've ever known. And I'll always be your friend, and thank you for being mine. How much longer can you be gone from the Keep?"

Sare glanced at a nearby sundial. "You're right to ask, I should be back soon. My father will want to know how I have found you both. And people might wonder where I've gone. I have less time alone now than I did when you first came. It seems that I'm … watched over more since I was hurt so near to death. Even my sisters attend to me more often than they did, as if they're afraid I'll burn so badly again when I'm alone, with no Obra to save my life. But I'll come back with her tomorrow. No one questions my going out with her; I've been doing it since I was small, to learn her healing skills. After that, I'll just have to slip away whenever I can. I'll come as often as I can, I promise."

Jenora saw her out through the garden gate, and heard her lock it from the outside. She went back into the house, smiling as she rubbed gently at a bruise on her shoulder. *Well done, Princess. Perhaps next time we should try swords!*

◆   ◆   ◆

Aaren was awake and alert when Obra and Sare arrived the next morning. He reported that his head no longer pained him, and insisted on going out into the garden after Obra changed the dressing on his injury. The sun beamed down upon him, mitigating the pallor of his face and seeming to lend him strength. He ate ravenously when food was prepared, until Obra had to warn him not to task himself too much. She left soon after, pronouncing him fit enough and well on the road to his full health.

Sare kept him in the garden when Obra was gone, and drew him down beside her on a shaded bench, and smiled at him. "You look almost like one of the Dark One's bandits, with that strip around your head. You know Jenora will be leaving soon, in the next few days. What would you have her tell your mother?"

"Only that I am alive and safe. Not where I am, I think. If she knew ... I can't say for certain, but it might be too easy for someone to learn that from her. My mother has never been a strong person, and since my father died..."

Sare nodded. "Jenora and I agree, but we wanted to know if you felt the same way. And now, another matter, if you're up to considering it: My father wanted me to ask you what you plan to do if Jenora can learn who's behind the attempt on your life."

Aaren reflected for some while before answering. "I know what I *should* do. I will be of age in the spring; I should then strike back, return to Edge and take my rightful throne, and punish the person responsible. That is what a King would do, what my father would want me to do. But now..." He lifted her hand, still clasped in his. "Now, I can't say that is what I *want* to do. Think of this:

If I am no longer King of Edge, then am I still bound to wed your sister?"

Sare's mind raced, bedazzled by such an idea. *We could go to Alatia, or even Seahale... But do I trust him? I know how impetuous he can be... And he has burned me all my life, nearly killed me, by carelessly using his power... But even this last time, he was not sure he would hurt me, we both only wondered... And we could be together, where no one knew us except as who we say we are...* She closed her eyes, and took a deep breath. As much as she ached to follow that path... "But what about Jenora, and your mother? Could you just leave them that way?"

He was surprised to find that he didn't need to ask what she meant; their minds had worked together, reaching the same point at the same time. He sighed. "And what of Edge?" he said. "I know. How could I leave my country to whatever fate awaits her, to whatever plan these plotters might devise? I spoke from my heart without my head, as Jen has always counseled me not to. Forgive me yet again, if you can."

Sare dropped her gaze, and asked, almost under her breath, "Would you ... wish to be free of your betrothal? If you were free, would you - would you still want me?"

Aaren's reply was not in words. When he let her go, both were breathless, and stared at each other in wonderment. He spoke first, through kiss-swollen lips. "I would want you for all my life. I feel as if I will *have* no life, without you. However we were bound by fire from birth, for good or for evil, I know *you* now. I love *you*, and that is the bond we have now. I swear that I will never - hurt you - again. I swear it on my life!"

Sare looked into his eyes, green peering into blue, for a long time. "I believe you," she whispered.

They sat, holding each other close, on into the afternoon, saying small things or nothing at all, knowing the time for other, greater decisions would come. But not yet.

Chapter 24
Alyda

When Jenora rode into Edge, the city was adorned in mourning. Every building dangled its black pennon or hangings, and many of the smaller businesses were closed and dark. She had expected this, and taken care to blend in. Around the sleeve of the shirt Sare had lent her (Cillistra's, as were the riding pants she wore), she bore a simple black band.

As she rode through the streets, she passed few people, and fewer still who recognized her. Without exception, all these watched her pass with expressions of mute sympathy.

When she reached the palace, the guardsmen admitted her with few words and similar looks. She handed Canticle off to an equerry in the courtyard, and entered at the Hall of Portraits. As expected, each of the old Kings was draped in black.

Wildon stepped out of the throne room as she approached it, and stopped when he saw her. "Lady Jenora! I am ... surprised to see you here. When you vanished, the same night that the Prince... Well, we could not help but wonder, and worry, if some evil fate had also come to you." It was almost, but not quite, a question.

Jenora answered him coolly, with just the right hint of sadness. "I was outside the palace when the fire began. I came back only in time to be told where it struck, and whom, by someone who had been inside. In my grief, I thought only to go home, and be comforted by my sister and her family. I am sorry if I caused anyone worry, especially the Queen. May I see her? I wish so much to reassure her that I am well."

Wildon's sympathetic smile slipped only a tiny fraction. "I am sorry to say, no, she cannot receive you now. This great loss, coming so soon after the last, has left her inconsolable and drained her even further. For a few days, we even feared for her life. She is confined to her bed, and only Vernor sees her for now. Mayhap next week she will be improved, but ..." He let the idea trail off into uncertainty.

"I understand. If you see Vernor before I do, please tell him that I wish to see her soon, would you. And now, I believe I should visit Master Leland."

"Of course. And be certain that I shall deliver your message." The Hawk strode off down the hall without looking back.

Jenora continued on as if going to the practice fields, but turned at the next corridor and climbed the stairs to the highest floor. She went down that hallway and stopped before a narrow window. Opening it, she leaned as far outside as was safe. Years ago, she had learned that by doing so, she could look through the window set in the next wing of Greybeal, into Queen Alyda's bedchamber and see if the Queen was in, or abed.

Today the bed was empty. Jenora was about to withdraw and close the window when the Queen stepped into view. She was dressed as if for bed, with a light robe over her nightdress, but she was broad awake, pacing the floor and wringing her hands. She stopped beside her nightstand and lifted a bound book, then slapped it back down and resumed her pacing.

Confined to her bed, Jenora thought as she closed the window. *Appears more like confined to her chambers. Well, wait until tonight, Lord Wildon.*

It was dark out on the roof of the palace, but there was just enough moonlight for Jenora to pick her way along very carefully. She hesitated when she reached the angle between the wings, and felt her way around it until she was again sure of her footing and destination. When she stopped, she was directly over the Queen's window she had looked through earlier in the day.

She uncoiled the rope from her waist and tied it securely to the corbel just below the roof's overhang. This would be the tricky part, much more so than climbing up from the corridor window had been. *Ah well, just like one of Leland's wall-scaling exercises.* After knotting two loops into the rope, one hooked around her left elbow and the other her left wrist, she carefully hung by her hands from the edge, placed her feet against the wall, and began letting the slack of the rope out slowly.

When she reached the Queen's second-story window, she planted her knees on its ledge and drew a thin dagger from her boot. It was only a moment's work to slip the simple lock once she'd inserted the dagger through the mortise. She straightened her legs, suspended again between her feet and the tautened rope, and swung the window open. In seconds, she was inside.

As she slipped the loops from her arm, she could hear the Queen's soft breathing from the bed in the corner. She crossed the space and stood over the bed, looking upon the older woman in the glow from the dying fire across the room. *Forgive my stealth, your Highness, but this was not to be delivered openly. I hope it will be a most welcome surprise to you.* She slipped a sealed letter from her blouse, and laid it very softly upon Alyda's sleeping bosom, then as quickly and silently as she came, went out the window and back up to the roof. In less than half an hour, she was between the sheets in her own chamber, smiling as she dropped into sleep.

◆   ◆   ◆

When Queen Alyda awoke and sat up in her bed, something white fell to the floor, catching the early-morning sunlight. She picked it up, and caught her breath when she recognized the seal that held it closed. Breaking the wax, she quickly unfolded the single page and read it with eager and disbelieving eyes.

Mother –

First, know that I am alive, and safe among friends whom I trust. The body found in my bed was the man who lit the fire and tried to kill me, the guardsman Malcomb. Jenora rescued me, and took us both to a place of safety.
Next, know that there can be no true safety for me, or possibly even for you or Jenora or our kingdom, until we discover and stop the person behind my "death." Therefore, I beg

you to keep secret the fact that I am alive, as you value my life. When the time comes, I will do what a King must do. But until then, please keep yourself safe and well. And remember that, no matter how difficult it may be to be a Prince, or a King, I will always be here for you.

Your loving son,
Aaren

Alyda read it through twice, as a great well of joy rose up in her, dispelling the empty darkness that had filled her heart for a week and more. *He lives!* She basked in the wonder of that joy for a long while. Then she stopped, and gave thought to the other part of his message, the still-present danger to both him and the kingdom.

He was right; she must keep his life a secret for now, and not let her happiness show to betray him. Beyond that, what could she do to help him, to hasten his return home?

Perhaps I could learn more if I behaved more like a Queen, instead of – her mouth turned down wryly – *instead of a broken-hearted old widow!* She rose from her bed, read the letter once more, and reluctantly thrust it into the coals of last night's fire, watching as it flared and was consumed. Then she pulled on her bell-rope. When her chambermaid appeared, she seemed surprised to see the Queen up and about so early – and issuing such crisp, sure commands. "Build up this fire, and draw me a bath. Then bring me my black velvet gown, the one with the ermine, and the robe that matches. And send a page to ask Lord Wildon if he would meet me in the throne room at his first convenience." The girl bustled about to obey, and Alyda stood looking out her window at the palace, and the city beyond, and the surrounding countryside. *Well, my son, if you are to come home and be King, then I can try to be a dowager Queen Mother to match you.*

✦   ✦   ✦

When Wildon entered the throne room, Alyda was already there and waiting for him, upright in her own high seat, dressed in finery and wearing her own diadem, with several lords and courtiers seated around the room. *Gods*, he thought, *she looks every inch the Queen. What's happened to her?* He stopped before her and bowed. "Your Highness, I am pleased to see you looking so well."

Alyda stood and stepped down to take his left hand. "Lord Wildon, I wish to thank you personally, from my heart, for all that you have done for me and for the kingdom since King Trever's death. Without you, I do not doubt that neither Edge nor I would have come through this awful time nearly as well. Know that I - that all of us - are deeply grateful to you, and that whatever boon we can ever grant you is yours for the asking."

Wildon felt the floor shift beneath him, and realized that the reeling was inside his own head. "My Queen ... I - I thank you, gratefully, but ... but are you dismissing me from your service, or ..."

Alyda released his hand and smiled. "Oh, no! Nothing of the sort. I will rely on your strength and judgment as much as ever. No, I have simply decided to resume my duties as Queen. I have mourned my husband and - and my son - enough for now. Edge needs to see that the Crown still stands, that even if the Telcien line is ended, the monarchy will continue. Next spring, I will convene a Council of Regents to choose a successor for me, when my time comes. Until then, I think it very important to show the people that they have a royal house they can still depend upon, don't you agree?"

"Yes, yes I see that. But your Highness, do you truly think you are ... ready to do this? So soon after the Prince's tragic accident –"

"My son's death was not an accident." Her voice and her eyes had a touch of flint beneath them, something he had rarely seen since the day Aaren was born. "Lord Wildon, that will be one of the first duties I charge you with: discover how Prince Aaren died, and why, and at whose behest. We must know, and bring this plot to light and justice, as soon as it can be done."

Wildon drew himself up and purposefully hardened his features, reining in the turbulence in his head. This might not, after all, be so hard to deal with. She had in fact given him just the leverage he needed to turn this debacle aside before it got entirely out of hand. He raised his voice so as to be clearly heard by all in attendance. "Plot, m'Lady? Surely you cannot mean that. Who could plan and carry out the deliberate murder of the Prince? And to what purpose? Do you actually believe that there could be such intrigues going on in this court? Perhaps your thoughts have become confused. Consider carefully what you are saying, your Majesty. Loose ideas can be extremely ... dangerous."

Alyda's voice became more strident. "I am speaking of danger, Lord Wildon. Danger to the kingdom itself. My own life – or even yours – could be endangered." She looked into his face more intently, as though trying to peer past his eyes and his words, deeper into what lay behind them. "Until we know the names and causes behind all this, nothing, and none of us, is safe."

He shook his head, and permitted himself an expression of mingled bafflement and pity. "My Queen, it grieves me to hear this. I had thought you recovering, coming back to yourself and to Edge, but ..." He went to the doors, and called out them, and stood aside as two guardsmen entered. He kept them standing by while the Queen's personal attendant was summoned, all the while watching Alyda and daring her to speak. When the woman arrived, he turned his back to Alyda and spoke only to the three others. "I am saddened to say, the Queen's grief has unsettled her mind. She must be returned to her chambers immediately, and there made comfortable again."

"My *mind!*" Alyda strode toward him, her voice rising. "I have never thought so clearly! Lord Wildon, you forget yourself. My son was murdered. How can you, or anyone, deny it?"

Wildon turned back to her. "Your Highness, we understand how strongly you feel your loss. But all the world knows that Prince Aaren died by some evil happenstance, nothing more. To say otherwise is foolish, and endangers the peace we've worked for so hard."

"How can there be peace while someone schemes and kills at will, even against the Crown? All our lives may be threatened!" She was nearly shrieking at him now. She knew that she had lost control of the situation, but felt powerless to control her anger. She had never liked or trusted Wildon. "There *was* a plot to kill Aaren, I tell you! Someone wished him dead, and gone from me! It may be that you, of all men, know more –"

"Enough! This is madness!" In the silence following Wildon's shout, everyone in the room stared at the

Queen, at her upraised fists and reddened face. She dropped her hands and stood still as death.

Wildon softened his tone, making it reasonable and cajoling. "I am sorry for what we must do, your Majesty, but we do it for love, and for thought of your safety." He looked carefully into the faces of his witnesses, and saw there what he wished to see. "Take her, please. Gently."

Alyda stood aghast. She, too, could see his triumph in the faces about her; there was no help for her there. Straightening to her full height and swinging her ermined robe more tightly about her, she stalked from the hall, followed by her servant.

Wildon stopped the guards as they prepared to follow. "Watch over her carefully. All her needs are to be attended to, and everything done for her comfort. But she is not to leave her rooms, and no one is to visit her without my permission. She must be kept safe."

When he was alone again, he stepped up onto the dais and stood beside the throne that had been Trever's, lost in thought and smiling to himself. *I believe we may indeed call a Council into session – and sooner than next spring.*

Chapter 25
Assassin

The eldest princess stepped carefully in the darkness, picking her way through the brush and long grass along the river's edge. She took another sip from her flask and tucked it into her skirt pocket. There was enough moonlight to see her way without much danger, though she had to lift her skirts above the blackberry vines and their thorns. The silvery light transfigured all the mundane things of her world, making the stones and the trees and the rushing water things of magic. This, and the thought of her destination, brought her a smile and a growing warmth inside, and quickened her breathing and her pace.

When she found the tall bush of holly, she held it aside with a fold of her cape protecting her hand. She felt the familiar prickling of its spines along her back as she slipped past.

The small clearing beyond was empty. Nothing moved among the shadows of the sheltering trees. She looked carefully around with a growing annoyance. *He's not here, the cur!* She stamped her foot.

A black shape slid out of a corner only a few feet away, appearing from the darkness itself as if summoned by her footfall. She gasped and jumped back as a hand grasped her wrist.

"Ah! Your heart quickens at my touch. Just as it should." There was no mistaking the deep, mellifluous voice.

"You *beast*." Cillistra lifted her hand, and Michael easily stopped it short of his face. "You nearly killed me with fright! Why were you hiding from me?"

He chuckled and took her in his arms. "I had to be sure you were alone. After all, it wouldn't do for some sorry man-at-arms to find us together, would it? Then some - accident? - might have to befall him."

For just an instant, she pulled away from him, uneasy at such callous talk. Things had been different after that night in the mountain; they were tied together now more strongly than ever before. In a very real way, she knew she now carried a part of him inside of her. Michael had even, it seemed to her, altered his methods somewhat, and was not as quick to solve his problems with killing. Though perhaps that was just her wishing it to be true. In any case, she felt she understood his position much better than she had. She was a far different person than the haughty, naive princess he had wooed the year before. She felt that she understood some of the necessity for change, even violent change, if their dreams were to be realized.

The death of Aaren had been a wonderful stroke of good luck. She was sure, she quickly told herself, that Michael felt as fortunate as she did about that un-foreseen tragedy and its advantageous effect on their plans. Why, in a few more months she could drop the guise of grieving fiancée and begin openly seeing "John Winters" again.

But his hands were already touching her, moving over her with power and possession, setting her flesh alight where they passed and lowering a dim blanket of longing over her mind. As his lips came to her own, she sank weightlessly into the grass and the darkness.

Some time later, as they lay amid crushed cowslips and scattered garments, she felt his beard tickle her ear when he whispered, "I have news. Something you may not wish to hear."

She rose up languidly, resting her arms on his chest. "What sort of bad news?"

"Things have changed again. Your fine fiancé, the Prince, is still alive."

Cillistra sat up. "Aaren? Alive? How could he be?"

"I don't know how." Michael glowered. "But it seems your father and your youngest sister are keeping him safely penned right here in the city, in a house on the north side."

"My sister? That's ridiculous. Sare has no gift for secrecy. And how could you possibly know?"

In the moonlight Michael's face tautened. "I know because I have eyes that see for me throughout Faires. Some of them are not ... noticeable even to people who are on their guard. And they follow and watch over every member of your family everywhere, at all times. So I can assure you, he is alive, and your sister aids him. He was injured when he arrived, you see."

Cillistra could scarcely believe it. "You have us followed? You watch us - even me?"

He laughed. "Most especially you, minnow. You're more slippery than the rest, and more dear to my heart. I wouldn't ever want anything to happen to you." He was silent a moment. "You can see that this changes everything. If Aaren is alive, then you are still betrothed, and all our plans are for naught. We were so near to being able to meet openly, and then marry, even such a short time after his death, and now we are no better off than we were a year ago. But there are things we can do to change that unhappiness."

Her mind raced, and the images it produced were frightful. Surely he could not be about to suggest what she imagined. "What sort of 'things'?"

Michael sat upright and pulled her close. "The only people in Faires who know that he lives are the King, your sister, and old Obra - and a city guard who may suspect Aaren's identity, but cannot be sure. If the Prince were to disappear, only they would miss him. And if he disappeared without a trace, where could they turn? They could only question each other, to no avail. Leaving us free to continue our lives as we wish, and to one day unite the kingdoms, with no obstacles. But for such a task, I would require someone that I trust as much as myself."

She stared at him. "You are asking me to kill him." She said it flatly, as an unadorned and unblinking fact.

Michael's voice grew soft and cold. His eyes were as dark as the sky under which they met. "I told you when you learned who I am that I must sometimes do hard things to win my way in this world. This is such a time. If you and I are to be together, ever, the Prince must be gone. I can remove the body, with your help, but I cannot reach him. He is watched over; the house is guarded by men who know not why they are posted there. My Shadow could fight his way past them, but that would cast off all secrecy. No stranger would be admitted near him, neither by your sister nor Obra, nor especially by Aaren himself. But you are of the royal house, and can go where you please. He might be surprised if you came to him, but he would not fear you. If you were found near the place, no one would question you. And his Palatine is away from him now, home in Edge. If she returns too soon, it will be much more difficult."

She pondered this, her thoughts a whirl of conflict. *Could it come to this? Could this be what I agreed to, that night? If I do not, what then? Could I live without what I have here, now, beside me?* She looked into his eyes, and saw the stars dimly reflected there.

When he spoke again, it was barely above a whisper, as though the same thought had struck him with pain. "Only you can set yourself free, my love. Set us free."

She closed her mind, closed her eyes, and touched his face. "I - will."

The next evening, just at dusk, Cillistra was watching when Sare left the Keep carrying a basket much like Obra's, but one that Cillistra knew was full of food. She had been watching earlier too, when Sare filled it in the kitchens.

In moments, she was out the postern herself, following her sister through the streets. Sare took no particular care to see that she was not followed; obviously she had made this visit very often, and never seen any reason for genuine stealth. She grew more cautious as she approached the isolated house, but Cillistra merely lagged farther behind and stepped into the nearest concealment whenever Sare looked around.

She was in position to see clearly when Sare unlocked the rear gate in the wall surrounding the house, and went through without pausing to lock it again.

Cillistra slipped into the garden the instant she heard the house door close behind her sister. She cast about quickly in the fading daylight, and found a hiding place between a bench and a tree it stood near. Her heart and breathing were much faster than her darting movements warranted; her emotions throbbed along in time, at high key.

"It must be done after dark, the moment Princess Sare leaves," Michael had told her. "I will be waiting at the back gate just after moonrise. The guards are ever only posted at the front. Admit me when you are done, and I will bring help along to dispose of ... all our troubles." *Meaning Aaren's corpse,* she thought, and touched the long dagger on her belt. *If being John Winters so long has made my love too fond of euphemisms, at least I can look directly at what is real. I have come to kill my betrothed, the Prince and rightful King of Edge. I know what I shall do, and why I must. I've come through a sleepless night, and far too many hours of troubling my soul today, to look away now.* She settled into the narrow space as comfortably as possible, to wait.

Darkness descended slowly, and she saw lights kindled inside the house. It was the earliest part of autumn, and the night was pleasantly warm. She sipped from her flask - not too much, just enough to settle her nerves. Soon crickets began chirring from the garden's secluded corners. The warmth and the sounds were soothing, quieting even thoughts as turbulent as Cillistra's. Soon, without knowing it, she closed her eyes. Minutes later, she was asleep.

She opened her eyes to see the full moon shining down into them. Springing up with a jolt, she struck her shoulder against the bench and fell back against the tree. *The moon! Michael has been waiting for – Gifter knows how long! Perhaps hours!* The enormous tension in which she had built her resolve to do murder was heightened by the disorientation of abrupt awakening from sleep. She peered around the broad tree trunk. No lamplights showed in the house; all was still. Sare must have left some time ago. With rising panic, she darted across the lawn to the door. It was unlocked. She entered, pulse racing, drew the knife and paused to let her sight adjust itself.

The moonlight shone through a pair of long windows on one wall, illuminating a large room with two doors on its opposite side. As she took her first tentative step into the room, one of the doors opened and a figure emerged. *Aaren! It must be now!* Raising the dagger, she charged.

✦   ✦   ✦

When they had finished the dinner she had brought, Sare and Aaren cleaned the dishes and the kitchen, then retired to the solar and played several games of Quoins. After Sare won – for the fourth time – Aaren put the playing cards back into their slipcase and set them aside. "There's no defeating your luck tonight. I won't try anymore. It's getting dark, so I suppose I should see you safely on your way home."

Sare smiled enigmatically. "Your own luck isn't so bad as all that, tonight. I have a small surprise for you, if you're polite enough."

He raised his eyebrows. "Really? And have I been well-bred enough to meet your high standards, m'Lady? You know that I love surprises."

"Just barely enough." She took his hand. "You know that everyone in the Keep is bustling around, preparing for Carola's wedding. They're all much too busy to keep track of my whereabouts. I'm certain that if I were to stay away for a few more hours, absolutely no one would even notice. So if you like..." She glanced down, suddenly unable to meet his eyes. "... I could stay with you for a while." A faint blush arose from her neck into her scarred cheeks.

"If I like? Love, if your meaning is what I think it is..."

She quickly shook her head, still looking down. "Oh. No, I'm sorry, but I don't mean quite - that. It's too soon; we're not sure what's going to happen to us, are we? And because of my sister, and things in Edge, your mother ... it just wouldn't feel - right, would it? And besides, I truly don't know if I am ... capable." She blushed again, this time furiously carmine. "No, I only meant that I could sleep here beside you, for a few hours, if you want me to."

Aaren reached out and gently raised her chin until he could look into her green eyes, his tone completely serious. "I would like nothing better than to sleep with you beside me, for as long as you can stay." He stood up smiling, stretched his arms wide, and gave an exaggerated yawn. "In fact, I was just thinking that I would turn in as soon as you left."

Sare stood too, and laughed. "Then don't allow me to keep you up any later, please." She sat on his bed while he closed the door. He sat beside her, took off his boots and jerkin, and lay back.

She looked down at him. "Do you usually sleep in your shirt and breeches?"

"No. But it seemed ... safer. And what do *you* plan to sleep in?"

She blew out the lamps, stretched beside him and laid her head on his chest. "Just as I am. I don't want to have to wrestle back into this dress when I leave; I might wake you. And you're right, it's safer this way."

His arm drew her close, and he kissed her. "Very considerate. Thank you. Do you want a blanket?"

"No. You're warm enough." She turned onto her side and snuggled back closer against him, drawing his arm over her and clasping his hand.

Aaren kissed the nape of her neck and flexed his knees up behind hers. He smiled, remembering a campfire years ago.

Sare whispered, "What are you thinking of?"

Aaren started. "Well, actually I was thinking of Jenora."

Sare thought on this. "Do you love her?"

"Of course," he replied. "But not like that. She is my Palatine, and my truest friend. We never – well, once –"

"Once what?" Sare turned back to face him.

Aaren frowned. "I have known her nearly all my life. We have had years to grow close to each other. But the love I feel for you is so different, so powerful. I do not feel that way for her, nor she for me."

Sare believed him about his own feelings, but knew that his brave Palatine might not have the same heart, though Jenora would never admit it. Sare reached up and touched his cheek. "It's all right, my love. I'm not jealous. I know your love for me as I know my own for you. But you still haven't answered my question."

Aaren hesitated. "It was nothing, really. One time a few years ago we kissed, and then, well, I held her much as I held you a moment ago. Nothing more, and the following day we agreed that it had been childish, and not to think on it again."

Did you indeed agree to that? Sare wondered. *And how many nights has Jenora thought back on it with pain?* She ached for her warrior friend, and marveled at Jenora's bravery and loyalty. She rolled over again and pulled his arm close. She bent her neck and kissed the fingers she could reach. She pressed his hand more tightly into herself, and smiled. "Good night, my darling."

"Good night, love."

When Sare awoke, the moon gleamed in through the solar's windows. Aaren had turned over in his sleep sometime, because he lay on his back beside her, breathing deeply. Relieved at not having to disentangle herself or wake him, she carefully rolled off the bed to her feet. It was only a few steps to the door, which she could see clearly in the moon's light. As quietly as she could, she opened it and stepped through. The instant she closed it, she heard the shuffle of feet coming at her across the floor.

She stepped forward, seeing the dark form lunging, its upraised arm stabbing down at her. Without thinking, she caught the falling wrist, turned into the body behind it, and swung it down and around with a strength that surprised her, sweeping the body across her hip and sending it to the carpet with a heavy thud. She heard a small object clatter off a table leg nearby.

She backed away, her hands raised to ward off another attack. *Just as Jenora showed me!* she thought with a touch of pride. When she bumped up against the fireplace, she quickly felt along the mantle for the lamp and spills kept there.

The figure on the floor was slowly getting to its feet. Sare lit the spill against a glowing ember and managed to light the lamp, blinking in its glare, before her opponent could fully rise. In the sudden, guttering light, she found herself looking into her sister's face.

Both could only stand transfixed and wonder. The question between them went unasked - "What are *you* doing here?" - because neither could bring herself to ask it first. Finally Sare spoke up. "I stayed to see him off to sleep." Cillistra just stared at her, a strange, wild look in her eyes, laced with disbelief. Sare couldn't hold back her secret from her sister any longer. "This is going to sound mad, but I love him, Cill, I truly do. I have ever since I first met him. I'm so sorry if that hurts you, but I can't help it. And -" she swallowed "- and he loves me, too. I don't know what you want to do, what you want *me* to do, but I guess we have to talk." Cillistra's look hadn't changed, and she was still breathing heavily. Sare rushed on, "You *can't* tell Mother and Father, not yet, there's so much more at stake than just us, you know."

Cillistra tightened her lips and said nothing, but sidestepped, trying to brush past her sister and stalk out. Sare caught her arm and swung her around. "You can't just leave! We have to talk about this!" They scuffled for a moment, tugging back and forth. "Did you follow me here? Did you -"

Sare stopped; her foot had struck something on the floor and sent it skittering into the circle of lamplight. She looked down, then bent and picked up the dagger. When she looked up, Cillistra's face was ashen-pale.

"What was this for? Oh, Cill, you couldn't! Did you really mean to - to hurt us? Does he mean that much to you? You've never said so, I've always thought you were marrying him because it was agreed, because it was best for Faires, not because you loved him! I thought you loved John! Please, *please*, tell me! Would you really have used this?"

Cillistra was silent a moment longer, her face twisting through several emotions. When she spoke, her tone was brusque, but mocking. "Yes. I came here to kill him, but not for the reasons you think. Hear it all, if you must! I never loved ... that *boy*. I love the wisest, mightiest man in all the world. Yes, John Winters, as you know him, or think you do. But he is not some simple merchant. He is Michael, the Dark One himself, and he will rule all this land! And he wants *me*! For that to be, your foolish Telcien princeling must die. So I came to kill him, in his sleep, if I could. But you, you *stopped* me." She sounded amazed. "Have you learned warrior's ways now?"

Sare was dumbfounded, but found the constancy to raise her head proudly and say, "Yes, I have. Enough to hurt you if you try again. I won't let you near him, Cill. I mean it." To accent the point, and bolster her own resolve, she raised the hand that held the knife.

Cillistra stared back at her with disbelieving eyes, and broke into a bitter laugh. "Well, then I shan't try again. I'm leaving, leaving here and leaving Faires. I have better things waiting for me. Keep your hot-faced Prince. Keep the kingdoms, too - if you can! Be Queen, and have a long and happy life together - if you can! Raise yourselves an army of stammering, whey-faced brats!" Tears welled, but did not fall from her sparkling eyes.

And she was gone, with a rush of air and a slamming door. Sare dropped the dagger and heard the door behind her open as tears began to spill from her own eyes. "You're the brat," she whispered, then turned into Aaren's uncomprehending arms and began to sob.

◆   ◆   ◆

Cillistra passed through the garden thinking only, *Michael is waiting.* The thought gave her a shiver of dawning fear. *How angry will he be? Well, he has me now, for good or ill. And if he won't take me away with him, I'll – I'll leave alone!*

She stepped through the gate. Immediately, a hand was at her elbow and Michael's voice was in her ear, fluid and ironic. "Why so long, minnow? Did the Prince actually put up a fight?" She could hear his anger as well, barely held in check. She tried to shake her arm free, and his fingers clenched tighter.

"No, but my sister did. And ... the Prince still lives. We must leave here quickly. I will tell you what happened as soon as we're safe."

His free hand caught her left shoulder and held her motionless, facing him. His fingers lightly caressed her throat. "You will tell me what happened *now*." The irony was gone from his tone, the anger more evident.

"Sare never left. I tried to go in and do it, to kill him for you; for us." She stopped, shaking her head in wonder. "She's fallen in love with him. We fought, and it came down to killing her or leaving. We argued, and I told her that she could keep the bastard." Her eyes flashed in the moonlight. "I told her I had the only man worth having in this miserable kingdom, John Winters, the Dark One, and that she was free to rot in hell with her Telcien swine."

He leaned close, so that their faces almost touched, and she could see the death rising beneath his black brows. "You told her *what?*"

Somewhere, she found a courage she had never tapped within herself, and was able to reply. "I agreed to kill for you, and I tried. I agreed because I love you. I failed because I love my sister. If you must kill me for that, then do it, quickly, before I can be afraid. But if you ever loved me, then we can go, now, and make our own lives. Do you need to be John Winters any longer? What do you need with Faires' royal house anymore? Are you not strong enough to come and take the city, whenever you please? Let us go, and be done with all of them!"

For a moment Michael's hand tightened, cutting short her breath. Then it relaxed, his gaze softened, and to her surprise, he kissed her deeply and with passion. When he drew back, he was grinning in the moonlight. "I knew I had chosen the right woman! Yes, we will go, and all that I achieve will be yours. But first, I have another solution to your ... indiscretion."

He motioned with one hand. Something moved out of the darkness across the narrow street, something the size and shape of a large man. Silvery mail on its arms and legs reflected the silvery light as it came closer. It had a man's face, but like the face of a corpse: loose, expressionless, grey as death, with unblinking, dead-white eyes. She knew that if Michael sent his Shadow into the house, the two lovers would be dead in moments.

It stood before them, oblivious to her presence, attending only to Michael. It was slack as the loosened string of a bow, a weapon waiting to be used, to which idleness had no meaning. Michael began to make a gesture toward the house.

"No!" Cillistra put one hand against Michael's chest, the other against the golem's. Both were hard, and dark, and strong. Both halted at her touch, their gazes riveted to her.

"Do not do this. She is my sister. I cannot just let you kill her! Please, my love, can't we just go, away from here and out of this city? I beg you!"

At the mention of her sibling both figures took a half-step back, eerily in unison. Cillistra followed. She had never been afraid of the golem; somehow it was a part of her lover that she couldn't fear, or hate, no matter its actions on Michael's behalf. She stood, her hands flat against them, suddenly overwhelmed by a sense of wild joy. It wasn't the blast of pleasure that she sometimes got (and secretly wondered if it was caused by Michael). It was a sense of letting go, an abiding love for them both, for it seemed to her that they were almost the same person. Live or die, tonight she had made her decision, and she had chosen Michael. The feeling seemed to course through her hands and into them. Michael and the golem took another of those strange half-steps backward. Again Cillistra followed, never taking her hands away or her eyes from Michael's. The three stood, swaying, in the darkness and the moonlight.

Finally, nodding, Michael stepped forward into her arms. They stood together for a long time. The sounds of movement inside the wall galvanized them to turn away from the cottage. Michael gestured to his Shadow. It turned as though on wheels and followed them down the street and away.

Chapter 26
Weddings

When Jenora rode into Faires, the city was adorned in celebration. Even more than on the occasion of her first visit, its apparel was splendid with gaiety. Every building sported Fairen flags; every flowerpot held sprigs of yellow broom. It took her a few minutes to remember that broom figured in Lord Garret's family crest. The roadside firepots were smoking away, mingling green and white smoke with yellow. Banners and streamers linked building with building along the main road, all the way to the Keep. Each bore the traditional Fairen symbol for a marriage, two linked rings against a scarlet chalice.

The guards who admitted her through the main gate were dressed in full armor, gleaming with fresh polish, and each wore a loop of green-and-white braid at his shoulder. The stableboys were in their finery again, and their domain was already crowded with strange horses and carriages, arrayed with unfamiliar coats-of-arms.

When she entered the Keep, she found many more faces than usual turned her way, and recognized far

274

fewer of them. With Princess Carola's wedding only two days away, obviously many of the attendees had chosen to arrive early. *Give them their due; I would leave home early too, if I had to travel far in the fall. But I bet they're eating King Gearld's larders empty already.*

She waded through the bustle of servants and guests, and waited for several minutes in the King's antechamber while a page announced her and awaited Gearld's reply. When she was finally allowed in, she was astounded to find Aaren and Sare inside with the King and Queen Signe.

Seeing the concern on her face, Aaren spoke up. "Don't worry, I slipped in here hooded and cloaked, pretending to be some wedding guest from Qualls. It's so busy around here, no one even noticed me." The other three each greeted her warmly, and saw her settled into a chair beside Aaren. He looked to Gearld for permission to speak first, and received a nod. "So, Palatine, how did you find Edge? And how is my mother?"

"I have answers for both questions, and the news I've brought back may answer many more besides. In brief, your mother the Queen is well, and knows now that you are, too. But I was never allowed to meet with her personally. She seemed to be nearly a prisoner when I arrived – I observed her briefly – and the next day, after I had delivered your letter, I heard that she held audience with Lord Wildon. By that afternoon, she was officially restricted to her chambers, and allowed no visitors whatever. They say she has become deranged; you won't believe the rumors I heard circulating before I left."

"You're certain she hasn't been harmed?" Aaren's voice held a dangerous note she had heard before.

"Yes, I was able to look in upon her later, the same way I did the first day. She is sound of body, at least. But that is not the greatest of my news. Hear me out, and see if your conclusions match my own.

"Less than a week later, the day before I left, Lord Wildon convened an emergency Council of Regents. He gathered as many major nobles as he could in such a short time, more than enough for a quorum. He announced that Queen Alyda was indeed of unsound mind, as a result of her double bereavement, and therefore unfit to rule. He asked them to judge his Regency, and if they found him fit, to name him King. And they agreed! I heard it was that weasel from the south riding, Becton, who urged his case most strongly.

"In any case, he has taken the power, and while I was packing my horse to return here, the announcement went about that he will be formally crowned after the Harvest Masque next month."

"Only five weeks from now," Aaren murmured. He was deep in thought, his face hollow under knitted brows. The others let the silence stand, doubtless considering the implications just as the Prince was.

After a few minutes, he lifted his head. "I agree, m'Lady, this answers many questions. It's clear now who wished me dead and out of his path to my throne. And I find it equally clear that I cannot allow him to succeed. We will discuss that in a short while. But we also have news for your ears. Things have also changed here in Faires." Again, he looked to King Gearld, who stood up and seemed to mull some weighty matter before he spoke.

"Cillistra is gone," Gearld said. "She left night before last, taking nothing but the clothes and jewelry she wore. And worse still, we know with whom she left: she has allied herself with the Dark One." He sighed. "My daughter ... consort to our greatest enemy."

Jenora sat back, overwhelmed. "Lord King ... how could..?"

He waved to Sare, and asked in a choked voice, "Tell her, please." As he turned his back, Signe went to him, slipping her arm about his waist.

Sare quickly told Jenora about Cillistra's visit to the safe-house, and everything that had been revealed in that awful moment. When she finished, the King and Queen had composed themselves and were seated again.

Aaren stood. "It seems that shock has compounded upon shock today, and none of us are much the better for it. But I have something to offer in the balance, and a favor to ask as well. Your Highnesses, will you hear me out?" Gearld looked up in surprise, and then nodded his assent.

"I have never spoken of this to you, because it was never my right to do so. I was bound by my duties as Prince, to both our realms. Now, because of all these upheavals, my bonds are loosed. Or at least -" he glanced at Sare "- are of a new kind. To be forthright: I fell in love with Princess Sare the first time ever I came here."

Gearld and Signe turned to stare at their daughter in astonishment. Sare looked up at them, nodded nervously, and then stared resolutely at the table in front of her. Jenora grinned.

Aaren continued, "I have had the great fortune to discover that she loves me in return, even when ... when I have given her reason to feel otherwise. While my betrothal to Princess Cillistra was so necessary to our lands, we could not act on our feelings. But now..." He stepped forward, and knelt before the King's chair. "Will you have our kingdoms joined in another, better manner than we planned? Will you have me for your son, and husband to your *youngest* daughter, in the eyes of the law and all the world? I have already asked Sare, and she has given me her answer, abiding on your consent. Will you consider it?"

Gearld looked from Aaren to Sare, then to Queen Signe, to find her eyes turning to meet his. Their gazes locked, and for some moments they sat while some communion passed silently between them. Signe raised her eyebrows as if to say, *Well, why not?* Gearld shook his head as if to clear it, sighed deeply, and turned his regard back to Aaren.

"I have often wondered what it would be like to have a son. Your betrothal to my eldest, and Carola's to Lord Garret, brought me the opportunity to know. When Cillistra left so horribly... But perhaps, indeed, the Gifter does his work in strange ways, beyond understanding. If you speak truth – and it seems my daughter concurs that you do – then her mother and I agree that we have no objection. Our nations deserve the peace this will bring us, and perhaps we all deserve it too." His hand came down with a clap on his chair-arm. "It will be done. But how can we set a date, with you still in hiding?"

Aaren tried, unsuccessfully, to rein in his smile. "I will not be in hiding much longer, I think. But you are right to ask, and I do want to be married before I deal with ... other matters. So I think it will have to be done in secret, and remain secret for a short while, until we can announce it to the kingdoms. And with that thought, I propose this: Why can it not be done now, while you have the clergy and all the preparations here in the Keep? Why not immediately after Princess Carola marries Lord Garret, the day after tomorrow?"

Another look passed between the King and Queen. Signe turned to Sare. "Daughter, would you wish it so? In secret, and in such seeming haste?"

Sare looked up levelly, her smile clear and untroubled. "I have already told the Prince that I would, if you consented. I ask for no other husband, and accord with his reasons for marrying secretly. I can think of no happier time to marry than on the day my sister does. Please, Mother, Father, let it be so."

Gearld stood, and raised Aaren up with him. He beckoned Sare to him, and clasped their hands together, a brighter smile lightening his face. "It will be. You two have brought some happiness back to one of my darkest days – notwithstanding the happiness I owe my middle daughter, whose wedding, at least, I can attend openly!" He hugged Sare, and shook Aaren's hand. "Now, my again-son-to-be, I seem to remember you said something about another favor to ask."

Aaren's face darkened for an instant, becoming almost grim. Then he shook his head and looked back evenly. "I don't want to dampen our better spirits now, but I have a usurper to contend with. Perhaps, with your leave, we can discuss it after the weddings."

Princess Carola's wedding day was one for even Fairens to remember. She was a resplendent bride, wreathed in linen and silk and cloth-of-gold, and the glow of love and happiness. Lord Garret was a groom to match her, in deep-blue velveteen trimmed with gold braid, his mustache sprucely trimmed and upturned by his immutable smile. When they exchanged rings and kissed, the chapel erupted in cheers that followed them both out the doors and across the courtyard to the great banquet hall. If there were any whispered discussions among the guests about Cillistra's absence, the noble couple never heard them.

Jugglers and musicians preceded them into the hall, and continued their entertainment while the army of servants began serving the first courses of the wedding feast. If anyone noticed that King Gearld and Queen Signe were not among the celebrating company at first, no audible comment on the fact arose. The revelry simply commenced without them.

The King and Queen, accompanied by Obra, were still in the chapel, behind doors now closed and protected by a pair of the most trusted guards.

The High Chaplain also stood unmoved from his place atop his step, waiting with folded hands as Gearld opened the door to the antechamber. If the cleric was surprised to see Aaren and Jenora come in to stand before him, he hid it well.

The outer doors opened a moment later, to close again behind Sare. Aaren regarded her with wonder as she crossed the floor and ascended the steps to his side.

She was dressed as he had never seen her, in a long gown of pale green silk, trimmed with ermine and embroidered with golden thread. There was gold tracery in her fine shoes as well, and in the lacework of her mantle and veil. The tiny shells and quills sewn into the velvet cape across her shoulders, a deeper green, echoed the golden tones with their own muted colors.

She stood with eyes lowered and took his hands. Behind them, Gearld broke the silence. "These are the two we spoke of yesterday, your Grace. We trust you to keep their secret, until all can be revealed to all, including yourself. Do you agree, now that you know their identities?"

The Chaplain cleared his throat and nodded. "I do. And if I may be bold, Sire, I can venture a guess to the need for secrecy. Very well." He shifted to more formal language. "Thou, Prince Aaren of Edge, and thou, Princess Sare of Faires, do thee come to be wed by our laws and the providence of the Gifter?"

Aaren leaned slightly closer to Sare and whispered in the same formal speech, "I have never seen thee so lovely as today. May I speak for us?" She nodded, and he drew himself up. "We do."

They knelt and dutifully answered the questions the Chaplain posed about their ages, their families' consent, and their lack of blood or legal ties that might prevent the marriage. He discoursed briefly about the need for felicity and fidelity in matrimony – exactly the same text he had spoken over Carola and Garret. Then he laid his hand atop their joined ones.

"Sare, Princess of Faires, and Aaren, Prince of Edge, shall thee be joined in wedlock, ever truthful, ever faithful, ever loving and kind, each to the other, as long as life abides in you both?"

Their voices made a joyful union: "We shall."

"Then rise, and exchange the rings that seal thy vows made here."

They stood, and Sare slid her ring onto Aaren's hand. It was gold, and bore an emerald that was almost the exact shade of her eyes. "Now and forever, my sole and beloved husband."

He drew forth his ring, also of gold and inlaid with pale chips of sapphire. He lifted her hand and slipped it over her finger, for once never seeing the scarring there. "For all the days I live, my sole and beloved wife."

The Chaplain laid his hand over theirs again. "Thee are man and wife. Be ever joyful, and let this bond never be broken." He stepped back and smiled. "Husband, know thy wife. Wife, know thy husband."

Carefully Aaren lifted Sare's veil, seeing only her smile and the joyous tears welling in her eyes as he bent to kiss her.

The witnesses applauded loudly, and swept the couple into their various embraces. Jenora struggled to find her voice as she clasped Aaren close. "My ... my King, I've never been so proud of you as today. Love her well, and know that you both have all my love, too." She turned away quickly to hug Sare.

After thanking the bishop and seeing him out, Gearld swept Aaren up like a bear, nearly off his feet, and then set him down. "Welcome, my son. Be good to her." He turned to begin separating Sare and Signe. "Come, m'Lady. All the gladness this wedding brings, we must take to the other feast before we are missed too long. We shall be festive enough for both, and see to it that you four are provided with all that our too-happy guests receive." He chuckled. "Enjoy yourselves as you should, as if we were with you. Obra, watch over them and serve them well. When the crowds begin to dwindle, we shall rejoin you and continue. Until then." He bowed low and formally, took Signe's hand in his elbow and marched from the room.

When Carola's reception was over, and Rodolpho was politely ushering the last guests to their rooms or to the gate, the royal party retired to private chambers, joining Aaren, Sare, and Jenora, Obra having turned in herself. Garret and Carola were amazed to see Aaren there and alive, but the story was soon told, with much weeping and hugging.

They were able to doff and loosen some of the more restrictive formal garb and have some quiet talk, joking and relaxing. When everyone was settled and the best wine was poured, Aaren rose to his feet.

"This will be the last of the toasts, I promise you." He laughed with the others, then continued. "I wish this last to be my thanks to you all, for all that I have found here in Faires. I thank you for the haven and the help you have given me when my need was great." He bowed slightly to King Gearld and Queen Signe. "I thank you for the love and comfort I've found, and pray to keep for all my life." He inclined his glass to Sare, who blushed and smiled. "And I thank you for the friends – and now family – who have come into my life." He bowed to Carola and Garret, and raised his glass. "May I treasure you all, always, as I do at this moment."

Everyone assented and drank. Aaren laid aside his goblet, and took Jenora's hand in his own. "And to the friend who has most sustained me, who saved my life and brought me here to you, who made all of this possible, I can give only..." He paused as his voice faltered. "... only my love, and my undying gratitude – and one thing more."

He turned and went to an oaken chest in the corner, and took from it a long parcel wrapped in blue silk. Coming back, he laid it in Jenora's hands. She looked him a question to which he only nodded, then quickly unwound the covering.

It was a sword. Sheathed in a gleaming scabbard chased with gold, its quillions were set with gems, and its pommel held a great ruby. Though not as large as the Rageblade, it was longer than most swords, with an extended, hand-and-a-half hilt bound in fine leather.

Amazed, Jenora drew its blade forth three handspans. It glistened in the lamplight as Aaren spoke. "For more than half my life you've been my shield and my blade, truer than steel and finer than gemstones. This was made by the greatest swordsmith in Faires. May it serve you as well and unfailingly as you have me, in the spirit whose name it wears." He pointed, and Jenora peered closely at the exposed forte. Engraved there in simple letters was the word FRIENDSHIP.

She slid it back as Aaren stepped forward and embraced her. "My Prince - my King - you've honored me. I promise to always use it with the same honor. Thank you."

When he stepped away, she could see, along with his love, a shadow of troubling in his eyes. "You will have reason to use it soon," he said. "In four weeks, we go home; back to Edge."

The silence this engendered was broken by Gearld, asking the questions they all would have asked: "So soon? How will you deal with Lord Wildon, if he has the backing Lady Oswin tells us he has?"

Aaren's smile was gone, replaced by an expression so serious he looked somehow older. "Two days ago, we talked of a favor I would ask of you. That favor is the linchpin of my plan: I ask you to provide me a force of men, picked from your own armies, to help me press my claim to my crown. It must be at your judgment, of course; I would never ask you to leave Faires' defenses weakened to tempt your enemies. Shall we discuss it now?"

The King furrowed his brow, speaking more to himself than to Aaren. "True enough, these are perilous days. Perhaps now more than ever, with the Dark One privy to -" He shook his head and looked up. "But he is in flight at this moment, and we are better forewarned against him than before. The only way I know to stand against him is to stand united." He considered for a moment more, then stood and laid his hand on Aaren's nearest shoulder. "I have today welcomed two sons to my family, you no less than Lord Garret," to whom he nodded. "What either of you would ask of me, I shall endeavor to do. Come to me tomorrow, and we will decide how best to see you to your throne, and finally bring peace to our lands."

Aaren smiled again and nodded, and pressed his hand over the King's.

◆   ◆   ◆

Three weeks later, Jenora found Aaren in the drilling yard, and stopped to watch him. He was armored, wearing breast-and back-plate, gauntlets and greaves, and a visored helmet. The man facing him wore armor too, and wielded a halberd against Aaren's two-handed sword. Aaren was pressing a strong attack, driving the other man before him. Both weapons were blunted, but Aaren's blade chewed a deep notch in the halberd's haft when his opponent blocked a hefty swing.

The halberdier knew his business. He swept the sword aside and thumped the butt of his pole into Aaren's chest, forcing the Prince back a step. Instantly, he swung his weapon's head down, trying to hook Aaren's ankle and trip him. But Aaren lifted his foot just in time and stepped inside the halberd's arc, and banged the pommel of his sword against the other man's helmeted head. The soldier fell; before he could scramble up, Aaren's swordpoint was at his throat.

The man laid aside his polearm and raised his visor. "Well struck, your Highness. Will that be enough for this afternoon? And may I get up now?"

Aaren also uncovered his face, grinning. "More than enough. Thank you for the practice." He extended his hand to help the man up. "You may return to your other duties. And thank Master Roman for the loan of you, would you?" As the soldier left, Aaren noticed Jenora and came over to her.

She linked her arm in his and walked beside him. "I agree, that was well done. You almost surprised me, you were going at it so ... fiercely."

Aaren stopped to pull off his helmet, shaking out his sweat-matted hair. He seemed to consider the observation for a moment. "How could it be more serious? We leave tomorrow. King Gearld has given us the best of his standing army, to do with as we see fit. Do you realize how much that might weaken Faires? Especially if we fail, and they do not return? We've been planning and provisioning and drilling for weeks. So much is in the balance with this one stroke, and Jen ... I just don't know if we can do it. If I can really *be* a King, when there's no other choice, and everything hinges on me."

"You can. You will. Aaren, this is something we've trained in all our lives. All these years we've been together, we've prepared for a time like this. It's the purpose of a Palatine to follow the King into battle, and bring him out again safely, you know that."

She took both his hands. "So listen to me now, and believe. I will gladly go with you tomorrow when you lead us over the mountains. I will follow you, and every man in this army will follow you, to Edge and whatever is waiting there. You *are* the King, and everyone will know it. You have the right, and all our belief. Trust me. You will prevail."

Aaren turned away his face, blinking, then took her arm again and resumed their way back to the Keep. As they approached, they saw Sare coming out to meet them. Aaren stopped and his voice came to her ear soft and deep with feeling: "How could I not?"

Chapter 27
Return

The sun was already climbing higher in the east when Aaren halted his forces as they emerged from the Waist. The light shone down through the few and wispy clouds upon the broad floodplain, the escarpment, the sea beyond, and upon the fields and structures of Edge. Greybeal Palace seemed to wait, its windows curtained and doors closed, for whatever the day might bring.

Aaren turned in his borrowed saddle and looked back over the ranks forming up behind him. The Fairen knights rode on both sides of the foot soldiers. Sunlight gleamed from the breastplates everyone wore, identical to his own, and from the points of the polearms.

The young King raised his voice so the rearmost could hear him. "We must descend as swiftly as we can, before the alarm can be given. Horsemen at the canter, so the foot may keep up. Engage no one who does not challenge you. Anyone left behind will be on his own." He paused, looking from face to face, all lifted to his.

"Bear with me and well, my friends. There is a kingdom and more to be won this day."

Jenora rode up to his side as he turned back again, and smiled at him. "I believe we are ready, my King. Fortune favor the right."

Aaron donned the visorless sallet that hung from his cantle beside the sheathed Rageblade, buckling it under his chin. Jenora's smile vanished. "But, your Highness–"

"I want them to see my face." His tone brooked no argument. He raised his arm, and a moment later led the column down from the Nethals.

The first people they encountered were a group of peasants working the fields of the westernmost holding. It was a tribute to the years of Trever's Peace that they did not flee at first sight of the approaching army. The troops were within easy bowshot before an older man, veteran of the past wars, recognized the pennons flying from the riders' lances.

"Fairens! Faires is invading!" His shouts stirred the field hands, and several ran toward the manor on the Road. Another called, "Wait!" when he saw the colors Jenora carried. The remaining workers made way, retreating into the tall grainstalks, while the warriors went by.

The vanguard had already passed the fields when a woman's voice rose above the tramp of boots and hooves: "It was Aaren, I tell you! Prince Aaren! He is alive, alive and returned to us!" Jenora smiled again as they continued down the Road.

They passed other farm folk, some of whom fled while others followed. By the time they reached the city bridge, there was a large and excited host behind the rearguard, some still carrying their tools, stirring the dust and jabbering among themselves. Aaren's name, and Jenora's, and Wildon's, figured prominently in this talk.

The first challenge came when they approached the bridge.

The usual four-man sentry posted on the bridge had been increased to eight, armed with halberds, commanded by a captain of guards. This worthy had already gathered his men at the structure's far end; they handled their weapons nervously as he stepped onto the wide, heavy planking.

"Come no farther! Know you that we have been warned of your coming. Already the city has been alerted. The defenders of Edge are coming, soon. If you do not come in peace, we few may die alone. But we do not *stand* alone."

Aaren and his leaders had drawn up during this speech. While the ranks behind her shuffled into order, Jenora opened her visor and laughed softly. "Well spoken, Captain ... Gallen, I believe? But whether we mean you peace or not depends largely upon you."

"Lady Oswin, is it you? Truly?"

"Come forward if you must, to know me better – and to know your rightful King, as well."

The captain's glance moved from Jenora to the man beside her; his jaw fell upon his gorget, beneath a face suddenly pale. "Your Highness! If I am not deceived, what means all this? We thought you dead, these past months."

"Deceived you were, but no longer. I seek only to come home, to what is mine by right. This army means no harm to any, save to those who wish us ill." Aaren leaned forward in his saddle, speaking lower and more directly to the man before him. "The choice I offer you cannot be an easy one. Your duty must be your decision. Do you bar our way?"

To Gallen's credit, he hesitated only a moment. Then he stepped off the bridge, motioning his men to both sides of the path. A snap of his fingers brought them all braced to attention before he spoke. "Pass and enter, your Majesty, and welcome. Welcome home!"

Aaren nodded to Jenora, who turned and gave the orders to form up for crossing. The bridge was only wide enough to admit four horsemen abreast, or six men on foot. Jenora and the Fairen leaders moved along the flanks, rearranging the troops into order. When this was done, she returned to the fore and raised her lance to the vertical. Its pennon snapped out in the breeze, spurs were set, and the assembly moved onto the bridge. So, with colors flying and friends at his back, King Aaren of Edge crossed the Wendlow, home to the city he was born to rule.

A shout went up from the walls. The city gates swung open. A host of warriors poured out, with officers riding on their flanks, and formed up into pike squares across the plain. The late-morning sun turned their body armor into a solid, shining barrier, and their weapons into the glistening spines of a steel hedgehog.

At his signal, Aaren's column stopped short. The Fairen commanders rode up beside him. They conferred quickly, as an armored man galloped forth to meet them.

He was big and dark, and he drew rein just near enough to be seen and heard clearly. He bore an air of authority; a scar etched one cheek and turned the hairs white where it touched his beard. His voice echoed from the wall behind him.

"Enough! Return the way you came. There is nothing for you here but your deaths!" He affirmed the threat by drawing his sword, a long curved blade with a wicked point.

Jenora leaned over to speak in Aaren's ear. "I recognize his blazon, my King, though not the man. He is a major of the northern mercenaries the kingdom has hired in the past."

"Nor do I know him. Speak with him, m'Lady."

Lady Oswin rode forward a few paces. She rose up in the saddle, tall and proud, and her words carried to every ear. "We come on behalf of Prince Aaren, son of King Trever, and rightful King of Edge. Make way before us!"

The major snorted. "I see no prince. We serve Lord Wildon, Regent for Queen Alyda, and no other! I see only a herd of Fairen cattle, bearing false colors and lies. Begone!"

Most of the allies had crossed the bridge. At a signal from the Fairen colonel they began spreading into a battle-line along the riverbank, on either side of their leaders. The tension in the morning air grew, laying on a kind of stillness that muffled the sounds of men and horses moving onto place.

Jenora returned to Aaren's side. Behind him, she could see the captain of archers arraying his men. Those with crossbows were already turning their cranequins; the longbow men were poking arrows into the ground before them, fletching up, for rapid fire.

She looked into Aaren's troubled face. "My King, he will not back down, no matter what our claim."

"No." Aaren's tone was flat. She noticed his hands, resting on his saddlebow. The right was toying with the clasp of his silver bracelet. "M'Lord..."

Aaren seemed to come back to himself, and stilled his hands. "No." He shook as if chilled. "Give him one more chance to avoid combat. We have no wish to re-enter our city in blood."

Jenora nodded, and addressed the major once more. "We say again, Prince Aaren seeks only to return home. Give way, and let us pass in peace."

The northerner spoke no reply, but swung the sword above his head in an obvious signal. All along the ranks of mercenaries, the long shafts swung down to point at Aaren and his friends; they were suddenly facing a glistening hedge of sharp steel. A moment later, it began moving toward them.

"Arms forward!" Jenora's voice galvanized the men on both sides. The Fairen officers moved away to their assigned positions as she lowered her lance. The footmen moved as one, bringing their polearms to bear on the approaching force. Jenora turned to Aaren for the command; he did not hesitate.

"Advance! Archers, fire!" His orders were scarcely spoken before the first flight of long arrows passed over his head, a whispering shadow that fell among the mercenaries and thinned their numbers. The cries of wounded men began to rise above the sounds of tramping feet.

In the next moment the pikemen clashed like conflicting waves in the sea, crashing against each other and falling back, dispersing as bodies fell. The ordered lines disintegrated into chaos, men heaving and thrusting with spears longer than themselves, tearing holes in each other's ranks.

The archers fired at will now, choosing their targets with care as the Fairen foot soldiers rushed into the breaches, following Aaren and Jenora and their mounted officers. A wedge of pike and halberdiers split the riders up, and more charging mercenaries assailed them.

Jenora spitted one man on her lance, jerked it free and thrust it again into the foes swarming around her. Suddenly something snagged her shoulder, biting through a gap in her armor. She felt a wrenching lurch, a stunning impact, and she was lying on the ground.

She rolled over, sick and dizzy, wondering why the fatal thrust had not yet come.

An angry whinny made her turn her spinning head. Canticle reared only a few paces away, slashing with both forefeet at Jenora's attacker. The man was fending off as best he could, backing away and trying to strike past the horse's hooves and barding.

Jenora rose to her feet while her vision steadied. Her shield and lance were gone; she drew Friendship, caught her balance, and advanced.

Before she could join the struggle, it ended. Canticle lashed out a vicious blow that glanced from the mercenary's helmet and ripped downward. The man fell screaming, clasping both hands to his devastated face. Jenora gave him a stroke of mercy to the throat, and leaned against her panting, twitching horse.

"Good girl. Brave girl." She stroked Canticle's side and neck, calming the animal with hands and voice. The fighting had moved away from her, farther up the plain and nearer the city.

Her strength was returning by the moment. She paused long enough to tear a strip from her undershirt and pad the wound in her shoulder. It felt deep, but hadn't stiffened enough to be too much a hindrance.

She climbed up into the saddle and patted Canticle's neck. "Come on, girl. Let's get back into the fight."

✦   ✦   ✦

All around Aaren, men were dying. They fell before blade and spear and battle-axe, stabbed or slashed or split from crown to chin. The carnage reflected in his wild eyes, and darkly distorted from the rounded pommel of the Rageblade, filled him with dread and awe. His mount smelled the blood and tossed his mane, nostrils flaring.

Both lines had dissolved into melee, noise and mud and struggling bodies twisting like foam in the eddies of the Wendlow. Men in ragged clusters stood shield to shield, hacking with sword or axe, survivors spinning off to form new groups. Pikemen pushed and strained to upset each other, grunting from the repeated impact of metal on metal. The halberdiers chopped and thrust, hooking riders from the saddle and smashing through armor with cleaver blows. A dull heat rose from the battlefield and the steam held the scent of fresh death.

Horses and men alike slipped and skated in the red, ghoulish mud underfoot. His own horse misstepped and went to its knees, nearly unseating Aaren. As the animal lurched up, a heavy blow rang off Aaren's backplate and flung him across the horse's neck. The beast stumbled forward, saving his master's ringing head from the whistling path of the halberd's return swing. He heard it pass a finger's breadth from the back of his skull, and thrust aside the last of his hesitation.

Straightening and drawing the Rageblade, Aaren wheeled his mount as tightly as he dared, cutting backward as he turned. The magical blade's sweeping arc carried it through the polearm's hardened shaft with no perceptible resistance, through the halberdier's light helmet and deep into the man's skull almost before Aaren could direct it.

He wrenched it free of the falling corpse. His shoulder blade throbbed as dented metal rubbed his bruise. The sword hummed softly, vibrating the bones of his hand and forearm with suppressed power whispering to be unleashed. He didn't have time to be disturbed by the seduction of his own anger as two more mercenaries rushed him. He struck out, and again, and turned his mount in a half-circle, seeing that the Fairen honor-guard at his rear had fallen. To a man, they lay maimed and dead on the churned ground. As their killers stepped carefully past, the blade began to sing, casting glittering crimson droplets over the dead.

He looked over his wounded shoulder in time to see another cluster of Fairen troops go down. A massive warrior he had come to know pulled himself up the shaft of a pike to cleave an assailant between the eyes before he died. Wildon's men formed up to attack the young Prince suddenly alone in their midst. His entire sword arm was thrumming with the Rageblade's song.

He looked all around. Jenora was nowhere to be seen amid the milling figures, the glinting steel, and the screams. Everything was too bright, too loud, too red. In the back of his mind he remembered this feeling, but the rising whine of his father's sword drowned the memory stillborn. A fury brighter, louder, redder than the day rose up in him. This was the feeling that King Trever had described, when they had talked after his Age of Trust ceremony. He softly spoke the word he had learned from his father that night, which turned his rage to power.

The blade grew radiant from hilt to point, the tiny pendulum carved in it casting a ruby glow on his hand.

And it screamed.

Aaren swung it through the air over the cooling corpses of his guard. The advancing chaff fell before the scythe, smoking. More pressed in, and he wheeled his horse again and swung the screaming blade. The dead flew back, and struck down the living.

Aaren rode over them. Malice roared in his weapon and his soul; he felt a surge of righteous power and hatred he had not dared hope to feel again. As he knew he was meant to do, he called on the power of the sword and cast it forth against his enemies, blindly secure that *this* flame would not hurt the woman with the emerald eyes. A shout rose behind him as he devastated a knot of pikemen, broken bodies and melted weapons flying from his path. His teeth were clenched in anger, and he had the sudden, not quite sane knowledge that the weapon was not drawing on even half its potential. There was a door waiting to be opened. His awful grin widened. The rage claimed him completely and he flung back his head and prepared to drag forth the rest of the fire.

Suddenly Jenora was beside him, raising high the colors of Edge snatched from a dying hand.

"The battle has turned, my liege!" she shouted, but as she came abreast of him, her grim smile withered on her bloodied lips.

At the sound of her voice Aaren's head snapped down, his eyes crawling with blue tendrils of fire. The bracelet on his wrist glowed with a heat that tested the limits of its protective powers. Very far away the shouting grew louder as Fairen leaders rallied their men. Jenora looked into the eyes of the Prince that she loved, saw him not, and knew despair.

"My lord! Oh Aaren, not this. Not now." Her voice could barely be heard above the howling of the enchanted blade.

But in the one tiny spot of coolness adrift in the raging sea of his mind, that place the fire never touched, Aaren did hear. The minute threads of blue fire withdrew through his eyes to the place in his soul that no one, not even he, ever saw. The flames of the Rageblade also flickered and died, screaming thinly in frustration as he sheathed it. Behind Jenora, the archers drew sword and rushed across the bridge to bolster the rally.

"My Gifter," he gasped, and reached for his companion. She caught him when he would have pitched from his saddle, and held him clumsily by the armor while his mind cleared. The sounds of fighting grew more sporadic, and Aaren raised his head.

In moments, it seemed, it was over. He found himself reined up at the city gates. There were cheering allies all around, Jenora at his right, and the flag – his flag – above him. The Rageblade crackled and pinged softly as it cooled in its scabbard. He felt he was looking at everything distantly, through a thin veil. The mercenary major, with blood and fear on his bearded face, knelt and asked for quarter. Almost distractedly, Aaren granted it with the smallest gesture of his mailed hand, as befit a King. The afternoon sun was warm on his armor, the river sang behind him, and he had come back to his people, having somehow carried the day. His home was once again his.

Only Wildon remained before him.

✦   ✦   ✦

Wildon was amazed at the stillness. He stared at the filthy, panting man before him, but could not hear the man's labored breathing. He peered about, seeing the familiar furnishings and decorations of the throne room, looking into the familiar faces clustered there, and heard nothing. Some of the faces appeared to be speaking to him, or to the soldier before him; no voice came to his ears.

He turned his head and gazed out the high window to his right. The branch of a plane tree crossed the window, and a small grey bird sat on the branch, its throat rippling. But he heard no song. *How strange, that doom and disgrace should be so silent...*

Then a hand tugged his sleeve, and a well-known voice harried his ear. "Majesty. My Lord! Are you ill? Please, my Lord, tell us; what would you have us do?" Wildon turned to look into the man's face, and after a moment, recognized him; it was Becton. And with that recognition, sound and motion seemed to return to the room. He found that he could also speak, and faced the messenger.

"You say that none of the officers or men of the city's army so much as raised sword to the boy? *None?*"

"No, Highness. Rather, they bent the knee before him, and quarreled to carry his banner, and proclaimed him through the streets with cheering. Listen, my Lord! You may hear the cheers even now, approaching the palace. Only we few, worthy of our hire, stood against him; the carrion birds pluck at our fallen while we speak."

One of the nobles – *why can I never recall his name?* – spoke up. "It must be true, your Majesty. It *is* the Prince, returned in triumph to claim his throne!"

Wildon glanced around him, at the purple velvet of the armrests between his fingers, the tapestry at his back. He turned again to Becton, who nodded bleakly. "We must go, your Highness. The houseguards will shield us, and there are boats to take us downriver to Seahale or Qualls."

Wildon was suddenly standing. "Flee? Flee before that beardless *boy*? And to what, a life of hiding and exile? Is that your counsel to me, Chamberlain?"

He stepped from the dais, brushing past his courtiers. Pulling a silver piece from his purse, he lifted the mercenary's hand and laid the coin into its palm. "Your duty is done, with this news. Go and tell your fellows that they have served me well, and their service also is done. As is your habit, go, and fight another day, for another master. Becton, go with him, and see that all are paid in kind. Then run! Your service, too, is done."

Becton stepped forward. "But your Majesty, you must come!"

"Leave me! Scatter, you sheep, run for your ovine lives! If he comes, and if he is a man, he will find a *man* here, on his feet and bearing a sword - with no devil's flames upon it. Begone!"

He strode to the wall behind the throne and snatched down one of the crossed swords hanging there. When he turned, the hall was empty.

Going to the window, he looked out, resting the sword's point on the toe of his boot. The sun gilded the plane tree's brown leaves and peeling bark, and lit every eave and stone of Greybeal, every rooftop of the city's northern side. It was, he thought, quite lovely.

A sound drifted on the wind. He wondered for a moment before realizing its nature. The messenger had not exaggerated; he *could* hear the cheering as the boy-king and his rabble came closer. And the bird was gone. *Well, soon enough, my "Prince."*

Absorbed as he was in the hateful sound, Wildon did not hear the tiny rustle of tapestries as a cloaked figure slipped into the room, through the door left open by the departing courtiers. It glided silently over the floor tiles with surprisingly few paces, and was at Wildon's back in a heartbeat. Its arms lifted. The sound of its sleeves falling back, revealing skin-tight mail on its forearms, was the only warning Wildon received before the grey hands closed around his neck. The fingers bit into his throat, crushing his larynx and stopping any cry he might have made.

He heaved against that grip, managing to turn his head just enough to see his murderer's face. Even as he thrashed and struggled his vision began to fade, and he died with the sight of lifeless white eyes, and the sound of a voice in his mind, perhaps Dark Michael's, perhaps his own: *The price of failure.*

After a moment, the golem laid the body at the foot of the throne. Without another glance it slipped away, leaving a sunlit room and a mystery, and the sounds of jubilation drawing near.

Chapter 28
New Home

The party from Faires was met at the palace gate in Edge with all the heraldry and fanfare due the new young Queen. They had traveled through the Nethals just ahead of the first winter storms. Sare, although tired and surprised at the assembly, gathered her composure and lifted her head high, nodding to the cheering crowds as her horse passed them. There was a great deal of curiosity about her, but she was used to the whispers and pointing, and handled it with equanimity.

The Fairen escort of men-at-arms took their tired mounts off to the stables, and Aaren and Jenora greeted the rest of the party in the main hall. Aaren and Sare immediately fell into each other's arms and Jenora stood back, beaming at them. Sare released her husband and turned, introducing her traveling companions.

"You remember Rodolpho, of course." The majordomo bowed stiffly. "I borrowed him indefinitely from Mother to help me settle in with the new household. And this is Ilaine, have you met before? She's been taking care of me since I was a little girl. Aric and Jiselle are with Rodolpho."

Aaren stepped forward. "Welcome to Greybeal Palace. Please consider our home yours as well. I'm sure you are all tired, so I have taken the liberty of setting up temporary rooms for everyone. We can sort out all the details after dinner. Stephen, our steward, will show you where the rooms are."

Stephen and Rodolpho looked each other over critically. Finally, Stephen said "This way, if you please," and led all but Sare out toward the Riverside wing.

"That may be sticky," commented Jenora, after they were out of earshot. "Stephen has served Queen Alyda for longer than I've been alive."

Sare sighed. "True, but if I'm to feel comfortable here as the new Queen, I thought that I might need some familiar faces. Not that the staff here would be anything but helpful, I'm sure. But...."

"You did the right thing." Aaren took her hand. "Stephen will always have a place here, and he'll just have to work it out with Rodolpho. The smartest course for him now would be to make himself indispensable. After all, he knows everyone's name, and where everything is."

The three went up the stairs and down the hall to the royal chambers, followed by a porter with Sare's valises. Aaren threw open the doors and Sare gasped. Every table, windowsill and shelf was covered with lit candles. The tiny golden flames danced in the draft from the open door and threw brilliant reflections into the heavy gilded mirrors.

"Fire has drawn us together, mostly in tragedy," Aaren said. "But whatever it is that binds us, burns in my heart brighter than any magicked flame. I love you. Welcome home."

She turned and embraced him again. After a long moment, he loosened her grip and held her at arm's length.

"Jenora and I will be in my council chamber. I thought you would like to bathe and rest. Join us as soon as you like. Just ring for Stephen and he'll show you the way." The porter set her bags out on the bed and quickly withdrew. As they turned to leave, Jenora hurried over to Sare and hugged her fiercely, favoring her still-sore shoulder.

"Welcome home indeed, my Queen." She rejoined Aaren in the doorway.

Sare stood in the middle of the room, surrounded by the tapers. "Wait," she called. Tears were streaming down her face.

"What is it?" asked Aaren, alarmed. "What's the matter?"

"Nothing. Nothing's the matter. Or, everything. I don't know. I don't know how to be a queen! I don't know how to be a wife! I don't know anything!" She turned around in the middle of the room. "It's beautiful, but I don't know where anything is, and I'm afraid to be alone." She was sobbing, and they rushed to her side and held her. "I feel so stupid and childish, but will you stay with me?"

"Of course we will," murmured Aaren. "We'll always be with you."

Chapter 29
Wil

The summer sun's first rays flickered redly through the alders onto Wil's sleeping face, lending his dream its angry hue. Wil's eyes raced back and forth under his closed lids, and sweat stood out on his furrowed forehead. He moaned in his sleep. Somewhere close by a woodpecker struck up its syncopated breakfast rhythm, and Wil awoke with a start. He sat up, rubbing damp grit from his eyes. His back was very sore from the root of the ash under which he had slept.

He stood, brushing the twigs from his cloak and the dreams of fire from his head. He sighed; his growling stomach commanded his attention more than the dream. The dream had been his constant companion for as long as he could remember, not that he could have described it in any detail. It was simply the sharper nightly echo of the dull terror that he lived with every day, the muted roaring and unfinished, forgotten words in his mind that drowned out his ability to think coherently for very long about any one thing. He didn't think about the dream much. He didn't think about anything very much.

Stooping down, he picked up his worn leather pack and rummaged about in the bottom. He found the last handful of the early acorns he'd gathered three days earlier. Cracking one between his teeth, he shouldered the bag and shuffled up the road toward the sounds of water he had heard the night before.

He crossed a mossy wooden bridge and paused in a shaft of sunlight. Munching the last of the nuts, he dropped the pieces of shell one by one into the small river (hardly more than a stream really) and watched silver fish dart and wriggle beneath the rippling surface. Leaning against the rough, bark-covered rail, Wil closed his eyes and let the sun warm his face. The knots in his back began to loosen, and he stretched his arms up over his head, smiling. Maybe it would be different in the next town. Maybe he wouldn't ruin it this time. Maybe he'd find a place to stop for a while and rest.

Unfortunately, his stretch dislodged the pack from his shoulder and it tumbled to the planks, precariously teetering on the edge. He lunged for it and managed to just brush the edge of the strap as it tipped over the side and landed with a splash in the water below.

"Oh ... *damn!*" He ran across the bridge. He stumbled around its end and down the bank, looking out into the water for his pack. For a moment he couldn't see it, then he looked farther downstream and saw it snagged on a half-submerged branch. The current was stronger than it looked; it had swept the pack almost around a small bend in the river.

Wil ran down the sandy bank and waded out to his knees in the icy water. He fished his pack off of the branch and brought it back to the shore. Sitting on a log he shook the water off the pack and opened its flap. The meager contents were as soaked as his feet, toes squishing forlornly in his low boots. He thought wistfully of his mood just moments before, and glanced back at the bridge, but he couldn't see it from where he was sitting. He tipped the pack and poured the water out between his feet.

It would take all day to dry his belongings. He looked around for a flat sunny place. Of course, he could build a small fire. That would be ... that might be ... his breath quickened, and he squeezed his eyes shut. Great Gifter, there'd be nothing wrong with a simple *campfire*. But the roaring in his head was insistent, and as always, ultimately triumphant, and the fear took him into its tender, gleeful arms and squeezed him until he screamed.

And that was how the dark men on horseback found him, curled on the bank of the river, eyes squeezed shut, screaming hoarsely in the tranquil morning glade.

The trip was an aching blur. He remembered being thrown across the back of a black Percheron, his wrists bound. The men had spoken little, and never to him. The dust of their passage choked him; his head bounced painfully against the flank of the horse as they galloped. He passed out more than once, both the terrifying abduction and the infinitely more terrifying roaring in his mind blanking out periods of time. Eventually, he wasn't sure how much later, they slowed and stopped.

He was roughly jerked from the horse and dragged into some sort of large stone building. It was damp inside, and cold. They hauled him down a flight of stairs and through a bewildering series of corridors, sickly lit by guttering torches. The smell of the burning pitch mixed with the smell of human excrement and fear. Suddenly Wil began paying more attention. This was no village jail, no round-up of vagrants and drunks. This was a dungeon, and the screams filtering shrilly into his ears were cast in madness.

They pushed him into a dark stone room; he stumbled and fell into a pile of mildewed straw, skinning the palms of his hands on the rough floor. Slamming the wooden door and sliding the bolt, the riders left him there in the dark, the flickering light of a torch in the hall sending muted ghost flames dancing under his door. He pushed himself into a corner and stared at the orange light, eyes huge. Soon his screams joined those of the other madmen, and he fell again into the oblivion of his fire.

◆   ◆   ◆

Michael rode up to the stone entrance and swung gracefully off of his mount. A stableboy hurried out and took the reins from his black-gloved hand, leading the horse away. Michael stood for a moment gazing up at the enormous mossy, black-streaked stones of the building: Hollow House. It was originally called The Hollow Log Inn, after its namesake lightning-blasted stump off on one side; Michael had purchased the building under his guise of John Winters, extended it underground, and converted it into a sanitarium. *What a generous man I am,* he thought, mounting the wide stone steps to the entry hall. *Donating the funds needed to keep the poor madmen and women out of harm's way.* The two burly guards bowed their heads as he passed, muttering, "My liege" and hoping not to be noticed.

He was met in the hallway by a tall, emaciated-looking woman with skin so pale he could see the tracery of veins beneath. Her hair was white, and the irises of her eyes were a delicate pink and utterly lifeless, though her movements were quick and precise. He nodded to her, and smiled.

"Rebecca. You are looking well. Tell me all the news." He placed his hand on her shoulder, enjoying her involuntary shudder. She hated to be touched.

"My Lord," she began, her voice a fluted whisper. "Everything is well ... in. The staff ... is delighted ... to have you for." The odd cadence of her speech and incomplete phrases were normal for her, but her shudders under his hand were growing more pronounced, the blue vein at her right temple throbbing noticeably. She clenched her jaw and pulled her lips back, showing teeth too large, too white, for the rest of her face. Michael realized that she was smiling, and dropped his hand in distaste.

"Very well then. I'm told we have several new guests. Anything of use?"

She turned, and beckoned him to follow with one of her quick, birdlike gestures. "As a ... matter of fact," she said, leading the way down the stairs. "Mostly the usual ... sort, but two I thought ... you'd be ... interested..." He waited for her to finish the sentence, but she did not. The damp air flowing up the stairs caught her colorless hair and wafted it behind her, glinting in the torchlight. Michael smelled something sweet, and acrid. He swallowed, grimacing.

They entered a long, low-ceilinged room with a wooden table near the door and several sets of manacles bolted along the far wall. Two men stood chained there, one large, hairy, and naked, and the other wearing clothes that looked disheveled and slightly singed, but otherwise normal. A guard stood by, idly toying with a torch in a sconce in the wall to the right. At their entrance he straightened, the smirk on his face wiped clean and replaced with stiff attention.

Rebecca glanced at him, then at the prisoners, noticed the disheveled one was unconscious and the other snickering and rubbing his back against the wall like a bear on a tree trunk. "Been playing ... with the guests ... Randy?" she whispered to the guard.

"No ma'am. You know I wouldn't," the man stammered, looking straight ahead.

"Then why is our ... man Wil ... so out of sorts?" she asked. "I'd ... hoped ... to introduce ... him. To our ... honored..." She walked over to stand before the guard, tipped her head to one side, and looked at him with her dead pink eyes. Sweat ran freely down his face. "We'll just have ... to have a little ... talk, later." She tipped her head the other way. "Won't we?"

"I swear, I didn't -" he stammered

"Hush," she whispered. "You ... may go now ... Randy."

He turned and walked stiffly through the door, not daring to meet the gaze of anyone in the room.

Michael shook his head fondly. "It's always such a pleasure seeing you work." He smiled and nodded toward the two chained men. "Now what do we have here?"

"The rough looking ... gentleman on the left. Raped and killed ... seven, as far as we. In Seahale." She glanced at Michael. "The sort you ... sometimes find..."

"Yes, well, that's just fine. Has he a name?"

"Bugger!" screamed the hairy man, laughing and rubbing his back harder against the wall. "Bugger *you!*

Bugger *her*! Bugger!" He laughed again, panting, and blood ran down his buttocks and over his meaty calf.

"That's all ... he seems to know ... how," Rebecca whispered sadly. "Randy and ... the boys call him."

"Bugger!" screamed the man again.

"Delightful," Michael murmured. "Have him prepared. And the other?"

"Wil. Found him ... in the forest ... no idea. Has quite a ... problem. Fire. Fear. Fire." She tipped her head and gazed at the crumpled man. "But, there is ... something. Something ... else. I thought you..."

Michael walked over to Wil, ignoring the raucous shouts of his cellmate, and taking off his glove he placed his hand on Wil's forehead. He left it there for a long time.

"You were absolutely right to send for me." He straightened. "He could be useful." He moved back to the door. "Clean him up and bring him to me. I'll be in your study." His cloak swirled as he strode from the room.

"Of ... course," she whispered.

✦   ✦   ✦

Wil was dreaming again. But it seemed like such a nice dream this time. The ceiling over the cot on which he lay was made of dark, oiled wood. The room smelled of cedar and incense and, slightly, something sweet. He was warm. The awful guard was nowhere to be seen. He sat up and swung his feet over the side of the cot. He was very dizzy, and couldn't seem to focus well. There was a desk, and a man behind it, reading a book under the gentle yellow glow of a lamp. Out the window the evergreens faded into mist at the slope of a mountain.

"Where am I?" he said, still trying to focus.

The man looked up, folded the book, and stepped from behind the desk. No matter how he tried, Wil couldn't focus on his face. The man pulled a chair over and sat down in front of him. Blurrily, Wil thought the man smiled

"You're safe, Wil. Everything is going to be all right." His voice was deep and reassuring. "How do you feel?"

"Dizzy."

"Well of course you do. That's the draught my friend Rebecca gave you. Do you know who I am, Wil?"

He shook his head. "I'm sorry."

"No need, no need to be sorry. My name is John, John Winters, and I'm here to make sure you get better." He smiled again.

"Oh, I'm fine. I didn't mean to, that is, I'm sorry if I, uh..." Wil didn't know what to say. It was the strangest dream he could ever remember having. It was doubly odd, because he never remembered any of his dreams. Of course, he guessed it was probably normal to remember them while you were having them. He still felt very confused.

"Wil, I don't want you to worry about a thing. You've had a rough time, I think. Do you know why you're here?"

"No."

"Because you're always afraid. Do you remember being afraid?"

"No!" Wil said, a little too loudly. Maybe this was turning into the wrong sort of dream after all.

"Well certainly you do." John's voice was low and coaxing. "You're afraid of fire. Isn't that right, Wil? Afraid of fire?" The man gently placed his left hand on Wil's forehead, and said some words that Wil did not understand. There was a sharp pain between his eyes. "Here it is," the man said, "all your memories and terror of the fire." The man pulled his hand back and held it, palm up, and dancing in its center, perfectly in focus, was a tiny yellow flame.

Wil shrieked. The roaring and muted chanting in his mind almost, but not quite, drowned out John's voice. "Yes, the fire is very frightening, Wil. But you know what? You know what, Wil?" he murmured over the sound. Wil tried to back away, but his spine was already to the wall. He stared at the fire in the man's palm, pupils wide, moaning in the back of his throat.

"You can take the fire." Wil shook his head wildly back and forth as the man lifted his hand toward Wil's face. "Yes you can. You can take the fire into yourself and make it yours. If you swallow the fire, Wil, bury it deeply in yourself, you won't have to see it anymore." He caught Wil's head in a powerful embrace with the crook of his right arm and pulled Wil's head close to his chest. He was very strong, and try as he might Wil couldn't twist free.

"Eat the fire, Wil. You have to," he said in his gentle voice. "It's the only way." Again he pushed the flame toward Wil's face. Wil screamed, and as he did the man forced the fire into his mouth.

It burned. His tongue blistered and his teeth cracked. His throat convulsed once, twice, and suddenly the pain was gone. The fire (*and something else?*) slid down his throat and vanished as if they had never been. John released him, and he slumped back in shock. The fire was gone. And so, remarkably was the roaring in his mind. The crippling fear that had been his constant companion for as long as he could remember simply faded away. He stared through his dizziness and his obscuring tears at the blurry face of the man who had helped him. Gingerly, he touched his tongue to the roof of his mouth. The burnt flesh had been magically restored. He began to cry.

"I know, I know," John soothed him. "It's overwhelming, isn't it? Come here and sit with me." He took Wil's hand and led him over to a large hearth on the far side of the room. They sat down on a soft bench by the fire, crackling merrily amongst the pile of logs on the grate. It felt wonderful. Wil stretched his hands out and warmed them against the gentle, ruby heat.

✦   ✦   ✦

This day, like most, Cillistra rose, dressed, and had breakfast with Michael. He seemed short-tempered. The serving girl carrying in a tray of toasted bread stumbled and spilled it onto Michael's boots.

"Clumsy fool!" Michael snarled. The girl bent down to pick up the bread, looking stricken. As she reached across his boot, he kicked her backwards, sending her sprawling.

"Michael!" Cillistra cried, as he scooted his chair back with an impatient snort. She was about to remonstrate with him, but caught the look in his eye at the last moment. She knew that look, and he waited a half-second to be sure she recognized it before turning and striding from the room.

"I'll be back tomorrow," he said, without turning around, as he passed through the doorway.

Cillistra sighed. His dark moods were getting more and more frequent. His impatience was legendary, but lately ... well, things were going to have to change soon. She knew that he still didn't feel his troops were strong enough to face Faires directly, and there was always the burning unspoken hatred he felt for Edge's boy-king Aaren. They didn't talk about that, hadn't since that last night in Faires.

She was sure he still resented her for thwarting his plans that night, but their relationship had become more complicated since then. She loved him as much as ever, and reassured herself that she wanted the same things he did. Her former life seemed empty and silly in comparison to this new adventure, and she knew that one day, at Michael's side, she would rule. She let her mind shy away from the specifics of how that might be accomplished, though. Sometimes she missed her family, and the comforts of the castle. She closed her eyes.

"Ma'am?" asked the servant meekly.

Cillistra opened her eyes and shook the cobwebs of thought from her mind. "Here." She bent down. "Let me help you clean this up."

She finished her morning preparations and pulled on her long riding boots. It was time to meet the new man, Wil, at the stables and try again to teach him the basics of horsemanship. To her surprise, Cillistra found herself growing fond of the bumbling newcomer. Wil was guileless, and possessed of a cheerful demeanor that she almost always found infectious. Most of the other denizens of Michael's camp seemed deadly serious, fawningly obsequious, or disturbingly inhuman. Wil was the first person besides Michael and his Shadow with whom she felt comfortable. Michael had been pleased to put Wil under her care, directing her to have him trained in the rudiments of swordplay, riding, and stealth. Michael's Arms Master handled the fighting and skullduggery, but Cillistra had taken it upon herself to teach Wil to ride.

"Hello Cillistra!" Wil called, waving, as she approached.

She smiled and walked up to him. She was just an inch or so taller than he. "Hello, Wil. How fare you today?"

"Wonderful! We got up really early today and did 'maneuvers'." He arched his eyebrows. "And then we came back to camp and had a huge breakfast. We had bacon. Would you like to see me low-crawl?" he asked, beginning to stoop down.

Cillistra laughed and caught his shoulder, straightening him up. "Perhaps another time, Wil. What do you say we saddle up and do some riding? I seem to have the whole day free, and I thought that it might be nice to get out of camp for a change. I packed some lunches." She patted the saddlebags slung over her shoulder. "Perhaps we could have a picnic. I used to love..." she trailed off.

"What is it?" Wil's concern trembled in his voice. "Are you sad?"

Cillistra shook her head. "No, I'm not sad. I guess I'm just ... remembering. Sometimes remembering certain things ... well..."

He put his hand on her shoulder. "I know. Remembering isn't always very nice." He looked so serious.

She placed her hand over his and found her smile again. "Michael won't be back for ages, and I have nothing else to do, so let's grab a couple of guards and take the day for ourselves, shall we?"

Wil's face lit up. "That would be grand!"

✦   ✦   ✦

The following months were the happiest Wil could ever remember having. After his initial transfer to his new friend John's camp, deep in the mountains south of Faires, he saw things of which he had never dreamed; and while many of the denizens were terrifying to look upon, all treated him with the greatest respect. Especially Cillistra, John's beautiful consort. She was so kind! He hoped that someday he could repay all of her kindnesses.

And the training! He was coached by true warriors in the arts of stealth and personal combat. He was to be one of John's right-hand men. He fell into bed each night exhausted and sore, but full of joy. He had long dreamed that he would someday find a family. He didn't know what he had done to deserve all this. And the best part of all was that he was never afraid.

The food was wonderful too, but he was having quite a lot of trouble with heartburn. He didn't dwell on it, it was such a tiny thing compared to everything else, and whenever he seemed to be getting moody, John would cheer him up and the hot fullness in his belly would be much better. For a while.

One morning in late fall, John came to see Wil in his tent. John sat down in an x-framed folding chair across from him and gazed levelly into his eyes for several moments. Finally, he spoke.

"How are you getting along, Wil? Are you happy here?"

Happy? Wil was flabbergasted. "Yes! Everything is wonderful! You are the best friend I've ever had! I don't know how I can ever repay you."

John smiled. "I'm glad you feel that way. Because the Arms Master says that you've been doing extraordinary work. And I need a brave man to go on a special mission for me. It could be very dangerous. What about it, Wil? Are you up to it?"

Wil plunged down off of his bed onto one knee, eyes full of tears. "Of *course*! I'd, I'd be *honored*!"

John smiled and put his hand on top of Wil's head. "I know. I knew it when I found you, Wil. You are destined to play a great role in things." He stood. "Walk with me."

They left the tent and began strolling down to the training yard. "Wil, I have an enemy. Every moment he lives, I long to smell his death. He thwarted me once, and forced me to change some very important plans. This upstart King needs to be taught a lesson he will never forget. As long as he lives." They came to the gate, and were met by the Arms Master.

"Take my friend Wil here and outfit him for a journey. He's going to Edge, tonight, on a special mission for me." The Arms Master nodded. John turned to Wil. "You will be admitted to the palace as an emissary from my beloved Cillistra, with a message for her sister and her husband. Show them this." He handed Wil Cillistra's ring, bearing the seal of the house of Proudlock.

Wil took the ring and nodded, eyes shining. "But what is the message?"

John reached over and grasped the back of Wil's neck, then suddenly drew their heads together so hard Wil could hear them crack. The pain was immediate, followed by a wave of dizziness and nausea.

"This is my enemy," John hissed, and the stars in Wil's eyes were replaced by an image of a young, dark-haired man with striking blue eyes. "You must get close enough to touch him. After that, you'll know what to do. But you must be close enough to touch him!"

The burning in Wil's belly was growing more intense by the moment. For just a second he thought he felt something *move* down there. For the first time in weeks, he felt the vaguest hint of the old terror. "I ... I think I'm going to be sick," he gasped, still reeling from the blow of his friend's head.

John released him, eyeing him critically. Wil pressed his hands over his eyes, his stomach heaving and hot, and a distant sound of crackling in his ears. He gasped deeply, and the sound retreated; he took another breath, and the burning and the nausea passed.

"Are you all right?" John asked.

Wil lowered his hands from his eyes. His mind cleared. "Yes," he said hoarsely. And then more strongly, "Yes. I'm ready."

"Good. Then off with you. Go down and requisition a horse and supplies. The good Master here will be along shortly to help you finish your preparations."

They watched him go. "He wouldn't get past the defense of a one-armed farmer with a dull pitchfork," commented the Arms Master.

"He doesn't have to," replied Michael. "He is too obviously a fool to arouse much suspicion. All he has to do is get close."

"And if he rejects your little secret in his belly? He almost did just now."

"No, I don't think so." Michael spoke softly, almost to himself. "It's tied, you see, to the thing he fears the most. He'd never choose to face that again. Not for anything."

The Arms Master shrugged, then strode off to prepare Wil for his journey over the pass.

Wil was almost disappointed. The trip had been completely uneventful. He had been greeted with cheer by the two merchant groups he had passed, and they had been his sole encounters the entire trip. Now he sat nervously in an anteroom, flanked by guards and under the suspicious eye of an officious steward. He heard raised voices in the next chamber, and craned his neck to try and see what the announcement of his presence had stirred up.

"Don't you move," the steward said.

Wil slumped back down. This wasn't how he'd expected it at all. He'd presented the ring, been stripped of his weapons and hustled into this tiny waiting room, and what seemed like hours had passed with nothing further happening at all. His stomach was really starting to hurt.

A striking chestnut-haired woman warrior swept into the room and came to a halt in front of Wil. He stared up at her, mouth agape. She looked him over with a critical eye. "Thank you, Stephen. He's been searched?"

"Nothing but the clothes on his back, m'Lady," the steward answered. The guards on either side of Wil rose, dragging him to his feet.

"Fine. You," she pointed to Wil, "come with me."

He followed her into a larger room hung with tapestries. In the center was an oval table. Around it sat several people; but the one that made Wil gasp and clutch at his stomach was the curly-haired, lightly bearded man at the head of the table. *The enemy. Aaren.* It was he!

He lurched forward and tried to get near him. He hadn't made two steps before the warrior-woman grabbed his collar and drew him back with a strangled cry. Several of the people at the table had jumped to their feet at his sudden movement, but he still had eyes only for the enemy. He struggled weakly in the woman's grasp.

"You just settle down, friend," she growled in warning, tightening her grip on his collar. Wil's face started turning red. He couldn't breathe, and there was the smell of smoke in his nostrils.

"Jenora, let him have his say—" said the scarred woman at the enemy's right hand.

But she was interrupted by a voice that brought fire flooding into Wil's brain. Suddenly the enemy was the farthest thing from his mind, as he turned in horror to face a man he had never thought to see again.

"Kill him! He is an assassin! Extremely dangerous!" screeched Vernor, his chair tumbling over behind him as he leapt to his feet, face suffused with blood, his right eye alternately wandering and then snapping back into focus. "In the Gifter's name, Jenora, kill him now!"

Wil heard the fire blossom to a crackling crescendo in his mind, as his old Master gestured lividly before him. Aaren was forgotten. This, in front of him ... it was his nightmare. It was as if no time had passed at all. He could still smell the fresh earth of her grave, could still see his Master's skin blacken as the fire burrowed into it, could still hear the awful, guttural syllables of the curse.

The curse. With dreadful inevitability, he began again to chant the words his Master had taught him nearly twenty years before. It needed to be finished. Their old power gripped his tongue just as it had that long-ago morning. And as his insanity burned behind his streaming eyes and the terrible words poured out of him, Wil vomited up the fire, its scorching heat seeming to purify him as it traveled up and out of his body. He almost didn't notice the shriveled thing that came up with it, a tiny poisonous blackness that screeched thinly as it died on the flagstones at his feet, too far from any target to fulfill its assassin's destiny.

Dimly he sensed the warrior releasing him, and dimly he saw the smoke pouring from his old Master's robes. Still uttering the horrifying words, croaking them through flame-savaged lips, he felt a dull soundlessness that started at the back of his head, enveloped the roaring of the flames, and silenced them.

◆   ◆   ◆

Jenora stood over the crumpled body of the stranger, the pommel of her dagger bloody from her blow to his head. The room was in chaos. Guards rushed in at her back, Aaren and Sare hurried to the aid of Vernor, and Leland was gingerly turning over the stranger's body with the toe of his boot, sword drawn and ready. Her instant assessment was that the danger had been nullified, but that Vernor was still struggling with whatever enchantment the stranger had unleashed. Jenora felt two emotions stab through her as she knelt at the magician's side opposite Aaren and Sare: first, relief that the King and Queen had escaped harm, and second, a self-directed rage that she had let the danger get so near.

Both emotions were replaced by horror as she saw Vernor. He was dying, twisting black snakes writhing under his skin, burning him from the inside. Violently, he pushed Sare's comforting hands away from him. His right eye had rolled completely back into his head. He turned his left, bloodshot and mad, on the King and Queen, and spoke to them in a high, garbled voice.

"So I won't live to see it end! Very well, spawn of the Tempter, but know you now that it was I who laid this curse upon you." He coughed, and sooty bile spattered his robes. The heat was beginning to radiate from him in waves, and Aaren and Jenora drew back slightly. Only Sare reached out for him again, to be rebuffed by his frantic claws.

"Don't you touch me! You, girl, I cursed with fire, and your husband as well. Your fathers took from me the only light in all my world, and for that crime they shall pay a hundredfold. Your lines end here, and with them your kingdoms!" He coughed again, longer this time, his face blackening and flaking before their horrified eyes. "Spawn of Proudlock: burn in Hell! Spawn of Telcien: burn there too! And may your cursed fathers scream from the grave as my retribution takes their children, as my Gwenlyn was taken from me!"

With that, the fire inside the mage burst forth, and consumed him. All three fell back this time, and then everyone fled the room as it became choked with bitter smoke. Jenora scowled, grabbed the collar of the stranger and dragged him out too, in the event that her blow had not been severe enough to kill him.

Slowly the pieces of the puzzle were found and fit together. After five days Wil regained the ability to speak, but was unable to make much sense. Scraps of his ramblings seemed to be almost coherent, but then he would lose his way, and end up crying quietly for hours. Once Jenora and Leland grudgingly acceded that he was no further threat, Sare spent the most time with him, practicing whatever healing she could on a man whose injuries seemed mostly to have afflicted his mind.

Mostly he just wanted to sit by the fire. Above all else, this seemed to calm him and bring him peace, although no one had any idea why. Sometimes he spoke of his childhood, and of Vernor. He spoke often of his wanderings, and his great friend John Winters, who had helped him to swallow the fire. He became confused and agitated whenever Aaren was in the room, and so Aaren did not visit him.

Chapter 30
Favors

Sare and Aaren were in their library one evening a few weeks later, playing cards. The demands of the throne had been light that day, and they were taking advantage of the time to be together. Jenora came up the hall outside the library and heard her friends laughing softly together inside. She almost turned away, to give them their peace, but a powerful loneliness welled up in her and she stepped into the doorway and leaned against the frame, arms crossed over her breast. Aaren was laughing and shuffling the deck, his hands quick and strong. Sare was laughing too, her beads tumbling over her shoulder as she said, "No, you're the cheater."

Sare caught Jenora's reflection in the dark window glass and she looked up, her smile welcoming her friend into room. "Jenora! You're just in time. I need someone to help me keep an eye on this lout. I believe he has an entire extra deck up his sleeves."

"Me!" sputtered Aaren. "Jenora, you *know* her." He rolled his eyes.

"Who are you rolling your eyes at?" demanded Sare. "Certainly, she knows me, and you as well."

"Yes, I do, and I wouldn't be caught playing cards with either one of you." Jenora went in and curled up on a settee by the fireplace, her long legs tucked under her, facing her friends.

"Ooh! You dare talk to your Queen that way!" squeaked Sare, getting up from the table and stalking toward Jenora. "The royal decree is... *tickling!*" She launched herself at the Palatine, and they both toppled shrieking to the carpet.

"I can see..." Aaren began, but was drowned out by their squeals. He got up, crossed the room, and stood over them. "I said, I can see that I'm going to have to break this nonsense up." He reached down and pinched Sare on her royal posterior.

Sare yelped and rolled free. "Oh, Jenora, I can see that this is going to get ugly." They turned and looked at Aaren with predatory gazes.

"Uh oh." Aaren began backing away, but the women were on him in a flash, the three of them tumbling over the rug, laughing. As usually happened, Aaren and Jenora ended up in a more serious wrestling match, and Sare ducked out, breathing hard, and watched the two of them squirm and grasp and try to go for the pin. It was a game they had played since they were children. Aaren ended on top, with Jenora's wrists pinned on either side of her head. She struggled for a moment, then nodded, red-faced and panting.

"I can see that Sare has been teaching you some proper moves. Good for you, my Queen," Jenora said, craning her neck to see Sare.

Sare was on the settee, lying on her stomach, disfigured chin on the back of her folded hands, smiling

gently at both of them.   Aaren sat back, releasing
Jenora's wrists.

"At ease, Palatine," he said archly, got up and went
to sit beside his wife. He began rubbing her shoulders.
His bracelet caught the glow from the fireplace and
sparkled. Sare closed her eyes. Jenora rolled up against
the side of the settee and leaned her head against Sare's,
the coolness of the beads familiar and perfect against her
face.

They stayed like that for a long time. As the fire died
down, Aaren stretched out next to Jenora on the
hearthrug, and dozed off as she rubbed his shoulders in
turn. He snored softly. Behind her, Sare braided and
unbraided the warrior's hair.

"Jenora?" Sare said quietly, so as not to wake Aaren.

"Mm?" answered Jenora in a sleepy voice.

"I'm afraid for him." Jenora turned her head to look
at her friend. "For all of us," Sare added.

"How do you mean?"

Sare paused. Jenora turned fully around. She drew
up her knees and hugged them to her chest, gazing at
Sare, waiting. "I've been talking to Wil," Sare began.

Jenora narrowed her eyes.

"Don't judge him too harshly," Sare whispered.

"He is one shade from the color of Dark Michael's
minions," Jenora said flatly.

Yes, I suppose so. The gift he received from The
Dark One was powerful. Although I don't think that it
was intended the way it turned out."

"Certainly not. He was undoubtedly sent here to kill
Aaren. You know how Michael hates him."

"True, Jenora, but that's not what I meant. When
Wil was finally released from his fear, he did it himself.

Do you remember when that ... that *thing* came from his mouth?"

"I didn't see that, I was behind him, but I heard others describing it."

"From several things Wil has said to me, I believe that he was still carrying his fear within him, that The Dark One merely forced it deeply inside him, for reasons I can't yet fathom. And when Wil saw Vernor..." Sare shuddered, and Jenora reached out and took her smooth, scarred hand in her own. "When he saw Vernor, he was somehow able to let it go." Sare's eyes took on a faraway cast. "To let the fire run through and around him. To let it burn, but not kill the part in the center of himself." She shook her head. "Anyway." Sare stopped, tears slipping down her rippled cheeks.

Jenora unfolded herself from the rug and sat next to her friend on the settee, wrapping her arms around the crying girl.

"I'm so afraid," Sare said again, voice catching. "What Vernor said he did, this curse we carry ... I knew as he said it that he was telling the truth. And something terrible is going to happen, I know that too."

"Perhaps his mind was torn by the fire that was killing him," suggested Jenora, but it didn't sound very convincing even to her.

"No, he knew. Aaren and I know too, but he doesn't like to speak of it." They looked at the dozing man before them, mouth slightly open, one hand curled back like a sleeping baby's. "We are moving toward something awful that spells the end of our families, and our kingdoms. That was Vernor's curse." Fresh tears sprang forth, and she wept against the warrior's shoulder.

"I refuse to believe that a dead traitor can kill the people I love most dearly," Jenora said fiercely. "Curse or not, our fate is ours to change."

Sare looked up. She sniffed and wiped at her tears with the back of her sleeve. Her eyes were bright, and full of pain, but also full of resolve. "Jen, I think I know a way to do just that. Vernor said that we would be the last of our lines, that we would perish in fire and our lineage would perish with us." Jenora nodded.

"It's true," Sare began, "that Aaren and I have been unable to ... to conceive a child. We've tried, but I believe that my womb must be as scarred as my countenance, and because of that, Vernor's curse has begun to come true. But it doesn't have to be that way." She gripped Jenora's arms fiercely, her words, obviously pent-up and waiting for this release, tumbling out of her in a rushing whisper. "If we could have a child, to raise here and be the royal heir to the combined thrones of Edge and Faires, that part of the curse would be broken, don't you see? And if that part were broken, then maybe the rest of it, the terrible thing that we all feel growing closer every day, that could be broken too!"

Jenora shook her head. "I don't understand. Is it possible for you and Aaren to –"

"No," Sare said softly, "it's not." She looked back up into Jenora's eyes. "But I am sure that he may sire children, and that might be enough."

Jenora's voice rose sharply. "What? You can't mean some other woman? He loves only you! And you could never –"

"Shh," whispered Sare, putting a finger to Jenora's lips. "This sort of thing has been done before. And I don't mean 'some' other woman. He does love me, and would never even consider the idea himself. And next to each other, more than anyone else, we both love you."

Jenora sat back, stunned. "Oh no. Oh, Sare, you can't mean this. He would never ... I couldn't ... you ... oh, no." She looked over at Aaren's sleeping form, and blinked back her own tears. "You don't know what you're asking," she whispered.

Sare, tears streaming freely down her face, answered, "Yes, my love, I do know. How could I not? I know your heart better than anyone. And I know his." She too looked at Aaren.

"But he doesn't, I mean, he'd never... I couldn't do this to you! I love you!"

"And that's why you must do this. Because you love me. And that makes it hard. And because you love him. And that makes it harder. I know, Jenora. I know.

"If it was just for me, I'd never ask this of you. If it was just for us, just Aaren and me, I'd never hurt you this way, place this terrible burden on you. But it's not. It's not, Jenora. There is a conflagration in the future, a fire coming that is so huge, and so awful, and I don't know if we can stop it. But I know I have to try. We have to. I don't know any other way. Be my friend. Be his Palatine. Please."

Jenora, eyes wild, stood abruptly, shaking her head, tears dropping to her tunic. "I have to think," she whispered. "You ask so much ... too much..." She turned and ran toward the hallway. She stopped at the door and looked back. Sare's face was in her hands; she was sobbing. The fire behind her was almost out. Jenora turned and ran down the corridor.

◆   ◆   ◆

It was a windy day. Sare walked alone in the Grove of Peace just outside the palace kitchens. The sky alternated frosty blue and tattered grey as the last of winter blew in from the sea and up the long slopes of the Nethals to the West. She drew her maroon cloak about her and stood watching the wind ruffle the water in the pond. The first buds were still some weeks away, but there was a subtle awakening in the bare plants that shook in the chill breeze.

Her eyes were distant. Looking up at the side of the palace, she wished longingly for Jenora to be at her side, talking or just walking with her. But the weeks following their conversation by the fire had been strained, and neither woman had mentioned the subject again. A fleeting movement in the south tower caught her eye. *Wasn't that the stairwell to Vernor's old rooms?* She had never actually been up there, but it had been pointed out to her. She was suddenly sure that she recognized Wil's shaggy head as he passed a tall window. She swung her cloak around her and went to the tower's outer door.

She found him sitting on the stairs with his hands on his knees, and his chin on his hands. Beside him were the remains of a small meal. He smiled nervously as she ascended the stairs.

"I, uh, I hope it's all right, me being here," he stammered.

"Of course, Wil." She sat a step below him. They often talked these days, and she was the only person in the palace he seemed comfortable with. He was obviously lonely, and her company was something he appeared to count on. "Do you come here often?" she asked.

"Yes," he said simply. "I like it up here. You can see far from different windows." He looked behind him, up the stairs, at the great oak door to Vernor's study. "I never go in there, though."

"Why not?"

"Well... I guess I don't know. Never wanted to. Have you been in there?"

"No, no I haven't." Sare craned her neck and looked up at the door with him. "Would you like to go in together?"

Wil swiveled his head back and gaped at her. Finally, he answered softly, "All right."

The room had not been touched since Vernor's death. It was cold and dusty, and smelled of things pickled in jars and ground from the plants of foreign lands. Wil breathed deeply and smiled, gingerly walking about the room and peering at glass philters and tarnished copper bowls and huge leather-bound books. Sare watched him from the doorway. He continued around the room, touching things. He found a book bound in a slightly scorched blue cover on one shelf and laughed aloud, pulling it down and turning the familiar pages.

"Do you know the ways of magic, then?" Sare asked.

He turned to her with a guilty start. "No. Not really. Well, I remember some of the things he taught me, but I was never any good." He looked back at the book in his hands. "I remember this one, it has simple spells for beginners." He smiled, closed the book, and put it down on the workbench in front of him. He stood awkwardly, as if not quite knowing what to do with his hands.

"Wil, do you know about the spell he cast on Aaren and on me?" she asked, as gently as she could, but knowing that her voice quivered slightly.

Wil frowned and began plucking at the sleeve of his tunic. "No. I really don't like to think about it." He set a pendulum on the workbench rocking with his knuckle, and began pacing the room again.

Sare hated pushing him, but felt powerless to stop herself from pressing on. "But, Wil, if a part of the curse didn't come true, that would make the rest of it invalid too, wouldn't it? Wouldn't it break the curse if you could stop its main part from happening?" She was pleading with him, and despaired at the incipient hysteria in her voice.

"I don't know!" he cried, his back to her, tearing at his shirtsleeves with agitated fingers. "I was only a boy!"

"But you said you knew magic! You must have some idea!"

He swung around, anger and pain writ plainly on his face. "Stop it! Why are you–" He stopped abruptly, his friend's tears stilling his tongue.

She sank against the doorframe, and slid to the ground. Her sobs were muffled behind her clasped knees. "Oh I'm so sorry, Wil! I have no right. I'm sorry. I never meant to hurt you. It's just, it's just that..." She trailed off bitterly.

He wavered for a moment, agonizing, then lurched across the room, knelt, and embraced Sare awkwardly. "There, don't cry." He patted her shoulder. "Maybe it would," he finally said, without much assurance. "Maybe it would help." She flung her arms around him and hugged him fiercely. Not knowing what else to do, Wil continued to hold the shaking woman.

A week later Wil appeared outside Aaren's council chamber. He sulked, glowering, in the hall until Stephen came upon him and asked his business. "I need to see *him*," he growled, pointing to the room with his chin.

"I see," Stephen replied, frostily. "Well. And this would be regarding..?"

Wil just stared back at him and pursed his lips.

"Very well." Stephen's eyes narrowed. "Wait here." He knocked at the door and entered at Aaren's command. "That ... assassin is here to see you, your Majesty. Should I call the guard?"

"No," Aaren said, looking up from a stack of correspondence in front of him, "that's all right Stephen." He stroked his chin, puzzled. "Send him in." The steward paused, looking troubled. "Really, it's all right. I don't think he means Edge, or me, any further harm."

Stephen hesitated a moment longer, then nodded. "Of course, Highness." He stepped back into the hall and stared long and hard at Wil. "You may go in." Wil moved to enter the chamber, but Stephen did not step aside. "I'll be right outside," Stephen whispered fiercely, and finally moved, just slightly. Glowering, Wil pushed past him into the chamber.

He stopped at the foot of the table. Never raising his gaze from his own shoes, he muttered, "I want to leave." There was an uncomfortable silence.

"You want to go back to Michael?" Aaren finally asked.

Wil raised his eyes to Aaren and quickly dropped them again. "Perhaps."

There was another long pause before Aaren spoke. "You are free to stay in Edge as long as you want, you know. I understand Sare has struck up a friendship with you, and there will be no punishment for your ... actions when you first arrived. You were obviously under the influence of the evil –"

"That's enough!" Wil growled angrily, looking up. "You will not speak of him to me, ever. He is a great and powerful man, and your twisted words dirty his name."

Aaren stood abruptly, slamming his palms on the table before him, and growled back, "As King I will speak however I please in my own palace, and strongly caution any *guest* to mind his place." The men stared into each other's eyes. Finally, Aaren nodded. "Yes." He straightened and crossed his arms. "Yes, I see that your notion to go from us is sound. There can be no peace for you here. I grant you leave. Take a horse and provisions. And may the Gifter smile upon you." Wil turned and opened the door. "Because," Aaren finished, "the Dark One will kill you the moment you set foot back in his camp."

Wil's shoulders stiffened. "Mayhap. But I'd rather die by his hand than live a moment longer in your shadow." He shouldered brusquely past Stephen and stormed down the hall.

◆   ◆   ◆

Aaren walked out the next day into the first warm morning of spring, and headed to the stables to see his troubled guest leave. He was met in the courtyard by Jenora and Sare, who turned angrily to him, both speaking at once.

"You can't possibly let him go –" cried Sare.

"I won't allow this man to leave –" began Jenora

"Stop." Aaren held up a hand. "One at a time. Sare?"

"He intends to rejoin Michael, Aaren. You must know that his life is worth nothing once he returns from his failure here. Sending him away is tantamount to a death sentence."

Aaren turned to his Palatine. "Jenora?"

"Whether they kill him or not, we cannot allow an assassin and spy to simply waltz into our halls, soak up valuable tactical intelligence, and then go blithely back to the monster that owns him. It goes beyond foolish, my liege, it is positively dangerous."

They both seemed ready to add to their arguments, but Aaren raised a finger for silence. He looked at Jenora. "What could he have learned here that would be of any value to our enemies? He has been confined to the palace itself. Has he been privy to planning sessions? Has he counted our horses, or assessed the readiness of our troops?"

"No," the warrior admitted, "but you know as well as I that any information is valuable to an enemy. We cannot know precisely what he has observed, and should it give Michael even the slightest edge, it would not be worth allowing this ... *assassin* to leave."

"And what could he know that a dozen others who pass daily, unmolested, from Edge's gates might not know?"

Jenora did not have an answer.

Aaren turned to his bride. "Have you spoken with him?"

"Yes. His faith in his benefactor is shaken, but not broken. He still believes, or wants to believe, that it was Michael who cured his madness. He intends to return and throw himself on the mercy of that fiend!"

"And what would you have me do? Chain him in the stockade? Though he's simple, he seems more than master of his own mind, and much as we might disagree with his loyalties, they are his own. We cannot force him to stay against his will unless we wish to imprison him for his crime."

Sare glared at him, small hands bunched into fists at her sides, and finally asked, "Do you want him to die then? For what he almost did to you? For loving our enemy?"

There was a moment of silence. He looked at them both, fully in the eyes, and softly asked, "Is there anything further that hasn't been said?"

Jenora crossed her arms and stared back at him. "No."

Sare dropped her gaze and said nothing.

"Very well." Aaren waited until they both looked up at him. He spoke with authority now. "Then my decision stands." He left them and went to Leland, who was leaning against a wooden gate outside the stables, waiting. "Is he prepared to go?"

"Aye," nodded Leland, adding, "he asked for a sword."

"Give him one. And get him out of my sight."

"Aye, your Highness." Leland snapped to attention. "Right away, m'Lord."

Aaren continued into the stables and saw Wil cinching the saddle girth on his mount, under the watchful eye of the head groom. Wil turned at Aaren's approach and gazed at him stonily. Aaren stopped in the dusty barn, smelling the horseflesh and hay, early light spearing in diagonal beams, until his eyes adjusted and he could look fully in Wil's own glowering eyes. After a moment he turned on his heel and tramped back to the palace, not speaking a word to anyone.

◆   ◆   ◆

Sare and Jenora sat in Jenora's apartments. The sun was long past the Nethals, and a fire warmed them from the hearth. Jenora sat at a small table. She oiled a dagger and ran it over the whetstone in her left hand, checking the edge every so often. Sare lay on her stomach on Jenora's bed, chin on her clasped hands, staring into the fire.

"Did he do the right thing, letting Wil go?" Sare asked without looking up.

Jenora took her time answering. "Yes. It was the right thing, because he truly is the King, and the decision was his to make." She shook her head. "I sometimes forget that Aaren is who he is. Times like today I marvel at how he has taken to his position. It is his job to make hard decisions, and ours to give him the best advice we may, and then support him, no matter what.

"Would I have done the same thing, had it been my place to say?" She laid down the blade and stone, and wiped her hands on a cloth. "Probably not. But I cannot help but respect the difficulty of the judgment, and his choice is one I stand behind. He is my sworn liege."

"And mine, as well as my husband." Sare sighed. "I weep for Wil, and hope against hope that he sees his way to some other direction than the one he has chosen, but I agree. Aaren was right to let him go. We can't let this sense of doom force us to forget who we are."

They both sat in silence, the crackling of the logs the only sound. Jenora got up and came over to the bed, where she sat next to her friend. After a moment she laid her hand on Sare's forearm. "We need to resolve this."

Sare tensed, staring at the flames. Then she turned, sighing again, and sat up to lean against the post at the foot of the bed. "I'm so sorry about the last few weeks."

Her scarred forehead creased as she carefully chose her words. "I've missed you terribly. I wish I could un-say what I said that night. But," she continued, "I am still so frightened of what lies ahead. I don't know what to do."

Jenora closed her eyes. She breathed deeply, twice, and opened them again. "I've missed you too," she said simply. Lying down, she curled up and put her head in Sare's lap, staring at the fire. Sare stroked her short hair, her cool fingers contrasting with the warmth of the hearth on Jenora's face.

"I really hated you for even asking me that," Jenora began. Sare, wisely, held her tongue and let the warrior speak her mind, though the words tore at her heart. "I mean, how *dare* you? The closest friend I have ever ... it was entirely too much." Yet she left her head in Sare's lap, and the young Queen held her breath, her hand stilled and trembling against Jenora's cheek. Finally Jenora spoke again.

"And that's what it is." Her voice was matter-of-fact, her words unadorned. "It is too much. I, too, sense the enormity of our future, and the terrible risks lying in wait. But I also know what is right and what is wrong. What you ask is wrong, Sare, and whatever destiny is thrown our way by Gifter or Tempter, this thing you ask would not aid us. It would destroy us. I will fight for you, and I will die by your side, but I will not do this thing."

The fire crackled and popped softly across the room. The sound of Jenora's slow breathing whispered against Sare's dress. One by one Sare's tears slipped from the scars on her chin and dropped, glistening, into Jenora's hair, where they sank after a moment, leaving tiny spots of darkness in the reflected glow of the firelight. After a while, Sare raised her friend up, wrapped her in her arms, and laid her face in the crook of her neck. They rocked, silently, a string of Sare's beads clinking softly against Jenora's cheek.

Chapter 31
Free

Wil rode into the canyon and stopped. He whistled as he had been taught, so that the sentries would know he was not a foe. Two burly outlaws rode out from behind their concealment and looked him over. One jerked his head that Wil should follow, and led him up to the camp. Wil's mount and gear were taken, and he was put in an unclaimed tent with a guard outside. An hour later the Arms Master came in, looked at him shrewdly, and performed an unpleasantly thorough search. Without saying a word he flung Wil's clothes back at him and strode from the tent, taking the borrowed sword away.

Methodically, Wil dressed and sat back down on the narrow cot. His mind was curiously blank; he felt no fear or hope. He didn't know who Dark Micha - John Winters really was, and he didn't know what his fate under the leader's iron hand would be; but he knew he owed the man his very life. So he waited.

Darkness fell, and a guard brought in camp rations and a flagon of water. Wil ate obediently, and later he obediently relieved himself when the guard led him to the latrine. Then he was put back in the tent. He grew tired and slept. The next morning he awoke feeling slightly dizzy, but otherwise as calm and empty as the day before. He rubbed his hands over his face and sat with his elbows on his knees, head hanging, until mid-morning when the gravel outside crunched under the unmistakable tread of his master.

Michael threw open the flap and stepped into the tent, followed by the guard who took up a position behind him. He was dusty, and wore a sword and riding clothes. Wil guessed that he had just now returned to the camp. Michael looked expressionlessly at Wil, who fell to his knees on the packed earth and bowed his head. There was a long moment of silence. Eventually, Wil looked up. Michael had not moved at all. They gazed at one another. Finally, Michael broke the silence. His voice was even, but began an almost imperceptible slide toward something more dangerous.

"My enemy is not dead."

Wil looked back at the ground, and shook his head.

"And you are not dead."

Wil shook his head again. There was an even longer pause than before. Then Wil heard the slither of steel as Michael's sword was pulled from its scabbard, and he looked up to see death in Michael's deranged eyes.

Michael's cheeks were mottled with color, and his breathing had grown ragged. He held the sword before him with trembling hands, pointing it at Wil's heart, then drew it back with a sudden inarticulate howl. Wil watched in utter astonishment as Michael swung around and cleaved the guard's head from his shoulders. It landed with a wet thud in the dirt between them. With enormous eyes, Wil watched as Michael hacked at the gory torso again and again, screaming and cursing. Momentarily he stiffened, and then, his mad fury abated, he staggered from the tent, calling hoarsely to his Arms Master: "Send him to Rebecca."

"Oh, we've been a ... bad..." whispered the albino, stroking Wil's cheek gently with one pink nail. She cocked her head to the side. "Michael is ... so very..." She looked briefly at the guard holding Wil, the odious Randy. "Take him to the empty ... cell and prepare him," she whispered. "We have so much to talk..." She straightened. "You can... handle that simple... can't you Randy?"

"Oh yes, ma'am," he answered quickly, twisting Wil's arms up behind him so forcefully that his shoulders popped. Wil moaned.

Rebecca smiled. "Then run along."

Randy propelled Wil down the stairs to the familiar dank corridor, arms locked behind his back. As they turned the last corner and came to the door of the interrogation room, Wil flinched as Randy pushed his head past a torch set in the wall.

"Oh that's right," Randy snickered, releasing his prisoner briefly to unlock the door. "We have a little problem with fire, don't we?" He pushed the door open and kicked Wil into the room.

Wil stumbled but did not fall. He recognized the room, saw the manacles set in the far wall, and suddenly decided that he had had enough. He had tried his best to do what - John - had set him to do. And in spite of the great gift that his friend had given him, Wil couldn't ignore all of the other evidence that led him to believe he was about to be tortured for information he didn't have, and then killed at - Michael's - order. The lethargy and hopelessness that had gripped his mind for far too long lifted. It was time, he decided, to take his fate into his own hands.

Wil squared his shoulders and began to turn around just as Randy's mailed fist drove into the side of his head. His vision obscured by stars and overwhelmed by the blossoming pain in his left ear, he nonetheless clearly heard the sound of the guard's girlish chuckle. At the second blow Wil did fall down, landed hard and ended up crouched on his hands and knees, head hanging, trying to regain his senses as he watched blood drip from his chin and spatter on his hands.

"Alley-oop!" shouted Randy as he planted a boot in Wil's midsection and flung him against the wall. Something in Wil's chest make a sound like a snapping twig. While he lay gasping and trying to get his wind back, Randy sauntered over to the wall and drew out a torch from its sconce.

Grinning happily, he turned and went back to the prone man, waving the flame back and forth in long whooshing arcs. "Uh oh - looks like trouble!" He smiled more widely as he watched Wil's eyes track the sizzling pitch. "Big trouble, I'm thinkin'." He stood over Wil, swinging the torch back and forth above him.

What happened next surprised Wil almost as much as it did Randy. Lunging out with his right leg, Wil kicked the feet out from under the guard just as he had been taught in a lesson with Michael's Arms Master. As Randy pinwheeled his arms and began to fall, Wil snatched the torch from his hand, exploded up out of his crouch, and jammed the flaming end up as hard as he could into the guard's crotch. Both men screamed in pain, Wil from his cracked rib and Randy from his savaged groin, and they toppled over together onto the rough floor.

Wil landed on top, and heard Randy's head crack against the flagstones. He heaved the guard up by his shoulders and gave him another crack for good measure. As he scrambled to his feet, Randy's eyes rolled back to their whites, and Wil fumbled the short sword from the man's scabbard. He staggered to the door and leaned heavily on it, resting momentarily and still trying to get back his breath. He knew he didn't really have the time – other guards were undoubtedly rushing to the sounds of their commotion – but he thought if he didn't take a moment to gather himself he would simply pass out.

Peering out into the corridor a few moments later, he was surprised to see it empty in both directions. *Could it be that screams are so common here that no one takes any notice?* he wondered, limping quickly back toward the stairs. He traveled unmolested up them to the main hallway of Hollow House. Glancing toward the front door he realized that night had fallen, and was dismayed to see two guards lounging in the entrance. There would be no escape in that direction. The hallway led the other way into gloom; he could just make out three or four doors, and it seemed to turn right at the far end. Cautiously he slid down the nearest wall, trying to make himself as small as possible to the guards' view.

At the first doorway he listened, heard voices, and moved on as quickly as he dared. He was staring so intently at the guard posted near the stairway that he didn't notice the second door opening until he bumped into it, his short sword clattering. Stepping past the door, he came face-to-face with Rebecca. They stared at each other in surprise for a moment, then her pink eyes narrowed, and she screeched, "Guards!"

Wil shoved the door into her as hard as her could, knocking her back into the room; a small velvet packet of glittering steel instruments scattered from her hand to the carpeting. Seeing the guards from both sides bearing down on him, Wil quickly followed her into the room and threw the enormous bolt he was relieved to find on the inside. As the men shouted and hammered on the locked door, Wil turned around to find Rebecca slipping quietly toward him, white hair in a crazed nimbus around her suddenly savage features, clutching a tool that had two tiny pronged hooks on the end.

She lunged at his face and he raised the sword instinctively, as it was the only thing in his hand. Its point came up and met the plunge of her stab, skewering her bony arm midway between elbow and wrist. She shrieked and dropped the hooked tool, pulling on his blade. But it was at a bad angle, and as near as he could tell she was trapping it between the bones of her forearm as she hysterically tugged away.

Wil wasn't about to let go of his weapon, and so he too pulled back hard. There was a revolting sensation of metal scraping bone, and suddenly the blade was free; her arm was spouting blood as she tumbled to the ground, her hand barely attached. She hit the floor and writhed, screaming, holding her mangled arm with her right hand.

Wil looked frantically around the room, hearing the guards redouble their attack on the door at the sound of her cries. It was the same room he remembered, the one in which Michael had fed him the fire. Wil ran to the windows, and seeing that they were not designed to open, he picked up a chair and hurled it through the glass. Retrieving his bloody sword, he knocked the remaining shards clear and clambered out into the rainy night.

He staggered off toward the woods at the base of the mountain. There, at last, he began to feel safe. This was something he knew: running at night, hiding in thickets, living in the forest when it wasn't safe to go among men. He'd spent the better part of his life in his own company; and without the fear and fire clouding his thoughts, and with all he'd learned from Michael, and Cillistra, and Sare, and the experiences of the last months, he felt that maybe he'd gained something more valuable than his sanity. He'd found hope.

With sudden clarity, he knew that he would head north. That was not a very specific destination, but it was more than he had had in a long time. He turned and vanished into the wet trees without a backward glance.

Chapter 32
Night of Dreams

A gibbous moon waxed with an oily sheen in the unseasonably cold autumn night. Sickly grey clouds tore themselves against the stars. The land and the sky waited numbly for the frightening and unknown future the next day would bring. Darkness curled around the Nethals and flowed into the isolated houses of the people who lived in their shadows. It seeped into their rooms. It lay with them in their dreams.

◆   ◆   ◆

Picking her way carefully over and between the familiar moss-covered stones and alders, Jenora took her hand from Friendship's hilt only long enough to grasp an occasional branch for support. Early morning sun shafts cut the dusty air, and she slipped between the diagonal spears of light with all the silence and stealth Leland had taught her. A brook chuckled nearby, but the sounds of her footsteps and heartbeat lost their struggle to blend with the forest sounds.

The figure in the ebony mask whirled into an en garde just as she thought that for once, she had gained surprise. With a sound of whispering steel, she was upon him.

Their blades met high, and a single blue spark sent the illuminated dust-motes spinning into troubled eddies. Jenora drew back into a midline feint, then struck from the side as the small black-masked form barely countered, deflecting her thrust inches from his ribs.

Both paused for a moment, her fierce brown eyes scouring vertical holes in his mask. Jenora noticed subliminally that the glossy black curls that usually adorned the mask's sides were gone. A host of small discrepancies were adding up in her mind ~ stature, speed, a peculiar hesitance; but she wanted this combat more than anything she could remember. Her soul cried out to kill him, kill him now, and with an indrawn breath she drove her sword straight to his stomach.

At the last second, far past the point at which she could have held back (though she never would have), her opponent's weapon dropped silently to the leaf-covered loam. With both black gloves he grasped Jenora's hands and pulled the blade deeply in.

The figure slumped forward onto its knees, upright only by leaning into the sword protruding from its midsection. In shock, Jenora staggered back, staring at the crumpled form. With the barest tremor, it reached up and removed the mask.

Sare's features were unmistakable. She looked up at Jenora, tears tracking slowly around the scars of her face. In one fluid motion Sare pulled the sword from her belly, only it wasn't a sword anymore. It was a key.

There was blood on Jenora's hands and arms, smeared all down her tunic and leggings, but on Sare there was none. Jenora's own abdomen pulsed, and she realized that the blood was her own.

In an intricate syncopation, her blood and Sare's tears dripped onto the leaves.

◆   ◆   ◆

The kitchen was a shambles. Chickens ran about squawking on the countertops, stock frothed and boiled over on the stove, and the first curls of black smoke began seeping out of the great main oven. The chef was passed out in the corner, empty wine bottles strewn about his legs. Rodolpho took a final incredulous look at the disorderly panorama and stormed out into the dining hall, only for some reason it wasn't the dining hall, it was the stables. Anxiety increasing, he tried to find his way back to the house. Damn this "palace," as they called it. Nothing set out properly, staff invariably somewhere other than where you needed them, and that Stephen fellow nipping about at his heels like a mongrel cur.

He found his way, somehow, back to the main building, but the corridor he was in was oddly long, miles long in point of fact, and he broke into a trot trying to find the end of it. That really made him cross; one made a point to never let the staff see one in any state other than calm efficiency, and Gifter forbid if he ran across a member of the royal family.

Suddenly, the door in front of him was the correct one. He took a deep breath, pushed it open, and walked calmly out into the dining hall. Thank goodness things in here seemed to be running more smoothly. Guests were properly seated at their proper places, the wait-staff looked attentive but not overbearing, and the Queen ~ well, actually the Queen looked rather odd. Shocked, that's how she looked. Shocked, and offended.

Gifter save us, Rodolpho thought, what's happened now? Have I remembered to give her the key? Yes, that was all right. Everything else looked normal. The room was a bit on the chilly side. At least, it felt that way to him. Suddenly, with the horror of inevitability, he stopped and looked down.

He wasn't wearing any pants.

◆   ◆   ◆

Aaren was climbing. He slid his hands up over the rough surface of the cliff face, and dug his fingers into the chill cleft between two rocks. He had been climbing for some time now, though he could not say when or how he had started. His limbs ached; his joints cracked with each movement. He was getting very near his goal.

The climb was doubly difficult because of the darkness. He was climbing by touch alone, feeling for each root and toehold. A light wind blew, pushing fish-scale clouds through the sky and tugging him away from the rock. He held on and continued to ascend. Within minutes he reached the top and carefully dragged himself over. He rested a moment, and then rolled to his feet.

He stood at the easternmost end of the Nethals, not far from the Waist itself. Almost two years earlier he had been here, with an army at his back, hoping to recapture a lost home. Now the pain and fear of loss-to-come were blades contorting in his soul.

He looked south. The figure of a man rose into the night, perched on the very lip of the precipice. The glowing semicircle of waning moon turned the scudding clouds half white, half black. It gave enough light to clearly show the man's garments and curls of ebon hair. But regardless of his movements, his face remained in shadow. Aaren moved closer, and heard a deep voice speaking words he almost recognized in a language he didn't know. He found himself running.

The shadowed man's voice intensified. Something glittered and swung from his neck like a pendulum, like a shower of blood. The clouds were gone; the wind in Aaren's face grew as if the air itself fled in terror from this being. A horrible urgency gripped Aaren's heart. He had to reach him, had to stop him...

The dark man cried out one last fearful word and flung high his arms, and the valley below disappeared beneath the foaming crest of an enormous crimson wave.

✦ ✦ ✦

"Stop!" Michael screamed, again, as his brother turned with a smile and stepped into the road. The carriage, as always in the recurring dream, thundered around the corner as if sprung from Hell itself, and the boy was battered beneath steel-shod hooves and splintered wood. The driver never slowed at all.

Jacob's body uncurled like crushed grass in the churned and crimson mud. One pale arm, spattered with dark earth, pointed toward Michael, pleading with him, or remonstrating against his negligence.

Breaking free of his paralysis, Michael rushed forward (checking the road first, he reminded himself bitterly) and knelt in the mud beside him. The boy was obviously, horribly dead. Haltingly, tenderly, he picked up his brother, vainly attempting to gather the broken pieces to his chest. Jacob's head lolled at a ghastly angle, dripping blood into the icy street. He was fast growing cold.

Beneath Michael's shock and grief was a rapidly swelling denial: This would not happen. Not again. He began chanting the ancient stolen words. Scooping the mud from the street, he packed Jacob's wounds, then kept on, slathering the bloodied grey soil over every inch of his brother's body. The words of the spell gathered Michael's power, drew it from him and focused it, and the cold form in his arms hardened, and became smooth. Michael stopped.

The golem opened its white eyes, and regarded him calmly. It reached up with strong, gentle fingers and tore out Michael's throat. As his lifeblood gushed out over the grey figure, the golem took Michael into its arms and rocked him, cradling him as gently as Michael had held Jacob. They closed their eyes and rocked, waiting.

◆　　　　　◆　　　　　◆

Cillistra walked through the streets of Faires like a ghost. All around her, people were working or playing or standing about. A shopkeeper to her right was handing pastries to a pair of well-dressed ladies in exchange for a silver penny. Three plainer women stood gossiping in the shadow of an alehouse sign at the next cross street. Children ran across her path and down an alley, laughing wildly at their game. A dairyman drove his cart down the center of the roadway; his great horse's shoulder brushed past Cillistra with a rush of air, and a small yellow dog ran yapping at its heels. But none of them, people or beasts, took the slightest notice of her.

She stopped beside the gossiping trio, and tried to speak to them. No sound came forth. She clutched at her throat, sucked in a great breath, and tried again: nothing. She could not utter the smallest word. She stepped forward and reached to take the nearest woman by the arm. All three vanished as if they had never been.

Cillistra turned and looked back the way she had come. The shopkeeper and his customers were gone; dark smoke rolled sluggishly from under his broken awning. The dairy cart lay on its side in the street, its wheels broken and its jars of milk shattered and spilt all around.

She heard a sound from the alley, and turned down it. Three steps in, she stopped and gasped in horror. The sound was made by two large rats, gnawing at the naked corpse that lay sprawled upon the refuse there. It was one of the children,

353

her throat slit. Cillistra could still utter no cry, no scream. She turned and ran up the street, terror stabbing into her very bones.

She rounded the corner and stopped again. It was the Avenue of Flags, and it was littered with bodies. She found herself racing past them, trying not to see them as they lay in their blood, headless, disemboweled, pinned to a wall by a broken lance.

She reached the Keep without going mad. Its gates were broken, and she slipped through them. If possible, it was worse here: corpses were everywhere, most of them armed, and killed as violently as the townsfolk. A line of them led up the steps to her home. Shuddering, stepping over and around them, she started to mount the stairs.

A hand fell on her shoulder. She gave a soundless shriek and whirled about. It was Michael.

His look was full of concern for her. His lips moved, and after a second, his words came to her: "It had to be. It had to be." He said it over and over again.

She looked down, dimly seeing the body at her feet. It lay on its face, its arms outstretched and a sword near one hand. It wore the colors of the royal house over its armor.

Cillistra looked away; she could not bring herself to see. She suddenly realized that Michael's hand upon her was dripping blood down her arm, that his garments and the sword in his other hand were splashed in blood. Dimly, she realized that some of the blood was his. A grievous wound on his throat pulsed gently down his chest and arm.

She turned her gaze down again. The corpse was still there, and this time she forced herself to see ~ to see the crown that lay beside its head. Michael's hand fell away. She looked up to see where he had gone, but he had vanished like the rest. Far away, near the edge of a distant square, she could see two figures approach each other and embrace. They dissolved into flames.

Suddenly, as she lifted her face to the sky, she found her voice. But all that came forth was a howl that shook the stones themselves.

◆   ◆   ◆

Sare was walking in the roof garden, at home in Faires, her eyes reflecting the oranges, pinks, and reds of the sunset. The purple and peach clouds were spectacular. The fountain was splashing quietly behind her. Her father was suddenly there, as happens in dreams; he walked toward her, smiling, and sat on the bench by the fountain. He patted his knee, and she went to him and sat on his lap, the way she had as a child. He kissed the top of her head.

"There's Da's best girl."

She curled up under his beard, and laid her head against his chest, listening for the great, safe, beating of his heart. But there was no sound. She squirmed closer, frowning, but his breast was silent, and did not rise and fall with breath. She noticed his crown overturned and lying at his feet. Alarmed, she raised her head, calling out in a childish voice, "Da? Da!"

"Stop," he said, putting a finger to her lips. "It's all right."

She looked into his calm gaze, her own eyes troubled. "But..."

"Shhh," he whispered. "What have I always told you?"

She swallowed. "That I am your best girl!"

He smiled. "Yes. That too. But you must remember that the Gifter in his wisdom saw fit to give you great courage, and great strength. Without it you could never have become the amazing young woman your Da loves today. Carola will be fine, and Cillistra..." He trailed off, his eyes full of sorrow. "But you, Sare, need to remember your strength, when the time comes."

"When what time comes?"

"When all our time comes," he said. "You are the key."

355

"The key to what?" she started to ask, but again he put his finger to her lips and held her close as they watched the ruddy disk of the sun disappear into the darkness.

✦　　　✦　　　✦

At last the sky pearled to chill grey over the sea. The darkness unwound grudgingly from bedposts and crept back out windows over the glittering frost. For a moment Alyda lay perfectly still, ruddy sunrise staining the walls of her bedroom. For just that moment, just one or two heartbeats, the night's illusions remained. Then the chill from the linen of the great empty bed reached over and caressed her arm, her breasts, her belly; and the last of the phantoms blew away in tatters, like mist before a cold wind.

Hugging her thin arms to her torso, she rose and walked over to the full-length mirror and stared in at the haunted woman who huddled there in the cold. Her long hair was snarled from sleep, her eyes sunken and dull.

"Stop." It was a whisper.

Whether she was talking to herself, to the cruel, lingering memories of Trever, or to her own certainty of onrushing calamity was unclear. As the rest of the palace began to stir and rise; the Queen stooped, shaking, before the cold glass.

Chapter 33
Biddings

Michael stood dripping on the white bones of the grotto. Some things had changed over the years that he'd been coming here. The icy swim through the narrow tunnel was a little more difficult for his fully muscled adult frame, and he had to stoop in some parts of the grotto. Some things never seemed to change, though: the leprous green light, the crunch of the bones beneath his feet, and the bickering of the Pendulum.

...Greybeal. The Sword will play a pivotal role.

Enough! We have gone over this before. We simply cannot see the effect...

...or the Lion Gems. The other lost relics...

Michael is here!

Yes. Our prodigal...

"Hello, Michael." He felt the faint whisper of the Touch. "You've been away a long time."

"You've received your deaths," Michael said flatly.

True. But we need more! If we could...

...time of resurrection. The extended Touch has almost reached the critical capacity for us to...

Death! DEATH!

Twenty months had passed since the traitor Wil had returned and maimed Rebecca. Michael had spent that time in his retreat, building his army. He could wait no longer. The time had come for him to gather his troops and make the first assault. His warriors were few compared with his foes, but most now had the power of the killing gaze, which would make up for much of what they lacked in numbers. And the reptile-men had been trained, motivated, and augmented with a force of creatures that lived in the remotest reaches of the forest beyond the unnamed western mountains. They were large, bearlike, and possessed of enough intelligence to make and wield weapons. But he needed one more thing.

"The time is ripe for war," he said. "I have gathered my army. With your help they have become strong, the match of any of my enemies. But what use are such fighters against walled cities and fortresses? I need a lever, a lever of such power that no fortification can stand to it. I have neither the time nor the resources for an extended siege."

...Orestius mendos. Carapath est dumia...

The creature of the bog perhaps?

...with no thought to our allies in the West...

Yes. Perfect.

"We know of a creature. The fortifications will pose it few difficulties. It is very old, however, and angry when disturbed. You will need to tithe it, in a very particular way."

Michael smiled. "I don't think that will be a problem."

✦   ✦   ✦

Cillistra awoke to a cacophony of voices and clashing metal, birdsong and wagon wheels, horses and clattering wood. It sounded almost as if a battle was underway somewhere below.

Michael was not beside her. Rising out of the wide bed, she padded to the nearest window and leaned out, the stone chill against her fingers in the morning air. The embrasure was too narrow to show her much; but she was able to see men, mounts, and equipment moving about with great activity on the ridge below.

She turned back to the room. The slanting light of this spring morning shone brightly enough to show her all its richness, the tapestries warming its thick stone walls, the heavy brocade underfoot, the dark woods of the chests and cabinets. In the four years since she came with Michael to this fastness in the mountains, this room had become her home.

She opened her wardrobe and quickly slipped on a warm, deep-blue gown and her sturdiest shoes, then descended the stairs into the anteroom and went outside.

It was like stepping into a maelstrom. Everywhere she could see, Michael's warriors and retainers were on the move. Wains and weapons heaved or glinted at every hand; stacks of pikes lay beside her own doorway, and horses snorted steam as they shuffled past her.

She moved among them carefully, as there was still snow lying about; it stayed late into the year at this altitude. She received several nods and salutes as she looked about for Michael. After all this time among his minions, she scarcely noticed the difference between the human and the inhuman any longer.

She found him at the northernmost bourn of his
redoubt, where the heights fell away into sheer cliffs. She
stopped for a moment just to watch him, silhouetted
against the morning, giving orders to those who
clustered about him and scurried away to do his will.
Taking a deep breath, she smiled and hurried forward.

Michael's lieutenants made way for her. He turned
before she could touch his sleeve, and raised a hand to
stay her. Glancing at the man beside him, he rumbled,
"Tell Rebecca to be ready, and meet us there just at
sunset. At sunset, and no later, you understand?" The
man nodded and hastened away. So, it seemed, did all
the others; in a trice, she and Michael were alone.

She stood beside him and looked out over the
crenellations, carved from the living stone to resemble
simple boulders, at least from a distance. The view from
this parapet was astounding, and Cillistra had never
tired of it. There was nothing below them for hundreds
of feet, down to the scree and snowdrifts among the
trees at the cliff's base. The land beneath swept out for
nearly a thousand unbroken leagues, the whole vastness
of the Steppes to the west, Michael's undisputed realm.
She could see the faint glistening of the streams that
crossed the plain, and wild grains waving in the soft
breeze. Far in the distant haze, she could just make out
the highest snow-capped peaks of the western
mountains.

Michael slipped his arm about her waist. "An early
rising for you, minnow."

She looked up into his face, noting the grey that had
lightly crept into his hair and beard this year past. It
accented the cragginess of his features, and the dark
warmth of his brown eyes. "How could I sleep with all

this bustle? Something has happened, hasn't it? What is it? Something bad, or good?"

He grinned and turned his gaze back to the forest beneath them, the great emptiness beyond that. "Nothing bad, little one, nothing bad at all. Quite the opposite." She could feel a tension, a caged excitement, in his touch. "Something quite magnificent, in fact. We are finally ready, you see. You shall be going home very soon. Home to rule, with me."

She stared, and drew away slightly. "Home? To Faires? You mean it truly, I can see that you do. I didn't know..."

"Yes." He looked back at her. "All the mustering and harboring are done, the waiting ended. All I need to take my place in this world is at hand - or at least, all but one last thing. We leave today, on our way to Alatia. Near there, tomorrow night, I will take possession of that one last tool I need. We will try it in Alatia first, and if it works..." He took her by the shoulders. "... then by this time next month, you will be sitting upon the throne in Faires. And by the end of summer, in Edge as well!"

She was stunned. She had known his ambitions all along, and known for five years that they were undimmed. He had often been away from her, and she knew that he had been making preparations for this time. Still, it came upon her as though it had no warning. She realized that she had been avoiding thinking of this inevitability. But now was no time to shy from destiny, she chided herself. Out of the turmoil of her thoughts, two questions arose. Looking into his eyes, she dared to ask the first. "May I go with you tonight? I never have, you know, but this time ... may I?"

He considered it. "I don't think that would be a good idea, minnow. There will be violence, and I need all my wits about me. I don't want to have to think of protecting you at the same time."

"Please, Michael. The time has come for me to be a part of all that you do." She stood back and faced him fully. "Who do you see before you today?"

He gazed at her long and hard, and then broke into one of his rare smiles. "I see a woman who will sit on the throne at my side. I see the most beautiful creature the Gifter ever put upon this world." He reached for her, but she pushed him away, not smiling back.

"And what don't you see?"

Again he appraised her, this time a bit more thoughtfully. Finally, he nodded. "I don't see the squeamish, silly girl I knew years ago in another life. I don't see doubts, or lack of resolution. I don't see cowardice or weakness." He put his hands on her shoulders and nodded. "All right. But take heed: whatever you see, keep your place and your silence. There will be things outside your ken done tomorrow night. Understood?"

She nodded, gathering her courage to make her second request. "Will you promise me something, as you love me? Promise me that - when we take Faires - that none of my family will be harmed."

For an instant she saw his rage kindled, with the rush of terror she always felt when she angered him. She knew, every time, that he was truly capable of killing her, however he might regret it afterwards. Then as quickly as ever, it faded, leaving only a dangerous light in his eyes, and she breathed again as he spoke. "It will be war, Cillistra. The strongest leader cannot warrant against what may happen in war. I do promise to command all my forces as you ask. Beyond that, no one can say." He held her gaze until she looked away.

He grinned again then, and twirled her around as though they were dancing. "If you plan to come with me, you'll need to make haste! Go and pack yourself for travel, and I'll send to have your horse exercised and made ready. We leave at noon!" He swatted her on one haunch as she hurried off, his deep laughter following her all the way back into the mountainside.

At dusk, Michael reined up his horse on the road to Alatia, and everyone else stopped as well. The setting sun cast an orange glow across the steppes and bathed the Nethals in its ruddy light.

He and Cillistra, escorted by two soldiers and his Shadow, had ridden ahead of the army encamped on the muddy trail behind them. Cillistra had been amazed at the size of that force, when she had first trotted out to join Michael the day before. The ranks upon ranks of men, unmen, horses, war engines, and supply wagons had covered half the plain, a frightening and thrilling vision. She had no idea that Michael had assembled such a host over the years; it almost rivaled that of Faires, if not Edge. When Michael gave the order to move, the earth had literally trembled beneath them.

They had left as the army began setting up its second nightly bivouac. There was a sixth rider with their group, a naked man bound to his saddle, with a sackcloth over his head. The golem led this captive's horse behind its own.

They were stopped now at a place where a narrow trail emerged from a dark wood to join the road. After a moment Cillistra heard a horse moving up the sloping trail toward them. Rebecca emerged from the trees, riding a dappled cob, its reins held somewhat awkwardly in her right hand, and came to Michael. Cillistra noted that the albino's left hand rested crookedly across her lap. Knowing the story, she suppressed a smile. *Good for you, Wil. And Gifter speed you, wherever you are.* She had always loathed Rebecca.

"My Lord ... you are ... just in. Everything below ... ready..."

Michael nodded curtly and turned to the men-at-arms. "You two remain here. My dear, you follow Rebecca." And to the golem: "Bring him."

Without even sparing the princess a glance, Rebecca started her mount back down the trail, and Cillistra went after her, wrinkling her face at the sickly-sweetish smell ahead. In seconds, they had left the daylight completely behind. Cillistra could barely see Rebecca's white hair bobbing before her as she ducked under branches and felt twigs snagging and releasing her cloak. She could hear Michael and the other two riders behind her, but could not see them when she chanced to turn her head.

They rode for perhaps a mile, downhill all the way, before Cillistra began to sense a faint, growing light ahead, and to smell burning wood. Moments later, they emerged from the trees and brush.

They were on the shore of a huge marsh, extending into the distance much farther than she could see in the darkness. A fire burned nearby, heaped high but giving off little smoke and hardly more light. Rebecca dismounted on its far side; Michael tied his and Cillistra's horses to the nearest tree, then swung to the ground and helped her off as well.

She looked around to see that the golem, soundless as always, was also afoot, and reaching up to its prisoner.

With no hint of effort, it heaved the man down from his saddle to the ground; the man's cramped, bound legs failed him and he crumpled. The golem dragged him over to the edge of the marsh, next to the fire, and stood holding him up.

Michael removed something from his saddlebag and strode around the fire to join Rebecca. He looked up over the flames, and pinioned Cillistra with his gaze. "I remind you of your promise. You *would* come here, and I saw no reason why you should not. But no matter what transpires, speak no word, no word at all – on your very life. This is not for you."

She could only swallow and nod. The look in his eyes was unholy, and Rebecca was breathing rapidly with excitement. *What Tempter's work is to be done here?*

Michael beckoned to his Shadow. The golem dragged the bound man over to its master's side, laid him supine and retied his arms and legs to stakes driven into the ground. Michael unrolled the black cloth in his hands and brought forth its contents: a brown leather pouch, a long leaf-shaped knife, and something dark and spindly.

He handed the pouch to Rebecca. She reached inside it and drew out a handful of yellow powder. At Michael's signal, she cast it into the fire. The flames leaped higher, emitting a foul smoke. Michael raised both his hands, and Cillistra could see both objects he held now. The brightened firelight glinted off the knife's blade in his right hand. In his left was a severed human hand, withered and crooked, its sere blackened skin flaking off in spots. *Gifter protect us!* thought Cillistra. *A Hand of Glory!*

Both Michael and Rebecca were speaking now, but the tongue they used was none Cillistra had ever heard, not even among the inhumans. Flamelight danced over their faces, at once grim and exultant. When they paused in the chant, Rebecca threw another palm of powder into the fire.

The spell-casting went on for several minutes, with first Michael's voice incanting, then Rebecca's answering. Her reedy voice was much stronger during the incantation than it ever was in normal conversation, though no less displeasing. Finally, they stopped. Rebecca drew back a step, and Michael bent over the prisoner.

Cillistra, on the far side of the fire, sidestepped to see them better around the curling flames. Michael pulled the cloth from the man's head, revealing the blond hair and pale eyes of an Alatian. Those eyes were filled with terror as Michael touched the Hand of Glory to the man's forehead, and drew it slowly down his face, the long, dead fingernails leaving shallow furrows in the fair skin.

The man whimpered through his gag when the Hand continued down his throat and chest. Michael was murmuring now, in the same lost language as before. He dragged the Hand over the captive's belly, all the way to his manhood, shriveled with fear. Michael laid the Hand in the center of the man's chest and held the athalme over the bound right arm. He spoke a single word, and thrust the point beneath the prisoner's skin.

Cillistra gasped but could not look away as Michael drew the blade down, opening a long, deep cut that welled forth blood. He drew the knife out, spoke the same word and made an identical cut on the left arm.

The Alatian was choking, weeping with pain and writhing away from Michael's touch. Michael moved down and sliced incisions in both bucking legs, muttering the same foul syllable each time. Then he stood and nodded to his Shadow.

The golem untied the man, lifted him into its arms and glided smoothly to where Michael pointed, toward the tarn. Michael and Rebecca were chanting again; his back was to Cillistra, but Rebecca's face was clear. Her head was upturned, her eyes closed, and a smile that could only have come from the Pit itself stretched her moving lips.

The golem stopped when it stood ankle-deep in the bog. Lifting the bleeding man high over its head, it waited. Michael and Rebecca also raised their arms, and shouted a final horrific command.

Without a sound, the golem threw the Alatian far out into the marsh. Cillistra heard the splat when he landed, but she could barely see him twisting and moaning in the rank mud and weeds. Michael pulled a burning branch from the fire and held it high.

Suddenly the Alatian stopped thrashing. His gagged voice rose up in muted screams of horror and revulsion, and he began sinking from sight. With renewed vigor he kicked and wrenched and heaved, and Cillistra clearly heard the sound of a snapping bone echo across the water to her. *Is he in quicksand? But what is that other sound, ugly and ~ unnamable, beneath his noise?* She realized that she had been slowly backing away all this time, and was now standing against the underbrush of the woods.

The man's screams stopped when his head vanished below the surface. Michael's Shadow sloshed back onto the shore and stood beside its horse. Cillistra looked from it to Michael to Rebecca. They showed no sign of having finished their work; no, they were standing expectantly, waiting with shortened breath for something, for something more to happen.

Motion, out in the fen. She thought perhaps the dying man had flailed himself up for an instant. Then a wide expanse of the bog slowly began to rise. The mud and water sloughed away, and something blacker than the ooze, blacker than the night itself, bubbled up like a small hill.

It sat, heaving and barely visible even in the torchlight, until Michael shouted again. The – thing – began to roll forward, coming to Michael's summons.

Cringing back into the stabbing brush, trying to move, suppressing the impulse to just *run*, Cillistra barely stifled the scream that bubbled in the back of her throat.

◆ ◆ ◆

A fortnight later, word reached King Aaren in Edge: Dark Michael had come out of the Steppes with no warning, and utterly sacked the city of Alatia.

Chapter 34
Invasion

King Gearld of Faires awoke to an odd sensation. For a moment, he wondered if the valley was suffering one of its rare earth tremors. He looked about and saw that neither the floor nor his wall hangings moved, so that could not be it.

The feeling was still there as he sat up, softly throbbing all through his bed and the wood beneath his feet. Beside him, Queen Signe turned in uneasy sleep.

He dressed quickly and strode through the halls. They, too, carried the strange vibration in their stones; all the Keep faintly hummed with it.

When he reached the outer passage, Gearld was moving faster. Something prodded him with the first unsettling spur of alarm. He was climbing the stairs to the battlements when he identified the tremor as a sound.

It came more clearly and softly through the open air, but could still be felt as well when he came out onto the western ramparts. Soldiers were clustering there from all over the castle's heights. They came to attention when the King approached, and gave him way to the best vantage.

Gearld looked out over the city. Much of it was still in shade, with the sun only beginning to color the highest rooftops as it cleared the Nethals. An unusual tumult was coming from the western gate: voices were raised from outside the city wall, and the gate sentries were shouting back. But these were not the sounds that had awakened him.

Gearld peered farther, past the quiet fields and manors with smoke rising from morning fires. He looked west along the river and the Road, toward the steppes beyond. His gaze was caught by a rider, a horseback figure pounding full-tilt toward the city amid a haze of road dust.

The sun rose higher at Gearld's back, and something appeared out near the river's bend. A shaft of sunlight winked back to him in a thousand pinpoints, twinkling like the star-crowded sky of mid-summer. A gust of wind breathed in his face and brought him a stronger draft of the sound that he felt, ever increasing, through his hands upon the wall.

He straightened with a frown. "Captain of the watch!"

A man stepped forward. "Your Majesty?"

Gearld turned to him with no trace of his usual amiability. "Have the western gates opened for that rider. When he enters, bring him to me. Bar the gates again. Wake the trumpeters and sound the muster. Send to the armory to issue full weaponry to each man reporting there, and have my armor and sword brought to me here."

He turned back to the west. "Those are drums, and that is an army."

An hour later, the first fires broke out.

The streets of Faires swarmed with people; most of the folk from the surrounding countryside had come within the city walls. Shopkeepers had dropped their counters and bolted their shutters; the smith had barred the iron gate to his mews.

King Gearld stood on the rampart of the town wall and watched the fires bloom. He could see figures running through the fields. They carried torches, and wherever they went, fire arose behind them. Already one manor and the land around it were ablaze.

The King could see the enemy clearly now, rank upon rank of horsemen behind only three squares of pike. Before the pikes marched the drummers, pounding long drums with deep bass tones. Behind the horses came something indistinct, a dark, shifting mass like storm cloud or roiling shadow.

Gearld gave orders while he watched, deploying the men who were arriving in numbers. His armor grew stuffy in the rising heat of the day; but it did not chafe nearly so much as his swelling anger against the enemy he could not yet engage.

The burning was a calculated act of terror and contempt. *Flee before us while your homes burn*, it said. *All your wealth is naught to us; we tread on it and leave only ashes.*

The walls on both sides of the King were lined with men, fully armed and restive. The Keep's own garrison was manning its posts in full strength. Glancing over his shoulder, Gearld saw the troops moving into place, and saw as well his wife and daughter watching at a high window.

"Majesty!" The captain's voice called him back. He followed the man's pointing finger to see that fighting had erupted at the nearest manor.

Old Lord Falder and his son were defending their home; the two nobles and their housecarls fired arrows from the windows. Two of the torchmen were down in the grass.

"Your Highness, should we not send them aid?"

The same thought was in Gearld's mind. His men-at-arms were ready, his knights were assembled near the gates below. At a word they could charge out. . .

A team of horsemen broke off from the advancing army and sent a flight of arrows from their powerful horn bows. As the shafts plunged into the manor's walls and windows, two men fell back from sight. They were replaced in seconds by two women: the elder Lady Falder and her daughter, a girl of thirteen, both firing crossbows.

The captain pressed closer to Gearld's elbow. "My King, the entire family is there! We must help them. We..."

"No." Gearld spoke gently, with the full weight of his kingship. "We cannot. That force will be upon us soon, and we must not waste our strength. We must make our stand here, and defend the city." He looked away, his throat twisted nearly closed with pain. "There is much more to lose than my old friend and his family."

Under cover of the horsemen's fire, a torchbearer reached the house and flung his brand into a low window. In moments yellow flame glowed from other apertures. Cries and shouting could be heard above the drumbeats, and the main door flew open before a pair of running boys. They were cut off and cut down before they could cross half the broad lawn.

More people sprang from casements and doorways. Some tried to flee into the planted lands; others tried to fight with what weapons they had. All fell in blood.

One brigand spurred his horse with a shout up the house steps and through the door. A howling quartet followed him, raising a tumult of screams and crashing inside. After several minutes, three rode out again with blooded swords flashing in the red light. They rejoined the mass and the army moved on, leaving the great house to burn.

Gearld watched in vain for sign of life as his old comrade's home was consumed. He closed his eyes against the sight. The drum sounds filled his ears and shattered thought. They were a throb in his bowels and marrow, the very pulse of his outrage and fear.

He opened his eyes. In moments, it seemed, the enemy had reached the city. They were spreading out into a battle-line before the gates. Their drums shook window glass everywhere behind him.

When they stopped, Gearld felt his heartbeat stutter without their rhythm to master it. The silence pressed into his ears like wool, a palpable weight.

Silence... Silence was not what he expected. From the ramparts, the King could clearly see the front line of bearded raiders, in their hodge-podge of leathers and furs and body armor. The sun came to his eyes from helmets and polearms and curved, naked swords. From shoulder to belt, each wore the black sash that marked him forever as Dark Michael's creature.

But these were not the howling savages Fairens had come to know and hate from their murder and banditry. Where they should be shouting threats, waving their weapons and building their courage, they sat or stood, just out of bowshot, in silence.

Gearld could feel his troops' eyes upon him as he scanned the foes' ranks. Understanding struck him like a bolt. *They're ... afraid!* The faces he could see were uneasy, far more so than the coming battle warranted. They shone dully with chill sweat, and their bearers glanced at each other, or backwards, and swallowed. *Are they afraid of us? What does this mean?*

He looked to the rearmost lines, and saw with revulsion that many of the faces turned his way were inhuman. And among them...

Michael! He wore no mask today; there was no mistaking him, or the grey skin of Michael's Shadow on the horse beside him. *The Dark One himself is leading them! He –*

Even as Gearld thought, Michael raised his hand and gestured strangely. A shadowy, amorphous mass, barely discernible behind him, suddenly moved forward and his troops divided, fairly leaping aside to clear its path.

No light reflected from its surface as it rolled ahead; none could say if it were liquid, solid, or vapor. It moved like a huge flood of pitch, like the densest, darkest night fog ever imagined, straight for the city walls.

When it passed Michael's foreline, it spread out until it was many rods wide, without losing a span of its thickness. Gearld shook off his bewilderment and rallied his men with a glance and a command.

"Archers! Stop that thing!" Arrows and quarrels followed his pointing finger. They vanished into the cloud, and the bloodless holes of their passage closed behind them. They slowed the nightmare not at all.

It flowed up to the wall and stopped inches away. A host of bulges appeared in its surface, swelling and rising to the height of a man. Smoothly, and with no sound, each bulge separated from its neighbors and became independent black globules. Each globe tilted forward and flattened against the wall.

Every man at the parapet craned his neck, peering down the wall's face. The King saw, with growing apprehension, that the black things were oozing like dark water into the interstices between the wall's blocks. They stretched themselves, running higher and deeper into the tiers of stone.

A strange crackling, crunching sound rose in the unnatural stillness. Crumbled mortar began sifting down over the alien things. They ceased thinning and grew taut, straining against the wall stones like a web of black cables.

Beneath his feet, Gearld felt the battlement shift. Long seconds passed, and he began to doubt the reality of the tiny movement; then it came again. He glanced around him, seeing the sickness of horror on each pale face turned to his.

He looked down again. The dark things were dappled and whitened with mortar now. The blocks they enwrapped could be seen to move, inching out of the positions they'd held for centuries. The catwalk suddenly lurched, and remained tilted back toward the street.

"Fall back! Back to the Keep!" Even to himself, Gearld's voice sounded terrified. Some soldiers began moving; others stood staring at him in disbelief. "At once!"

Abruptly, men were running with a clatter of arms, shouting directions and fear to one another. The walk heaved again, and someone fell screaming onto the flagstones below. The retreat became a rout, a mad scramble for the stairways. Gearld reached the stair and tried to regain control of his men and his own fright. The uproar and jostling were overwhelming, drowning his orders. So gripped by terror were some that they pushed roughly past their King without regard.

A tremor ran through the city wall. Like a man going to his knees it fell, in a crash and rumble of stone. The soldiers who remained between the gate tower and the passages to the Keep vanished into the haze of dust that rose immediately.

In the singing silence that followed, King and commoner alike stared at the shattered heap, shocked as though each had himself taken a mortal wound. The rattle and hiss of settling dust and pebbles came from the wreckage, and were joined by the moans of survivors among those entrapped.

Abruptly Michael's army cheered, a deafening roar of triumph. Even as the alien things slithered through the rubble, seeking and finding human food there, the pikemen and horse charged through the breach, into the streets of Faires.

King Gearld stood at one of the Keep's high towers and surveyed the rape of his city. Bitter smoke ascended to him, and the screams of men and women and children.

All the long afternoon, Michael's killers had stormed through Faires. Their archers had swept the walls and rooftops of men. The mounted knights and the city garrison had fought in the streets and alleys, bravely and to the last; what resistance the burghers could offer had been crushed. Homes and shops were burning, and the gutters ran with crimson rain. *My people! I have failed, and you bear the price. The Gifter's mercy to us all!*

Now he could see, in the distance, a file of people and carts, moving up the road into the Nethals. The ones in the lead were already nearing the Blinder. Whole families, or the remnants of them, were on the move, fleeing with only what they could carry or pull, fleeing to Edge. He could only hope that they would survive the trek and the evils between the two cities.

Now he could only watch as the devils reformed their ranks outside the Keep itself, beneath the very walls of his home. Their numbers seemed undiminished; indeed, more men, laden with heavy planks and timbers, were coming over the wreckage of the city wall. Their faces, flushed with victory and bloodlust, grinned up at him like wolves. Michael and his Shadow were among them, still at the rear, just out of bow-shot. The golem sat immobile, looking at nothing at all. Michael's face was upturned, smiling grimly, and Gearld felt that the dark, hooded eyes bored into his own, tearing at his mind and will.

He turned away and called to the captain of the King's Guards. That worthy came at the trot, his immaculate armor belying his grim demeanor. A young man to hold such a position, he took it the more seriously; this day's events clearly bore heavily upon him.

"The Guard stands ready, my liege. Our defenses are prepared, and each man knows his place. We may yet turn the tide on these fiends."

Gearld had aged since that morning. The jesting king was gone, leaving a man whose words came with effort from a face bitterly darkened. "It is not the Dark One's troops I fear. He has brought true fiends, creatures of the dark, among us. How can even the best of men stand against them?" The King shook his head and spoke more firmly. "Who are your best archers?"

"That would be Erik and Verlan, m'Lord. They are at the battlements even now."

"Look sharp, and when the attack comes, position them as well as you may to either side of the enemy's point. Tell them they may fire at will, but their chief duty is to watch the Dark One and stand ready." Gearld turned to the stair and started down, the captain a pace behind. "They are to use all their skill to bring him down." He paused a moment; when he spoke again, his voice had resumed its earlier gravity. "Whatever happens, that monster is not to enter the Keep."

By the time they reached the ramparts, Michael's forces were moving. In a horrible repetition of the morning's events, men and unmen alike stood aside to let the unearthly black being pass. It slithered forth and stopped beside the wall of the outer curtain. Once again, it divided its alien body into spheres, and flattened each sphere against the stones. *Again, you demon?* Gearld thought. *But this time, you'll find us not entirely unprepared.*

As it began spreading and branching along the wall's face, Gearld gestured to the men lining the parapet to his right. They hurriedly rolled forward two great cauldrons of boiling water, mounted on wheeled cradles. The men stepped to either side of each cauldron, grasped long wooden handles attached to the cradles, and heaved up on them.

The water poured smoothly into the channel at the edge of the parapet, coursing out through the machicolations and showering down the wall onto three of the black things. The creatures recoiled, drawing in their tendrils and hunching into balls. But after a moment, they uncurled and began insinuating themselves among the stones again.

King Gearld beckoned five of his archers to the battlements. Each man brought several arrows wrapped with oil-soaked cloth. As the archers nocked their missiles, a page quickly moved down the line, igniting the cloths with a torch. As one, the men raised and sighted their bows, and sent a volley of flaming shafts into the nearest branching globes.

The arrows struck with a splat and a hiss, as though fired into a stream. The flames vanished instantly, causing no more harm than the shafts shot into the creatures that morning. Even as the archers reloaded, relit, and fired a second harmless flight, the King and his men could hear the crumbling of mortar, and feel the tiniest shifting through their feet.

Gearld waved his arm in summons again, and to his left more troops rolled out another cauldron, this one reeking of hot oil. They poured it into the channel, and it fell the long drop down the wall to strike two of the beings - now no longer spheres, but black netting covering a wide expanse of stone.

The oil worked. The webbed things it spattered sprang free of the wall, curling in upon themselves in voiceless agony. They writhed and twisted, and began to melt eerily, turning liquid, then fading and steaming into a black mist.

A cheer went up from the parapet. Gearld had to shout to be heard above it. "More flaming arrows! Fire into the oil!" The archers leapt to comply, and set more of the beasts alight, igniting the oil splashed over the ground. For a moment, it seemed the Keep might have carried the day.

But it was too late. With the dreadful grinding and rumbling heard once before this day, the wall of the outer curtain began to crumble. Stones began falling out of the lower tiers, where the remaining black things pulled. Cracks spread upward, clear to the corbels beneath the battlements. A gap appeared in the wall itself; it broadened, more blocks breaking loose and falling.

The cheering stopped. Men began leaping away from the widening breach. With a roar, the topmost stones broke free and dropped, carrying with them the walk and crenellations – and several men, including the archers Verlan and Erik. When the cloud of dust began to settle, it revealed a mound of dirt and rubble, leading up to a rift some three armspans wide at its base. Michael's brigands raised their hellish war-cry, and charged up the mound.

In moments the inner ward was chaos, filled with plunging bodies and flashing weapons and cries of pain and rage. From his vantage near the iron-clad door to his own chambers, King Gearld could see his personal Guards spearheading a charge into the thickest of Michael's forces. The barbarians split before that wedge of hand-picked stalwarts. They fell to both sides, were steadily pushed back toward the break in the wall. The rest of the garrison forces, taken unaware by the wall's collapse, began to rally and reassemble.

And Dark Michael himself rode through the rift, his Shadow beside him, and his own picked bodyguard swarming up around him.

The black-armored riders plunged into the King's Guard with lance and sword and axe; the rally died as the cream of Faires' warriors did, with horrifying quickness. Gearld saw the young captain himself go down. In moments, the fighting was at the very doors of the Keep.

The King turned away from the doom below, and turned the key in his own lock. When he entered his chambers, Queen Signe ran to him.

"My Lord! We heard from one of the chamberlains that – that the Keep is fallen! Is it true? We've prepared ourselves, as you see, but Gearld; how can it be?"

Gearld turned from relocking the oaken door, and saw that Carola and her husband were with them in the room. He saw also, with relief, that all were dressed for travel.

He strode across bedchamber and anteroom, to the inner door. "It is far too true, and it happened because we could never contrive against the things The Dark One has brought against us this day. And now we must go, on the instant, and escape with our lives and no more, if we may. Come."

Garret already had their cloaks over his arm. He helped his wife and the Queen don theirs, and draped his own loosely about him. When the King drew sword, he took his own blade to hand.

Gearld nodded to him. "I shall lead, and you take the rear. We may well have to cut our way free." He looked at Garret. "Never hesitate to kill, if you must." He might have picked a stronger man to help guard his family in such a situation, but there was no denying the resolve in the young man's eyes. *So be it.* He opened the door, checked that the way was clear, and led them to the stairways.

They descended slowly and watchfully. They met no one at all on the first three flights, though the sounds of fighting grew louder as they moved downward. Those sounds could mean only one thing: some of the invaders were even now inside the Keep.

As they neared the second-story landing, Gearld held up his hand and all four stopped. All could plainly hear the footsteps and jangling of an armed man running up the stairs toward them. As the King raised his sword, Garret stepped out from behind Carola and the Queen, his weapon also at the ready.

The man swung around the curve of the stair into view; he was armed with an axe and armored only in bloodstained mail, with a torn black sash flapping at his waist. There was no mistaking him for a knight of Faires.

He saw the royal family as they saw him, and tried to strike at the King with his axe, but his blow was hampered by the stair's newel. Gearld's was not. He laid the bandit open from throat to collarbone, and shoved the falling corpse back down the stairs with his foot. He turned to the others, whispering urgently. "Quickly! There will be more behind him. It may already be too late!"

They came out into the audience-hall, to find themselves in a scene of utter melee. Everywhere were men locked in desperate combat, knights, houseguards, invaders, and even squires and servants. No quarter was offered by anyone on either side; all were fighting in the last extremity, to the death. The floor tiles were already slick with blood and cluttered with bodies.

Gearld was lifting his sword and preparing to advance into the thick of it when Garret tugged at his arm. "My liege!" He turned, and saw where his son-in-law pointed. The way to the scullery door was unblocked. It connected to the great kitchens, which in turn let out into the courtyards – only a few paces from the secret doorway that led to the Keep's postern gate. That way lay escape, and safety for Carola and Signe. Gearld hesitated only for a heartbeat, and then motioned them ahead of him to the door, now bringing up the rear himself.

They passed through the scullery and the kitchen. Garret carefully opened the outside door, peering around it and watching for several moments before stepping out. The fighting in the courtyard was on the other side of the Keep, giving them perhaps a few minutes' respite in which to reach the hidden door, and the postern beyond.

Garret slipped out and ran to sweep aside the curtain of ivy that concealed the postern door. As he worked its lock and swung it open, Carola dashed across to him. Queen Signe was outside and following behind when shouts rang out in the kitchen, followed at a run by four of Michael's warriors.

Still inside, Gearld slammed the courtyard door as he spun about with his back to it, drawing his dagger into his left hand. He kicked a stool into the legs of the nearest invader, and hacked at the man's throat when he fell headlong. The second came on in a howling rush, his sword high – a mistake, for Gearld stepped inside its sweep, and plunged his dagger into the bandit's heart.

The dagger slipped from his hand before he could withdraw it from the falling corpse. He parried the low slash of a sword with his own, and shoved its wielder back into the fourth assailant. He pressed his attack while they untangled themselves, managing to kill the third man. But he took a deep cut in his left arm from the last brigand, who flung himself on the King as Gearld staggered back from the blow.

Both fell, tumbling over a carving-block and rolling across the floor in a scatter of cutlery. When they stopped, Gearld's sword was gone; his attacker still had his, but it was pinned to the floor under Gearld's shoulder. The man heaved and twisted, trying to pull it free, while the King's free hand groped along the floor for a weapon – and found one. He snatched up a large boning knife. His opponent managed to catch Gearld's wrist as it came up, and for a moment they were locked, immobile.

Gearld swung a blow as hard as his wounded arm could make. His gauntleted knuckles crashed into the other man's nose, and as he reeled back, Gearld threw him off and lunged with the knife. It sank home, and Gearld held it in through the man's death-throes.

The King was rising to his feet when a horrible shock plunged through him from behind. He tried to turn, but could not; something was holding him in place. There was no pain, only the stunning blow and a frightening weakness sweeping over him, until his killer, who had come in unnoticed during the fight, wrenched the blade from his body. Gearld sank to the floor, his blood spreading under him, feeling the life rush out of his limbs. He tried to get up against the weakness, tried to hear through the roaring in his ears, tried to see through the strange darkness filling his vision. For just a moment he was sure he heard the sound of his youngest daughter's voice, which was strangely comforting because he knew it wasn't real, that she, at least, was safe. Then the darkness and the roaring were all there was.

◆   ◆   ◆

The towering brigand watched as the fallen King died at his feet. Reaching down, he hacked the head from its body, and clutching it by the grey hair held it aloft, laughing shrilly.

"Bugger!" he screamed, racing back the way he had come to show his grisly prize to his master.

Chapter 35
Desperation

Three days later, when the refugees from Faires began straggling in to Edge, Queen Signe, Carola and Garret were among them. They were taken at once to the palace.

Queen Alyda, Aaren, and Sare met them as they entered. Sare rushed to her mother and sister, a fearful question showing, unasked, behind her look of concern. The Queen could only nod, and then be embraced by both her daughters as they wept together.

Alyda drew Garret aside. "What is wrong, Lord Garret? The King ..?"

Garret's face was grim, without any of its normal animation. He looked down as he replied, "He is dead, your Highness. A servant who escaped the Keep just behind us says he saw the King's head carried out and his body dragged into the courtyard, where the Dark One's creatures cheered and danced around him. Then they took up his limbs, and they ... I cannot say it, m'Lady. I have no words."

Aaren's face had gone pale, with furious spots of color dancing high on his cheekbones. His eyes had grown lustrous and very, very blue. "Nor any need for words," he ground out between his teeth. "The time for words is past."

Alyda, knowing her son, put a gentle hand on his arm. It was rigid with anger. "Aaren," she said softly. He jerked his head toward her. For a moment she expected to feel the familiar warm flush of his projected anger, and when she did not, she realized just how firmly he was holding his power in check. It made her even more concerned, because a grip against such fury could not be maintained forever. "The horrors are best forgotten for now, until we can exact a price for such things from those fiends." She held his gaze until she could see her words penetrate. "Come now my son; your wife needs you, as does my fellow Queen." Slowly, Aaren nodded.

Sare turned, sobbing, into Aaren's arms, and Carola into Garret's. Signe looked up at Aaren and Alyda with her face misted in tears, and drew her dignity about her. "We come to beg asylum with you, as you once did with us. Our home is lost. Our - our King is lost, and with him our protection. We ask only for sanctuary, by the laws of our peoples."

"Of course," Alyda said, going to her. "But not just sanctuary; please consider this your home now, for as long as you wish to stay. Our home is yours. And we will make a place for all the others who escaped poor Faires as well, here in the city. Jenora will return tonight. She is at her sister's manor, and will certainly have heard the news there. She will command whatever is needed to see your people sheltered and fed."

Aaren stepped forward and raised Signe's and Carola's faces, to catch their eyes with his own. "I make you a promise, here, now, for you all to remember. Michael and his monsters had best enjoy Faires while they have it; they shall not hold it long. We will punish them for their crimes, and you shall return to your city soon, to make it your home again. I swear this. Believe me."

The Queen and her daughter nodded. Aaren stepped back and pulled Sare close again. He pressed his face into her veil, and murmured another promise, so softly that only she heard. "I also swear this to you: no more fathers shall die at that demon's bidding."

Aaren had brought to him the last desolate stragglers who came through the pass. He asked only a few questions, and received the answers he expected: Dark Michael and his army were in fact regrouping. They were not wasting time, settling in to enjoy the spoils of Faires, but were organizing and equipping themselves to push on – through the Nethals and into Edge. The last few refugees who arrived in Edge, soldiers of the garrison who had fought in a protective rearguard at great cost, reported that already scouts were moving ahead into the pass, spying out the way for the march that would follow.

When Jenora came into the King's council room that afternoon, she found Aaren there with his commanders seated about the table. Every countenance was grave. When Jenora had taken her seat at his right, Aaren stood and addressed them.

"From the news these last men brought me, it is clear that we have perhaps two or three days, at most four or five, to prepare ourselves for Dark Michael's attack. He will be upon us as quickly as he can march his forces through the mountains. Here and now, we must decide what action is best to meet his threat. All thoughts will be entertained, but we must choose a course, and move swiftly to implement it. What say you?"

The captain of the palace guard cleared his throat, frowning. "Your Majesty, won't his force be smaller than the one he brought against Faires? Surely he will leave behind troops to occupy Faires and prevent the mounting of an attack from his rear."

"Aye, almost certainly he will," Aaren said. "But the fighters who came last out of Faires reported that he was bringing in still more troops who had taken no part in the battle for the city. They were probably reinforcements he had held ready out in the Steppes. They will more than make up for any garrison he must leave behind." Aaren's mouth turned down. "They also report that most of those reserves were not actually ... human."

The general who commanded all the standing army of Edge ran a huge hand through they grey bristle of his beard, then placed both hands flat on the table in front of him. "I, too, have heard the report from the survivors of the rearguard, and believe it. Some say they have the strength of ten men each, that they do not even bleed when cut, or that they can freeze you in your tracks with a glance. I don't know what to believe, but I can tell you this: they fight as men possessed. I have thought much about it since this morning, and say what I know to be true: though we surely outnumber him, the forces we have now cannot withstand the ones he will bring against us." He paused to let everyone present silently digest that grim thought. "So I ask: how can we increase our strength? The guard is already merged with my army, raising my numbers by one hundred. Can we muster volunteers and mercenaries in time to meet this assault? Master Leland –" he swiveled to face the Arms Master "–

you have always trained the citizen volunteers; how many are there now, and how quickly can they be readied?"

"Fewer than three hundred, General. They can join your army at a day's notice, and many have arms of their own, mostly bows and swords. But I fear these peaceful times have lulled most of our citizens into other priorities besides preparing for invasion. Far too few have come forward and been trained. The news from Faires will surely swell my ranks. But the newcomers will be untrained, only a rabble in arms to throw against the Dark One."

"What about mercenaries? Are they available to be hired?"

Aaren spoke up. "Bluntly, no. The mercenary warriors Edge has used in the past are understandably reluctant to enter our service again. The fault for that is mine. Too many were killed when I was forced to fight through them, three years ago. I have, however, sent a request to Seahale for troops. In it I point out that Michael shall certainly not be appeased with only our two kingdoms. If he is not stopped now, sooner or later he will move against them, too, as he took Alatia before attacking Faires." He smiled wryly. "I hope they will see that helping us is in their interests as well. If they come, they will be here the day after tomorrow.

"In addition, Lord Garret has taken personal responsibility for all the survivors of Faires' army. He is organizing them into a single unit, and seeing them armed and supplied as well as they possibly can be. Might these added strengths be enough to turn the tide, General?"

The older man pondered that carefully and at length before answering. His eyes were piercing but distant, his bushy brows drawn fiercely together. He shook his head and met his King's eyes. "Seahale's army has never been large, and I cannot imagine them conscripting more just to come to our aid. Until they arrive, I won't be able to say with assurance, your Highness. I can only say that, with Leland's forces and mine, they might."

Aaren considered it, and then nodded. "Very well then; let us hope, but not assume, our neighbors will see clearly their own advantage in helping us. We must go on to strategy and logistics, then." He turned and met the gaze of every person at the table. "General, I want you to lead the army itself, and any from Seahale as well. Master Leland and Lord Garret will captain the men they already lead.

"I will take overall command of the force we raise, with Lady Oswin as my second." He paused, noting the general's furrowed brow. This was not completely unexpected, but he'd hoped not to have to address this issue. Respectfully, and with all of the authority he could wrest from the memory of his father, Aaren turned to the general and said, "Andrew." The general's head started back, the unfamiliar intimacy, in that voice, from that chair, reminding him powerfully of the king who'd come before – as Aaren had intended. "You have questions."

The general stared hard at the young King. Ghosts or no, it was his duty at this table to prepare the kingdom he served for war. "With all respect, your Majesty, I question only your ... inexperience. I served under your father, rest him, in the wars with Faires. Your only battle to date – and Lady Oswin's as well – was the one that restored you to us."

Aaren nodded gravely. "And that battle was won as much by sorcery as by skill; I know." He glanced at the Rageblade hanging from his chair. "But even my father had never known war before he led you in those days, General. He was proven in the heat of battle, as you were, and as the Lady Oswin and I shall be. We have been through ... much together, and have been tempered more than you can know. We will not fail.

"And I have another reason for giving the High Chamberlain such a responsibility. She has worked and trained with the volunteers fully as much as Master Leland, and is well known and trusted among our citizenry. They know she speaks for me in all things. She will be someone our irregulars will gladly follow."

Jenora added, "Trust me to rely on your judgment and wisdom, General. I know when to defer to experience."

The general stared hard at them, his eyes in that clear and distant place where battles were measured, lives and kingdoms tallied. Finally, he nodded his assent; if he had further doubts, he kept them to himself.

The tension in the room relaxed noticeably. The young guard captain raised a question of strategy. "If I ask something too artless, pray forgive me. I have held my post only through these past days of peace, and I am new to times of war and invasion. Is there some way we can surprise our enemy in the pass itself, or even close the pass and so cut off his advance? Such tactics been used before, have they not?"

Leland answered, "They have. The pass itself is narrow, as we all know, with no space except around Lake Fount wide enough for two armies to engage. The only full battle of the wars between the kingdoms took place there, when I was a young man. There are other places in the pass that might admit of some ambush –" He glanced at Aaren and Jenora, mutely asking forgiveness for stirring pained memories; "– but nowhere that a true assault can be mounted from any side. We could only harry his progress."

Aaren added, "And Lake Fount is more than a day's march into the mountains, and offers no worthwhile defensive ground from either direction. The great battle there was outright slaughter on both sides, as Master Leland can attest, and ended with no clear victor at all. It is no place to make a stand against the likes of Dark Michael.

"As for closing the pass, that could probably be done. With sufficient time and workmen, a landslide might be started on the cliffs above the Waist that would seal it with tons of rock and rubble. But consider: It would have to be done perfectly, lest it leave the enemy a way through or around the blockage. Even if it were done correctly, what would prevent Michael, with his resources of both men and creatures of darkness, from simply removing it? We've all heard of the monsters that brought down the walls of Faires; could they not do likewise to a wall of loose stones?" No answer to that came from the grim-faced warriors around the table. Aaren seated himself again, and slid his chair up. "Does anyone have anything to add?"

Leland leaned forward. "I agree that we should consider other plans. If we tried to close the Waist, at best we might buy ourselves only a few days, at the cost of the days we would spend engineering a rockfall. And further, there *are* other ways through the Nethals besides the pass itself. We fought several skirmishes during the wars in places where we or the Fairens sought to slip through." He paused. "Indeed, the battle that turned Vernor against both kingdoms occurred at one such place."

Jenora shifted in her seat and studied the faces around her a moment before speaking. "Agreed, then, there is no reasonable way to stop or assault Dark Michael before he leaves the mountains. I say, then, that we must meet him at that instant, before he can descend to attack the manors and the city itself. We have no great walls like Faires to hide behind, no great Keep to retreat to; and look what short work he made of *those* when they stood in his way." She looked to the each of the others, trying to read their expressions. "Our best opportunity is to be upon him at his weakest moment, before he can properly form up for battle and array his forces. If ours will truly be weaker than his, our only chance may be to strike at them when they are ill-prepared to receive us."

Silence sat among them, as they each pondered the weight of her thoughts and the risk of her suggestion. Finally Aaren broke the stillness, and stood again at the head of the table. "What say you? General, Leland; you have more experience of war than any here. Is there a better way than this, which we can choose and move upon today? We dare wait no longer to begin."

Leland said, "I would be willing to lead my volunteers in such a blow. I will tell you what I know: this is no time for caution. If we try to hold back, to keep something in reserve, we will fall. The Dark One has cast the die, for himself and for us. We must destroy him, or bow to him. I will endeavor his destruction, with you."

The general cleared his throat, and sat motionless for several moments. Finally he raised his eyes. "I see no better way. But let us meet him on the western plains of the kingdom, just below the opening to the pass, where we can array our forces to maximum advantage on familiar terrain."

The captain thought on this, nodded, and sat back straight in his chair, as did Jenora, their eyes on the King. The general spoke first. "I am with you, my liege." He stood deliberately and saluted, followed by Jenora, Leland, and the captain. Aaren, blue eyes flashing, nodded once.

"Then let us begin."

All that day, and all the next, were taken by preparations. The army was mobilized, the volunteers mustered, and the armorers and provisioners redoubled their labors. All afternoon the smoke poured from the chimneys of the forges and ovens; all night the glow of their fires seemed a false dawn in the streets of Edge, until the true dawn outshone them.

The streets themselves were currents of activity, as people and animals, carts and tumbrels and great wagons, flowed back and forth and across them. In the fields the soldiers massed and organized their companies, arranged their weapons and equipment, and received newly made additions to their arms and supplies.

Others were on the move for other reasons. Many of the residents from outlying manors and small farms had come into the city, fleeing the approaching danger. As well, more timid city dwellers were leaving Edge by the eastern Road, toward Seahale and points south. The apprehension was not yet near to becoming a panic; but dread was a presence everywhere, threatening to become a contagion.

When Aaren summoned Jenora, she quickly left Leland and Garret to continue putting their forces in order, and reached the Palace in a matter of minutes. He was outside the west wing in a courtyard, looking past

Vernor's tower to the Nethals with his face closed and tense, his eyes hooded beneath drawn brows. Sare stood a little way off, her face as grave as the King's. Aaren turned at her voice. "You sent for me, your Majesty?"

"I did." He held up a rolled parchment with a broken seal. "I received this not an hour ago, from Seahale." After a moment, he nodded at what he read in her face. "No; they are not coming. It's very ... diplomatically phrased, about how they must look to their own defenses in light of what befell Alatia and Faires, and deeply regret that they can't spare any troops now, and wish us the best of fortune. They are not coming. We are on our own."

They considered in silence for some time before Aaren asked, "What does this mean for the strength we can bring to bear against Michael? You've been commanding the muster for the past two days; you've seen what we have and what we do not. Tell me the truth, my Palatine, my Chamberlain: can we hope to defeat him?"

Jenora did not answer at once. Finally, she touched his arm and raised her eyes to his. "We can hope, your Highness. We have nearly the largest force Edge has ever assembled, led by some of the ablest fighters we've ever had. Every man knows what he's fighting for, and what the cost of failure will be. I can only say we will use every tactic and stratagem the best can think of, and we will never yield. If Edge falls, it will only be because we have fallen first."

He stared at her face for a moment, then turned away again. His gaze roamed the Nethals as though he could see past the Waist, past the lake, to the very heart of the enemy coming his way even now. "You offer me strength when I most need it, my friend, as you always have. I respect your honesty as well. Thank you." Sare had come up behind him, and laid one hand softly on his shoulder.

He settled into silence that lasted several minutes more. He turned to Sare, and a look passed between them that Jenora couldn't read. When they turned and moved back to the palace doors, he bore the air of a decision reached; but his face was grim and closed. Sare stepped up to Jenora and kissed her lightly once on the cheek, held her eyes with a tiny smile and went past Aaren into the palace.

"The moment the scouts report that Michael has entered the Waist, we'll move to meet him," Aaren said. "And tomorrow morning, as quickly as we can arrange it, I want the Palace evacuated. Especially I want Queen Signe and my mother to go, and to take Princess Carola with them. Sare will follow when we've seen the rest safely away; it is our duty to remain until our people are safe. I will join you then, before the battle commences." He paused at the door. "I think that it will *be* tomorrow, Jen. He's coming, and we have only today and tonight to prepare. Come and help me."

Chapter 36
Rageblade

It was just after midnight when Aaren rode into the eastern mouth of the Waist. He glanced up at the half-moon almost directly overhead, by whose light he picked his way along the river's bank. It was a waning moon, flickering in and out of sight through the fish-scale clouds moving on the light breeze from the west. It reminded him of something he couldn't quite grasp, and he shuddered as though the winds were cold, and looked away.

Less than a half-mile inside the narrow passage he stopped and dismounted. He stood unmoving for some time, listening and watching every shadow. When he was certain that none of Michael's scouts were anywhere nearby, he cast about in the uncertain light for some moments, until he found a spot near one side of the road where the ground was soft enough. He untied a spade from his harness and began digging.

It took him less than half an hour to make the hole long and deep enough to suit him. Returning to his horse, he drew the Rageblade from its scabbard on his saddle, and carried it back to the hole.

He knelt and held the great sword over its grave for some time, hearing it hum and murmur with pleasure at his touch. It tried to reach out to the place inside him, drawing up a rising heat to join it. He knew, he had always known, about the danger the sword represented. The wild savagery of its purpose called to its like, the wild flame that burned in him. He ached to drop the sword, but his heart was torn by what that would mean. Once he dropped it in, the die was cast; there was no other course he could follow.

But there is no other course at all, is there? I've known that since this morning. No, for much longer. There never was another way for this to end. He opened his hands and let the Rageblade fall. It chimed a dashed, forlorn note as it disappeared.

In a short while, the hole was filled and carefully hidden with strewn grass and his horse's prints. The spade was slung back into its place behind him as he rode away, back to Edge. *Now there remains only resolve, if I have the strength for it. And if I do not, I doubt that I will live to regret my weakness for long.*

◆   ◆   ◆

Two hours past dawn, workers in the western fields that adjoined the Road were startled from their labors by two horsemen coming down it from the mountains. The first flashed by at full gallop, pelting toward the city without a word or a glance to either side.

The second rider came some distance behind, passing at a trot and shouting: "To the city, all of you! Dark Michael is coming! Flee while you can!"

His warning was obeyed without exception or hesitation. In moments the word was spread from the Road to the farthest fields, from manor to manor. Before the first scout reached Greybeal, a line of people, peasants and gentry alike, was forming on the Road and flowing toward the city.

Aaren was summoned from his chambers while the rider was still dismounting. Throwing a quilted blue robe over the long shirt he had slept in, the King raced down to meet the man being brought to him. When they came together, the scout fell to one knee and bowed his head.

Aaren waved his hand brusquely. "No time, man! What news have you?"

"Your Majesty, Dark Michael and his army broke camp before it was light. The moment they could see their way, they moved onward. His vanguard entered the Waist less than three hours ago."

Stephen, only half-dressed, was standing at Aaren's elbow, awaiting the order that followed the news. "Wake Lady Oswin and Lord Garret and bring them to me. Then rouse the rest of the house and get them moving, as we planned yesterday. I want everyone ready to travel in two hours - or less. Then bring up the wagons and carts and load them, and get them on their way."

"Yes, your Highness." He was already moving away when Aaren called him back. "Stephen ... I want you to go with Queen Alyda, Queen Signe and Lady Garret. You are to personally see them safe to their destination, and attend to their every need, no matter what transpires today. Do you understand?"

Stephen looked into the King's haggard face and hooded eyes a moment before answering. "Yes, m'Lord.

I understand. I shall do my best for them, always, on my life."

Aaren smiled faintly. "I know you will, and I thank you. See to them now." He turned and mounted the stairs, to dress quickly and waken Sare.

Inside of an hour, the palace was in turmoil. Hastily packed bundles were thrown into carts outside the main gate, where a steady stream of people filed out onto the Road and away. The clanging and shouting were subdued, though, Sare thought. *No laughter.* The children were hushed, and their parents grim.

As she passed the temporary armory in the east courtyard, she saw Garret readying the last of the Fairen soldiers. Slipping out a side door, she walked over to where he was arranging the dole of weapons among his men. Seeing the Queen approach, he broke off and joined her.

"Lord Garret," she said, taking his hand in both of hers.

"My Queen," he bowed. "What brings you here?"

"I just wanted to pass along the news of my mother and Carola's safe departure. And their love." She leaned up and kissed him on the cheek.

He smiled. "Thank you, Highness. That takes a great load off of my mind. Is their aught I can do for you or the King?"

"No, I think not. Other than that which you are already doing, leading the men of Faires into victory against the Dark One."

His smile grew taut. "Yes, your Highness. We will prevail, or die in the attempt." He saluted, impulsively kissed her scarred cheek in return, and strode back to his duties.

Sare had turned and began walking back to the doorway when she noticed Rodolpho being fitted with mail and greaves along with several other Fairens. She went to stand beside him, and waited until he glanced up.

"My Lady," he said solemnly, standing to greet her.

"What are you doing here?" she asked. "You're not a warrior, Rodolpho."

He nodded. "But where else could I be, your Highness? There are no household duties to perform, no errant stableboys to herd out of the kitchens. Indeed, there may be no house to serve at all should I not choose to take up arms in her defense."

"Of course, Rodolpho, of course." Sare smiled at him. I just never thought of you in ... in armor."

He gave a tiny smile in return. "Just because I turned down your coverlet as a girl doesn't mean I wouldn't lay down my life for you as my Queen."

She threw her arms around him and hugged him fiercely. After a moment, he returned the gesture, patting her gently on the back. "Rodolpho, you are a marvel," she whispered into his neck.

He released her and nodded. "As the Lady says."

◆   ◆   ◆

The sun was well up in the sky when Aaren rode onto the mustering field west of Edge, and stopped his horse close beside Jenora's. All around men were hastening to fall into the ranks assigned them. Last-minute volunteers, coming to join now that the threat was real and imminent, strapped on swords or carried bows, axes, or pikes as they straggled in from the city and the surrounding houses.

Aaren could see Garret at the head of his Fairens, who already stood at attention and awaited the command to march. Behind Jenora, the regular army was almost equally ready, and Leland was herding the latecomers into his volunteer company.

Aaren leaned from his saddle and laid his hand on Jenora's, at once both offering strength to her and drawing it forth to himself. "There will be little or no time later, my dearest friend. If there is not, know that you have been ... everything that I could ask for, as comrade and confidant and ... more. You have meant more to me than anyone but Sare, from boy to man to King. Know that, and know that you have also my trust, and ... my love."

Without waiting for a reply, he spurred away, leaving Jenora holding out her hand as though to draw him back. Her hand fell slowly to the pommel of her sword. Aaren stopped before the men now arrayed at attention, and wheeled his mount to face them, shouting now to be heard to the last man.

"Time is short, with none to waste in windy speeches. Each of you carries with you all the hope of Edge this day. I can think of no better shoulders on which to set such a burden. I know you will not fail us, and I shall not fail you. I return to the palace to arrange a final surprise for our enemy. I will be with you shortly, before the battle is joined; look for my signal. We will stand together against this evil. And we will prevail!"

He raised his hand to them as the cheers swelled from their throats, and rode along their forefront to the Road and then away, as the cheer rose behind him. Jenora looked after him until he went through the palace gate; Aaren never once looked back.

Chapter 37
Pyre

At the eleventh hour he sent the last of the staff to the wagons. The rumble and clatter of their departure echoed through courtyard and halls. The great stones and beams spoke ponderously into the silence as he sat down and covered his face. Tapestries hung purple and heavy, muffling the last of the hoofbeats into a steady, vibrant stillness. The buildings waited in the cumbrous morning grey.

Finally Aaren took his head from his hands and sat back. He looked about the hall as though it were an unfamiliar dream-room, moved his chair back from the table and stood. The scrape of oak on flagstones settled softly into the farthest corners.

Outside in the open yard, the bronze sundial cast the minutest finger of black. The King turned and walked from the palace, into the gardens.

She was in the Grove of Peace, her favorite part of the gardens, as he knew she would be. She sat on an ironwork bench amid trees and birdsong. Her carefully tended lilacs and dogwoods dropped their scents gently to the springy turf; there was no wind. She turned as he approached, her beads and feathers rustling and clicking with a sound to cleave his heart.

"All safe and gone, my love?" Her smile was for him, alone of all men, full of warmth and affection and – this day, of all others – understanding. It left him wordless.

He stood before her and took her hand. He tried to speak; the welling of love and pain took him by the throat and stopped his breath. The strength that had held him erect all morning failed, and he sank to his knees at her feet. She leaned close and stroked his hair. He looked up, vision narrowed until he could see only her eyes, shining and green as the promises of every spring of his life. His hearing focused, closer and closer, until he could hear only the susurration of her garments and her touch, and the murmur of her voice.

"It must be soon, now, mustn't it?" Sare asked.

Aaren could only nod. The strange sensation of urgency was pressing into him more with each moment. Yes, Michael was approaching. Aaren could feel every foot of the Dark One's advance in his own flesh, and knew within an armspan exactly where his nemesis trod. The vanguard was emerging from the Waist just *now*. Within the half-hour, the bulk of the army would be nearly through, and ready to descend upon Edge, and it would be too late. But there was still some time.

Sare rose from her seat, and drew him up with her. "Then come and walk with me. I would spend the time with you, and enjoy the beauty of the day."

Aaren held her hand. They strolled along the lanes that circled the pond. A breeze rose to ruffle their hair and chime in Sare's ornaments; the noonday sun of autumn was perfectly warm and bright.

But the tension inside each grew steadily, until it could no longer be ignored or denied. They stopped simultaneously, and turned to face each other.

Aaren looked down into the strange serenity of Sare's scarred, smoothed, dear face, and for a moment felt only wonderment. "How can you know such peace? The time is upon us; if we wait longer they will be safely through. It must be now." Despair burst again within him. "Would it were a thousand years!"

Sare touched his cheek with fingers neither moist nor trembling. "Because it must be, my love. I think we've always known this time would come." She slipped her amulet over her head, its stone flashing gold in the sun. "I feel almost as if I had been waiting all of my life for this. And I *am* at peace with it – as you must be. For me. For our kingdoms. For all these things we love. You must be King, now, and do this thing."

Carefully she laid the amulet upon a nearby bench. "For Jenora," she said, and turned back to him. "Now kiss me, and leave me, with love, and remember me always. I'll never ask more than that."

He swept her against him, tighter and tighter until his arms throbbed. He kissed her with all the passion and despondency in his heart. In his mind only one thought echoed: *How will I live, if you are gone?*

He let her go and slowly stepped back, one pace, another, touching her fingers as long as he could. In their touch he could feel a vibrancy now, like the air after a lightning stroke, flowing between every part of their two bodies. When their hands fell separate, he stopped. He raised his palms toward her. Between them, she seemed almost to shimmer with a faint, blue glow. She closed her eyes. "Farewell, beloved."

His bracelet dropped to the path beside him. The power rushed into him like a storm, more wild and uncontrollable than he had ever known it could be, like the darkness of death itself, more than any man could ever contain. It surged down his arms to his hands, reaching for her in a mad, all-consuming wave.

And as it burst between them, he sprang forward and flung his arms around her, with a cry of hopelessness and loss that echoed throughout the grove.

◆   ◆   ◆

Sare's face was pressed against his chest, her arms were imprisoned by his, her soul blasted by the enormity of what he was doing. *No! Aaren, you can't!* She tried to twist herself free and away from him, but found that she couldn't move. Then in a flash of wonder, she realized what was happening to them.

Their enclasped bodies were entirely enveloped in the shimmering blue haze. She could not see through it; there was nothing beyond it to see. She tried to speak, but had no voice. Their bodies were flickering and... fading somehow, but there was no pain. There was a strange sensation welling up inside her. In seconds, it filled her being completely with the throb of its power, and she knew it for what it was.

This is the truth of what we are, Aaren and I. The power was never his alone. This is not something he has done to me; he cannot do this without me. I am the key. She felt their hearts begin to beat in time, and just for a moment, thought of her father's smile.

An inner sight came to her, showing her where the force of their union must go. She felt the link between the energy soaring in her flesh and the Rageblade, buried inside the Waist, where the center of Dark Michael's army marched over it. She heard it respond and call to Aaren – no, to *both* of them – and heard its dim, inhuman joy sound within the distant metal as its own magic rose to meet theirs.

A lifetime of fear had fallen away from her, almost unnoticed. Without question, she knew what she must do; and now, for this instant alone, she knew how. She gathered the whole of the fire into herself and shaped it. Knowing the price to be paid, she breathed a silent prayer for them both. She held Aaren as tightly as her fading arms were able, drew together the power between them, and cast it forth.

And a pillar of blue flame roared up into the noon sky.

Chapter 38
Desolation

Jenora and the army were growing uneasy as the sun rose higher. They could hear the tramp of Michael's forces, dimly, when the wind was blowing down from the Waist. The more seasoned horses, used to battle, could smell armed men and other war-mounts, and unearthly things as well. They shifted and stamped, restive with both impatience and fear, like their human companions. For the tenth time, Jenora loosened Friendship in its sheath.

A young runner rode up on her left. "The archers have finally caught up with us, m'Lady. Where would you have them deployed?"

She considered the area about her, and the question. "Place them to our left, on that small rise; it will give them a clear field of fire. Tell their captain to watch my flags carefully, and have every man ready for rapid fire. I intend to attack the Dark One as soon as his lines begin to form, and I'll begin by sending as many flights into his men as I can in the shortest time. That may hasten them down the slope to us before they can properly harden their line."

The boy saluted and rode off at a gallop. Jenora turned her gaze back up the hillside. *Every trick I can muster*, she thought. *But will anything be enough to take this day? How many of us will even live to see the sunset?* She looked back over her shoulder, toward the city gleaming in the late-morning light, the green fields and manors, the great bridge in the distance. No plume of dust marred the Road's unbroken surface anywhere. *The archers have caught up. But where, my King, are you?*

Just as the sun rose high enough to send unbroken streams down into the Waist, the first of Michael's troops stepped forth. There was no more of the covert or furtive about the Dark One's actions or intentions on this day. His standard-bearers led the way out of the pass, followed by cohorts of pike and infantry. There was no pretense that these were mere brigands; their armor and weaponry - much of both stolen from poor, sacked Faires - gleamed and shone in the late-morning light. This was an army, come to take what it would. No light of mercy could be seen in any of the faces now emerging from the shadow, whether those faces were human or not.

If they were at all surprised to see the full forces of Edge awaiting them in the valley, they never betrayed it by the slightest pause. They began to spread into a battlefront, widening and deepening as more of them came forth. And even as they did, a horse, black as its rider's garb, pushed through the ranks and came to the fore.

Jenora started at the sight of him. He raised his hand, holding a sword that Jenora recognized; it was

King Gearld's. Above his head, it caught the sun. *The sun –*

Suddenly, there was no sun. Shadow fell over invader and defender alike. Jenora looked to the sky, and saw that out of nowhere, a single leviathan cloud had come instantly into being. It covered the entire pass, from the Waist to the heights, and stretched out over the edge of the valley as well.

It was like no cloud ever seen by mortal eyes, a deep, inky blue, and it stood supernaturally still. No wind ruffled its fringes, nor moved it from its place. As all watched, stricken motionless with awe, red-orange flames appeared at its edges and spread inward until they merged at its center. The color of the burning cloud began to change, now copper, now bronze, now gold.

Beneath this vision, men on both sides began to waver, and raise their arms to shield eyes that could not look away. At the core of the cloud, the blaze suddenly turned pale blue. The blue spread outward, replacing the golden fire and growing painfully bright to look upon. It expanded, nearer and nearer the edges, *now –*

And the cloud exploded.

It burst downward in a howling blast of blue fire, a column wider than the gap between the mountains. It struck into the nearest end of the Waist – and the center of Michael's forces. They never had time to scream. The balefire simply obliterated them: their mounts, their weapons, their armor, and their bodies. Only those in the vanguard, already clear of the pass, and the few who were farthest to the rear, were outside its lethal radius. Even for some of those, survival lasted only another snatched breath or two.

The flame crashed into the cleft and erupted up the sides, washing over the stones and sending lethal splashes flying in all directions. Everywhere it touched, earth and water and living things vanished into puffs of mist, nearly too faint to be seen. Men who were only grazed by errant tongues of it screamed as their armor flowed, molten, over their flesh. The rocks split and melted, and from the earth fire also spewed, many feet high, yellow and crimson and steaming. It engulfed more of Michael's creatures, and floods of seething lava welled forth and swept among them. Much of Michael's army, men, half-men, and things from dismal and nearly lifeless places, all were blasted away in the space of only a few heartbeats.

And just as quickly, the blaze was gone. The blinding blue fire flickered and died, and the dark cloud overhead began to tatter and fray. In the Waist, nothing remained. The shattered stones on either side still flowed at their edges, blackened all around, gaping a furlong wider than the pass had been only a moment before. Within, nothing stood, neither man nor horse nor tree nor blade of grass. Only the slowing lava moved in the scorched perdition that lay between the peaks, bathed in rising steam where a reach of the Wendlow had disappeared. The stench of a great burning, and of burned flesh, began to seep down into the valley.

For long moments, Jenora sat as rigid as all her army, stricken mute and motionless by awe and the horror of what they had witnessed. Her mind could scarcely compass it; her heart knew, and refused to know, what had truly happened.

Canticle whickered and shied a half-step. As she did, an arrow whistled past Jenora's arm. She looked back along its path, seeing the clutch of Michael's archers and infantry moving down the bank to her right, where they had been protected from the fiery cascade. Shaking her head, Jenora looked about her more. All along the hillside, her surviving enemies were picking themselves up and trying to make order from the chaos that had fallen on them. Pikemen were reassembling their squares, archers were nocking their shafts, and cavalry were remounting. In the center, Michael's standard suddenly rose. *The Dark One's army is badly damaged; but it is not yet finished.*

She beckoned to her trumpeters. "Sound the charge! We must be at them, while they still reel from the blow! At them – *now!*" Friendship seemed to have flown from its sheath and into her hand. Leveling it at the enemy, she spurred Canticle into full gallop, pelting up the slope with the sound of the horns trailing behind her.

A roar went up from the soldiers of Edge. Their foreguard rippled, broke into a wave of shouting, rushing men and horses and flags, flowing up in Jenora's wake.

They crashed into Michael's scattered troops. Jenora reached them first; the archers on her right sent a flurry of arrows to meet her, but none found their mark. She slashed to right and to left at the men clustering about her, hacking her way toward the black ensign only a score of long strides away.

Her knights were just behind her, the pikemen and foot soldiers at their heels. They formed no battle-line; there was no solid front of foes to cast themselves against. Instead, they dispersed and threw themselves into a dozen or more disordered fights, all along the hillside. The black-sashed enemy had no choice but to fight or surrender. There was no hope of retreat through the boiling, smoldering Hades that had been the Waist.

Only a few of the survivors had time, or the presence of mind, to throw down their weapons and ask for quarter. Most of them were embroiled in combat before they could make any other choice. The men of Edge attacked with a savagery they had seldom shown before. The years of peace with Faires had forged many bonds across the mountains. Many of these men had lost family and friends in the rape of Faires, or seen them arrive, injured and destitute and shrunken with fear, to seek refuge in Edge. Only moments before, these same men had fully expected to die this day, to give their lives in a bootless attempt to spare Edge the fate of Faires. Now, astoundingly, they held the source of so much terror at the same pitiless extremity. And so the battle quickly turned to slaughter.

In the thick of it all, Jenora faced a mounted and fully armored soldier, one of Michael's picked guard. He spoke no word, but set spur and charged with raised battle-axe.

She flung Canticle forward with equal speed. *Only one chance to get under that weapon*, she thought. The horses collided chest-to-chest; Canticle's footing was better, and the warrior's grey was thrown back a step. Its rider's axe swung wide as he struggled to keep his balance. Jenora drove Friendship's point into his exposed armpit, and he folded over the pumping artery as she swept past.

The flag was before her; its bearer rushed forward, striking at her with its standard as if it were a weapon. She chopped through the shaft with one blow, and killed its wielder with the backstroke. She rode over the corpse, and suddenly Michael was right in front of her.

He was on horseback, though the dirty smears on his armor showed where he had fallen. His mount seemed to favor its right foreleg; it must have gone down when that flaming thunderclap fell from the sky. His face, too, was smudged and grimy. His eyes met hers, and knew her, and saw her resolution. He snatched out his sword.

She smashed into him before he could set himself, driving back his mount, battering at his half-raised shield with her own buckler and striking over its top with Friendship. Her blow rang off the edge of his sallet. His horse placed its weakened leg into a hollow; Canticle, straining against the black, also stumbled, and both horses went down.

Falling free of saddle and stirrups, Jenora lost her shield as she landed and rolled. She stopped and got to her feet, looking about for Michael. He too was up again, trying to hold and mount the grey horse that belonged to his fallen axe-man. His own horse struggled in the declivity, unable to rise.

Jenora rushed him as he put foot to stirrup, slashing two-handed with her sword. Michael flung up his shield desperately, and Friendship ripped it from his arm and sent it flying. As the grey shied away from them, he managed to draw the sword he found hanging in a saddle-sheath, the axe-man's reserve weapon.

He barely had time to raise his guard before Jenora came on, striking and lunging with all her strength and skill. She saw fear in his gaze as he blocked and parried. She drove on, forcing him to back up the embankment of a small cliff. *Now, monster! Now, many debts shall be paid.*

The golem thundered into the valley like Death incarnate. The first of the soldiers of Edge to behold it drew back in horror; their hesitation cost them their lives. Leaving a half-dozen foot soldiers dead or dying in its wake, Michael's Shadow pulled its charger into a tight turn and raced straight toward the next mounted group.

The golem had been near the rear of Michael's forces, hastening stragglers through the pass with its presence. The awful fiery blast had descended not fifty yards from where it had ridden. Every man and beast around it had perished in seconds. Not possessing life in the true sense, it had flung itself to the boiling mud where the river had been and buried itself as deeply as it could while the inferno raged above.

The golem finally emerged from the holocaust a charred and smoking, somehow smaller version of its former self. Its limbs were twisted out of true, and its right leg no longer bent at the knee. Great black flakes of skin crackled off to reveal more blackness beneath.

Unable to see, it had reached up and scraped at the char of its eyes until the white showed again, dim and smudged. It had staggered down the slope of the pass until it found a weapon and a live mount, then galloped ahead to aid its master. It knew Michael was alive. He had to be, or his Shadow would also have perished.

Two of the four horsemen it approached met it at a gallop from either side. The one to its right was beheaded. The other planted his broadsword between the golem's ribs. The force of their passing tore the blade from the knight's fingers. Michael's Shadow wheeled, seemingly oblivious to the sword protruding from its side, and rushed the other two riders. One man panicked and loosed a poorly aimed crossbow bolt, which went well wide of its target. The other spurred his horse to meet the golem. He too fell before the creature's blade. The remaining pair made short work, the smell of their blood mixing with the sour smoke that followed the golem as it wrenched the blade from its side with a spurt of grey ichor, and raced off again toward the main conflict.

As it plunged into the melee, two well-trained pikemen braced their weapons against the earth and brought the golem's steed screaming to the ground. Michael's Shadow leapt from the saddle but landed badly, its right leg refusing to act as much more than a crutch. Struggling to its feet, it carved a swath of destruction through the men around it, steadily moving toward the rise where it had finally sighted Dark Michael. Its swordsmanship was undamaged and still quite lethal, but by the time it got to within thirty paces of its master, it dripped its dull ichor from a dozen deep wounds.

The space around Dark Michael was clear. Only the girl warrior, Jenora, faced him. But she was driving him, pushing him back against the cliff. Already he bled in several places where her blade had cut him. Sword-to-sword, Michael was clearly outmatched, and nearing defeat with every second.

Faster than a human eye could follow, the golem snatched up a loaded crossbow from the carnage at its feet and aimed it at the woman's back. Its gnarled, blackened finger pressed the trigger.

◆   ◆   ◆

Michael felt the power of his arms failing, his balance slipping as he backed up the slope. He faced a madwoman, tireless and driven, agile as a cat and deadly quick. She handled her great sword with horrifying ease, cutting and thrusting as though it were weightless. Again and again she had sliced past his guard, and his strength flowed out with every drop of blood through the stinging wounds. Only the power of his magic, bolstered by his small skill with the sword he held, kept him upright.

He *twisted* his mind, glaring at the warrior, but nothing happened. He had feared as much. The screaming of the Pendulum had nearly driven him from his horse, back in the mouth of the pass, and was only slightly less alarming than their utter silence since the fire had stopped.

Her blade swept in and knocked the helmet from his head, opening a long, shallow gash from temple to scalp. He backed away, swinging wildly – and found himself trapped against the stone of the cliff face.

She struck the sword from his hand with contemptuous ease, and her voice filled with triumph as she lifted her blade to cut him down. "Now, beast, you die *now!*"

Blood was flowing into his eye, he could hardly see. He knew – he could *feel* – that his Shadow was somewhere near. He needed its power – he needed *all* his powers – or Death would claim him. With a sensation like steel bands snapping and recoiling upon him, Michael hissed the ancient phrase and recalled the life force from the golem.

◆   ◆   ◆

The golem felt the crossbow's string slip free just as its arms went nerveless and dropped. The bolt flew only a few feet and plunged uselessly into the ground. The creature found itself stretched on the earth, feeling the life and power rushing from it and back into Michael's body. Its head had fallen so that it could see Michael and Jenora, frozen in an instant's tableau, only a few armspans away. As the seared mud of its shell began to dissolve, a small white withered hand emerged from the streaming muck, stretched toward its unseeing master. It felt an awful pain across its chest. A tremendous longing sang in sympathy to the pain, and the tiny hand scrabbled feebly in the bloody soil. His brother was in trouble, and he had to... had to....

Sight faded, limbs stilled, and it sank, already putrefying, into the bloodied soil on which it lay.

◆   ◆   ◆

Jenora had begun to swing the deathblow when Michael abruptly flung himself off the rock face and crashed into her. They tumbled back down the slope, locked together. She felt his hands tearing at her body-armor, his teeth snapping at her throat, seeking her veins. He was like a panther, with a sudden, eerie strength that poured from him like darkness. She brought up her knees and barely managed to buck him off as they next went head-for-heels. He rolled away from her, and they skidded to a stop at the base of the scree.

Michael had landed near a cluster of corpses, some ten paces away. As she scrambled to her feet, he found a double-bitted war axe among the fallen weapons, and rushed her with the bloody blade raised high.

She feinted right, then sprang to her left and away, barely escaping the sweep and impact of the axe. She backed away as he came on. Her foot came down on the hilt of a sword – her sword. She stooped and flung a palmful of dirt into Michael's dark eyes, giving her an instant to scoop up her weapon.

Her hurried parry, coming up from the ground, managed to deflect the axe-blow that would have split her skull. Her return stroke cut his right knee – and slowed him not at all. She gave ground, blocking his attacks, but finding her counterstrikes blocked with equal skill. *He's stronger than before, faster; he even looks larger, somehow.* There was a savage, inhuman cast to Michael's face now. *And he's not bleeding anymore, not even from his head wound.* She caught the haft of the axe full on her blade. Michael began pressing down with unthinkable force, grinning at her amazement, bowing her backward.

Jenora lashed out with her foot, striking full on his wounded knee. He staggered for a moment, and she slipped free from the engagement. The axe's edge sliced the skin away from the back of her left hand as it whickered past.

He swiped at her horizontally, and she sprang back. Rolling his shoulders, he smoothly changed the gut-stroke into an upward swing, turning it to a great overhand blow descending on her head. Friendship swung up from her right hip, caught the axe, and turned its course and momentum down to her left. It struck the earth as her shoulder brushed Michael's chest. Using one of Leland's tricks she pressed her sword down atop the axe, driving it deep into the ground.

Michael stooped, his face a grinning deathmask, wrenching at the axe. Just as he freed it with a shriek of triumph, she swept her sword up in a merciless slash across his exposed throat. It should have been a killing blow. The bright blood drenched her arm and shoulder as she stepped back. Michael merely laughed, mirthful bubbles frothing from the pumping gore of the wound, let go the axe and raised his hands to his throat, as if to stanch it. Already the founts of crimson had diminished, the edges sealing together like wax.

Without thinking Jenora braced her feet and swung with the strength of all the slaughtered Oswins in both her arms. Friendship's blade sheared through skin and flesh and spine, and before she had time to even think on what she had done the Dark One's head landed in the dust at his own feet.

But still the upright body stood, clawing for her with its gore-spattered hands. At their feet, Michael's head snarled. Reflexively, Jenora plunged Friendship into the beast's heart. It stopped, clutching at the blade, and then simply stood, swaying. Jenora wrenched the blade free. Finally, the body fell to its knees, and toppled over beside its now-stilled head.

Jenora stood over the twitching corpse, Friendship's point in the dirt and her weight upon it; it seemed the steel was the only thing supporting her. Her blood ran over its hilt and down its blade, blending with her enemies' before reaching the ground. He didn't move again. Michael was dead.

It was the pain in her hand, suddenly making itself felt, that brought her mind back to the world. She lifted her gaze from staring at the fallen relic of the enemy that had so long given focus to her life. Men – her men – were gathering about her. They shouted in the distance, telling the news, and rushed toward her. But as they neared they slowed, and stopped some paces away, forming a ragged circle. Their faces mirrored their mute incredulity; it was as if Jenora had struck down the Tempter himself, leaving his body settling in the afternoon light at their feet. Mythic beings do not die before mortal eyes.

Lord Garret slowly raised his sword into the air, and with it his voice. "Oswin! Lady Oswin and King Aaren!" Others took up the cheer, until it rang off the cliffs of the Nethals from the soldiers circling Jenora to the ones standing guard over the survivors of Michael's army. "King Aaren! And Lady Oswin!"

Jenora sank to her knees, leaning against the upright sword. The shout surrounded her, filled her ears. "Lady Oswin! For Oswin and King Aaren!" Her hands covered her face as tears of grief poured from her, coursed through her fingers and down her hands. "Oh, Aaren ... Sare. Why didn't you tell me?" Even when her page came and tried to bind her wounded hand, she wept, and would not be distracted or consoled.

The shouting died down, and was replaced by a hushed murmuring of troubled voices. Jenora looked up from her exhausted anguish and wiped the tears from her eyes, smearing blood and dirt across her face. She stood as the crowd parted, and a lone figure picked its way down the hill from the Waist.

Cillistra's long hair flowed out behind her, wafted aloft by the warm coppery air of the battlefield. She had been among the decimated rearguard that was just now emerging from the inferno in twos and threes; her boots were covered with char and ash, as were her traveling clothes. She was still very beautiful though, and carried herself with the nobility that had once been hers.

The crowd of triumphant warriors fell silent. The only remaining sounds were Cillistra's footsteps, the thin moaning of the wounded, and the distant popping of superheated stone as it cooled in the Waist. Cillistra stopped and knelt by Michael's body. She turned his head over and closed the eyes, now faded and dull in death. Face drawn and rigid, she rose and faced Jenora. "You killed him?"

"Yes." The word was a whisper. She was so tired.

"And Aaren?"

Jenora stared at her. "I don't know. The fire was his, was theirs..." She stopped. "Mayhap they're all dead." There was a horrified murmur from the crowd.

Cillistra nodded. "Good." She gathered up Michael's head in her arms, and began walking away.

An outraged swordsman raised his blade as she passed through the circle of warriors, but Jenora stopped him with a raised hand, saying softly, "Hold, soldier." She swallowed. "Let her go." They all watched the smudged, erect figure pick her way over bodies and stones, heading north. Eventually she was merely a speck in the distance.

Jenora turned back to the faces of the victors, struggling to comprehend the day's events. She took a deep breath.

"Care for the wounded. Gather Michael's remaining stragglers and bring them down to the stockade." She drew Friendship from the ground and bent down, wiping the blade on Michael's cloak. She sheathed it, costing her nearly all her remaining strength. She turned and looked down the valley to the east. "Let's go home."

EPILOGUE

In the shadow of Greybeal Palace, at the base of a gentle slope from its western walls, lay the royal gardens. Amid the lush flowerbeds and shrubs, an avenue of white stones spread to circle a vast fountain set with a bronze figure from mythology, a huge man with the head of a lion. From the fountain's hub flagged and cindered paths spoked out in many directions, leading off into the garden's reaches.

One of the cinder tracks to the north meandered up a low hill and sprouted sheltering evergreens on either side. These increased in size and number from the trail outwards until they blanketed the hill. Near the hillcrest, a sound sifted through the stillness of the trees. It might have been the wind, though not a branch stirred; it might have been a swarm of insects, though there were none nearby.

Farther along, the sound grew. It muttered and throbbed through the earth and evergreens. Over its crest, the hill descended into a bowl-shaped glade. A sylvan pond at the bottom mirrored its surrounding trees and shrubbery, the hills on three sides, and the man-made grotto above the far end. Flowers bloomed along the lanes that circled the pond; ivies climbed the elevations and twined around the shade trees. A sense of peace was profound throughout the grove; only a soft breeze stirred the leaves or the water's surface. But that breeze's source drowned its whisper, shattered the peace, and commanded all attention.

From the midst of the wide path, its glow flung across the pool, a column of living flame rose into the afternoon sky. Wide as a man's outstretched arms and just over twice as high, it was blue, almost incandescent at its heart, paler at the edges, with aquamarine tongues leaping from its peak. Dimly, indeterminate shapes flickered in and out in the core of the flames. The column's sound filled and rebounded in the little vale. A throaty roar, hinting at voices, and pain, and terrible conflagration, had continued unabated since its awful birth.

High overhead a kestrel dipped and swooped on the warm currents of air over the Pillar. It veered away to the Palace's nearest tower where it landed smartly on a window ledge. Intrigued, it cocked its head to one side, looking through the dirty pane at a flash of light from within.

The room hadn't been touched. Inside, a film of dust had gently begun to accrue, layer upon layer, dulling the gold lines of the pentagram in the floor and its silver circle. The dust softened the horns of the cat-like skull, obscured the titles of the old magical books, and lined the dry copper basin. The room was very quiet, and almost completely still.

Pyre

On a workbench in one corner, behind an overturned glass jar and a stack of tarnished brass rods, stood a simple pendulum. It alone was untouched by the grey dust, its wooden frame gleaming dully in the light from the window. A single beam of ruddy late-afternoon sunlight glanced into the room, reflecting from the pendulum's silver weight.

The weight flashed as it hit the sunbeam, tossing the red light back out through the window at each arc of the pendulum's agitated swing.

Eric J. Hull has published poetry and stories in various magazines and websites. He also designs games, and once told a serial improvisational story every night for over three years. He lives in the Pacific Northwest with his wife and son.

Outside of fanfiction, **C. M. Stultz** has previously published *Shadow of the Beast*, a dark-fantasy novella based upon his boyhood experiences in France. He lives and writes in Washington (the state), surrounded by diverse family and friends.

If you enjoyed *PYRE* , we hope you will also
enjoy the following preview of

ASH
The Pendulum: Book Two

available soon from Amazon

ASH

Chapter 1
Cillistra

She was cold, she was dirty, and Michael's glowing head was keeping her up at night.

In the first few days she'd been too overwhelmed by the grief and horror of that last battle to do much more than huddle in the forest, weeping. But her thoughts were beginning to clear now, and she needed to figure out what to do next.

She continued moving north, staying in the foothills, the Nethal peaks to her left glimpsed through the fir boughs. The second night after leaving Edge she found a stream at the bottom of a shallow ravine, and drank. Carefully, she washed Michael's face in the cold water.

The emptiness in her belly barely registered; her thoughts were of fire and savagery, her memories of her horse screaming as it lay writhing in the smoking char of the pass.

"Oh Michael...." Fresh tears ran down her soot-smudged cheekbones and soaked into her tunic. She sat on an old nurse log next to the stream, cradling his head in her hands. She stared at his face, tried to see the monster there, but she couldn't. Of course it was gruesome; it was unthinkable that she should be here, holding her husband's head, alone in the middle of the forest. But the weeks leading up to this had been so full of horrors, and her dreams so awful, she no longer had the strength to make the distinction between the normal and the horrific. Michael's eyes were closed and his lips were slightly parted, and she missed him so badly that she knew nothing else.

Whatever magics he had employed in the final cataclysm still surged in his remains, and at night the head glowed softly. It wasn't the blue balefire of the deceiver, Aaren, and it wasn't the sickly nameless color Cillistra associated with the casting of Michael's dark magic. It was softer, more gentle, the gray luminance of the moon through a fog. It didn't frighten her at all, but it startled her each time she noticed it, especially at night.

She shook her head, dark tresses greasy and tangled, her tears falling on his face. She had never been very good at thinking things through. Since her childhood as the eldest princess in the royal house of Faires, she had acted impulsively when she had to make decisions at all. She'd been quite spoiled, even after she'd fallen in love with Michael, forsaken her family, and followed him into the mountains. For in spite of all else that he was – murderer, monster, victim himself of the dark forces that ultimately consumed him – he had always treated her with tenderness and love. He had spoiled her, too.

She had no idea why she had taken his head from the battlefield. It wasn't a matter of thinking. Mostly she just couldn't bear the thought of him surrounded by his enemies. She didn't understand why the warriors from Edge had let her go, but they had. She had felt their hatred on the back of her neck as she walked stiffly away, wondering if she would also feel their arrows.

What was she going to do? She could never go back to Faires, or to Edge; her name was reviled in both places. Everyone she had ever cared about was dead, or hated her. She rocked slowly back and forth, sobbing now, holding Michael's head tightly against her chest.

She shuddered and took a deep breath. Sunlight on the stream sparkled through her tears, and her feet were cold, but her hands were warm where she held him. Night was approaching.

She wiped her face with her sleeve. She knew that she wouldn't survive too many more nights in the woods. Hunger or predators or a misplaced step down a hardscrabble gully would take her, and she'd die alone.

She continued rocking. Gods, how she needed a drink. She smiled wanly, thinking of Cook's hard apple cider, stolen and sweet and hot as it hit her throat and dulled her pain. Yes, she wanted a drink. She wanted one very much.

And that was enough. It was a goal at least. What would he have said to her now? How would he have comforted her? She looked down at his handsome face, the dark curls soft against her fingers. *Buck up, Minnow,* he would have said, *get off that beautiful, lazy ass of yours and do something about it. The world won't come to you. If you want something, you'll have to take it.*

Yes.

She hugged Michael's head tightly to her side as she struggled up the loose earth on the other side of the ravine. Pausing at the top, she looked down to the east. There was an old road some few miles away that she didn't recognize. It went south, probably back to Edge, and north into an area she was completely unfamiliar with. She'd spent her entire life on the other side of the Nethals, in Faires, and any geography lessons she had taken as a girl were long forgotten. She squinted, frowning.

She had a small purse under her belt with enough gold to buy her passage with a caravan, and some to spare. She squared her shoulders. She'd need to spend one more night in the forest. But tomorrow she'd reach the road, and with luck find some friendly strangers. *And if they aren't friendly, I'll probably know them,* she thought, smiling a small tight smile.

And maybe they'll have something to drink.

Cillistra imagined that the truth needed little embellishment to garner her the sympathy and anonymity she sought. She would use her middle name, and most of her own story. There were so many people with terrible stories following the battle at the Waist that hers would seem tragically common.

She would be Penelope, a stable girl from the fallen royal house in Faires. Her father had been killed in the battle, and she could cry real tears over that part of the story, her overwhelming feelings of guilt adding bitterness to her grief. She was traveling north to seek refuge with an aunt and uncle, her only remaining family. *Yes, that sounds just about right.* She carefully wrapped Michael's head in her cloak, and started down the hill.

The first group she encountered on the road the next morning looked little better than refugees themselves, four men, all on foot. She came upon them resting by the side of the road as she rounded a corner. They started from their simple breakfast at her sudden appearance, but no one said anything. Cillistra looked them over crit-ically. They had no weapons larger than daggers, and they looked as if they might have been beaten.

"Hail," she said simply.

The largest one got to his feet. He had a thick black beard, and the side of his face was puffy and bruised. "Hail," he replied. They regarded each other with narrowed eyes.

"Where are you journeying?" she asked, her voice neutral, but with a deliberate ring of command in it. She didn't like the looks of them; in fact, she had the impression that they may have been mercenaries working for Michael, but she didn't recognize any of their faces.

"Why is our business any of your concern?" The big man scowled. Evidently they didn't re-cognize her either, if they had been Michael's.

Cillistra paused. These angry, suspicious men would not make fair traveling companions. "No concern or interest at all," she replied. Staring directly into his eyes, she strode past him and up the road. She did not look back. She did listen, however, and was relieved to pass the next bend without hearing any sounds of pursuit.

There was a carved wooden sign two miles farther on: *Innswitch 10 miles.* She looked up and down the empty dirt road, the midmorning sun dappling through the leaves at either side. If she didn't find anyone to travel with, she would reach Innswitch by nightfall anyway. There would be lodging there, and food.

And surely there would a tavern.